"The students deserve a clean, safe place for their learning... Don't you agree, Levi?"

His head was spinning over all the words she managed to get out in a few seconds. He started to answer her, but she began talking again.

"As soon as the paint dries, we can get the shades back up on the windows and then I can start hauling in the boxes of books. I'm excited, Levi, because it's looking like we'll be done on time."

"*Ja*. That it does. You're a good worker."

He didn't know why he said those words to her. She was a "good worker." That sounded so impersonal, like he was speaking to one of the male helpers. But his compliment brought a light blush to her cheekbones and Levi found himself wanting to smile.

"*Danke*. I just want everything to be perfect for the students."

"With your enthusiasm, I'm certain that it will be."

Mesmerized by the sparkle of hope reflected in her blue eyes, Levi found it hard to look away from Sadie.

An Amazon top ten bestselling historical romance author, **Tracey J. Lyons** was a 2017 National Excellence in Romance Fiction Award finalist. She sold her first book on 9/9/99! A true Upstate New Yorker, Tracey believes you should write what you know. Tracey considers herself a small-town gal who writes small-town romances. Visit www.traceyjlyons.com to learn more about her.

Books by Tracey J. Lyons

Love Inspired

A Love for Lizzie
The Amish Teacher's Wish

Visit the Author Profile page at Harlequin.com.

The Amish Teacher's Wish

Tracey J. Lyons

LOVE INSPIRED
INSPIRATIONAL ROMANCE

LOVE INSPIRED®

INSPIRATIONAL ROMANCE

Recycling programs for this product may not exist in your area.

ISBN-13: 978-1-335-48878-7

The Amish Teacher's Wish

Copyright © 2021 by Tracey J. Lyons

This edition published by arrangement with Harlequin Books S.A.

For questions and comments about the quality of this book, please contact us at CustomerService@Harlequin.com.

Love Inspired
22 Adelaide St. West, 40th Floor
Toronto, Ontario M5H 4E3, Canada
www.Harlequin.com

Printed in U.S.A.

But I will hope continually,
and will yet praise thee more and more.
—*Psalms* 71:14

This book is dedicated
to the loving memory of my dad;
Theodore J. Pinkowski—gone but never forgotten.
Cheers, Dad!

Chapter One

Miller's Crossing
Chautauqua County, New York

Sadie Fischer should have known better. After the rains they'd had this past week, the hillsides were muddy. She probably should have stayed on the main road. But, *nee*, she was in a hurry to see her friend Lizzie Burkholder and to deliver the latest supply of quilted pot holders she had made for the store Lizzie ran with her husband, Paul. A schoolteacher here in Miller's Crossing, Sadie helped her *mamm* with small quilting projects during the summer months when school was not in session.

As she hurried along the old cow path shortcut through the field at the bottom of the hill below the *Englischer's* church, Sadie was glad her students couldn't see their teacher now. It hadn't taken long for her haste to catch up with her. A few steps onto the path, and her feet started sinking into the soggy earth. She always chided her students for trying to take shortcuts in their schoolwork. She couldn't help but smile, thinking how they'd be the ones wagging their fingers at her now.

Looking down, she grimaced. Her feet were almost ankle-deep in the murky water. The soles of her shoes were caked with mud. Her *mamm* would have her doing the dishes for months if she caught her in this predicament. Oh, Sadie could almost hear her *mamm* scolding her now, reminding Sadie to pay attention to where she was going.

Of all her siblings, Sadie was the most talkative and the most distracted. In her *mamm*'s words, she was a *blabbermaul*. She couldn't help being chatty. As the youngest, she'd learned at an early age to speak up in order to be heard over the din of her sisters and brothers. She had three of each. When the others were busy with chores, she'd also learned how to fend for herself and to take shortcuts.

Clinging tightly to the bag filled with the pot holders, Sadie attempted to lift one leg and then the other out of the sloppy mess. She hoped she could make her way out of this quagmire and back to the main road.

"Oh, dear," she murmured, looking down to where the mud now bubbled around her feet. Her movements only caused her to sink farther into the soft ground.

Blowing out a breath, she looked around for something to grab hold of. Spotting a low-hanging tree branch a few feet away, she thought she might be able to grab hold of that and pull herself out. Although, she'd need to find a safe place to put her bag. Lifting her arm, she flung the bag high into the air, watching it land on a dry spot in the field a few feet away from the cow path.

Next, she stretched her right arm as far as she could for the branch, her muscles straining against the effort. The leaves tickled her fingers, and her heartbeat kicked up. She was so close to getting out of this mess. She had the first bit of the branch in her hand when suddenly it snapped free, sending her backward. Sadie let out a yelp as she fell with a splash into the mud.

"Nee! Nee!"

She sat there looking down at her blue dress now covered in mud, the cool wetness seeping through the fabric. A honeybee buzzed around her head. Without thinking, she swatted at it, splashing more mud up onto her prayer *kapp*. She wanted to cry. But crying wasn't in her nature. However, getting out of the many messes she always seemed to end up in was.

Once again, she looked around for something she could grab hold of to pull herself out of this muck. When she couldn't find anything, it seemed like the only thing to do might be to give up what remained of her pride and crawl out onto the drier part of the field. She made a face at the idea of getting even dirtier. Still, she was just about to give it a try when she heard the sound of a wagon.

Craning her neck, she spotted a long work wagon coming up over the rise in front of the church.

She waved her arms in the air and shouted, "Help! Help!"

At first, she wasn't sure the driver could hear her, so she yelled louder. "Help! I need help!"

She sent up a prayer of thanksgiving as the wagon pulled to a stop in the church parking lot. A man jumped down from the wagon. He was too far away for her to tell if she knew him. He stood with a hand shielding his eyes from the sunlight, looking out over the field. Maybe he couldn't see her.

Sadie waved her arms over her head, hoping to catch his attention. "I'm over here! Over here!"

She breathed a sigh of relief when he began to run toward her. By the time he got to her, she had only managed to dig herself even deeper into the mud. That's what she got for trying to get up on her own.

"Miss, are you all right?"

"*Ja.* I'm just stuck in this mud pit." She tried to laugh but couldn't quite manage it.

"That you are. Here, let me help you up."

When he moved closer, Sadie realized she'd never seen him before. The depth of his hazel-colored eyes struck her—hues of blues, greens and browns all mixed together. His fine cheekbones were cut high on his face, and his hair was a touch lighter brown than most of the men's around here. She also noticed he wore his suspenders fastened on the outside and not on the inside of his pants like the men in her community.

A million questions flew through her mind. Where had he come from? Why was he here? Was he just passing through Miller's Crossing? And if so, where was he headed?

He raised an eyebrow, his mouth pressing into a thin line. "Miss, I don't have all day to stand here while you make up your mind about staying or letting me help you out of your predicament."

Surprised by the abruptness in his voice, Sadie replied in her best schoolteacher voice, "There's no need to use that tone with me."

He drew back his shoulders. *"Es dutt mir leed."*

Sadie narrowed her eyes, wondering if his apology was sincere. His gaze softened a bit. "I accept your apology."

The wetness was seeping into her skin, and she looked down at the mess she'd made of herself. When she looked back up, she found the stranger extending his hand to her.

She hesitated, then took hold of it, surprised as his large hand swallowed hers in a firm grip. She let out a yelp as he tugged her up to stand beside him on the dry grass.

Sadie felt his warmth against her side and took an acceptable step backward. It wouldn't be proper for her to be seen out in a field, alone, with any man, especially with someone she didn't even know. She imagined the scolding she'd get from the elders who ran the school if they could see her now. No doubt not unlike the one she would get from her *mamm* when she saw the mess Sadie had made.

Due to her reputation within the community for being, what some would consider, too outgoing, Sadie had struggled to convince the board to let her teach the students in the first place. With no one else available for the last year, they'd reluctantly agreed to let her take over on a temporary basis. But with summer and harvest time nearing an end and still no permanent teacher found, Sadie had been given another chance to prepare for the upcoming semester.

She hadn't seen teaching as a lifelong endeavor, more as something to hold her over until she met the man who would become her husband. However, while all her friends had married off to eligible men in Miller's Crossing, Sadie had been left with suitors who were either too old or too young. So, for now, she was content to focus on *her* students. Though she knew it was wrong to think of them as hers, it was hard not to feel that way when she had no husband or *kinder* of her own yet.

Although if her parents had their way, Sadie would be forced into a courtship with Isaiah Troyer. The man was older than her, a widower with no children. She had no desire to be involved with him even if her *vader* thought they could be a *gut* match.

She knew the right man was out there. She just had to be patient in finding him.

Pushing those thoughts aside, she rubbed her hands together and thanked the tall, lanky man at her side. "*Danke.* If not for you, I might have had to crawl my way out."

His eyes took on a deeper brown hue as he folded his arms across his chest and looked down at her. "Then it's a *gut* thing for you I came along when I did."

"*Ja.*"

"I've got to be in town for an appointment. I can drop you someplace if you'd like." He studied her for a moment. When she hesitated, he shrugged and turned away.

"*Ja*, a ride would be nice. If you wouldn't mind," Sadie said. Hurrying to pick up the bag of pot holders, she followed him.

Halfway to the wagon, he paused so she could catch up. "Dare I ask why you were stuck in the mud?"

She blinked up at him. "I…um…I was taking a shortcut to my friend's house. And as you can see, that didn't end well."

"Am I taking you there?"

Sadie knew she needed to change out of her wet clothes before she did anything else. The pot holders would have to wait. "*Nee.* You can take me home."

They walked the rest of the way to the wagon in silence. Pausing alongside it, she put her hand on the seat to hoist herself up.

"Do you need help getting up?"

"*Nee.* I can do it," she assured him.

But when she put her wet foot up on the step, it slipped off, throwing her backward. If not for the grace of God, she might have landed on her backside again. She managed to right herself just in time.

The stranger rushed to her side, but Sadie waved him off. While she may have needed help getting out of the mudhole, she could handle getting into a wagon on her own.

"I'm fine."

Nodding, he walked around to the other side of the wagon and climbed up.

Sadie scraped her shoe across the dirt in the parking lot to give the sole a little grit, then managed to get up onto the seat without any more mishaps.

Settling a respectable distance away from him, she pulled her skirt in close, hoping to keep the seat free from the mud.

Blowing out a breath, she looked over the vista spreading out below the church. The view always filled her with hope and happiness. In her mind, this was the prettiest place in all of Miller's Crossing, even all of Chautauqua County, New York. Her family's Amish community had settled here back in the middle of the last century. Her ancestors had come from Ohio, leaving scarce farmland to make a living here.

Sadie wiggled around on the seat, trying to ignore the fact that the mud was beginning to dry. She looked down at the floorboard where drips of mud were falling off her shoes.

"I'm afraid I'm making a mess of your wagon."

The man didn't respond. He nudged the single workhorse along with a flick of the leather reins. He appeared to be focused on the roadway and not her. Only now did she notice the way his eyes were narrowed as if he were in deep concentration, and there were grim lines around his mouth.

A smile could make those disappear.

"I'm Sadie Fischer."

Keeping his hand steady on the reins, he said, "I'm Levi Byler."

In all his days, Levi had never seen a young lady looking such a sight. Mud covered most of her, and streaks of dirt ran through the loosened strands of her blond hair. A smudge of mud was drying on her chin. He had to hand it to her. Most women he knew would be crying right about now. But Miss Fischer sat there smiling at him like nothing had happened.

Her light blue eyes seemed to take in the sight of him. Levi swallowed. He knew better than to be sucked in by a woman's ostensibly innocent smile. He struggled to ignore the ache in his chest. The hurt of his recent breakup was still too fresh. On most days since that horrible time, he managed to go about his business quietly, but then there were days like today. He'd taken a wrong turn on his way to Miller's Crossing and ended up on this road.

He was coming to help his cousin Jacob Herschberger with his shed business and to heal his broken heart. Levi hoped that lending his expertise as a craftsman would not only be useful to Jacob but also aid in his own healing. He figured if he kept his hands busy, then his mind wouldn't wander to the past.

Pushing those thoughts aside, he stole a glance out of the corner of his eye at the woman sitting next to him. He supposed it was a good thing he'd come along when he did, otherwise there was no telling what would have happened to Miss Fischer.

"Where are you headed?" she asked.

Concentrating on the unfamiliar road ahead, Levi did his best to ignore the soft, friendly lilt of her voice. Her tone reminded him of the woman who'd broken his heart.

Keeping his answer simple, he replied, "I'm going to help out a family member."

"Does this person have a name? I know all of the Amish families around here."

His emotional situation was not her fault, so Levi answered, "Jacob Herschberger."

"Oh, his wife, Rachel, is a cousin to my best friend, Lizzie Burkholder. Lizzie is from the Miller family, the same ones who first settled this area. She and her husband, Paul, have a furniture and art store in Clymer," Miss Fischer went on. "Lizzie does beautiful watercolor landscapes. I wish I had half her talent. The only thing I can make are quilted pot holders from my *mamm*'s fabric scrap pile. I sell them at Lizzie's store. That's where I was heading when I got sucked into the mud."

She paused and Levi thought she might be taking a break, but in the next breath she asked, "So, you'll be working on Jacob's sheds?"

"*Ja.*"

"That's a *gut* thing. I know he's been looking for help. He and Rachel have a small house on the other side of the village, close to his shop. Where are you traveling from?"

Levi gave her a sideways glance, wondering if she ever stopped talking. "A district near Fort Ann," he said, keeping his answer short hoping to satisfy her curiosity.

"Oh. That's a long trip for a horse and wagon. I haven't been anyplace other than Miller's Crossing, and of course the village of Clymer."

"I came in on the bus." He didn't feel it necessary to tell her that he'd picked the horse and wagon up in the village. Levi wasn't interested in anything beyond getting her to where she needed to be in one piece.

"That was smart of you."

"Miss Fischer, you still haven't told me where you'd like to be dropped off."

"I'm afraid my *mamm* is going to be upset when she sees me looking a mess and returning home with the bag of pot holders. You can leave me at the end of my road if you'd like. That way you won't have to hear her scolding me."

"In order for me to do that, you'll need to tell me where the end of your road is. I do need to be somewhere," he said in a soft tone, hoping to coax directions out of her.

"It's not that late in the day." She gave him a small smile. "But you are right. I'm the one troubling you, not the other way around."

He waited for a second, raised an eyebrow and asked again. "Miss Fischer, the directions to your house?"

"Ja." She pointed straight ahead. "Just over that rise, right on the other side of that cow fence, you will find my driveway."

Levi's patience was wearing thin. Perhaps it was the long trip he'd taken added to meeting this woman and wondering about his new job. With the pain of his past still fresh in his mind, he just wanted to be left alone. He didn't want to worry about Sadie Fischer. He wanted to selfishly drown in the sorrow of his heartbreak for a bit longer.

But his past had nothing to do with Sadie. She had needed help and he'd come along at the right time.

He wasn't sure if he wanted to leave her alone on the road. Levi didn't feel like being friendly, but he wouldn't leave someone in distress either.

He pulled up to her drive and looked over at her. The spark seemed to have left her. Her shoulders sagged as she turned to hop down from the wagon seat.

He started to apologize, and then suddenly it wasn't her face he was seeing. *Nee*, it was the face of the woman who had shunned him.

Levi blinked. The pain of betrayal welled up inside him again. No matter how sweet Sadie Fischer appeared to be, no matter how much she might need someone to be a buffer between her and her *mamm*, he had to protect his heart. He simply could not allow himself to be drawn in again.

Over her shoulder, he saw a long tree-lined drive leading to her family's property and in the distance the roofline of a house. The better side of him—the old Levi—was starting to feel a bit of remorse for his short temper.

"Please, let me drive you the rest of the way."

Chapter Two

"*N*ee. I told you I'd be fine and I will be. I know you've someplace to be," Sadie replied as she stood on the side of the road, making a sad attempt to straighten her soggy skirts.

She paused to look up at the man. She'd kept him long enough.

"I wish you a good day, Mr. Byler," she said in a soft voice. And she meant that. Crankiness never got one anywhere in life, which is why she always tried to find the bright spot.

"*Gut* day to you," he said, giving her a courteous nod before heading on his way.

Lizzie waited for the wagon to be out of sight. She shook her head, thinking that he hadn't had such a good start to his first day in Miller's Crossing. Deciding to pay him no more attention, she turned and began to walk to the house.

She passed the complex of white barns with black trim where her *daed* had the farm equipment lined up nearby. The hay baler was missing. No doubt he was out in the field working on the recent cutting.

Sadie smiled as a small flock of white hens skittered over to her, pecking around the toes of her shoes. Seeing them reminded her she'd yet to collect today's eggs.

Letting out a sigh, she hurried along, hoping to skirt around the backside of the house and enter through the mudroom before anyone saw her. She glanced back at her muddy shoe prints. Sadie hoped her *mamm* was in a *gut* mood, otherwise she'd be in for it. Her dirty skirts slapped against her stockings as she ran behind the house.

A movement in the shadows behind the screen door caught Sadie's eye as she stepped onto the cement stoop. It appeared she wasn't going to best her *mamm* after all. The screen door flew open, slapping against the clapboard siding. A tall dark-haired woman came out onto the porch, her face flushed. Sadie sucked in a breath.

Wagging a finger at her, *Mamm*'s voice rose. "Sadie Fischer! What mess have you gotten yourself into this time?"

"*Mamm.* I'm sorry. I tried to take the shortcut into the village and got stuck in a big mudhole down behind the *Englisch* church on Clymer Hill Road."

"And who dropped you off? I didn't recognize the wagon."

"How did you know I was dropped off?"

"I was coming in from the barn and saw you up at the top of the driveway. I'd have waited for you, but I had my hands full carrying a basket of eggs."

"I was going to gather those as soon as I cleaned up," Sadie told her.

"The day was wasting and your sister needed them for her cake mix." In a gentler voice, her *mamm* added, "You know better than to be alone with someone you don't know."

Sadie knew *Mamm* was right about that. She did her best to explain what had happened. "Levi Byler helped me out and then he kindly offered to bring me home. He's a cousin of Jacob Herschberger, so he's not really a stranger. He will be working at Jacob's shed company."

Her *mamm* gave her a sideways glance. "You are the schoolteacher, and you are held to a higher standard in the community."

"I do understand that, *Mamm*. But if not for Levi Byler coming by when he did, I'm afraid I'd still be stuck in the mud."

"Well, then you should have brought him down here so I could have thanked him properly."

Sadie nodded. She saw no need to tell her *mamm* that the stranger had been distracted and in a hurry to be on his way.

Looking her up and down, *Mamm* scolded her again. "Sadie, today of all days, you decide to take that shortcut! And you didn't get the pot holders delivered like you promised. Furthermore, you know we have your special dinner guest coming over."

Sadie made a face. She felt bad about the pot holders but didn't care much about Isaiah. She knew he was a man of means. He had his own farm, after all. But when it came to matters of the heart, a man's stature in the community shouldn't matter. Even so, her parents were set on making this match.

Sadie thought the man would be more appropriate for her sister Sara. She'd always acted years older than her age.

"I know what you're thinking, Sadie." Her *mamm*'s voice softened. "You think we should be more concerned with marrying off Sara. But worrying over you is what keeps your *vader* and me awake most nights. You've a way about you. And this traipsing off into the mud is yet another reason why we want you to have your future secured. You can't keep doing things on impulse."

Sadie met her *mamm*'s gaze, seeing both concern and love reflected in her eyes. She almost gave in. Sometimes she thought it might be easier to let her parents choose her spouse for her. But then she remembered that this was her life, and she was determined to live it her way. Even if it went against what her parents considered to be right. Sadie wasn't doing harm to anyone. She lived a good faithful life led by her church's teachings. She worked tirelessly to bring her beliefs into her classroom and to teach her students about acts of kindness and love.

"Think about what I've said," her *mamm* said.

The last thing Sadie wanted was to disappoint her parents, but on this one topic she would remain steadfast.

Sitting down on the stoop, she pulled off her shoes. "Yuck." She set them on the edge of the cement step. Then, standing, she rolled down her stockings and placed them with the shoes. She wiggled her toes, feeling the coolness of the air touch her skin.

"You might as well come inside the mudroom and leave your skirt here," her *mamm* said from behind her. "And anything else that has mud on it."

"*Ja.*"

"Get inside before someone else sees you." Her *mamm* held the door open for her.

Sadie walked past her into the small coatroom off the back of the kitchen and stepped out of her skirt, now heavy with the dried mud. She unpinned her prayer *kapp* and caught her *mamm* narrowing her eyes and giving her another stern once-over. Perhaps she'd really gone too far this time.

"*Mamm*, I'm sorry for making such a mess. May I go wash up?"

She nodded. "When you are finished, you come right back to the kitchen. Your sister and I have been working to get the food ready for *your* dinner. You can wash the dishes."

Washing dishes had always been her least favorite chore. Sadie expected nothing less as her punishment. Holding her prayer *kapp* in one hand, she headed upstairs to the bathroom just past the bedroom she shared with her sister Sara. She turned on the cold water in the sink and carefully rinsed the mud off the *kapp*. Hanging it on the rack to dry, she turned her attention to peeling off the rest of her garments.

She made quick work of washing up and then went across the hall to her bedroom to change into another light blue dress and apron. Once she had pinned a fresh *kapp* on her head, Sadie took in a deep breath, blew it out and prepared to meet her *mamm* in the kitchen.

Mamm greeted her in the doorway. "Ah. Here you are, all cleaned up. *Gut.* Now let's get you to work on those dishes."

"I'll get my clothes washed up after I've done the dishes," Sadie told her *mamm*, knowing that would be her next concern. *Cleanliness is next to godliness.* The old phrase popped into her thoughts.

Walking over to the double sink, Sadie made quick work of the first batch of dishes and then listened as her *mamm* and sister discussed the upcoming meal.

"We'll make mashed potatoes to go with the roast beef," Sara said. "We want to be sure to impress Isaiah. For Sadie's sake, of course."

Sadie's head snapped up. She heard something in the tone of Sara's voice that made her think that perhaps her sister might be excited about their dinner guest.

"Sadie," her *mamm* said, "when you've finished with the dishes, you can get out the tablecloth."

The tablecloth to which her *mamm* referred was only used on very special occasions. The last time it came out of the drawer was for her *bruder* John's wedding dinner. He and his wife, Rebecca, had had a small family ceremony here on the property two years ago.

Sadie began to worry.

She didn't want to be married off to just anyone. *Ja*, like every girl she dreamed of one day falling in love, but in Amish communities, courtships and marriages weren't always about love. A lot of times *vaders* picked the match for their *dochders*.

But she didn't need to be watched over by someone older than her nineteen years. Isaiah Troyer's first wife had died soon after their marriage. She shook her head. She didn't want to be married to an older widower.

She found the tablecloth her *mamm* wanted. Spreading it out on the table, she inhaled the delicious aromas coming from the kitchen. The roast smelled like onions and garlic. A pot of potatoes sat on the back of the stove, ready for mashing. Again, she thought all of this effort a terrible waste of everyone's precious time. But there was little to be done about this situation without causing a whole bunch of trouble.

The living room clock chimed four times. And then came the sound of a low rumble of thunder.

Her *mamm* let out a gasp and spun around from the counter where she'd been gathering the milk and butter for the potatoes. "Oh my! Sounds like there's a storm brewing."

Sadie ran to the front door and, sure enough, the sky to the north had taken on a very ominous appearance. Dark clouds swirled about. This time of year, with the high humidity and hot days, pop-up thunderstorms were common. But she had a feeling this one might turn into more than your run-of-the-mill storm. A flock of birds flew from the large oak tree in the side yard, their noise startling her. Even the hens seemed to be running for the cover of the henhouse.

"Do you see your *vader* out there?" her *mamm* asked.

Sadie looked up the drive. Trees swayed as a hard wind blew through them. Off in the distance, lightning flickered against the dark sky, followed by another roll of thunder. It looked like the strike was right near the schoolhouse. Sadie began to worry, not only for the school but for her *vader*. There was no sign of his wagon. He should be coming in from the field by now.

Relief flooded through her when she saw the barn door being rolled open and her *vader*'s form stepping outside. He struggled to push the door closed and then ran across the yard just as fat, round raindrops pelted the hard earth.

"We're in for it with this one," he said to Sadie as she held the door for him. "I saw Isaiah when I was coming in from the back field. He sends his apologies but he had to go home to his farm. He has animals outside in the pen. He needs to get them to safety. He said his knee pain was kicking up, telling him this storm could be a bad one."

Sadie held back her relief and managed to say, "*Es dutt mir leed* to hear that."

"*Dochder.*" Her *vader* raised one of his bushy eyebrows, giving her a knowing look. Leaning in, he whispered to her, "I'm not sure you are all that sorry."

"I'm sorry there's a bad storm coming," she said with a tiny smile.

Patting her on the shoulder, he said, "There will be another time for our special dinner."

Sadie turned her attention back to the storm. A shiver ran down her spine. The clouds blackened as the air churned. She let out a yelp when a branch broke off the maple tree in the front yard, landing on the porch steps.

"Come away from that door this instant, Sadie!" her *mamm* shouted as another crack of lightning hit close by the house.

Doing as she was told, she slammed the front door closed. And in that moment, she found herself praying that Levi Byler had safely found his way to Jacob's house.

Levi pulled into the parking area near Jacob's shed company just as the first wave of thunder rolled through Miller's Crossing. A man came running out of the large steel structure, and Levi immediately recognized his cousin.

It had been a few years since they'd seen each other at a construction safety symposium in Saratoga Springs. At the time, Jacob had hinted that his company was growing at a fast pace, while Levi had been preparing his own future, one that included marriage.

It amazed him how quickly things had changed. One day he was happy and the next he'd found himself alone, uncertain where his life should be heading next. When Jacob had called and offered him the work, Levi's parents insisted he move to Miller's Crossing.

While Levi was happy for his cousin's success, he still wished his own future had gone the way he'd planned.

"Pull the horse and wagon into the barn over there!" Jacob shouted, pointing to the structure on the far side of the driveway.

The leather strap tugged in Levi's hands when the horse shied away from a sudden gust of wind. Carefully, he led the beast and the wagon to the safety of the barn. Jacob followed him in and rolled the barn door halfway closed behind them.

Wiping the rain from his face, Jacob said, "You've picked a fine time to arrive."

Jumping down from the wagon, Levi started to unhitch the horse. "*Ja*, this storm came up pretty fast."

"I was hoping you'd be here earlier," Jacob said. Taking the reins, he led the horse to a free stall.

"I had to stop and help out a young woman. She was stuck in the mud way down in a field behind the church at the top of the hill."

Jacob paused, looked over his shoulder at Levi and raised an eyebrow. "A young woman stuck in the mud?"

"Sadie Fischer. Do you know her? She tells me she knows you and your wife."

"We know her. That one is fiery."

Levi pondered the comment. He supposed that was one way to describe her, though *chatty* came to mind.

"You'd do best to steer clear of her. Last I heard, her *vader* has been trying to get her married off."

Even hearing the word *marriage* made his stomach muscles tighten. A union such as that was now the furthest thing from his mind. It didn't matter what the young woman was like. Levi wasn't looking for a courtship anymore. The pain that his ex-fiancée, Anne Yoder, had put him through was still fresh in his mind and in his heart. Levi didn't think he would ever be able to bear the pain of a broken heart again.

He and Anne had seemed like the perfect match. Both of their families had agreed the marriage would be a good thing. But then Anne had abruptly changed her mind, leaving him for an *Englisch* man. No amount of talking to her had changed her mind. He felt badly for her *mudder* and *vader*. It was hard enough having a relationship end, but then to have their *dochder* leave the community... Well, he imagined that must have crushed their hearts.

As for Levi, he'd come to Miller's Crossing to work and to heal. Absently, he rubbed his hand over his belly as his stomach rumbled. He hadn't eaten much in the way of a meal since he'd left Fort Ann in the predawn hours this morning.

"You must be hungry after your day of travel. My wife, Rachel, is a *gut* cook. She'll have a hearty meal ready for us."

Levi had never met Rachel, although Jacob had talked about her at length the last time they'd been together.

Bright streaks of lightning slashed through the dark sky.

"Come, let's get to the house," Jacob shouted over the thunder.

Levi grabbed his travel bag from the back of the wagon, and the two men dodged mud puddles as they ran to the safety of Jacob's house. Once on the porch, they shook the rain from their hats.

Jacob and Rachel's home looked good and sturdy. Built on a slight knoll overlooking the shed company, the house had dark wooden slat siding, and a grapevine wreath hung from the front door. Through the side windows, Levi could see soft light coming from the lamps hanging on the wall near the doors.

Jacob held the door open for him, and Levi stepped over the threshold into a great room that served as the kitchen, dining and living room. Off to one side was a large stove where a young woman wearing a white apron over a blue dress stood putting the finishing touches on their meal.

Jacob followed him into the house, saying, "Rachel, Levi is here."

Jacob's wife turned from the stove. Her smile was warm and kind. "*Willkomm* to our home. You made it to the house just in time. I fear this storm isn't going to let up anytime soon. You must be tired. After dinner, Jacob can show you to your room. We've a small bedroom you can use for as long as you need it."

"Levi, this is my wife, Rachel."

"*Sehr gut* to meet you." Levi nodded to her. "I've heard so much about you."

"Pleased to meet you, too. All of Jacob's family is *willkomm* in our home. Nodding her head in the direction of the table, she said, "Come, come, dinner is ready."

Rachel carried the steaming pot of stew to the table, then they took their seats.

Levi dug into the meal as Rachel and Jacob caught

up on their day. It was obvious the couple loved one another. It occurred to him then that he might never get to experience this in his own life. He chided himself that this wasn't the time to worry about his future. He should concentrate on getting through the present. The exhaustion of the long day of travel had caught up with him, jumbling his thoughts.

Stifling a yawn, he thanked his hosts. "Rachel, *danke* for this meal. Jacob, if you don't mind, could you direct me to my room?"

"Ja. Ja," Jacob said, jumping up from his seat. "Right this way."

Levi picked up his travel bag from where he'd left it by the door and followed his friend down a long hallway toward the back of the house.

"Here is the room. I hope you find the bed to your liking."

"I'm sure I will." Levi was so tired he would be comfortable sleeping on a straw mat.

After Jacob left, Levi settled onto the single bed. He bent one arm under his head and lay there, listening to the storm. The thunder rumbled all around the house, sometimes so loud the windows rattled. He blinked into the darkness, holding his breath as he waited for the next strike of lightning. One hit close to the house, the flash illuminating the bedroom.

The storm rumbled away over the countryside. Then, just as it seemed that the storm had lost its fuel, it gathered energy once more and circled back around again. He hoped and prayed that the village wouldn't rise in the morning to find too much damage. After lying awake for a bit longer, he finally drifted off to sleep.

The sound of a voice calling his name jolted him awake, and thinking he was home, Levi shot out of the bed. By the time his feet hit the floor, he remembered where he was. The voice was not his *vader*'s but Jacob's.

Quickly, Levi got dressed and ran down the hall.

"Levi, come! We must hurry!"

Chapter Three

He met Jacob in the kitchen.

"I was out in the shop, and my workers came in and told me about storm damage throughout the area. We are going to head over to the schoolhouse. There's been a lot of damage there."

"Oh my! Sadie will be beside herself if something has happened to the school," Rachel said as she came up behind them.

Levi wondered what Sadie had to do with the schoolhouse. But there wasn't time to ask questions as they hurried outside into the early-morning light and hitched up one of Jacob's wagons, then joined the line of others on the main road heading toward Miller's Crossing.

Looking out from the wagon, Levi could see where the storm had cut a path. Trees were felled in single rows along one of the hedgerows, and sirens were going off. They had to pull off onto the shoulder of the road to wait as an ambulance and fire truck sped past.

"I fear there's been a lot of damage, Levi."

"Me, too." He hung on tight as Jacob took the next corner at a good clip. "You were lucky your property was spared," Levi said.

"The storm circled around my house. I'm praying most of my neighbors have escaped any serious damage." Jacob pulled in the reins, slowing the horse's pace, and said, "The schoolhouse is up ahead."

Levi sat up taller, trying to catch a glimpse over the three wagons that had stopped on the side of the road just ahead of them. He let out a low whistle at the sight of what, by his best estimate, had to be a one-hundred-year-old oak tree split right down the middle. Half of it lay on the lawn in front of the long white schoolhouse. The other half was twisted in large sections. Large limbs had landed on an outbuilding and on top of the roof on a section of the one-story schoolhouse.

Hopping down, Jacob attached the reins to a hitching post on the side of the graveled driveway. Levi followed him.

"Come on. Let's go see what we can do to help." Jacob led them over to the downed tree where a group of men had gathered. A few of them moved to the side to allow Jacob and Levi room to step in.

"I think we should break into groups," a tall man was saying. "One can start cutting the tree off the roof of the school and the others can see if the shed can be salvaged."

Out of the corner of his eye, Levi saw movement toward the back of the school building. Quietly he left the group to go investigate. There was no telling how safe the structures were under the weight of the trees, and he would hate to see someone get hurt. Pushing aside branches and stepping over twigs, he picked his way through the debris, coming to a stop around the backside of the schoolhouse.

He saw a flash of black. Was that a prayer *kapp*? A young woman raised her head, and there was no mistaking who she was.

Sadie Fischer.

Placing his hands on his hips, Levi looked at her. There were branches and twigs stuck all around her. He wondered how she even got in the spot to begin with. Even though she had tiny brown twigs sticking out from her hair, she looked a darn sight better than she had when he'd first met her yesterday. She lifted her head to look up at him, one hand holding a branch, the other shielding her face from the morning sun.

She narrowed her eyes. "Levi Byler, is that you?"

"Ja."

She frowned. "I don't need your rescuing today. As you can see, there's plenty of help to be had."

"I know that." Folding his arms, he widened his stance, trying to decide if he should help her out from the tangle of branches or go find someone else to help her.

She gave him a cross look, sucking in her lower lip as she wiggled around trying to find a way out of the brush pile.

"Ugh!"

"Geb acht!" Levi yelled.

Letting out a sigh, he dropped his arms and

stepped toward her. If she wasn't careful, she would fall and get hurt. Levi was a stranger in these parts and there was no way he'd be accused of letting this woman get injured his first full day in town.

"Let me take hold of that branch and then you can slide out."

To his surprise, she did as told, letting the branch slip from her grasp into his hands. Once he felt certain it wouldn't spring back and hit her in the face, he let go and then reached for her. Of course, she pushed his hand away, stepping out of the branches on her own.

"Danke," she offered, brushing some leaves from her apron and pulling the twigs from her hair. "I can't believe the damage the storm brought. I came here with my *vader* to check on the building, and we were shocked to see all the trees that are down. And our *Englisch* neighbors had a tree come down on their car. I think they've lost power, too."

"It was a big storm."

"Some are saying it might have been a tornado. I'm not sure. What do you think?"

He shrugged, once again amazed at how quickly she could talk. "I think it's too soon to tell. Straight-line winds for sure." He tipped his head, looking her over. It was dangerous being out and about in the middle of broken tree limbs. "What are you doing back here by yourself?"

"I came to check on the flowers." Her mouth dipping downward, she shuffled her feet along a brown patch of grass. "I think they are a total loss."

"Why would you be worrying about the flowers

at a time like this?" He was more concerned about the building coming down around her.

"The *kinder* and I planted them at the end of the school year. The flowers were a special project." In the next breath, she asked, "Are you here to help out with the cleanup?"

"I came over with Jacob. Some of his workers were talking about this damage."

"Probably Abram Schmidt. I have two of his *kinder* in my class."

Levi tried to put this all together. Obviously, she cared about the school a great deal, otherwise she wouldn't be here worrying about the plants. Was she some sort of assistant? "You help out here at the school?"

Sadie pulled back her shoulders. "I do more than that, Mr. Byler. I'm the teacher here."

Levi's jaw dropped. He gave his head a shake in disbelief. But she had no reason to tell him otherwise. He frowned, trying to imagine her in a classroom as anything other than a student.

"You seem surprised."

Remembering his own teacher, who had been much older than Sadie and a lot more stern-looking, he offered, "Well, you just don't seem the type."

He didn't think it possible that she could narrow her eyes any more, but she managed. In a firm voice, she asked, "There's a type?"

Seeing he'd upset her, Levi held up his hands, gave her what he thought was a friendly grin and said, "You know what I mean."

Putting her hands on her hips, she glared up at him, her blue eyes filled with indignation.

"I don't know what you mean," she snapped.

Sadie had better things to do than stand here talking to this man. Why did he have to be the one to find her out here? She hadn't been all that stuck. Not like yesterday, anyway.

"Levi! There you are. We were wondering where you'd gotten off to," Jacob said as he came around the back of the building. And then he noticed Sadie. "Sadie! What are you doing back here?"

"Checking on the flower garden."

He wagged a finger at her. "You shouldn't be worrying over that."

She knew that, not when the school was in such a state. But her first thought had been for the children and how they'd worked so hard on this project. They'd been looking forward to seeing the fruits of their labor. If the garden could be saved, then they would have some hope.

Jacob said to Levi, "We were just dividing up the workload for the cleanup."

Sadie looked at Jacob, was thankful he'd saved her from any further chatting with Levi. To think he'd been surprised that she could be the schoolteacher. Sadie was well aware that pride goeth before the fall, but she was a *gut* teacher. She took her time smoothing down the folds of her dress, waiting for her temper to settle. It wouldn't do a bit of good to show her annoyance. Today was a day when everyone needed to work together, even if part of that everyone included Levi Byler.

She focused on Jacob. "*Gut.* The sooner we get this cleaned up, the sooner I can get on with preparing for the upcoming school year. We've only a few weeks until the first day," she reminded him.

"*Ja,* I know." Patting Levi on the back, Jacob added, "Come on around to the front. We need to get you your assignment."

Sadie stayed a few steps behind as the three of them walked around to where Abram Schmidt was speaking.

"We're going to have the older boys remove the brush and smaller tree branches, while the men can cut the tree up into manageable lengths. The good news is the cleanup here will give us enough wood for next year's winter heating. The Lord does provide. And this will surely help with our next school budget.

"I think it best if we break up into three groups. One will work on getting the shed area cleared, one will work on the front and the other will see about damage to the school building," Abram went on.

Sadie looked around the lawn and noticed a few more buggies had pulled up in front. Some were loaded with saws and young men who'd come to help. Others carried women with baskets of food and thermoses. Confident the cleanup would be handled in a timely manner and knowing she wouldn't be needed there, Sadie headed off to join the women.

Rachel ran toward her. "Sadie!"

Sadie gave her a wave. "Rachel. *Gute mariye.*"

"*Ach*, I'm not sure how *gut* the morning is, what with all the damage in our community." Rachel wrinkled her nose.

"It is a *gute mariye* because no one was injured," Sadie reminded her.

Rachel gave her a thoughtful smile. "This is true. What do you think the damage is to the school?"

"I can't say for certain. I was out in the back hoping the flowers the *kinder* and I planted in the spring had survived. But I'm afraid all I saw were broken stems, and some of the plants were smushed underneath the tree limb that fell across the back."

"Those can be replanted," Rachel assured her.

"They can." Still, Sadie knew the *kinder* would be disappointed.

She linked her arm through Rachel's as they walked over to their friends. She said hello to a few of her students' *mamms* and was happy to see Lizzie Burkholder in the circle. Sadie broke away from Rachel to give Lizzie a hug.

"*Es dutt mir leed* my pot holders never made it to the store. I got myself into a bit of a mess while walking over."

Lizzie laughed. "You will have to tell me all about it."

"Well, let's just say it wasn't my finest moment."

Rachel came up to them. "Let's talk while we set up the food table. I see there are a few picnic tables we can use. You know how our men are. They will be hungry before you know it."

Sadie and Lizzie walked to where the tables had been set up in the side yard. They put out red-and-white-checked tablecloths as Sadie filled her friend in on yesterday's mess. Telling her how she'd taken the path behind the church and ended up stuck in the mud. By the time she'd finished recounting her day and how she'd been rescued by a stranger, the table was laden with sandwiches, salads and a big basket of apples.

Sadie kept her hands busy, but her mind was elsewhere. She was anxious to hear what the damage to the school might be and prayed they'd be able to open it in time for the new school year.

"Who is that man standing by Jacob?" Lizzie asked. "He keeps looking over this way."

Sadie glanced over her shoulder. Pulling her mouth into a thin line, she answered, "That is Levi Byler."

"Your rescuer," Lizzie said, her eyes widening in curiosity. Nudging Sadie in the side with her elbow, she added, "He's headed this way."

Turning around to face him, Sadie figured he was coming for some food. She guessed he might not have had time for breakfast. His strides were long and purposeful as he crossed the lawn.

Levi stopped in front of her, and the gaggle of women behind her grew quiet. Sadie knew they were going to listen in. She had no desire to be fodder for their gossip. Squaring her shoulders, she tipped her head back to look up at him. He did not look happy at all. Of course, there was a lot of work to be done, and perhaps he was still tired from his long day yesterday. Either way, Sadie was beginning to think one of Rachel's egg salad sandwiches was not going to help his mood.

Sadie pasted her best smile on her face, the same one she used when a student became unruly. Folding her hands in front of her apron, she asked in a cheery voice, "Is there something I can help you with?"

Levi wasted no time with his answer. "It appears that the work assignments have been given out."

A bad feeling wiggled along Sadie's spine. "I'm afraid I don't understand what that has to do with me."

"I am to work with the schoolteacher to get the schoolhouse ready for the new semester. And once that's done, I'll be overseeing the shed repair. Since you are the teacher, I guess this means you and I will be working together."

Sadie's jaw went slack.

Chapter Four

Behind her she heard an "oh" escape Rachel's mouth. Sadie didn't dare turn around. She knew Rachel and a few of the others must be grinning in delight over this turn of events. Her friends knew she was independent and enjoyed being in charge of her classroom. While she did have older students who helped with the lessons of the younger *kinder*, the setting up and running of the schoolroom fell to her.

Having to work side by side with this stranger would be a challenge for sure, even if he was a relative of Jacob's. She decided it was best to remain professional. After all, she was the teacher and she wanted the best for her students. Her discomfort over the matter shouldn't be of any concern.

Except that feeling didn't seem like it would be going away anytime soon.

Sadie blew out a breath, then said, "Well, why don't you grab something to eat, and after that, we'll take a look at the damage and make a list of what needs to be done in order to get the school fixed."

She followed him to the food table and did the neighborly thing by introducing him to the women who'd cooked the food. They piled his plate high with an egg salad sandwich and spoonfuls of two kinds of potato salad, along with a generous helping of her own *mamm*'s locally famous macaroni salad. A smile tugged at her mouth when she saw Rachel add a large chocolate chip cookie. She wasn't sure Levi would be able to eat everything.

But he managed. After he finished, he tossed his empty paper plate and utensils in a nearby trash can and gave her a half smile. "Shall we go take stock of what needs to be fixed?"

Nodding, Sadie couldn't help thinking again that Levi Byler needed to smile more. Smiles had a way of warming one's soul. From his stiff demeanor, she had a feeling Levi's soul was in need of some warmth. She walked ahead of him, leading the way to the front door of the schoolhouse, which was ajar.

As she stepped over the threshold, her breath caught in her throat, and her hand covered her heart. "Oh my," she breathed at the sight before them.

Shards of glass littered the floor where a window on the left side had been broken by a tree limb. The wood floor had puddles of water clear to the center of the room. Some of the educational posters on the wall had blown off and were lying in the water. One of the green blackout shades flapped in the breeze against the broken window.

Sadie paused to send up a fervent prayer of thanks that all her students had been safe in their homes when the disaster hit. This damage could be fixed.

Still, a sadness filled her. It was difficult to see the classroom that she'd grown to love and take comfort in looking such a mess. The storm had been ferocious. Sadie knew in her heart this all could have been so much more devastating.

Bending down, she picked up a paperback book that had fallen off a shelf. Setting the soggy mess on a desk she was standing next to, she turned to look at Levi. He, too, stood taking in the storm damage. Her gaze followed his up to a basketball-size hole in the roof. She could see clear out to the sky, now blue. They'd need to get a tarp on that right away.

Looking down at her, he said, "It could have been worse."

"Ja," she agreed, as he gave voice to her thoughts. "At least it's not a total loss like the shed appears to be."

When she'd gone out earlier to check on the garden, she'd carefully avoided what was left of the shed. They'd kept the garden supplies and some of the playground equipment out there, but all of that could be replaced.

She picked her way through the debris. Walking over to her desk, she found a notebook and a pen. Picking them up, she started making a list of what needed to be done. First off, *clean up.* Then *fix the window.* She was about to add *replace torn posters and damaged books* when Levi approached her.

"I'm going to see if anyone has a tarp stored in their wagon. At least we can get that hole covered up until we get the supplies needed to fix it."

"That sounds like a *gut* idea," Sadie replied. "Then we can work on the rest of the list."

He raised an eyebrow.

"Is there something the matter?"

He shook his head.

Twirling the pen between her fingers, she kept her tone even as she said, "Please don't tell me you have a problem with making lists."

Sadie, for one, liked lists. They kept her on track. Maybe Levi was the type of person who kept everything in his head.

"I don't. You give me what you come up with and I'll see that whatever is on there gets taken care of."

"Mr. Byler, I'm perfectly capable of helping out here. I know the students and what needs to be in place before they return in a few weeks for the start of the fall semester. It makes sense that I handle getting the ruined classroom supplies replaced. Besides, you're going to be very busy working on the building." Softening her tone, she added, "Unless you think you'll have time to go to the King's Office Supply and Bookstore to pick up what I'll need."

While she waited for his reply, Sadie looked beyond him, once again surveying the mess caused by the storm, only now seeing the torn strip of paper hanging from the wall. One of her most loved quotes:

Be Kind, Be Thoughtful, Be Genuine, But Most Of All, Be Thankful

Reading that reminded her she should be thankful for all of the help here today, including Levi Byler's.

It also reminded her that she loved this building and what it represented. Here was where the *kinder* came to learn not only their numbers and letters but how to be kind. She taught them about their faith, forgiveness and how to work together. They also practiced the Golden Rule, to treat others as you would want to be treated.

It pained her to see even one thing out of place. The *kinder* she taught were part of her community. Many were a part of her family. They deserved to come back to a building that had been repaired to its fullest potential. She owed it to them to see that that happened.

Besides, she didn't want to disappoint the school board either. It had been hard enough convincing them she was the right person for the job. It wouldn't do to have some storm come through and prove otherwise.

She knew full well the men of this community were strong, but the women could be counted on, too. Sadie could find a way for her and Levi to work together.

Levi watched various emotions play out on Sadie's face. Her expression had gone from determination to sadness and finally to acceptance. He didn't want to waste time arguing with her, but this project was the first one for him as Jacob's helper and he wanted it to go well. He had to make this work. It shouldn't be too bad. Obviously, this teacher wanted what was best for her students, as did he.

Of course, his way of tackling a project wasn't

necessarily making lists. He liked to get a feel for a job before stepping into it. He got the idea that Sadie wanted to get her lists made and then dole out the tasks.

Being a stranger to this community didn't make his job any easier. He didn't mind helping where help was needed, even if repairing the school hadn't been the reason he'd come to Miller's Crossing. But you never knew what life was going to hand you.

Levi came close to letting out a snort at that last thought. Life certainly hadn't gone the way he'd planned. He should have been married by now, setting up a home with the woman he loved. But the Lord had other plans. Levi knew better than to try to interpret what those might be. He had to trust in the Lord.

Letting those thoughts tumble from his mind, he looked at Sadie.

She had gone back to writing on her notepad. From the way her hand had moved three quarters of the way down the page, he surmised the list had grown a bit longer.

He realized that she would know better than he what needed to be replaced. Looking around, he took in the larger damage. The broken window, the hole in the roof. That roof damage in and of itself could lead to more work. He wouldn't know until he got up there how many shingles were damaged. And he had no idea about the books and other things that needed to be replaced.

Putting his hands on his hips, he said, "I think you

are right. It would be best if you took care of going to the office supply and bookstore."

"Danke."

He noticed a wisp of her blond hair had fallen from underneath her prayer *kapp*. She caught his gaze on her. Lifting her hand, she tucked the strand back in place. A light blush rose high on her cheekbones.

Levi looked down at the desktop. "Tell me what else you have on your list."

"Cleaning up the storm debris will be first because we won't know the full extent of the damage until we can see underneath everything. Then we'll need to clear out this room so we can scrub and paint." Letting out an exasperated sigh, she added, "There's so much to see to. I'm not sure this can all be done in a few weeks."

"There is a lot of help waiting right outside those doors," he said, pointing over his shoulder at the group of men, both old and young, who had come out to assist.

"Yes. You are right. I'm overreacting."

He shook his head. *"Nee.* This mess is hard to look at. But we'll all work to get everything fixed, and it will be better than before."

The schoolteacher gave him a smile.

Levi simply nodded in return. "All right then. It seems like we're making headway."

"We are. Do you think you could call some of those helpers inside to start moving things?"

Levi left her at her desk and walked outside to find Jacob. On his way over to the men, he noticed that more tables had been added to the area where he'd eaten earlier, forming a long row of communal seating. Someone had erected a blue pop-up canopy to cover the food, and it ruffled in the warm breeze.

He met Jacob in the front yard. "Sadie and I have come up with a plan for the schoolhouse."

"I'm glad to hear that," Jacob replied. "We've given our groups their tasks. We're lucky enough that some of the older students have come by to assist. I think they should work with you and Sadie."

Levi nodded. It would be *gut* for the boys to help rebuild their own school. "I think the first order of business is to get a tarp up on the roof," Levi advised.

"*Ja.* I looked in the wagons that are here and didn't find any. You should go into the village and pick one up at the hardware store. I've an account there for my business. You can tell him you're my cousin and you have my permission to add the purchases to my account. And let Herb, the owner, know that I'll be in at the end of the week to settle as usual."

"I can do that. Is the tarp all we'll be needing?"

"Why don't you pick up extra tarps? We can use them to cover up the school desks and other items that Sadie wants protected. I have some boxes over at my shop that we can put the books and supplies in. And I think among the men who came today, we have enough supplies to begin the cleanup."

Jacob and Levi agreed to have the crews start removing the tree limbs from around the school first, and then they would take the portion of the trunk off the roof. Jacob took his tools out of his wagon and then told Levi to use that to go into town.

"If you think of anything else we might need, don't hesitate to buy it," Jacob told him as Levi climbed up onto the seat.

"Would you mind telling me the best way to get to the village?"

"Sure! Turn left at the first intersection and then go two more intersections. You'll see the sign pointing the way to Clymer. Go through the stoplight and you'll find the hardware store in the next block."

"Danke."

Levi set off the way Jacob instructed. Here and there along the way were signs of storm damage. A tree had fallen into a portion of the road, causing him to maneuver the horse onto the opposite side. When he came to the first intersection, he waited for a pickup truck and two cars to go through before proceeding.

Eventually he made it into the village and parked the wagon next to a small hitching post. Hopping down from his seat, he took a look around. Clymer was a quaint village. He noticed the hardware store and bank, and down the road he spotted a three-story, redbrick schoolhouse. This one was for the *Englisch kinder*. At the main intersection, he noticed the grocery store. Good to remember in case he needed any sundry items. He also saw the storefront for Burkholder's Amish Furniture and Art store. A really nice dining table and bench set were displayed in the window.

The door opened and a couple came out. The man was tall and carried some sort of canvas. At first Levi wasn't sure why the couple held his attention, and then it dawned on him that the woman looked very familiar. Her dark hair and her height, the angle of her jaw. She looked just like his former fiancée.

Levi didn't think it could be possible for her to be so close to Miller's Crossing. This woman wasn't wearing dark skirts and a prayer *kapp*. She was dressed in blue jeans with a sleeveless white top tucked into the waistband.

Shock rolled through him as he stared at the woman he'd once thought he loved. *What is she doing here?*

Chapter Five

"Anne?" he whispered.

The woman looked across the street, their gazes colliding, and he realized it wasn't her. Upon seeing him, an Amish man, the woman quickly reached into her pocketbook. She pulled out her cell phone and held it at arm's length, pointing it at him, and quickly tapped her finger on the screen. He ducked his head, hoping to avoid having his picture taken. Though he felt certain she'd managed to capture his image.

Levi's knees went weak with relief as he realized this woman was nothing more than just another *Englisch* tourist. Still, his breathing was quick and shallow. He kept his head bowed as he tried to absorb the pain that tore through his heart. He'd been trying for weeks to shut that part of his life off. And today, in this very minute, like the ripples of water lapping against a shoreline, the sadness washed over him. He kept his head downturned and swallowed against the tightness gripping his throat like a vise.

Taking in a breath, he waited for the tightness to

ease. He exhaled, concentrating on the ache in his chest. Levi knew a few deep breaths wouldn't fix what ailed him. He wanted this feeling of hurt and betrayal to be gone. There was no place in his life or in his heart now for it, and yet for the moment the unbearable pain crippled him.

He stood on the side of the road with life's noises in the background. Car horns and kids playing in their backyards filtered through the fogginess of his brain. He knew deep in his soul that Anne had made her choice. He'd accepted that. She had moved on and he'd chosen to come to Miller's Crossing to help his cousin, with the possibility of maybe starting fresh.

He heard a car door close, then an engine start, and he lifted his head, looking up as the two tourists drove off. Squaring his shoulders, Levi pushed his pain back down and entered the hardware store.

Within seconds, an *Englisch* man came over to ask if he needed assistance. Levi asked for a tarp large enough to cover the hole in the roof at the Amish school in Miller's Crossing. The man, whose nametag read Herb, led him to the back of the store.

"Wow, this shelf is almost empty. I guess with the storm we've had a lot of people come in needing these," the man observed. Pulling a large blue tarp off the top shelf, he handed it to Levi.

Levi noticed right away that it was the last one. "I don't need to take this if there's a chance someone else might come in with a hole in the roof of their home."

"Thanks for the offer, but we have an order coming in tomorrow morning. The storm damage in some sections of Clymer is pretty intense," Herb said. "Can I get you anything else?"

"*Ja*, I'll add a couple cases of roofing shingles and nails." It wouldn't hurt to have them in case they were able to get started on the repair today.

He followed the man down another aisle, where they picked up the supplies. Back at the checkout counter, Levi told Herb this would go on his cousin Jacob's account. Herb seemed fine with that, looked up the information and then rang up the items. He printed out two receipts, handed one to Levi and put the other inside a ledger.

"If you need us to deliver any more supplies, just let me know."

"*Danke*. I'll tell Jacob."

"Do you have a wagon outside?"

"I do."

"Well, let me help you get this stuff loaded up."

Hefting one of the boxes of shingles onto his shoulder, Herb followed Levi outside and set it in the back of the wagon. Once everything was loaded, Levi headed back to the schoolyard. He imagined the crew would be about ready to get the tarp in place.

He was amazed at the amount of work that had been done in the two hours he'd been gone. The tree had been removed from the schoolhouse, and the older students had already started cutting the wood into smaller sections. Even from the driveway he could see a decent-size hole in the midsection of the roof. The tarp would cover that nicely until they could get back up there tomorrow. He parked the wagon with the others.

Jacob saw him drive in and came over to help unload.

"Looks like you've been busy," Levi commented.

"It's nice the older schoolboys are helping out. I think being a part of working on something that's for the good of the community keeps them grounded."

Levi agreed. When he was a young lad, he'd enjoyed working on community projects. It made him feel like he belonged to a larger family.

Hefting the heavy shingles onto one shoulder, he headed off toward the front of the schoolhouse, where he dropped the heavy shingles to the ground. Looking up, he noticed Sadie standing in the doorway speaking to a man he hadn't met. He appeared to be much older than her. With a gray beard and gray hair, the man stood with a slight hunch in his shoulders.

Sadie had her arms folded in front of her, and she wasn't smiling. As a matter of fact, he thought there might even be a scowl on her face. He wondered if the man was someone she didn't like.

Taking a handkerchief out of his pants pocket, Levi brushed the brim of his straw hat back and wiped the sweat from his forehead. The storm that had plowed through last night had left behind air thick with heat and humidity. The sweat seeped through his work shirt. Tucking the cloth back into his pocket, he walked over to the entrance. He was anxious to see what the interior looked like now that some of the debris had been cleared.

Sadie stood on the top step watching Levi's approach over the top of the man's head. Levi couldn't decide if the man was a relative or a neighbor. He overheard a portion of what the man was saying.

"I'm sorry I didn't come last night. The storm came in so fast."

"*Ja.* That it did."

Levi thought Sadie sounded agitated. He wondered why.

"Your *daed* was kind enough to invite me back to dinner on another night," the man spoke softly, shifting his weight from one foot to the other.

"Then I'll see you on that night," Sadie replied in a dismissive tone.

Levi took that moment to step up to them. "Hello," he said to the man.

With a half smile, the man met Levi's gaze and stuck his hand out to shake. "I'm Isaiah Troyer."

"Levi Byler."

"New to the area?"

"I'm here to help my cousin Jacob Hershberger with his shed company." Looking around, Levi added, "And to help with these repairs."

"I imagine the storm caught you a bit off guard."

"It was a rough night."

"And now you are helping out here. *Gut* sturdy men can be hard to find. The community is fortunate you came to visit when you did," Isaiah said with a tip of his hat. "There seems to be enough help here and I've got work to do at home." Turning his attention back to Sadie, he said, "I hope to see you again soon."

Sadie nodded, spun on her heel and went inside. Again, Levi couldn't be certain, but it seemed that she really didn't like that man. Following her inside, he

paused and looked around in surprise. The desks had all
been moved to one side of the room and the bookcases
were nearly emptied out, with the books stacked in
cardboard boxes. The exposed hole in the roof brought
in a lot of sunlight. That would be covered shortly.

The green blackout shades had been removed from
all but one window in the back of the classroom.
Sadie was working at getting the rest of the posters
down and rolled up to be stored away. The side walls
were bare, and there were still three left behind her
desk on either side of the chalkboard.

He let out a short whistle. "You've been busy!"

Sadie shook her head. "I didn't do this alone. I
had plenty of help."

"This is a *gut* start."

"It is. I'm thankful for all the students who've
come by. And the *mudders* have restocked the food
table twice now," Sadie said with a laugh. "If you're
hungry, you can go out and grab something."

"I'm *gut*," Levi told her.

She noticed the sweat on his brow and seeping
through his shirt. Even she was feeling the heaviness
of the humidity and had gone out a few minutes ago
to get herself something cold to drink.

"How about a lemonade?" she asked.

"I can get one if I'm thirsty."

"Okay," she said. *Suit yourself.* She turned around
to look at what was left of the posters on the wall. She
reached up to take the one with the alphabet down
from behind her desk. Except the tack on the top right
side held firm. Her first instinct was to give it a tug,

but she didn't want to tear it. Instead she grabbed for the back of her desk chair, planning to stand on it, but jumped when she felt a warm hand on hers.

She hadn't heard Levi come over. She spun around and looked up, ready to offer him a thankful smile. Except he stood scowling down at her. She bit her lower lip and wondered why he acted as though he didn't like her. Maybe she was being too judgmental. She did her best to be kind to everyone, including Isaiah Troyer. Of course, if she were honest, she did not want to do anything to make that man think there would be a union between the two of them.

His arrival here today indicated that he genuinely wanted to help out. This school was a part of his community. But the last thing she needed right now was a distraction. She wanted to concentrate on restoring her school.

"I can get this down," Levi said. "No need for you to climb up on the chair."

Stepping aside, she let Levi remove the last three posters. After rolling and wrapping a rubber band around each one, she gathered them up and placed them in the last open box. With that done, she only had to get the desks moved to the basement and the last green shade down. Then she could think about cleaning the room so they could repair, repaint and reopen in time for her to teach the three R's. Sadie let out a laugh.

Levi looked at her. "What's so funny?"

"Nothing. A silly thought I had, that's all. *Danke* for helping me get those posters down. Now I can move the desks downstairs, and we can begin the hard work."

"You know the menfolk can handle this."

"I do, but it's still my classroom. I'm able to use a paint roller and wipe a window clean."

"I'm sure you are. But you can't do any of those things until we have the repairs finished. By my best estimation, that will be sometime next week."

Sadie did her own calculation, determining they had exactly three weeks to get everything done. Two weeks to do the repairs would leave her with a week to get the classroom set up and ready for the new school semester. "That should work."

"Keep in mind, Sadie, that we still don't know the extent of the roof damage."

"Speaking of the roof," Jacob said as he strode into the classroom, "we've got a ladder so we can get up there, take a closer look and get the tarp on before nightfall."

Coming around from behind the desk, Levi joined Jacob, saying, "All right then, let's go."

The three of them went outside. Sadie stood off to one side. Raising her hand to shield her eyes from the brightness of the sun, she watched while the men took turns climbing up the ladder. Jacob yelled down for someone to bring up the tarp. Once that was done, they covered the hole. She ran her hand along her forehead to wipe the beads of perspiration away.

Someone bumped into her elbow, and Sadie smiled when she turned and saw Lizzie.

"Lizzie!" Sadie gave her friend a big hug.

"This heat is getting to me. Why don't you come over to the tent and have something cold to drink? I made my pink lemonade."

Sadie loved seeing her dear friend so happy.

Lizzie's transformation had been nothing short of a miracle. Ever since marrying Paul Burkholder, she'd been beaming. Right now, she was smiling from ear to ear. Even the scar that had marred her dear friend's face since the childhood accident that took her *bruder*'s life had faded into nothing more than a barely noticeable thin line.

"Let's go get that drink," Sadie said, sliding her arm through Lizzie's. She wouldn't tell her that she'd just had one. On a day like this, a person couldn't get enough to drink.

"This storm left behind a lot of humidity."

"That it did. Maybe tomorrow will be better for working outside."

"I know we shouldn't be complaining." Lizzie laughed.

They walked across the schoolyard to the shady area where the tents and tables were set up. The women were busy doling out the last of the salads and sandwiches from the coolers. Sadie knew they'd be refilled and brought back tomorrow. She let Lizzie lead her to the drink table, where Lizzie handed her a glass of the cold lemonade. Bringing the paper cup to her lips, she drank in the mixture of tart sweetness. Always a perfect fix to the heat.

Sadie turned and looked out over the yard. She could see the area where the *kinder* played kickball. Beyond that were the swing set and slide. Branches and twigs littered the area. But that would all be gone in a few days.

"Tell me how things are going." Lizzie picked up a drink and stood beside Sadie.

"We accomplished a lot today. And I feel that to-morrow, with the desks cleared and the books packed away, the men can get in and fix the window. There are a few spots in the one wall that need to be patched."

"I saw Isaiah Troyer earlier."

Sadie swallowed a mouthful of lemonade. She concentrated on watching the men put away their tools for the day. She wasn't sure how much Lizzie knew about the situation. But she had to talk to some-one about her feelings.

"*Ja.* He came by to check on me."

"That was nice of him, don't you think?" Lizzie asked, keeping her voice low so the other women couldn't hear them.

"What I think is that he is too old for me."

"He's the man your *vader* has chosen."

"He is, but my *vader* understands my feelings on this matter."

Lizzie looked at her sympathetically. "He can under-stand, but do you think it will make any difference?"

Sadie shrugged. "You know how I feel about find-ing the right man."

Lizzie's face softened with laughter. Her eyes lit up as she chuckled, recited Sadie's very thoughts on the matter. "He can't be too old or too young. He has to be your perfect Amish man."

They burst out laughing. Someone cleared their throat. Sadie swung her head around and came face-to-face with Levi Byler.

Chapter Six

She heard Lizzie's surprised intake of breath. Her own seemed caught in her throat.

Oh my goodness!

Sadie could only imagine what Levi must be thinking of her now. Although if the deep frown he wore was any indication, she might think he didn't approve of her requirements for a husband.

At that moment, Sadie couldn't help wondering if perhaps she was turning into one of those women who simply couldn't make up their minds about things like this. *Nee.* She knew what she wanted. Lizzie's words were Sadie's truth.

She coughed, then asked, "Are the men done for the day?"

"They are. Everyone is packing up and heading home. Most of them have evening chores that need tending to," he answered, avoiding making eye contact with her.

Sadie felt bad that he'd overheard a conversation

between two lifelong friends. Friends who very rarely kept things from one another.

"Well, Lizzie and I are going to help pack up here and then we'll be heading to our homes, too."

"Okay. Will you need a ride?"

She shook her head. "My *vader* is right over there." She pointed behind Levi to the place in the yard where her *vader* had pulled the family wagon in line with the others a few minutes ago.

"I'll see you tomorrow."

"I'll be here bright and early," Sadie quipped, giving Levi her best smile.

She watched him walk off, then turned to help with the last of the packing up. Lizzie was bent over a large red cooler, putting away empty plastic containers. Sadie joined her, handing her the last three left on the picnic table.

"I take it he heard what I said?" Lizzie wanted to know.

"I'm afraid so."

"You don't seem too upset by that."

"I'm not. He didn't mention our conversation, but I could tell by the look on his face that he'd heard us. I don't know Levi all that well. But from what I've seen so far, he tries to keep to himself."

Lizzie shrugged. "Maybe that will change as he gets to know us all better. He is Jacob's cousin, so he does have some family here. I'm sure once he settles in, he'll get more comfortable."

"Maybe." But even as she agreed, Sadie had a feeling Levi just might not be the outgoing type.

After saying her goodbyes to Lizzie and the other

women who'd been helping out under the food tent, Sadie went to meet her *vader*. He was waiting for her in the shade of a stand of maple trees. She waved at him. When he saw her coming toward him, he smiled at her.

"Good afternoon, *dochder*."

"Good afternoon, *vader*."

Nodding in the direction of their wagon, he walked with her over to where he'd parked it. "Did the day go well?"

"*Ja*. The men came out in full force. Tomorrow we can start repairing the inside of the schoolhouse."

Sadie caught him looking beyond her to where Levi and Jacob were getting into Jacob's wagon. Both men looked flushed from the heat and tired.

Sadie rubbed a hand along her face, feeling the warmth of her skin beneath her fingertips. The humidity had spiked. She prayed there wouldn't be another storm tonight. Unfortunately, this was the time of the year for them. She'd long gotten over her childhood fear of late-night storms and the thunder and lightning that came with them. The crops needed the rain.

"This cousin of Jacob's, did he help out today?"

Sadie gave a start at his question. It was interesting that her *vader* wanted to know about Levi. *"Ja."* She thought it best to leave her answer at that.

Her *vader* wanted a union between her and Isaiah Troyer. Sadie knew that wasn't going to happen. She feared her *vader* might be upset if he knew she was working with Levi Byler. Being the schoolteacher, her life required a different set of proprieties. She had a reputation to keep. Even though they were working among a lot of other community members, her *vader* might frown upon their partnership.

However, the only thing that concerned her was getting the school up and running in time for the new semester. She didn't care how that came about.

Settling herself onto the seat of the wagon, Sadie adjusted her blue skirt. The toll of putting in a long day's work was catching up with her. Her shoulders ached from moving the desks, and her feet felt as if they might explode out of her shoes. She couldn't wait to get her shoes and stockings off. She wiggled her toes in anticipation. As they rode past the white schoolhouse, she saw the blue tarp flattened against the roof covering the hole. She sent up a prayer of thanksgiving that today had gone well and that the Lord had sent an extra pair of hands in the form of Levi Byler.

"Did you happen to see Isaiah?" her *vader* asked.

"He came by to check on me," Sadie admitted.

"Gut."

"Vader—" she started, wanting to tell him to stop wasting his time and effort on something that would not happen.

His stern voice interrupted her. *"Dochder*, you have no idea how I wish you would abide by my decision concerning you and Isaiah."

"I understand."

He slapped the leather reins against the backside of the large mare pulling the wagon. "I'm not sure you do."

"Can't you please give me a little more time?" Sadie asked softly.

A breeze blew in from the north, bringing with it a hint of coolness. Sadie lifted her face, letting the air wash over her. She waited for an answer from her *vader*, hoping he would continue to allow her lenience in this matter.

"I know you're going to be busy at the school, and that's where your attention should be. The community needs you there. But that doesn't mean I'll be forgetting about my wishes where your future is concerned."

Sadie looked over at her *vader*. His jaw was set in that stubborn way he had when he was mad.

She didn't want him to be angry with her over this. There was too much at stake. Her future, for one. And her heart. She couldn't waste either on a man she would never love. She knew there were plenty of marriages built on love. Jacob and Rachel, and Lizzie and Paul came to mind. They'd all overcome obstacles, but in the end, they'd found their true love. That was all she wanted.

Blowing out a breath, she wondered if that kind of love was even in the Lord's plans for her.

A week later Levi stood in the schoolyard, the early dawn light casting soft shadows from the trees onto the lawn. The air was still and quiet. He liked working in solitude, without distraction. On his way here, he'd seen deer drinking out of a stream and red-winged blackbirds perched on the fence that ran along Jacob's property. The early-morning hours were the perfect time to reflect and meditate on the good word.

Unfortunately, some of today's thoughts were filled with words he'd overheard Sadie and her friend saying last week.

He found it interesting that she was so set on knowing what she wanted for every part of her life. Like how she wanted the classroom to look when it was finished and what she wanted in a husband. Mind you, none of the latter was any of his business, but he'd heard her words and there was no forgetting them.

Levi wanted to tell her, based on his life experience thus far, that there was no such thing as a "perfect" person, be they Amish or otherwise. Every last one of them had been born with flaws. It didn't take much to remind him the reason he was here had nothing to do with finding a proper wife and everything to do with putting his hands to work. Busy hands kept one's mind from wandering back to the past.

Of course, he could have stayed in his community. If not for Jacob's offer of employment, he might have done just that. Levi was a strong person. But he hadn't expected the turn his life took a few months ago to leave him feeling so unsettled. His *mamm* had been the one to encourage him to make a change. She'd seen the pain Anne's betrayal had caused and had told Levi a new start could be what he needed. Coming here to Miller's Crossing had seemed like the right thing to do.

Bringing his mind back to the task at hand, he rubbed his hands together, feeling a blister on the inside of his right thumb. It was his own fault. The preceding days had been filled with many tasks, and he hadn't been wearing the work gloves Jacob had given him. He'd been hammering away on the shingles, replacing some of the wood siding and even helping chop a bit of wood.

Levi rolled the ache out of his shoulders, aware of the heat. Not even nine o'clock and the August day was growing hot. He'd been in the schoolyard since sunup, hoping to get ahead of the workload. Swiping his sleeve across his brow, he walked around the back of the schoolhouse to take a look at where the shed once stood. He knew it would be at least two more days before he could get started out here, but he wanted to get an idea of the size of the original foundation.

He did a quick pace of the area. Walking heel-to-toe along the remaining slab, he estimated the structure had been sixteen by twelve feet. A decent size for storage.

Jacob had told him this morning that he didn't have a shed of this size in stock. They would have to build it from scratch. He also suggested that rather than constructing it at the shed company, they should work here, on-site. This would save them in shipping costs since Jacob contracted with a local transport company to deliver the sheds.

Levi wanted to get this project done. Then he could begin working with Jacob on his business. The shed company was doing really well, and he knew Jacob was anxious to expand. Levi wanted to support him.

Meanwhile, it was time to start repainting the walls inside the school. He said hello to one of the women who still came by to help with the food tent, which had decreased in size as fewer workers were needed. But the food and drinks were still welcomed by the remaining crew.

He walked along the side of the school, noticing how the new clapboards blended in with the old. The windows were open, letting in the summer breeze, and he caught a glimpse of Sadie inside talking to some of her students. He recognized an older boy from earlier this week.

"Miss Sadie, my *vader* said I should work with you today," the tall, lanky boy was saying.

"Thank you so much, Jeremiah. It's very kind of him to allow you to be here. We're going to start painting!"

Levi heard the excitement in her voice. He walked through the tall blades of grass and made his way around to the front door. Entering the room, he noticed that Sadie was indeed ready for painting. She had on a light blue skirt and matching blouse covered by a canvas work apron. Her hair was neatly tucked up under her prayer *kapp*. Three five-gallon pails of flat-white paint sat near the door, along with four rolls of blue painter's tape, paint pans, rollers and paintbrushes.

Surveying the room, he thought it might take the three of them the better part of a day to get this job done. He was pleased when a few others in the community straggled in. That meant he would be freed up to begin work on the shed.

"Mica! Josh! *Danke* for coming today," Sadie greeted the newcomers. Then turning to Levi, she explained, "I asked Josh Troyer and his friend Mica King to help us out, too. I hope you don't mind."

Seeing her delight in getting extra help made him realize that Sadie could be extremely resourceful.

"More hands make less work for us," he commented.

"That's what I was thinking. We should start by taping off all of the windows. Then we can get the paint on the walls. Once that is done, I can have the men help bring the desks up from the basement. Then we can get everything back in place. The room is going to look the nicest it's ever been when we are finished. The students deserve a clean, safe place for their learning. Don't you agree, Levi?"

His head was spinning over all the words she managed to get out in a few seconds. He started to answer her, but she began talking again.

"As soon as the paint dries, we can bring the posters back out and get them hung up and get the shades back up on the windows. And then I can start hauling in the boxes of books. I still have to get over to the stationery store to pick up the replacements for the books that were damaged. I'm so excited, Levi—it's looking like we'll be done on time."

"That it does. You're a good worker."

He didn't know why he said that. She was a *good worker*. That sounded so impersonal, like he was speaking to one of the men. But his compliment brought a light blush to her cheekbones, and Levi found himself wanting to smile.

"*Danke.* I just want everything to be perfect for the students."

"With your enthusiasm, I'm certain that it will be."

Mesmerized by the sparkle of hope reflected in her blue eyes, Levi found it hard to look away. But it appeared that she had her mind set on getting today's work started, and her attention quickly shifted from him to the young man standing next to her.

"The first thing we need to do is get the blue tape around the door and window frames," she said to Jeremiah. "Why don't you help me get that started?"

Eager to please, the young man's head bobbed up and down so hard, his hat nearly tumbled from his head. He managed to catch it in time as he followed his teacher over to the pile of supplies stacked near the door. Sadie pulled the protective plastic wrap off the rolls of tape and handed one to Jeremiah.

"Since you're one of the tallest, let's have you start with the entry door."

Jeremiah's reach went almost to the top of the doorframe.

Levi stopped him.

"Wait. Don't overreach or you'll end up hurting your back. Let me go find a ladder for you, Jeremiah."

Levi went outside and brought back in a five-step ladder. Setting it up, he said, "Watch your step, and don't go above the fourth rung."

Words from the instructor at the Ladders Last safety seminar he and Jacob had attended together in Saratoga last year came back to him. He never imagined he'd be using the lesson at a school. But, he supposed, *gut* advice could be put to use in just about any situation.

Confident that Jeremiah could handle the job, Levi grabbed a roll and began taping around the windows. Sadie worked along the floor and walls.

It took the better part of the morning to get all the tape up. Even though it was a pain to do, it would save them the time scraping the windowpanes and floorboards afterward.

Eventually, he heard a soft groan coming from the other side of the room and turned to see Sadie getting up from her hands and knees. Rushing over, he offered her his hand.

At first, he thought she was going to push him away, but then she took hold of his hand, saying, "*Danke.* I was down here far too long without a break."

He helped her into a standing position.

Sadie blew out a breath. "*Phew!* I'm glad that's done. Now we can get the canvas cloths on the floor and start this project."

Letting go of her hand, Levi followed her to the other side of the room. Together they unfurled the heavy canvas and laid the cloth out on the floor. Grabbing a steel tool that looked a lot like a can opener, he ran the tip of it around the rim of the first five-gallon bucket of paint. Setting the opener on the canvas, he carefully lifted the lid. The color was a simple off-white.

Peering over his shoulder, Sadie observed, "I really wanted a yellow for the new color. But they didn't have any and I didn't want to make the cost go higher by mixing a custom color."

Sitting back on his haunches, he looked up at her curiously. "Is yellow a favorite color of yours?"

She gave him a soft smile, nodding. "*Ja.* It reminds me of sunshine. But it's frivolous to have that here when most of the walls are covered with posters and bookshelves. Do you have a favorite color, Levi?"

Grabbing the handle of the paint bucket, he carefully tipped some into a heavy metal tray. He'd never really given color much thought. Most of his life had been surrounded by the simple colors of their clothing.

Concentrating on getting the paint into the tray and not onto the floor covering, he answered, "I suppose I favor blue."

"There are so many shades of blue."

He paused and said, "I like the color of the sky." *And your eyes.* He thought Sadie's eyes were about the prettiest blue he'd ever seen.

"*Ja.* The sky is pretty most days. Unless it's storming. But even then, it can be beautiful." Sadie's voice took on a wistful tone.

"We'd best concentrate on our work."

He stood, picked up the package of rollers and pulled them out. Placing one on a handle, he showed the boys how to glide the paint roller along the bottom of the flat metal pan.

"You don't want to get too much or else you'll have drips running down the walls," he advised.

Sadie nodded, adding, "And if you don't get

enough, then you'll have dry patches. We can't have that. Here, let me show you."

Reaching down, she took hold of one of the rollers and gently slid it into the pan. Once she had enough white paint, she moved the roller up and down on the wall.

"See how I'm making a W shape and how you're getting a lesson at the same time!" Sadie let out a laugh. "After you make that letter, you go back and fill in the space. Like this."

"This way you'll get a nice even coat," Levi finished, impressed with her painting skills.

"That's it exactly," Sadie agreed, smiling at him.

He felt the corners of his mouth turn upward and quickly busied himself with gathering a brush and container to pour some paint into. He didn't want to be drawn to Sadie, and yet he was finding it harder and harder to resist her charm. Turning away from everyone else, Levi began applying paint to the baseboard trim along the floor.

It wasn't long before he heard the light, sweet sound of someone humming. Sadie. Her voice sounded so lyrical. Levi listened to her hum one of the songs he remembered from his own school days. A little bit of light broke through the heaviness he'd been carrying around. He wanted to ignore the feeling, because he didn't want to attribute it to being around Sadie.

Levi didn't want another woman to work her way into his life. But the lightheartedness stayed with him as he dipped the paintbrush into the half-empty can. There was no denying the power of Sadie's positive attitude.

They worked until lunchtime.

"Come on, everyone. I believe you've more than earned a lunch break." Looking at Levi, Sadie said, "You, too, Levi. I know I've worked up an appetite, and I don't care if that doesn't sound ladylike. I'm starving!"

He saw the flush of her cheeks that came with working hard in the summertime heat. With a laugh, Sadie spun on her heel and hurried out the door, stopping at the water pump to the right of the building to wash her hands.

"Boys, don't forget, cleanliness is next to godliness," she called out as Jeremiah, Mica and Josh plowed by her.

They turned around and rushed back to splash their hands in the water after she finished. Levi waited his turn, then putting his hands together, he splashed the water up on his face. The coolness refreshed him.

They formed a short line behind Sadie to get a hamburger hot off the grill that Jeremiah's *mudder* had set up.

"I thought you might be getting tired of the sandwiches. So, I had my husband bring over our gas grill."

"*Danke*, Susan." Sadie patted the woman on the forearm. "Your thoughtfulness is much appreciated."

"*Danke*," Levi added. The delicious scent of the burgers caused his stomach to rumble loud enough for Sadie to hear.

"We'd best get you fed, Levi. I don't need you collapsing. And when you're ready, I want to talk to you about the new shed."

Levi blinked. They'd agreed to work together on the schoolhouse repair, and then he would be free to continue with the shed. The rebuild would be straightforward. A simple shed. Yes, he knew it was the school's shed, but they were on a tight schedule.

What could she possibly have to say about the shed project?

Chapter Seven

Sadie could tell by the look on Levi's face that he wasn't thrilled with her request. His mouth had taken on the same determined line she remembered from the day she'd first met him.

She pasted a smile on her face. Taking her paper plate with the hamburger and macaroni salad over to the picnic table, she joined the boys. After a few minutes, Levi sat at the opposite end of the bench.

It was clear he did not want to discuss the shed project over lunch. That was fine by her. She was content to enjoy every last bite of her hamburger. The boys sat across from them, inhaling their food.

"Boys. Slow down when you eat. I don't want you choking."

All three of them looked up at her, as if they'd forgotten their manners and that she and Levi were at the table with them.

"*Es dutt mir leed*, Miss Sadie," Jeremiah said. Nudging Josh with his right elbow, he added, "We're all sorry."

The other two boys put what was left of their burgers on the plate and nodded.

Leaning across the table, Jeremiah said, "My *mudder* makes the best burgers."

"*Danke*, son." Susan accepted the compliment as she joined them with her own plate. "Sadie, I cannot believe how much work you've gotten done in such a short time."

Sadie watched as the boys went back to eating at a much slower pace, then turned to Susan. "I've had a lot of help."

Susan glanced over to where Levi sat. "It was *gut* that you came along to our village when you did, Levi Byler. You've certainly been a great help to our Sadie and our school community. Though, I imagine your own community must miss you."

A look Sadie couldn't identify slid across Levi's face. Was it sadness or longing, maybe regret? She imagined he must be a bit homesick. Maybe not, though. It was hard to say, because she hadn't had any conversations with him about his life. She only knew the little that she'd learned the day he rescued her from the mudhole. And, of course, that blue was his favorite color.

They finished eating their lunch and returned to work. Levi got the boys set up painting the wall behind Sadie's desk while she continued to work on the trim around the windows. She was painting the lower half of the one by the entryway when Levi came up behind her with a brush in hand.

"I'll do the tops so you don't have to worry about standing on the ladder."

"That's very kind of you." Sadie grew pensive. Their close proximity brought her the perfect opportunity to learn more about him.

As she dipped her brush into their shared paint can, she formulated her questions. She enjoyed learning about people. One of her favorite classes to teach was history. For a few days she and the *kinder* got lost in learning about the people who had come and gone before them. She wondered again what Levi's people might be like.

"Tell me, Levi, what is your community like?"

His movements stilled. Sadie thought the question was innocent enough. She continued moving the brush up and down the trim in short strokes. Waiting.

"I live closer to the city than you do. But we have farmland and ten church districts," he said. "Some are smaller than others."

"And your family?"

"My family?"

"Do you have a large family? I know you're part of Jacob's family, but what is your immediate family like? Most of us around here have large families, and some live near their elders or in the same house if it's big enough. My friend Lizzie's sister lives in the house they grew up in, with her husband and *kinder*. Lizzie and her husband, Paul, moved into the village to be closer to their shop."

"I see. I have two older *bruders* and a younger sister. They are all married off."

"But you're not." Sadie drew in a breath, surprised when she voiced her thought. "*Es dutt mir leed.* That is none of my business."

Levi turned away from her, appearing to concentrate on touching up the paint on the windows. Then he said, "I understand. We're at a time in our lives when courtships are all our families want to talk about."

"Perhaps I spend too much time ruminating about the subject." Softly she added, "I know you overheard my conversation with Lizzie."

"Ah. *Ja.* I might have heard some of what you were saying." He raised an eyebrow, studying her.

A shiver ran along her spine. It wasn't an unwanted feeling. Still, Sadie found herself wondering at her reaction to Levi. She was about to tell him she'd no interest in the man her *vader* wanted for her, then changed her mind. She didn't think Levi would care to hear her thoughts on the matter.

Eventually she turned away from him, focusing on her work. The only sound in the room came from the movement of the brushes and rollers. Even the boys had settled into a rhythm. Sweat trickled down Sadie's back, and she longed for a wisp of a breeze to come through the open windows. All the while she wished she could take back her words about Levi's marital state. His family and his life before coming here were none of her business.

They continued working in silence until she looked up and realized the room was finished.

Sadie sent the boys home, leaving her and Levi to finish the cleanup. She was helping him fold the drop cloth when he finally started talking to her again.

"What are your thoughts on the shed?" he asked, taking her side of the folded cloth out of her hands.

Clearing her throat, she knew her idea might sound like extra work. "I want to add in two windows in the front so we can use them to start our seedlings for the garden. And I think some window boxes would be nice, too. This way the students can try out different types of plants."

"You have windows here." He pointed to the ones they'd just painted.

"We do, but they don't get the right light to grow seedlings in."

"It seems to be bright enough now."

"Yes, but this is the summer sunlight. The early-spring light comes in from that direction." Sadie nodded toward the east side of the room.

"And you can't use those windows?"

"*Nee.* The sills are not wide enough." She saw the stubborn set of his jaw and put her hands on her hips.

She would fight to the end for her students, and even though this might seem unimportant to him, for her this little thing was worth the effort.

Levi stared at her. She waited for his gaze to waver, and when it didn't, she broke the stare down by casting her gaze to the toes of her shoes. That was when she saw the paint spatters and knew her *mamm* would not be happy with her for making a mess of them yet again.

"Doesn't Jacob have a shed that we can use here?" she finally asked. "One with windows?"

"*Nee.* We're going to build this one on-site. He's swamped with business. Even before the storm, his orders were backed up, and now with people needing theirs replaced, he's running out of stock."

She nibbled on her lip, trying to come up with a way to convince Levi to add the windows to the new shed. "Is it the cost?"

"Nope."

"So, it's you not wanting to change your plans?"

"I guess it's been a long day and I don't have the energy left to think about changing any existing plans," he admitted to her.

Stubbing her toe along the floorboard, she grumbled, "I understand. But don't you think my idea is a *gut* one?"

"I do. However, it's not really up to us to make these changes."

She pondered his words, knowing the school board had put Jacob in charge of this project. He was a trusted member of the community. Surely, he would do this for her.

"What I want is to have an area for my students to work on their gardening skills."

Levi took the drop cloth over to the pile of leftover supplies. He fumbled around for a few minutes, tapping a hammer on top of the loosened paint can lid. Then he picked up the can and the drop cloth, brushing past her, and carried them out the front door.

Sadie hurried after him. Her patience thinning, and knowing the fatigue might be fueling her, she called out to him, "Levi! We're not finished with this."

He set the supplies in the back of his wagon. She saw the sweat breaking through the back of his shirt and knew he had to be as tired and worn out by the heat as she was. But that didn't stop her from wanting to know if he might at least consider her suggestions for the windows.

Resting an elbow on the side of the wagon, Levi pushed the brim of his straw hat off his forehead. Sadie tipped her head back a bit, looking up into his eyes. The blue-green color was striking in the afternoon light.

She ignored that thought, even though she knew many of her friends would consider him to be a handsome man. And she wouldn't be able to contradict them on that observation.

Her nerves became a jangle, a feeling she wasn't familiar with. Normally, she would plow through to make her point. But standing here, at the end of a long day spent working side by side, Sadie felt her conviction about the windows waver.

Nee. She must stop thinking like a schoolgirl and remember the interests of her students.

Using a soft, relenting tone, she asked, "Levi, will you please help me out here?"

He knew what she was doing, and while he might not trust her cajoling tone, he understood why she wanted him to make the changes. He supposed there wasn't any harm in bringing her idea to Jacob. She was right about one thing: the students' needs should come first.

Finally, he said, "I'll talk to Jacob."

He went back inside and brought out the rest of the cans, brushes and rollers. Sadie helped him clean up, until the exhaustion of the day caught up with her. Levi noticed her steps slowing on the last trip to the wagon. In two easy strides, he came alongside her, taking the can.

"Danke," she said, releasing the metal handle.

He squinted down at her, "Sadie, you've done a good day's work here. Let me drive you home."

"That won't be necessary. I rode my bike over this morning."

"Come on, it's too hot to ride it back home. The wagon will take half the time. I can put the bike in the back."

He saw her indecision, as well as her flushed cheeks. She had to be feeling the heat as much as he was.

She narrowed her eyes, as if she had a choice in the matter. "I don't want you to get any ideas about my needing rescuing, like the first time we met."

Biting back a half smile, he replied, "Nope. Think of it as a neighbor helping out a neighbor."

"All right. I left my bike near the pop-up canopy. Would you mind getting it for me?"

"I can do that."

After finding her bike, he wheeled it back and loaded it on the wagon. Then he offered her his hand, which surprisingly she took hold of. If he'd learned one thing about Sadie Fischer in his short time here, it was that she had an independent streak. Levi waited for her to settle in the seat, and then going around to the other side, he climbed in, as well. The wagon shifted under his weight and caused Sadie to bump into him.

She pulled away from him with a soft "I'm sorry."

Once back on her side of the seat, Sadie continued, "I guess I am more tired than I thought I was. You know how you go and go and go and then when you stop, you realize how much energy you've spent? That's how I'm feeling."

Urging the horse forward, Levi nodded. He did know. Right now, his shoulders and arms ached from all the painting. Sadie had to be feeling the same discomfort and yet she sat with her back tall and her hands folded neatly on her lap, looking out over the passing hills. Meanwhile, the blister on his right hand was still bothering him. He'd have to be sure to clean and bandage it when he got back to Jacob and Rachel's place.

"Levi, before I forget. We have our annual Miller's Crossing picnic coming up. You must be sure to come. You'll be able to meet more of our community. A lot of the older folks don't come out except for our gatherings, and of course the weekly church services. There will be lots of food and games," she went on. "I might even find time to make my blue-ribbon snickerdoodles! My *mamm* will, of course, make her potato salad, and there will be coleslaw and moon pies. I'm sure there will be a roasted chicken and bratwurst."

She groaned in delight. "My *grossmudder*, on my *vader*'s side, made the best bratwurst. She passed over a decade ago, but we still use her recipe at large gatherings." She rubbed a hand over her stomach. "All of this talk about food is making me hungry. Trust me, the day of the picnic will be filled with fun, and it's a *gut* time to catch up. Which reminds me, you never finished telling me about your people." She gave him a smile.

He knew she was trying to find out what brought him here. And he wasn't willing to share his personal life with her. Sadie didn't need to know about his past. He certainly didn't want her to get any ideas about adding him to her list of what she wanted for her perfect Amish man. He was anything but perfect.

He thought back on this time last year when his life had seemed cemented in place.

He'd been working with his *vader* on the family farm. Because Levi had always been good with the craftsman side of things, he'd been in charge of all the building upkeep. And he'd been in love with a young woman he'd known all his life. Levi thought Anne had been a perfect match. She was kind and gentle. When their families proposed the idea of their courtship, it had seemed like the most natural path for them.

They'd made plans for their wedding day, after which they were going to live in a small house near the back of Levi's family farm. He'd spent weeks cleaning and painting, inside and out. Because he knew how much Anne liked to work on her quilting, he'd set up a separate space off to one side of the living room for her to work in. He'd built a shelf along one wall with cubbies for all her fabric.

Levi had intended those white shelves to be her wedding gift. The only problem was Anne had had other plans. While Levi had been planning a life with the woman he loved, she'd been plotting to leave their community. Absently, he rubbed his hand over his chest, knowing nothing could remove the remnants of the dull ache that still lay inside his heart.

The day he realized Anne had gone still stood out in his memories. His plan on the beautiful sunny fall day had been to put the finishing touches on the house. But when he'd gotten there, he'd found a note taped to the front door. Her words seared into his soul. She was in love with someone else: an *Englischer*. Under the cover of darkness, Anne had left the community.

And in the blink of an eye his life changed.

For days afterward he found himself falling into a well of sadness he didn't think would ever end. Then came the anger. Anger at himself for believing in something that would never be. Anger at Anne for her deception.

Questioning his every move since the day they'd agreed to the courtship, he let his work on the farm go. He spent hours in prayer seeking an answer from the Lord and realizing there might not be one. Until one day his *mudder* came to him with the letter from his cousin. She was the one who convinced him to come here, telling him he needed a new outlook on life. And reminding him that the Lord never gave anyone more than they could handle.

Pausing in his thoughts, he brought his attention back to Sadie. He pushed down all those memories, all those thoughts and feelings, and gave a shrug. "There's not much more to tell."

"Do you miss them?"

He'd have to add *tenacious* to the list of words that described the schoolteacher.

"I've sent them off a letter or two. My *mamm* is *gut* about responding with news. Besides, I'm not sure if this will be a permanent move for me." Levi paused. He had no idea why he'd voiced that thought.

"Right, because you're here to help out your cousin. Who knows, Levi. Miller's Crossing might grow on you and maybe you'll never want to leave."

Her voice drifted off, leaving only the sound of nature and the occasional car zipping by them. Sadie seemed satisfied with their conversation, for now. This young woman was a force to be reckoned with. He'd seen how patient and kind she was with the lads helping them out. And she always, always had a smile for everyone. Levi could tell from the way she took care of the things in her classroom that she was a devoted teacher.

Though he had to admit, he couldn't imagine her scolding anyone, let alone a *kinder*. And her stubbornness? Even that had a soft side.

He knew he shouldn't be thinking this way. He'd learned a hard lesson this past year about trusting his feelings when it came to love. But even in this short amount of time, Sadie Fischer had worked her way into his thoughts. He would be better served focusing his attention on his work with Jacob.

Levi looked out over the landscape unfolding before them. Rolling hills and trees filled with lush green leaves lay on the tapestry the Lord had created. The air, though heavy with the summer humidity, was pure and clean. The rhythmic sound of the horse's hooves tapping along the road settled over him. Levi's mind wandered.

He imagined life here in Miller's Crossing, though tough at times, could in turn be filled with grace and beauty. The people he'd met so far were kind and caring. The nearby village of Clymer had buildings that were obviously cared for with pride. Levi didn't know where life was going to take him. He only knew to trust in the path laid out before him… the path that had brought him here. Still, he couldn't help battling with the changes in his life. He knew for certain he would use caution when it came to making decisions that would last a lifetime.

He suspected that the others, like Sadie, didn't know what to make of him, but like all Amish communities, they were welcoming. And the fact that he had family here helped. He felt he was doing good work at the school, which led him to an idea. One that might make Sadie's workload easier. And even as he had the thought, Levi knew he was going down an emotional path that he shouldn't be taking.

He still believed his life was meant to be lived alone. But that didn't mean he couldn't do something helpful for Sadie. After he dropped her off at her house, he'd take advantage of the lingering summer daylight and head back to the school.

Glancing to his right, he realized Sadie hadn't spoken in quite a few minutes. Her chin was tipped down, and he could see the even rise and fall of her chest. Her hands, though still together, lay limp in her lap.

"Well, I'll be," he muttered in amusement. She'd fallen asleep.

Laying a light hand against her forearm, he gave her the tiniest of shakes. "Sadie. Sadie. Wake up."

Chapter Eight

Sadie sat up with a start, blinking. She'd fallen asleep. How had she let that happen? She must have been more tired than she thought. Embarrassment flooded through her. How could she let herself be caught in such a compromising position? She worked at brushing the wrinkles out of her apron.

"I wasn't sleeping. I was simply resting my eyes." She couldn't believe she'd resorted to using one of her *grossmudder* Fischer's responses when caught napping.

"If you say so."

Sitting up taller, she quipped, "I do."

By now, Levi was guiding the horse and wagon around the last bend before her home. She could tell by the slant of the sun that it was nearly past suppertime.

"Oh, dear."

"What's the matter?" Levi asked.

"I'm late for dinner."

"We should have left the school sooner."

"But we were busy with painting. My *mamm* will understand my tardiness."

Her *vader*, on the other hand, might not be as accommodating. He liked to have everyone at the table at the same time each evening. Sadie often wondered how he could be so strict with his routine, while she liked to see how the day would unfold. She liked to think that was what made her a better schoolteacher. While she did use a lesson planner that the committee approved each semester, she also set aside time just in case an educational opportunity arose that needed further exploration.

Take last spring when the girls had wanted to know more about the painting Lizzie Burkholder did. Lizzie was getting quite the reputation for her watercolor landscapes. Sadie had spent a week on art, giving a little time each day to let the students dabble in the paints. Indeed, schooling should be used to teach the fundamentals, but Sadie would never subdue her students' natural curiosity. They were young for such a short time, and the adult world would be upon them soon enough.

And that thought brought her full circle to her *vader*'s concerns that she needed to concentrate more on her future beyond the classroom. Her gaze slid to Levi. He seemed intent on steering the wagon around the corner and down her driveway.

She wondered again why he hadn't brought a wife with him to Miller's Crossing. He seemed reluctant to discuss his family when she'd asked. While some might think a man like Levi wasn't the marrying kind, Sadie could tell he cared. Even though he was quiet and pensive, he'd been helpful to her these past days. When they were working at the school, she'd caught him watching over the boys, teaching them how to do things the right way. And he'd worked tirelessly alongside her.

The wagon came to a stop near the hitching post at the front of the house. Sadie hopped down. The first thing she noticed was that the barn had been closed up for the night. And the picnic table in the side yard had been set with the plastic red-and-white-checkered tablecloth. Her *mamm* and sister were busy setting out the food.

Sara looked up when she saw Sadie and Levi. Giving them a wave, she beckoned them over.

"Come. You're just in time. *Mamm* and I were just putting dinner out," Sara said. Taking the lid off of the beef stew, she added, "Our *bruder* William and Kara are coming over with their *kinder*. They should be here any minute."

As if on cue, Sadie heard the laughter of her niece and nephew. She turned to watch as William parked the buggy next to Levi's wagon. William and his family lived about a mile up the road at his wife's family home. Sadie was happy to see them.

"Kara! William! *Guten owed*." Sadie greeted them, giving the *kinder* a big hug.

"*Guten owed* to you, Sadie," her *bruder* said with a nod. He looked to where Levi was getting her bike out of the back of the wagon. "And who might this be?" he asked.

"This is Levi Byler. He's been helping out with the school repairs."

"*Ach*. That was a fierce storm." William held out his hand and Levi shook it.

Sadie looked back and forth between the two men. Her *bruder* was a clever one. Acting nice and neighborly when she knew he was, in fact, taking stock of the man.

"*Ja*, it was indeed," she agreed. "But we're moving along. Tomorrow I have to go to King's Stationery to replace the school supplies that were ruined."

She walked with Kara and the *kinder* while William stayed back to chat with Levi.

"I'm not sure your *bruder* is too happy to see you with that man," Kara commented.

Sadie made a face. Though she loved him dearly, and he was the eldest, William was not in charge of her life. "Levi offered to bring me home. We had a long day's work. I have to admit I was too tired to pedal all the way here. I appreciated the ride."

Sara met them halfway to the picnic table. "*Mamm* wants to know if Levi might like to join us for supper."

The suggestion caught Sadie off guard. It hadn't occurred to her to ask Levi to stay. She knew he had to get back to Jacob's, and that was at least a twenty-minute drive from here. She imagined he would say no. However, she didn't get the chance to invite him. William came over a few minutes later as Levi was driving off.

"He seems nice enough," was all William said.

Sadie nodded, thinking that Levi was indeed nice enough. Her gaze lingered on the roadway as she watched the wagon disappear over the horizon.

"Sadie, come, dinner is waiting to be served."

Sadie smiled at her *mamm* and approached the table. A large maple tree spread shade over the area, and she took a moment to drink in the scene. Her parents, two of her siblings, and the *kinder* all took their places on the wooden benches. She sat between her *mamm* and sister and joined in the thanksgiving for the food set before them.

The breeze floated around them, offering the first bit of coolness she'd felt all day. She wanted to tip her head back and take in the moment, but she tamped down the urge, instead spooning some of the stew onto her plate.

"How far have you gotten at the school?" Sara asked, handing Sadie the bread basket.

"I have a few more days before I can begin to bring in the desks and bookshelves. Tomorrow I'm going to the stationery store to get some supplies."

"William can take you. He has to run there himself," Kara offered. William and Kara ran a small quilt shop out of their home.

From the far end of the table, William said, "I'll pick you up at eight."

Sadie agreed, then finished the meal and helped with the evening chores.

The next morning, she was ready when William pulled into the driveway at eight on the dot. She settled into the buggy and bade him a *guder mariye*.

"I hope your morning is a *gut* one, too, Sadie," he returned.

She'd say it was. The humidity that had been plaguing them for the past week had finally broken overnight, leaving in its wake a clear blue sky and easy breathing. She glanced at her *bruder*—from this side, he reminded her a lot of their *vader*. Both men had the same long nose and graying beards, though her *vader*'s was almost all white now. William had the same shape to his eyes, although the color resembled their *mudder*'s.

He gave the reins a shake and the horse trotted off. Sadie sat back under the cover of the buggy.

"Sadie, I'm not going to waste any time. I need to speak with you about your situation."

She felt the tiny hairs on the back of her neck rise. This couldn't be good. "And what situation might that be?"

"This one between you and Isaiah."

She tried to keep her frustration in check. "As I've told our *vader*, there is no situation there."

"You know there should be."

"I know no such thing, William." She felt her anger rising.

Annoyance didn't do anyone any good. But now she had a feeling that William bringing her into the village hadn't been a kind offer. He'd been wanting to find a way to speak to her about her future, and a ride into the village was a good excuse. Sadie looked out the small window of the buggy. The horse moved along at such a speed that the trees and hillside whizzed by them.

"William, slow down!" She felt the buggy slowing. *"Danke."*

He mumbled, *"Es dutt mir leed."* A mere second passed and then he continued, "Sadie, you are the schoolteacher and as such you have to live up to a certain standard."

"William! Are you saying you think that I'm not good enough for the job?" Sadie felt flushed. She couldn't accept that her *bruder* would think such a thing of his own sister. She worked night and day during the school year planning and preparing for her students to get the best education they could under her tutelage.

"*Nee. Nee.* Of course not. But you have been ignoring *Vader*'s choice for you, and people are beginning to take notice."

"I don't care."

"You should care!"

"Don't raise your voice to me."

William let out an exasperated sigh. "Oh, Sadie. We, and by we, I mean our family, only want what is best for you."

"Maybe what's best for me would be for you to let me make my own choice in this matter."

"I don't want to see this cause you any trouble."

"See what causing me trouble, William?"

"Your being with Levi Byler. He's driven you home, not once but twice. And you are spending time working with him at the schoolhouse."

"For goodness' sake. Neither of those times count for anything. The first time he rescued me from that mudhole, and yesterday he was doing nothing more than being a good neighbor." Sucking in a breath, she breathed out, "As for being alone at the school, there are others there most of the time."

"*Most* of the time, but not all of the time," William pointed out.

By now they had traveled to the outskirts of Miller's Crossing. The stationery store was over the next rise and then a turn down a narrow, winding road. Sadie grabbed onto the handrail as William allowed the buggy to sail around the corner. Taking his anger out on the poor horse wouldn't help the matter.

"Slow down," she said once more. "Did *Vader* ask you to speak to me?"

"*Nee.* He did not. I'm the one who is concerned." William's voice softened as he slowed the horse coming into the parking lot for King's Stationery. He pulled into a space, tugging the brake back and setting it. Then he turned to look at her.

"Levi Byler seems like a nice person. And yes, helping you with the repairs is a *gut* thing. But you are the teacher. You know you have to be careful with your time and you shouldn't be unchaperoned. Just be careful. Okay?"

Sadie could see that concern softening the edges around his eyes and knew he only had her best interest at heart. She didn't like arguing and hated that they were starting this glorious day sparring over her future.

"Sadie, please consider my words."

"I will."

They entered the store. William headed off to the office supply section, and Sadie went to the aisle that had the classroom materials. It didn't take her long to find the two posters she needed, then she made a beeline to the books. She hoped they had a replacement for a title that had been destroyed by the rain.

She slowed her pace, enjoying the covers on display. An entire row was filled with Christian books with such beautiful art that Sadie paused to admire them. Then she saw a few gardening magazines and the *Farmers' Almanac*. Finally, she found the children's section and was delighted to see the book she'd been looking for. She added it to her basket, then she went up to the front counter to pay for everything.

Her *bruder* had gotten there ahead of her and was chatting with Amos King, the owner of the store and one of the school board members.

"*Gute mariye*, Miss Sadie."

"It's a fine morning, Amos. I think we're in for the best day of the week so far."

"I would agree." He smiled at her and then slid the book into a paper bag. "Should I add these to the school account?"

"Yes, please."

"My *kinder* are anxious to start the new school year. They were very upset to see the storm damage. But I assured them it would be taken care of in plenty of time."

"I've had a lot of *gut* people helping. Some of the older boys have been working inside with me on the painting."

"So I've heard." And as if to prove William's point, Amos added, "Jacob's cousin Levi has done *gut* work there. But please be sure to work in groups."

Sadie turned her back ever so slightly so she didn't have to see the look on her *bruder*'s face. She hated to admit when he was right. It was clear that the community members were indeed talking about her. Sadie didn't want to create any problems for the school board when it came to her personal life.

Sadie chastised herself. She knew better. She needed to give more thought to her actions.

Nodding at Amos, she gathered her things and headed out to the buggy. William came right on her heels. Thankfully he had the wherewithal to keep his comments to himself regarding what Amos had said.

William dropped her at the school, and Sadie thanked him for taking her to the store. "I appreciate the ride, William."

"It's no trouble. You'll think about what I said?"

"Ja."

Sadie waved him off, knowing that where Isaiah Troyer was concerned her mind was made up.

She walked along the pathway to the front door. She swung it open, fully expecting to find the blue tape surrounding the windows and floor trim. But that wasn't what she found at all.

Sadie stood in the middle of the room with her mouth agape.

"I don't understand," she whispered in amazement at the sight before her.

Chapter Nine

Sadie set the posters and book down on the desk. The desk right in front of her. The room was full of them! She spun around with her arms spread wide in happiness.

All the desks were in orderly rows, and the bookcases were set up against the wall near the door. Her teacher's desk was still absent, but that didn't matter. She wondered who she should thank for this gift.

The sound of voices came from behind the building. Sadie hurried out the door and ran around to the back, anxious to see who was there.

Levi stood with Jacob and two of the boys who'd been helping her out.

"Danke!" she blurted out. *"Danke! Danke!"*

"Miss Sadie, were you surprised?" Mica asked.

"I was very pleasantly surprised. *Danke* so much."

"It was Levi's idea. He'd already gotten the cleanup done. All the desks were set out. Josh and I helped bring up the bookshelves this morning."

"Well, that was very kind of all of you." Sadie

nodded to each of the boys and then raised her eyes to meet Levi's gaze.

His expression was unreadable She wondered when he'd found the time to do all of this work. It had been quite late in the day when he'd left her house yesterday and it was only midmorning now.

"Levi, I can't believe you found the time to do all of this!"

He was half turned away from her, as if he didn't want to meet her gaze. "I came back last night."

"You didn't have to do this," she said. His generosity touched her.

"I thought getting the desks back up here would push us along. Now you can concentrate on getting the classroom ready for opening day."

There seemed to be a different mood about him this morning. She couldn't quite put her finger on the change. But it was as if he didn't want to be near her. Sadie didn't understand. Maybe Levi was distracted thinking about the tasks for today. Either way, she was grateful for his effort.

"*Danke* again for your thoughtfulness."

While she'd been offering her thanks, two wagon-loads of lumber arrived, one with two-by-fours and the other with roof trusses. Sadie watched as the drivers pulled to a stop next to the old shed foundation.

Levi still hadn't agreed to add in windows. Deciding she could catch more bees with honey, Sadie flashed him her most radiant smile. She needed him to fix the shed the way it should be done. *For the children, of course.*

Not wanting to be in the way, Sadie left the men to carry on.

* * *

After seeing the look on Sadie's face when she'd come around back, he thought his late night, working by the light of one of the most brilliant moons he'd seen in a long time, had been worth it. After he'd dropped her at home, he'd come back to the school and finished taking down the tape, swept the floor, cleaned up a few cobwebs and hauled thirty desks up the flight of basement stairs.

Ja, he'd been exhausted, but it was *gut* exhaustion, the kind that came when you knew you'd done something that would make someone else happy. Sadie had been so tired at the end of yesterday, and while he knew she would work without complaint, he wanted to do something that would make today easier.

He hadn't meant to sound terse with his response just now, but Levi knew from hard experience that Sadie's feelings were softening toward him. The tells were there. The way she spoke to him with a lighter tone, the way her gaze grew steady when she looked at him. He knew the signs because those were the exact emotions he'd experienced with Anne.

Levi wasn't about to be taken in again. He had to be careful where Sadie was concerned, because she was beginning to grow on him.

"Levi!"

He turned to see Jacob coming toward him.

"I'm going to unload these wagons and then we'll be back with the rest of the lumber you'll need to get started on the shed."

"Okay. What were your thoughts on adding in the windows that Sadie asked for?"

"I still have to see if we have any in stock. I might have two older ones we could use. But go ahead and start with the framework as we originally planned. I don't want to have to redo the walls if we don't have those windows."

"That sounds like a *gut* plan."

Jacob gave him a wink, joking, "Do you want me to tell Sadie?"

"*Nee.* We won't say anything until we know for certain."

"All right then. On second thought, I'm going to send one of my workers back with the next load. I still have a month's backlog to deal with. I'm thankful you came out to Miller's Crossing when you did. I'm not sure how I could have been in all these places at once."

"I'm happy to help."

"You're more than helping, Levi. We'll talk more about the business when things settle down. Have a good day."

"You, too," Levi replied.

Watching his friend leave, he wondered what Jacob had meant. He heard the boys laughing behind him. Turning around, he found Mica and Josh horsing around on the pile of two-by-fours. They were pushing and shoving each other on and off the pile.

"Boys! Get down from there before you get hurt!" Levi didn't like to raise his voice, but he didn't have time to tend to an injury. "Come here."

Doing as they were told, the two of them scrambled over to him.

Folding his arms, Levi stared down at them.

Mica fidgeted in front of him. "We didn't mean no harm, Levi," he said.

"I understand. But we've got a lot of work to do today. Do either of you boys know anything about putting up a shed?"

"Nope," Josh said.

"How old are you?"

"I'm twelve and Mica is eleven," Josh answered.

Raising an eyebrow, Levi asked, "Do you know how to swing a hammer?"

Both boys nodded.

"*Gut.* Then let's get to work." Of course, Levi had no intention of letting the boys work with hammers and nails. He just wanted them to concentrate on helping him and not roughhousing.

They'd done well enough with the painting, but working with lumber required focus.

"I'm going to tell you what I need help with, and you let me know if you think you can handle it." Levi took an authoritative stance with his feet spread apart and his arms folded across his chest while he let his words sink in.

After a few seconds, both boys stilled.

"I'll need help carrying the wood over to the foundation, then I'll need someone to hold the pieces in place while I nail them in position. You think you can do that?"

Both boys nodded so hard their hats tumbled off their blond heads.

Clapping his hands together, Levi said, "Okay then, put your hats back on and let's get a move on."

For the next few hours, Levi had to delve deep

for patience. Mica and Josh took turns holding the two-by-fours while he pounded the nails in place. Though they were good helpers, they would wander off when he wasn't watching them like a hawk.

He didn't understand their behavior. Yesterday they'd been diligent while working with Sadie. Today they were acting like little *kinder*. Listening to them horsing around reminded him of his own childhood with his *bruders*. They'd managed to get into their fair share of trouble during chore time.

Putting the hammer back into the leather work belt he wore around his waist, Levi tilted his hat and wiped his brow with his sleeve. Blowing out a breath, he surveyed the work they'd done. It might be a good idea to nail the frame of the walls together on the ground and then push them up into place. For that he'd need the strength of a few men. Not as many as a barn raising required; just two would suffice.

He thought the boys might be happy to hear they wouldn't be needed for that part.

"Mica, Josh!" he called to them. "Come on over here. You've earned a break."

"Are you pleased with our work today, Levi?" Josh wanted to know.

"I am. You've done a fine job. Now, here's the thing, and I know you'll be disappointed, but I'm not going to need you for a few days. I'm bringing some men in to help me with the wall frames. It's a big job."

The boys did their best to look solemn, but then their faces broke out in grins. Saying their goodbyes, they bounded off across the schoolyard.

"Well, I'll be." Levi shook his head and laughed.

Some days he missed the freedom of being a young boy. The long summers spent fishing and playing in the hayloft. The time before the responsibilities of life intruded.

As Levi laughed to himself, he noticed Sadie coming around the back, picking her way through the construction debris.

"It looks like they were itching to leave you." Her comment came out in a chuckle.

He liked her laugh.

"They hung on longer than I thought they would. Let's face it, working with you inside is nothing like being out here helping lift heavy lumber. But they are *gut* boys."

"*Ja*. They are." Walking over to the pile of two-by-fours, she looked down at them. "I don't see any windows."

"Now, Sadie, before you go getting all in a huff, Jacob is going to look around to see what he has in stock."

Though she tried to hide it, Levi saw the satisfied smile cross her face. "That's very nice of him, and of you, to take my request seriously."

It was more that he didn't want to get bogged down arguing with her over the matter when there was so much work yet to be done.

She stood there with a look he couldn't quite figure out. Her eyes were scrunched up a bit as if she were deep in thought. He fiddled with the hammer stuck in his tool belt.

Finally, she said, "You're good with the *kinder*, Levi."

A jolt of surprise ran through him. He hadn't expected her compliment. With a shrug, he said, "I like them well enough."

"I can tell. It's hard to be patient when all they want to do is be allowed to run free. But you took your time with Mica and Josh today. That was nice of you."

"Danke."

She grinned up at him. "Like it or not, Levi, you are becoming a part of this community."

He didn't say anything. He still wasn't sure he'd be staying on here. But he did like the people, and they were friendly toward him. He was aware of how Sadie's *vader* and oldest *bruder* felt about him. Not that it mattered. Levi was not in the market to find a wife.

"Do you work on projects like this with the *kinder* in your family?"

"If the need arises."

He knew this young woman well enough to know she was trying to bait him into sharing more of his past with her. No matter how sweet she tried to be, Levi couldn't let himself fall into her trap.

"Sadie, I really need to get back to work."

"I'll let you go, but promise me you'll come to the picnic."

Chapter Ten

A week later, Sadie stood in the kitchen putting the finishing touches on the final batch of her blue-ribbon snickerdoodles and thinking about her last exchange with Levi. While she rolled the dough into one-inch balls and dropped them into a bowl of cinnamon and sugar, she realized he'd never given her an answer about whether or not he would be attending today's picnic.

Using a spoon, she coated the unbaked dough with the mixture. She'd gotten out of bed right before sunrise to avoid running the oven in the heat of the day. The entire house smelled like vanilla, cinnamon and warm sugar. Oh, how she loved the scent. Inhaling, she let the smells flood her senses with homey goodness and comfort.

It had been a busy month, but she was looking forward to the annual Miller's Crossing picnic. The day was much like a wedding celebration, but in her mind even better, because you didn't have to wear your Sunday clothes. Today was a day to celebrate life, community and friendships. And Sadie couldn't wait to catch up with her friends.

Setting the balls of dough on the tray, being careful to leave two inches between each one for spreading, she put them in the oven to bake.

She grabbed the chicken-shaped timer off the Formica countertop, setting it for eight minutes. While the cookies were baking, she had two other sheet pans cooling with a few dozen snickerdoodles. The sight of their crackled tops brought a smile to her face.

Sliding a flat spatula under each cookie, she carefully transferred them to a wire rack where they would finish hardening. Later, she would put them in a big red cookie tin. If anyone asked her what her favorite thing to do was other than teaching, she'd have to say baking these cookies. How could you not love a good old-fashioned cookie?

She wondered what Levi's favorite cookie might be. She remembered mentioning her snickerdoodles to him the day he'd brought her home from school. The same day her *bruder* had spoken to him.

Sadie didn't understand why her family couldn't leave her to make her own decision when it came to finding the right person to spend the rest of her life with.

Isaiah hadn't been around much at all. Come to think of it, she hadn't seen him since that day he'd stopped by to see the storm damage at the school. The day Levi had interrupted their conversation. She'd known he wanted to know who Isaiah was. But they didn't discuss those matters. Instead their conversations stayed focused on the school or the little bits when she could get him to talk about his family.

Sadie had tried on more than one occasion to get Levi to open up about his life. In her opinion, he was very good at keeping his life closed. She didn't know why this bothered her so much. His behavior toward her had continued to be polite, but still she found herself wanting to get to know him better.

The spatula fell from her hand, landing on the floor with a clatter.

She liked Levi Byler.

"Oh, dear."

"Sadie, what on earth is all the noise about?" her *mamm* asked, rushing into the kitchen to shut off the timer.

Sadie had been so lost in her thoughts that she hadn't even heard the timer buzzing.

"And who are you talking to?"

"No one." Giving her head a shake, she admitted, "Myself." She picked up the spatula, walked to the sink and rinsed it off.

"Well, your distraction almost caused your cookies to burn." Her *mamm* grabbed a pot holder off a nearby hook, opened the oven and slid the tray out, setting it on top of the stove. "Your *vader* should be in from the barn soon. He wants to get over to the picnic early. Remember last year when one of his prized cows had all that trouble with her twisted stomach?"

She sure did remember. They were two hours late to the fun because they had to help chase the cow around in hopes of getting the poor beast's insides to right. The entire family was out running around in the pasture behind the barn. Eventually the cow settled down. This year the day looked brighter and worry-free.

While she waited for the cookies to cool, Sadie cleaned up her work area. She put the ingredients back in their place, wiped the countertop clean and then washed up the bowls and utensils. Meanwhile, her *mamm* put the finishing touches on her potato salad.

Sara came into the kitchen carrying the wicker picnic basket. She looked extra pretty today. Sadie wondered who her sister had in mind when she'd chosen to wear her best skirts.

"It's looking like we'll have perfect weather for the picnic," her sister observed.

"*Ja.* The sky is blue with only fair-weather clouds. Did you find the bread I set out in the pantry last night?" *Mamm* asked.

"I did. I already put the loaf in the basket along with a pound of butter."

"*Gut.* I think that will be plenty. And did you get out the sacks like I asked?"

"I did," Sara replied, wrinkling her nose. "I'm not going to participate in the sack race this year, so don't sign me up."

"*Ach*, me neither," Sadie agreed with her sister.

"Your school *kinder* will be disappointed if you don't join them, Sadie. You know that's a favorite at the picnic."

Taking the lid off the cookie tin, Sadie started layering the snickerdoodles inside. "My *kinder* will

YOU pick your books –
WE pay for everything.

You get up to FOUR New Books and TWO Mystery Gifts...absolutely FREE!

Dear Reader,

I am writing to announce the launch of a huge **FREE BOOK GIVEAWAY**... and to let you know that YOU are entitled to choose up to FOUR fantastic books that WE pay for.

Try **Love Inspired® Romance Larger-Print** books and fall in love with inspirational romances that take you on an uplifting journey of faith, forgiveness and hope.

Try **Love Inspired® Suspense Larger-Print** books where courage and optimism unite in stories of faith and love in the face of danger.

Or TRY BOTH!

In return, we ask just one favor: Would you please participate in our brief Reader Survey? We'd love to hear from you.

This FREE BOOKS GIVEAWAY means that we pay for *everything!* We'll even cover the shipping, and no purchase is necessary, now or later. So please return your survey today. You'll get **Two Free Books** and **Two Mystery Gifts** from each series to try, altogether worth over **$20**!

Sincerely

Pam Powers

Pam Powers
For Harlequin Reader Service

Complete the survey below and return it today to receive up to 4 FREE BOOKS and FREE GIFTS guaranteed!

FREE BOOKS GIVEAWAY
Reader Survey

1

Do you prefer books which reflect Christian values?

◯ YES　◯ NO

2

Do you share your favorite books with friends?

◯ YES　◯ NO

3

Do you often choose to read instead of watching TV?

◯ YES　◯ NO

YES! Please send me my Free Rewards, consisting of **2 Free Books from each series I select** and **Free Mystery Gifts**. I understand that I am under no obligation to buy anything, as explained on the back of this card.

❏ **Love Inspired® Romance Larger-Print** (122/322 IDL GQ36)
❏ **Love Inspired® Suspense Larger-Print** (107/307 IDL GQ36)
❏ **Try Both** (122/322 & 107/307 IDL GQ4J)

FIRST NAME　　　　　LAST NAME

ADDRESS

APT.#　　　CITY

STATE/PROV.　　　ZIP/POSTAL CODE

EMAIL ❏ Please check this box if you would like to receive newsletters and promotional emails from Harlequin Enterprises ULC and its affiliates. You can unsubscribe anytime.

be happy with me cheering them on from the side-lines, *Mamm*."

"If you say so."

"I'm bringing kites for them to fly."

"I guess they'll like that, too." Her *mamm* made a silly face at her.

Sadie laughed.

The potato salad and cookies, along with ice packs, were put inside the picnic basket. The bread was carefully placed on top, so as not to be crushed. Added to the mix were their paper plates and eating utensils. They didn't need to worry about the drinks because the Schrader family had a special wagon they loaned out for weddings that held half a dozen five-gallon containers of lemonade, iced tea and water. Perfect for an event such as this.

Sadie could feel the excitement building. This day was so much fun and she looked forward to it every year. It was a time for the farmers to take a much-needed break. And it was the last hurrah for the *kinder* before the start of the new school year. Maybe Levi had decided to join in the festivities.

"Come, come! Your *vader* is outside with the buggy." *Mamm* thrust the picnic hamper into Sadie's arms, ushering both her and Sara out the door.

"You sure are in a hurry, *Mamm*," Sara observed.

"I don't want to waste a minute of this day."

They all piled into the buggy, and by the time they reached the glade where the picnic had been set up, Sadie could see they were not the only ones with the idea of arriving early. The edge of the field had filled with wagons and buggies. There were *kinder* running about, and *mamms* and *vaders* hauling baskets and blankets over to where a long row of tables and benches had been set up.

Sadie saw Lizzie and Paul, with Rachel and Jacob behind them. Sadie waved. Then her heart thudded inside her chest as she spotted Levi carrying several tins in his hands.

He'd decided to join them.

Trying not to appear excited by his presence, Sadie meandered over to the table where her parents were unpacking. She helped her *mamm* set their places and then took her tin over to the dessert table, three lengths long and already filled with cobblers, pies and cakes. *What a sight to behold.* Their community was blessed with so many wonderful bakers and cooks. The neighboring tables held a variety of salads. Sadie's mouth watered.

She felt the breeze ruffle her blouse, and then something light brushed against her back. She turned around to find Rachel standing behind her. Levi stood next to her, carrying the tins she'd seen him with a few minutes ago.

"Rachel. Levi. *Gute mariye.*" Sadie didn't know why it was happening, but she couldn't stop the heated flush of her cheeks. Her reaction to seeing Levi today was so schoolgirl. Quickly she busied herself taking the tin from his hands and setting it next to hers on the table.

"I recognize that tin." Rachel's voice penetrated the haze of Sadie's mind. "Did you make those blue-ribbon cookies?"

"I did."

"You are in for a real treat, Levi." Rachel nodded to him.

Levi stood there, shifting from one foot to the other, his gaze not quite meeting hers.

She wondered why, after all the time they'd just spent working on the school, that he suddenly seemed shy around her.

"Are you signing up for any of the events?" Rachel asked.

Sadie turned her attention to Rachel. "*Nee*, this year I'm doing kite flying with the *kinder*."

The trio made their way out from under the shade of the large oak tree and wandered over to the tables where Sadie's family was gathering. It was nice to see everyone. With her siblings getting married off and having *kinder*, her family was expanding. Her *bruder* William stood among the men chatting. He waved while Sadie joined the women. This was how it always was at these events, with everyone breaking off into groups.

Sadie joined Lizzie, Rachel and Sara under a shade tree. The four of them chatted for a bit about the weather and the school. Lizzie told them how good the store was doing and that her paintings were selling faster than she could paint them.

"The one of the fields where Paul and I had our first outing together is the most popular. We are looking into getting prints made. The *Englischers* like to have originals. But I have to charge so much for them. I'd really like to be able to price them so they are affordable for everyone who would like to buy my art."

"Lizzie, that is wonderful!" Rachel gave her a hug. "It's *gut* to hear of your success. My Jacob is so busy with the shed building that he's up at the crack of dawn and works by the light of the kerosene lamps at night. He's thinking of asking Levi to stay on full-time as a partner."

Sadie's heartbeat kicked up a notch. The thought of Levi being a permanent part of the community meant that he liked being here. And maybe he wasn't going to be running off anytime soon.

"Levi has mentioned that the shop is busy," she said.

All heads swung in Sadie's direction.

She waved them off. "Stop looking at me like that. He told me because I asked for windows in the replacement shed they are building at the school," she explained, fighting back another blush.

What on earth has gotten into me today?

"He said he'd have to wait and see what Jacob had lying around. That's all." She tried to talk her way out of the conversation.

"Oh my." Sara looked at her intently. "You are smitten with Levi Byler."

"I am not," Sadie denied, even though she knew her sister's words had some merit. But there was no way she would admit the truth in front of them.

Out of the corner of her eye she caught a glimpse of Isaiah joining the group of men where her *vader* and *bruders* stood talking.

She glanced back to her sister and saw Sara's gaze following the man and knew then and there that Isaiah Troyer had the wrong Fischer *dochder* in his sights.

Sadie knew that, in time, everything would work out for all of them. They just had to be patient. Not one of her finer virtues. She had no intention of marrying Isaiah, and there was no reason why Sara shouldn't be with the one who would make him happy. Sadie only had to convince their *vader* of this. She had faith that everything would work out as it should. It had to.

The bell rang, and they followed the crowd over to the picnic tables.

Their family had managed to crowd in one place at the table. Sadie elbowed her way in between Sara and her sister-in-law Kara.

"It seems that the entire community has come out for this," Kara commented.

"Ja."

Across from them sat Rachel, Jacob and Levi, with Lizzie and Paul lining the bench next to Paul's family. Levi chatted with Paul. Sadie heard him ask a question about furniture making. And then her attention was pulled away as Sara told her it was their turn to go to the food line.

Sadie tried not to pile her plate high, but there were so many delectable choices. She was so busy walking through the line that she didn't realize Levi stood across from her until she recognized the sound of his voice speaking to one of the school board members.

Glancing up from her plate, she watched him, thinking what a good fit he'd be for their community.

"If you don't stop your gawking, people are going to start talking about you."

Sadie jumped and turned to Lizzie, who had come up behind her. Out of the side of her mouth, she whispered, "I wasn't gawking."

Lizzie leaned in close, talking low so only Sadie could hear. "*Ja*, I think you were. He's not too old, heaven forbid, not too young, and as far as I can tell, he doesn't appear to be in a relationship. He could be your perfect…"

Sadie nudged Lizzie with her elbow, cutting her off. "Stop. This isn't the time or the place for this discussion. There are too many *blabbermauls*."

Lizzie cocked her head to one side, the corner of her mouth lifting in a knowing way. And then she moved ahead of Sadie in the line. Feeling an unexpected flutter of nerves in her stomach and her appetite diminish, Sadie left her spot in the line and went back to the picnic table. Some of her students came up to her along the way, telling her of their summer.

Little Mary Stolfus jumped up and down in front of Sadie, nearly knocking her plate out of her hand in her excitement to tell how she had gone fishing with her *bruders* for the first time.

"Mary, you could write a report on that for the class. I'm sure everyone would love to hear about your experience."

"Homework already!"

Sadie grinned down at the stricken look on the child's face. "Only if you wish to share. I'll tell you what. You can think about what you want to write and then when I give out the assignment, you'll be halfway done. How does that sound?"

"Like a *gut* idea." Mary clapped her hands together. "I've been practicing my letters with my *mamm*."

"You have?" Sadie's heart swelled. It was so wonderful to hear when her students took their learning seriously.

"Yup." Mary's blond head bobbed up and down.

"I'm very proud of you, Mary. I'll be flying kites after our meal. Come find me out in the lower field."

"I will, Miss Sadie!" With that, Mary ran off to join her friends.

Settling back in with her family, Sadie picked at her food.

Lizzie's words had left her with an odd feeling. She never wanted anyone, most of all Levi, to ever think that she was chasing after him, or any other man for that matter. Sadie wasn't like that. But she did know what she wanted, and she knew in her heart she would never settle for anything less. Shouldn't it be everyone's goal to find true happiness?

The minute the thought entered her head, she found herself face-to-face with Levi.

Chapter Eleven

Levi didn't think he'd ever tasted anything quite as delicious as Sadie's snickerdoodle cookies. He took a second bite, savoring the sweet, vanilla taste, and the sprinkle of sugar and cinnamon over the entire cookie was almost too much to bear.

"I see you're enjoying my cookies," Sadie observed from her side of the table.

"I am. And you know what I think?"

"I don't."

"I think there's a reason these won the blue ribbon."

"They've won the award on more than one occasion. I don't enter them in the bake-off anymore. It was time to give someone else a turn at the ribbon."

"Can you give me the recipe for my *mudder*?"

"I'll write it out for you and you can send it to her in your next letter."

"I'm sure she'll like that."

He noticed her plate sitting half-eaten off to one side and wondered if she was feeling okay.

Seeing his look, she commented, "My eyes were bigger than my stomach. There was so much good food on the tables that I wanted to try it all."

"The women in Miller's Crossing sure know how to cook. My stomach is full." He gave his belly a pat.

Sadie gave him one of her pretty smiles, saying, "But there's always room for dessert."

"Always," he agreed. He gave her a half smile.

"I've heard that Jacob is serious about wanting you to stay on."

The bluntness of her statement caught him off guard and wiped the smile off his face. One thing Levi knew for sure was that news in small communities traveled fast, and Miller's Crossing was no exception. Sadie had been after him for days to talk more about his life and what brought him here. He wasn't ready to discuss those parts of his life. Even though the pain of his breakup was easing, Levi didn't want to be caught up in another relationship that would leave him broken. He still wasn't able to trust enough to be sure about Sadie.

He still hadn't been able to figure out if Sadie was looking to settle down or simply looking to settle.

People were beginning to clear away their plates. Some wandered off to the creek, others gathered under the shade tree and some were getting ready to play a game of softball.

"Levi." She spoke his name so softly he almost didn't hear her.

"Ja."

"Will you be staying on?"

They were interrupted by a small girl whose exuberance brought a smile to his face.

"Miss Sadie, we're ready to fly the kites! Are you coming?"

Her gaze lingered on him. Levi wanted to tell her what she needed to hear. But he couldn't. He didn't trust himself to open his heart. Still, he found himself wishing the outcome could be different. Maybe they were meant to be only friends.

While he pondered that thought, Sadie accepted the outstretched hand of the girl. Standing up, she gave him a look that told him she wasn't finished with this conversation.

"Levi! Do you want to play in the softball game?" William called out to him from the field. "We need an outfielder."

"Go," Sadie said. "Have fun with the men."

"All right. You have fun with your kite flying."

"Come on, Miss Sadie!" the little girl clamored, tugging Sadie away from him.

He walked with them partway to the field, then broke off and headed to the ball field. He watched her disappear over the rise, wondering what would have happened if he'd met her sooner.

"Miss Sadie! Look how high my kite is!" Mary exclaimed, jumping up and down next to her.

Raising her hand to shield her eyes from the sun, Sadie looked heavenward, watching the kite dip and flutter in the wind. The tail with the pink-and-orange strips trailed out behind it, spinning in the breeze.

"I'm not having much luck with mine," said another girl. Beth Miller frowned at the tangled mess at her feet.

"Come, let me see if we can get yours going." Sadie walked through the blades of grass. Picking up Beth's kite and handing it to her, she instructed, "You need to hold it here at the crosspieces."

She took hold of Beth's little fingers, placing them where the cross pieces met and once she was certain the girl had a good hold on the kite, she added, "Now you run into the wind until the breeze captures your kite."

Beth looked up at her with wide, brown, doubt-filled eyes.

"Let's give it a try, shall we?"

Beth nodded and then, doing as she was told, ran like the wind. Her little legs pumped hard on the soft earth, and to her delight the paper kite got off the ground, sailing up into the blue sky. The other *kinder* who'd been watching and playing with their own kites let out a cheer.

Beth turned to Sadie, shouting, "I did it! I did it!"

And then without warning the kite lost its lift and fell out of the sky, landing halfway up an oak tree.

Sadie ran over to where Beth stood under the tree, crying.

"Oh. There, there, *liebling*." Sadie patted her on the back. "Wipe away those tears. I'll get your kite for you."

Without a thought, she hoisted herself up onto a low branch where the tail of the kite was just out of her reach. The fabric bows swayed in front of her, flirting with her. Sadie stretched her body tall and extended her arm as far as she could. The kite tail danced against her fingertips. She just started to grasp the string when her foot slipped on the branch.

"Get down from that tree!"

The familiar voice startled her, and she gave a shout as she tumbled backward out of the tree.

Her breath whooshed out of her as she fell hard against Levi. She spun around to face him. What on earth was he doing down here? She'd thought he was playing ball.

Oh my... Her heart skipped a beat as she looked up into his blue-green eyes. He looked frightened for a moment, and then she saw something else as he stared down at her. His gaze softened, taking in her face. His eyes lingered on hers and then his gaze dropped to her mouth. Sadie's breath caught.

Then he blinked and quick as a breeze the look was gone.

In the next instant she jumped out of his arms. She put her hand against the tree trunk to steady herself. Her heartbeat fluttered in her chest, and that fluttering had nothing to do with fear.

"Sadie! What were you doing up there?" he demanded.

"I was helping Beth get her kite out of the tree."

"You should have had one of the boys go up."

"I'll have you know, Levi, that I'm perfectly capable of climbing a tree."

"I don't doubt that, but when you have help nearby, you should ask."

She closed her eyes to keep her frustration from showing. How could he make her want to be near him one minute and then in the next make her so mad? Sadie swallowed, realizing she wasn't really mad at him, just unsettled by these feelings that popped up inside her whenever they were close to each other.

It would do no good to be flustered in front of the *kinder*. And in front of their parents who had made their way down the hill to see what all the commotion was about. Sadie's heart raced as she glanced at the faces of her neighbors, many of whom had known her for her entire life. And many of whom would like nothing more than to have something to gossip about during the next quilting bee.

It wouldn't do to have the schoolteacher be the fodder for their chatter. Sadie knew she should put her reputation first. But how did she do that while keeping her growing feelings toward Levi at bay?

Pushing away from the tree, she squared her shoulders. "You are absolutely correct." Putting on her sweetest smile, she asked, "Would you mind going up the tree and getting Beth's kite for her? Please."

"I'd be happy to."

He was up and back in less than three minutes, handing the kite to a very happy Beth, who took it from him.

"What do you say to Mr. Byler, Beth?"

"*Danke* for getting my kite out of the tree."

"*Du bischt willkomm.*" Levi smiled at the little girl.

The smile brought out the fine lines at the corners of his eyes and a dimple on the left side of his mouth. The look suited him. And Sadie wondered, as she had since the first day she'd met him, why those smiles were so rare.

He brushed the dust off of his dark pants and adjusted his straw hat.

"*Danke*, Levi, for coming along when you did," Sadie finally offered.

The smile disappeared.

Feeling the need to state her case once more, she said, "I didn't mean to scare anyone."

"I know you didn't." His tone softened. "Let's get back to the picnic."

She didn't understand his behavior toward her. One minute he was nice as pie and the next he was acting like he didn't want to be around her and then he was back to being nice again. There was something going on between them, and she felt Levi was battling with these same feelings. She didn't know how to reach out to him, how to deal with this new tension developing between them.

But Sadie was a firm believer in the Lord working in mysterious ways. Levi had been sent here for a reason.

She needed to find out why he was so driven to keep his distance from her. She had to know if there was something between them other than their shared desire to complete the repairs on the school property in time for the upcoming semester. Determination drove Sadie in her work, and her personal life was no different. One way or another, she would get to the bottom of this.

Levi walked ahead of her, leaving Sadie to accompany the *kinder* back up to the picnic tables. Lizzie came up to her, linking her arm through hers, and gave Sadie a reassuring pat on the hand.

"It seems Levi's rescue is drawing a bit of attention."

Sadie looked at her friend. "I saw the women watching us."

"Not just them, Sadie."

She followed Lizzie's pointed gaze, seeing where her concern came from. Sadie's *mamm* and *vader* stood on the knoll watching her walk up the hill. This would only make her *vader*'s case stronger for a match between her and Isaiah. Sadie had to find a way to head this off, and the sooner, the better.

Her parents met her at the top of the hill.

Her *mamm* rushed over to her. "Are you all right?"

"I'm fine. Levi was right there to break my fall. And even if he wasn't, I would have been perfectly capable of not getting hurt."

"You don't know that, Sadie," her *mamm* scolded. "You are always so impetuous."

"*Dochder*, it's time we packed up to head home."

She nodded at her *vader* and helped her *mamm* pick up their remaining leftovers. This day had left her a bundle of nerves. To hide the feeling, she busied her hands packing up the picnic basket and carrying it over to their buggy. Levi was helping Rachel and Jacob put their basket and softball equipment in the back of their buggy.

Spotting her, he waved.

Sadie waved back.

Off to her left stood her *vader*. She felt his gaze on them.

He came up behind her. "Come, let's get our things loaded up. We have evening chores to tend to." His voice sounded gruff.

A sinking feeling hit Sadie. Her time to be a part of deciding her future was running short.

Chapter Twelve

A week later Levi found himself face-to-face with Sadie's *vader*. The man had been waiting for him at the school.

"Levi, I'd like a word with you."

Drawing in a breath, Levi jumped down from the wagon seat. Pushing his hat back off his forehead, he walked over to Saul Fischer. The man straightened his shoulders. Levi stood a good head taller than him.

"What can I do for you, Saul?"

"I'm not going to beat around the bush. I'm here to talk to about my *dochder* Sadie."

"I see," Levi said, knowing full well where this conversation would be heading.

"I'm not sure what she's told you about her future. But my Sadie wants things she can't have. Right now, her job is to teach the *kinder* of our community. And she's of the marrying age."

Narrowing his eyes, Levi looked at Sadie's *vader*, trying to figure out where he was going with his thoughts. Levi didn't want to make a decision he might later regret.

"When you are married with *kinder* of your own, you will understand that a *vader* knows what's right for his *dochders* and *sohns*. I've chosen someone for Sadie. He's a *gut*, solid man with a home that's ready for a wife."

Levi folded his arms across his chest, thinking he must look as though he had none of those traits. He thought he was a *gut* person, but he didn't really know what his future held. He supposed to Saul Fischer, he could look like something of a drifter. A man that wouldn't be a *gut* fit for his *dochder*.

He knew arranged marriages were not uncommon in their culture. But he doubted the Sadie he knew would ever settle for something like that. He couldn't imagine her living with a man she didn't love for the rest of her life.

Levi thought about him and Anne. He'd been so in love with her, and yet he'd come to find out she'd not returned those feelings…leastwise not for him. Now that time had passed, he knew they never would have been happy together. He wanted Sadie to be happy. Still, at this time he didn't think he'd be the right match for her.

But he'd seen Isaiah Troyer. He didn't think the man was a fit for Sadie either. He couldn't imagine her spending the rest of her life with him, bearing his children.

And those thoughts would do him no *gut*. "I understand what you are saying, Saul."

"Do you? I know how Sadie can turn things to her

liking. But in this matter, I need her to abide by my wishes. I'm asking you to tread carefully where she is concerned. You would do well to remember her standing as the teacher in our community. She has a reputation to uphold. You two have been working here these past weeks, many times alone. If nothing else, I want you to steer clear of her."

With that, the man turned and boarded his wagon, leaving Levi to his work and his thoughts.

He should have told Saul that he needn't worry. Levi had no plans to rush into any kind of a relationship. He and Sadie were friends, nothing more. At least that was what he kept telling himself.

He'd barely had time to unpack his work tools when another wagon came into the schoolyard. This one carrying Sadie's *bruders* William and John. William jumped down from the wagon and came over to him.

"Levi! *Gut* to see you again."

"You, too."

"John and I were going fishing today on Lake Erie. We were wondering if you'd want to join us."

He declined the invitation and sent them on their way. There was no time to take a day off, not if he hoped to get everything completed on schedule. And he suspected that William and John were trying to learn more about him.

He expected nothing less of them. He'd have done the same for his sisters when they were getting ready to be married off. The difference here was Levi had no intention of asking for Sadie's hand in marriage.

Picking up the hammer, he pounded the nail into

the piece of siding he'd been putting up on the back of the shed. The wood was stubborn and he had to strike the nail three times before the head settled snuggly against the hearty oak slab siding. He slid the next piece of wood into place, continuing to pound the nails. Maybe if he worked hard enough and long enough, he could ease the thoughts of Sadie Fischer out of his mind.

But that was becoming harder to do. As each day passed, he wondered how the classroom was coming along. Levi knew better than to approach Sadie if she was working alone. Jacob had warned him off, and Levi suspected the elders were concerned that he and Sadie were spending too much time alone, even if it were for the *gut* of the *kinder*. And now with the visits from her *vader* and her *bruders*, he took these warnings to heart. Sadie was a respected member of her community and she didn't need any trouble coming from him.

Still, he found himself missing the sound of her voice and the way she laughed at the simple things. He envied the way she could be so carefree even when he'd seen the hard days she'd had. Sadie was well liked by her students and their families. These were all *gut* qualities. He smiled, thinking about how patient she'd been with the little girl at the picnic. Sadie could easily have flown that kite herself and then handed the string to the girl. Instead she'd taught the girl how to fly the kite.

The phrase *give a man a fish and you feed him for a day; teach a man to fish and you feed him for a lifetime* came to mind.

Nothing seemed to get Sadie down. She clearly loved her job and all of the *kinder* she taught. They adored her. That had been clear when they'd all come around her during the picnic.

She was a kind, decent person. Not what he expected to find when he'd come here. Sadie was nothing like his former fiancée. Though Anne had seemed committed to their relationship, it turned out she'd had other plans all along. He knew Sadie's life was firmly grounded here in Miller's Crossing. But that didn't mean he wasn't going to keep exercising caution where she was concerned.

There would be no more impulsive decisions when it came to finding love. Perhaps he needed to be forceful with his intentions where Sadie was concerned. If he told her there could be nothing between them other than friendship, maybe that would take some of this pressure off of them. He didn't want to be the cause of her losing her job. In his mind, it was too soon to have feelings for her, even though, no matter how hard he tried to deny it, his heart had begun to open up to her.

The one sure thing in his life was his faith in the Lord. Time and time again the Lord had provided for him in his moments of need. Pausing, he turned his attention to the Lord, asking for guidance and giving thanks for what he already had.

As he carried on with his duties, Levi worked in silence, stuck within his own thoughts, until he heard Sadie calling out to him.

"Levi? I know you're out here. I've heard your hammering all morning."

"I'm around back," he called out.

Putting his hammer into his leather tool belt, he walked around to meet Sadie.

All of his thoughts about using caution flew out of his mind the minute he saw her. She looked even prettier today than the last time he'd seen her. Her face had a healthy glow from being outside in the summer sunshine. She wore one of her famous smiles. She held a white envelope.

Narrowing his eyes, he focused on that, rather than on how lovely her blue eyes appeared today. "What do you have there?"

"My blue-ribbon snickerdoodle recipe, just like I promised."

"*Danke.* I know my *mamm* will enjoy making them. I'll send it along with my next letter."

He stood there, gazing into her eyes. His thoughts swirled around in his mind once again. Sadie deserved better than what he could offer. His heart had been broken and was barely mended. Maybe the breakup had been because of something he'd done… something he may be doomed to repeat. The last thing he wanted was to hurt Sadie. They'd already breached propriety by working without others around them. Levi recognized the fact that Sadie's job was important to her. Neither one of them should be putting her future in jeopardy.

Perhaps if she could see his flaws when it came to love, she would go back to focusing on her teaching.

"Levi?"

"*Ja?*"

"Are you going to take the envelope?"

"Sure, sure." In two strides, he closed the gap between them. Careful to keep his distance at arm's length, he accepted the recipe.

"This is coming along," Sadie observed as she took her time meandering to the other side of the building. Stopping in front of the shed, she turned to him. "*Danke* for the windows."

"Jacob found some extras."

"Admit it, Levi, this project is much better with the windows. Just think of all the plants my *kinder* and I can start out here. The light is perfect!"

"You were right in your thinking."

"I'm glad we can agree on that." She let out a laugh, clapping her hands together in triumph. "I can picture all those seedlings tilting toward the sunlight. This year I'm planning on doing more flowers. We need to replace the plants that were damaged in the storm anyway. We can start with the pansies and Johnny-jump-ups. Then we can move on to the marigolds and mums. I can just see their yellow and orange blooms lining the bushes around the front of the building."

"You're planning way ahead of the next spring season," he commented, realizing he'd grown used to hearing her talk in long segments.

"It doesn't hurt to plan or to use your imagination and dream about what something could look like."

They grew quiet. Off in the distance, a tractor engine started up. A few cars drove by the schoolyard. Sadie stilled. She looked up at him, her gaze taking in every inch of his face. By now he recognized that look. Sadie wanted more from him.

Levi swallowed. He needed to tell her there could be nothing more between them. "You got something on your mind, Sadie?"

Rolling her shoulders back, Sadie took her time forming her words. She'd been thinking about this moment ever since the picnic. Now the time had arrived, and she found herself feeling the unthinkable: tongue-tied.

Levi looked at her with one dark eyebrow cocked, his mouth in a firm line. She wondered if he thought she might be about to scold him for something.

Nee, this wasn't the case. She needed to talk to him about their relationship. Sadie knew she wasn't alone in sensing the undercurrent running between them. Her friends and her family had mentioned their observations to her. If others saw it, then there had to be more to it than just her wishful thinking.

"Levi, I…" She hesitated. This was going to be harder than she'd thought. Then she reminded herself how long she'd been fighting her *vader* over the Isaiah issue. If she wanted to have any hope of finding happiness in her future, then she needed to be brave.

"Levi, why are you here?"

A surprised look crossed his face. Then he asked, "Here? As in here at the school?"

"*Nee*, Levi. I think you know what I meant by my question."

She saw realization dawn on him.

"Ah. Here as in Miller's Crossing."

"*Ja.*"

He toyed with the handle on the hammer in his

tool belt. Sadie watched as he grew still again, his hands dropping to his sides. His eyes took on a deeper shade of green as he pondered her request. She wanted to grab hold of him and shake the words out. Why was he so stubborn when it came to talking about his past? What was he afraid of? Sadie wasn't some monster who wanted to hurt him. She did, however, long to know if he had been feeling the same way she had.

"I don't have time for whatever this is, Sadie. There's a lot of work yet to be done if my job is to be completed on time."

She stood even taller. "Levi, I'll ask you again. Why are you here? Surely you have a family who misses you and would like you to return to their community."

"Sadie."

There was a plea in his voice. She heard it, and her heart broke for whatever pain he was suffering. Whether or not he wanted to believe it, he had become a part of Miller's Crossing. Levi wasn't just some worker passing through. The *kinder* liked him. Her *bruders* had even begun to change their idea about the man. Otherwise they never would have invited him to go along on their fishing trip.

"Every time I think we're about to grow closer, you shut me off. Why is that, Levi?"

"Sadie!"

He looked shocked at her forwardness, but she didn't have time to waste wondering if whatever was happening between them was simply a figment of her imagination. Desperation was creeping in.

"Please, Levi. Tell me."

"Sadie…" He extended a hand to her. "Don't. Move."

"Why?"

Levi seemed to be focused on something behind her. Suddenly afraid, Sadie started to turn her head.

"Levi, what is going on?"

He brought his finger to his lips. Very carefully, he mouthed, "Skunk."

Sadie's mouth formed an O. She heard the animal rustling around behind her. Levi's hand grabbed her forearm as they both held their breath. Sadie tried not to notice how warm his fingertips felt or the way his steady pulse thrummed beside her.

She didn't know how much time passed. Seconds turned into minutes.

And then he released her.

He gave his head a shake and grinned down at her. "That was a close call."

Her hand flew up to cover her heart. "You can say that again! *Danke* for saving me. Oh, my goodness, I can't even think about how bad that would have been if the skunk had sprayed us."

Blinking up at him, she went on, "Last year one of our dogs got into it with a skunk in the back field. We went through a case of canned tomato juice trying to get that smell off him. *Gut* thing the grocery store had them on sale or else we would have had to empty out the pantry!"

Levi turned away from her. "Perhaps we should get back to work."

"Levi, can't we at least finish our conversation?"

Sadie sucked in her lower lip, waiting on his answer, holding out hope.

"I'm not sure that's a *gut* idea."

"Why?"

"Because."

She put her hands on her hips and glared up at him. "As I tell my students, *because* is not an answer.

"All right. How about because I can't tell you what you want to hear? The last thing I want to do is hurt you, Sadie. You've no idea how hard a relationship can be."

Sadie let his words sink in. "I know you would never hurt me." And then it dawned on her. "But you... You've been hurt by someone."

It was not a question. The soul-crushing look on his face told part of his story.

He shook his head as if to clear away the pain. "Please, don't push me on this."

She bit down on her lip, her heart breaking for him. She couldn't imagine anyone hurting a man so kind and giving. "I'm not pushing you."

"*Ja*, you are." His voice rose in anger. "It's like you're on some sort of self-imposed timeline." He paused, clenching his teeth together. Then his look softened. "I know your *vader* has someone in mind for you. Maybe you should consider his choice. Sadie, I'm not sure I'm the man who can be your 'not too old or not too young.'"

Her mouth fell open. He'd overheard the conversation she and Lizzie had had weeks ago, and those words had stayed with him. Sadie was ashamed at their silliness. She and Lizzie had been joking. But deep down, Sadie knew the words carried some certainty. She didn't want to settle. She wanted her own happily-ever-after. Even if he thought differently right now, Sadie knew she could have that with the man who stood before her.

"The day is getting on," he said. "We'd best be getting back to work."

She knew when to let something go, but this time she just couldn't leave it be. While Levi had built up a wall around his emotions that might seem impenetrable, she knew better. Her faith and her instincts were stronger than ever. This wasn't over yet.

"I don't understand why you are being so stubborn."

"Because you could lose your job over this," he said, waving his hand back and forth between them.

"Why do you say that?"

"Because we both know you're under scrutiny right now. Your position has not been made permanent."

"You don't need to remind me of that, Levi."

"Sadie, there is so much about me that you don't know."

"Then tell me," she pleaded.

He shook his head, making her angry and sad at the same time. "This isn't the time for us to begin anything other than a friendship."

His words stung. "You can't mean that." Sadie felt her lower lip tremble.

"Your *vader* has someone picked out for you. Perhaps it would be best if you went with his choice."

"That's a terrible thing to say to me," Sadie said, trying not to cry in front of him.

"I only want what is best for you. First off, your job here is part of who you are. I can't be the reason that would be taken from you. Second, we've only known each other a short amount of time."

"You don't always need a lot of time to know when something feels right."

"Sadie, please don't make this any harder than it needs to be."

She put her hand over her heart, trying to hold back the pain. She wasn't ready to give up. She wouldn't give in this easily. Deep in her heart, she knew they were right together. Isaiah Troyer wasn't the Amish man for her. Levi was.

Sadie tried one more tactic before letting him leave. "Levi, promise me one thing."

He stopped walking and looked over one shoulder at her. "What?"

"Promise me you'll think about this. The Lord brought you here for a reason."

His eyes clouded with emotion. Sadie could almost see the tiny break in the shell he'd put around his heart.

"I'll consider your words." With a shrug, he added, "I can offer you nothing more."

Brushing a tear from her eye, she watched him go. "Hope," she whispered. "You've offered me hope."

Chapter Thirteen

He felt like the worst of the worst, and burying himself in his work did little to alleviate that feeling. Ever since the conversation with Sadie, Levi had been taking on every extra hour of work he could get from Jacob and then some. He figured by keeping his hands and his mind busy, he wouldn't have time to think about Sadie. But just the opposite had happened. By cutting himself off from the community, he'd only had time to think.

Time to think about him and this woman who'd come into his life like a tornado. Her enthusiasm for life couldn't be missed. He envied her patience with her students and the way she'd thrown herself into getting her classroom ready for the new school year. She could be so carefree even when he knew she'd had a hard day.

Sadie was a force to be reckoned with, and the problem was Levi didn't know what to do with his feelings for her. He'd taken the coward's way out when she'd been brave enough to broach the subject of their relationship. He'd been nothing but honest with her, even though he didn't think he'd ever be able to share with her what Anne had done to him. The pain she'd caused, the way she'd ruined his trust and taken away his faith in finding true love.

He walked down the drive to the shed company from Jacob's house. Levi wasn't certain where his life was headed. One thing he knew for sure, he didn't like being in limbo.

Grabbing the doorknob, he pulled the side door open. The scent of fresh-cut lumber wafted by him. Some workers were busy doing finishing work, while others were on the assembly line putting together the framing for the walls.

No doubt about it, Jacob's business was booming.

"Levi! Just the person I've been looking for." Jacob headed toward him, removing his safety glasses and hearing protection. He clapped Levi on the shoulder. "Come on into my office."

Levi followed him and took the seat Jacob offered.

"How's all of this going for you?" his friend asked.

"*Gut.* Except for a few paint touch-ups, I'm finished at the school." Levi didn't feel the relief he'd expected over completing the job. It meant he'd no longer have a reason to see Sadie every day. The thought sent a jolt of surprise through him.

"Listen, Levi. There's something I've been wanting to discuss with you."

"Okay."

"I know you came here for temporary work. But my orders are not slowing down. Right now, I have half a dozen landscape and nursery companies owned by *Englischers* looking to stock my sheds, in addition to Troyer's big nursery right here in Clymer. And I've got more asking about the sheds."

Pushing his hat back on his head, Levi said, "You've been blessed, my cousin."

"I have been. These people don't want stock assembly line–type products. They are clamoring for Amish made."

Levi sat up taller in the chair. "I'm not sure what you're asking here, Jacob."

Steepling his fingers, Jacob speared him with a look of determination. "I want to share my blessings with you."

"I don't know what that means, exactly."

"It means I want you to go into partnership with me."

Levi settled against the back of the chair in shock. Though he'd known Jacob and Rachel had been discussing this, he'd no idea that a full partnership was what his cousin had been thinking about. Levi had expected the possibility of more hours, taking on more responsibility within the shop or maybe even overseeing projects, but this… He'd not seen this offer coming.

A partnership.

This could be life changing. Of course, it would mean relocating here permanently. He knew one person who would be delighted with this bit of news. He so wished this opportunity had come along even a year ago. But then, he reminded himself, a year ago he wasn't even considering leaving his community to start fresh. Now with his life in limbo, he had no idea what he wanted. Could this be the answer to his prayers, or would taking Jacob up on his offer only bring more heartache?

"Hey, Levi. I can see from the look on your face that my offer hasn't brought you the happiness I'd hoped for."

"*Nee, nee.* It's not that. I've so much on my mind, Jacob. So much to consider. And you and Rachel have been so kind to me these past weeks."

"Well, we like having you here. And you've been a tremendous help for me. And my Rachel likes having me home a few nights a week in time for supper." Jacob leaned forward. "Is there something else I don't know about?"

Levi knew the gossip concerning him and Sadie was quietly making its way around Miller's Crossing. Things like the prospect of a new couple never stayed quiet for long in any close-knit town, particularly an Amish one. Right now, he told himself, there was nothing more between them than a growing friendship, though he knew Sadie wanted more. Levi didn't know if he had it in him to give her that. He'd tried to explain that to her when he'd seen her last.

Maybe he was nothing but a coward when it came to love.

"Levi?" Jacob's voice interrupted his musings. "What do you think?"

"I'm not sure."

"If this helps any, I'm aware of the undercurrent between you and Sadie. I know it's none of my business, but if that's holding you back—"

"Jacob, I came here because I needed time to put my life back in order." Levi gave his cousin the short version of what had transpired between him and Anne. "I thought I'd found the love of my life last year and she ended up leaving me. I'm not sure I can be this man Sadie is searching for."

He knew he'd hurt her feelings the other day. He felt terrible about it.

"For what it's worth," Jacob said at last, "I think the Lord knows what He's doing and He sent you here for a reason other than to help out a family member and a friend."

"Funny those are the words you chose. Sadie said the same thing… Well, the part about the Lord bringing me here for a reason."

"You should listen to her." Jacob smiled. "So, you'll think about my offer?"

"I will."

"Levi, I really want to make this work. If you decide to leave, then I'll have to seek out someone else to buy into a partnership. I really want to keep this business in the family."

"I understand."

"One more piece of advice—you need to let go of your past. Otherwise you'll never find the happiness you deserve."

Levi knew the bigger part of this would be not only letting go of the past, but letting Sadie in. He wondered if he could find the courage do that.

Sadie stepped out the front door of the schoolhouse, taking in the glorious sight spread out before her. The fall semester had gotten underway a few days ago, and Sadie had been thankful for the distraction of preparing for this week. It kept her mind off of Levi. She hadn't seen him since the day he'd told her he couldn't be the one for her.

So now Sadie filled her time with teaching. Watching her students, both young and old, playing in the schoolyard filled her heart with gladness. The swings were full with the *kinder*. And the older ones ran around the bases playing a raucous game of kickball. She hated to end their freedom, but the lessons were calling. She yanked a braided string and rang the bell.

"Come on, everyone. The quicker you get inside, the quicker you can get to your work!"

Mary stepped out of the line, asking, "Miss Sadie, did you see how high I went on the swing?"

"I did, Mary. You've really improved."

"*Danke*, Miss Sadie."

She ushered the rest of the *kinder* inside. "I hope you all enjoyed your time outside. And now that we've settled in our seats, I want to go over the chore list with you." In addition, she had a special project for them to work on.

There were a few groans. She stayed behind her desk, waiting for them to quiet. "I've assigned the tasks based on what I think you can do best. You'll find your name on the sheet and then be responsible for that chore."

Mica's hand shot up. "What if we don't like the chore?"

"Then you'll do your best to complete it. Now, today I'd like us to start on our first class project of the school term. As you know, our building and shed sustained some damage over the summer from that storm. I'd like to break off into groups—the boys in one, the girls in the other. We are going to make thank-you cards for Mr. Byler and Mr. Herschberger. The girls will work on one for Mr. Byler and the boys will do the one for Mr. Herschberger. They did a great deal to make sure your classroom was ready for you. In addition, Mr. Byler built us a brand-new shed. When the cards are finished, you can each take a turn signing your name."

Sadie had already set up large pieces of paper on the project table located along the side wall. "Perhaps some of you older boys can help move the table away from the wall so there is space for you to gather around. "We'll have the girls work first since there won't be room for all of you at once. In the meantime, I'd like the boys to get out their chapter books and begin reading silently."

After she got the girls set up with paper, crayons and colored pencils, she walked around the room, helping the boys with their reading. She stopped by Josh's desk and worked with him to sound out a word, but when she got to Mica's desk, she noticed he hadn't even opened his book.

"Mica, why aren't you reading?"

He gave a shrug. "I have a headache."

Concerned, she inspected his face, then lay her hand lightly against his forehead, looking for any signs of a fever. "Would you like me to get you a cold compress to put on your forehead? That might help."

"Nee."

"All right. Stay here and rest at your desk. I'll keep an eye on you."

"*Danke*, Miss Sadie."

Moving down the line, she stopped a few more times to work with the other students. Noticing a half hour had passed, she switched the groups out. The girls were quick to open their books.

"Mary Ellen, could you please take little Mary and Beth over to the reading corner and read out loud to them?"

"Yes, Miss Sadie."

Mary Ellen was one of her oldest students and soon she would be aging out of the classroom. Next year, she'd finish up eighth grade. Sadie intended to have her assist her with the other *kinder* this year. The girl loved to learn and had an abundance of patience. Sadie hoped she might go into teaching.

She heard chatter coming from the craft table and went over to check on the progress the boys were making with their card. Oddly enough, Mica was bent over the table with a crayon in his hand coloring in some lettering. He elbowed Josh, who leaned in, cupped his hand and whispered into Mica's ear.

She found Mica's behavior odd, considering he'd just told her he couldn't read because he had a headache. She'd believed him and allowed him to skip his reading time. She might come off as a kind and easygoing teacher, but Sadie didn't like being lied to.

She needed to nip this in the bud.

"Mary Ellen, I need you to stop reading to the girls and keep an eye on the class."

Stepping behind Mica, she gave him a pat on the shoulder. "Mica, I'd like to have a word with you, outside."

She knew from the look on his face that he understood he was in trouble. A hush fell over the room as she led him out the back door, where her steps faltered as she came face-to-face with Levi.

"Levi! What are you doing here?"

"I'm finishing up with the painting on the shed. How are you doing, Sadie?"

"I'm fine. And yourself?"

She wanted to shake some sense into him. Here they were speaking to each other like they were polite strangers, when they both knew better. Mica squirmed. She'd nearly forgotten he was standing beside her.

"Mica, sit on the step, please, while I speak to Mr. Byler."

Doing as he was told, the boy sat on the bottom step awaiting his fate.

"I'm doing okay."

Longing to ask if he missed her as much as she'd been missing him, Sadie forced herself to watch Mica as he brought his knees up to his chest. Wrapping his arms around his legs, he rested his chin on his bony little kneecaps. Sadie didn't like to think that he might be afraid of his punishment. She had no intention of being overly strict. That wasn't her way.

She glanced over his head at the shed. It looked mighty nice with the spotless windows flanking either side of the door, and the whitewashed siding. Levi had done a fine job.

"The shed looks wonderful, Levi."

"*Danke.* I have one last thing to do and then I'm done."

She wondered if he felt the same pain she felt. A knot had formed in the pit of her stomach. She didn't know what to do with the sensations rippling through her. How could she, upon seeing him here, feel joy and sadness at the same time? Even after their last conversation, even after the days of feeling hurt and empty inside, why did her heartbeat still kick up at the sight of him? Sadie knew then and there whatever was between them hadn't ended as Levi had wanted.

The sound of the *kinder*'s voices coming from behind her jolted her back to reality.

"I'd like to drop by Jacob and Rachel's on my way home," she said to Levi. "Could you let them know to expect me?"

"Ja."

"Miss Sadie, can I go back inside?"

"Nee, Mica. We need to talk." She looked back up to find Levi watching her, the expression on his face carefully guarded. Sadie fought hard to tamp down her frustration with the man. This situation infuriated her and she didn't know how to fix it.

"I'll leave you to your day," Levi said.

He walked off, leaving her to watch his retreating back. The breeze ruffled the dark locks of hair skimming the top of his blue work shirt. Sadie took in his tall, lanky form, remembering the first day they'd met and what a mess she'd been.

She wanted to cry.

"Miss Sadie? Are you okay?" Mica asked.

She took in a deep breath, bolstering her courage. Looking down at the boy, she gave him a shaky smile. "I'm fine, *danke*." Gathering her skirt, she sat next to him. "Mica, I know you understand that lying, even a tiny fib, is wrong."

He nodded.

"I'm going to let you off easy this time around by sending your reading home with you tonight. You can read the pages and we'll discuss them tomorrow. I'll send a note to your parents so they'll know. I won't mention why."

He swiped a hand across his eyes. It broke her heart to see any of her students in pain.

"Mica, do as I've asked and all will be well."

"Okay, Miss Sadie. I'll try."

She patted him on his thin shoulder as they stood. Holding the door open, Sadie let Mica go inside ahead of her. She had one foot on the threshold when she thought she'd heard her name.

Turning, she saw Levi about to swing his hammer against a piece of wood. She waited, hoping he'd stop and look at her. But he didn't.

Squaring her shoulders, she followed Mica inside, closing the door behind them. She wanted to do nothing more than sit at her desk and lament over Levi. But there wasn't time to do that. She had a class to tend to.

The rest of the day flew by with math lessons and their first English assignment, which was to write about what they did over summer break. While they worked on that, she wrote the note to Mica's parents. She let Mary Ellen lead the class in the closing scripture, and then made sure each of them had signed their name to the thank-you cards.

Once the *kinder* were gone, Sadie neatened up her desk, grabbed the cards and, locking the door behind her, went to where she'd left her bicycle. She put the cards in the basket on the handrails and headed for Jacob and Rachel's.

The trip took about half an hour, and Sadie had been preparing herself for the final hill the entire time. Back in her younger days, she'd been able to ride up the steep incline with little effort. But now it loomed like an unscalable mountain in front of her.

Resting her feet on either side of the bike, she pondered the situation. She could easily get off and walk the bike up the hill, or she could take on the challenge to ride. While she stood there debating, she heard the creaking of a wagon coming up behind her. She turned to see if it might be someone she knew.

"Hey, do you need a lift?"

The bobbing of her head said one thing while her mouth said, "Nope. I'm *gut*."

Cocking his head to one side, Levi asked, "Are you sure? Seems like you're having trouble deciding."

She scuffed the toe of her foot along the side of the road, trying to make up her mind. If she remained stubborn and pushed the bike up the hill, it would be at least another twenty minutes before she arrived at Rachel and Jacob's place. Then the time for a visit would be shortened because she still had to pedal back to her house, which would get her home just in time for supper. But if she took Levi up on his offer, she'd have more time to visit with Rachel.

On the other hand, she didn't understand why he wanted to be with her. He'd made his feelings on their relationship clear. She didn't need to spend any more time with this man. A man who didn't want her to be a part of his life.

"Come on, Sadie, let me give you a ride."

Chapter Fourteen

He could almost see her mind working at coming up with a reason not to go with him. But finally, she got off the bike and took some papers out of the basket. She let him take hold of the handlebars. While she got herself seated in the wagon, he loaded the bike in the back.

Grabbing hold of the side rail to hoist himself up, Levi observed, "Maybe your *vader* should let you get one of those motorized scooters." Settling next to her, he added, "The youngies go whizzing by me all the time."

"*Nee*. He thinks they are too dangerous. And they sort of frighten me. Today I'm heading to see Rachel and to drop off a surprise for you and Jacob," she explained, keeping her eyes straight ahead on the road.

"What sort of surprise?"

"If I told you, it wouldn't be a surprise." She held her hands neatly over the papers in her lap.

Apparently, she would not be elaborating, so he asked, "Did Mica get into trouble?"

"I wouldn't call it trouble. We had a misunderstanding."

"I see. He's a *gut* boy."

"He is."

Levi understood Sadie's stiff attitude toward him and yet it still stung. He knew he'd been the one to put a halt to their feelings. It had been the right thing to do for both of them. She'd be free to find someone who could love her with his whole heart, and Levi...

Well, he didn't know what any of this meant for him. He'd done a lot of thinking about what Jacob had said.

Putting aside the hurt and pain of betrayal had taken a toll on his soul. And now he had this offer of a partnership from his cousin. An opportunity that, if he accepted, would mean he'd be living near Sadie. He'd see her at church services and picnics. He didn't imagine she'd be single much longer. Levi might have to reconcile himself to seeing her with someone else. Then again, he'd told her to move on, to accept the man her *vader* had chosen.

Knowing Sadie, though, he doubted she had any plans to settle on a choice that wasn't of her own making. His heart ached. Somehow this ache didn't feel the same as what he'd felt when Anne had left him. *Nee*, this pain held something different. A longing that didn't seem to go away. Sadie was literally within arm's reach. He knew all he had to do was turn and tell her his words had been a mistake.

He wouldn't do that. Sadie deserved someone who could love her with their heart intact. Levi didn't trust himself with his feelings. The hurt and pain of

Anne's betrayal still lingered, and he couldn't seem to let go.

"Levi?" Her warm, sweet voice broke through his musings. *"Bischt allrecht?"*

"Ja," he answered, even though he felt far from all right. Clearing his throat, he noted, "We're here. Shall I drop you at the house?"

"I'd like that, *danke*. But I do have that surprise for you. So, come inside with me."

She waited for him on the porch as he tied the horse to the hitching post. The afternoon sunlight spilled across the house, bathing her in a warm glow making his heart ache all over again. Sadie had to be the prettiest woman he'd ever seen.

Rachel burst onto the porch. "Sadie! I'm so happy to see you. I just made some iced *kaffi*. Jacob and Levi have been partaking at the end of these hot days. Would you like a glass?"

"Just water, please, Rachel."

"I'll bring out some of my sugar *kichlins*, too. I'm afraid they do not compare to your snickerdoodles," Rachel admitted with a laugh.

She headed back into the house, and Levi heard her call out to Jacob, telling him they were here. A shadow appeared behind the screen. Jacob swung the door open and came out to join them.

"Gute nammidaag, Sadie. Levi."

"Gute nammidaag to you, Jacob," Sadie replied, sitting in one of the rockers on the porch. "I've brought you and Levi a surprise from the *kinder.*"

"Ach. We don't need a surprise." Jacob raised his hands in front of his chest.

"This is one you will cherish, I promise."

After pulling two folded sheets of paper out of an envelope, she handed one to Jacob.

Levi stepped around him to collect the remaining one Sadie held out to him. His fingertips skimmed hers. For the briefest of moments, her soft skin brushed against his roughened hands. She pulled away, casting her eyes downward. His stomach clenched. What had he done?

"Rachel. Come see this card the *kinder* made." Jacob's face lit up with joy. "Show me yours, Levi."

Levi held the paper between his fingers. The *kinder* had indeed done a fine job with their artwork. The front of his card had a rather rustic drawing of the shed. He smiled when he saw the stick figures alongside. Each one had an arrow pointing at it. One had the name *Mica* written over it and the other *Josh*. Levi shook his head. He'd never forget working with those boys. Opening the card, he read each name. *Thank you* was written in block letters.

He'd never gotten a gift such as this. He looked up to find Sadie watching him. Her blue eyes taking in his face, she gave him a slight nod.

"I told you, you would like this surprise."

"You were right."

"Here's our refreshments!" Rachel came out onto the porch carrying a tray of drinks and the plate of *kichlin*.

"Sadie, did Levi tell you his news?" she asked, as she handed out the drinks.

Accepting the ice water, Sadie answered, *"Nee."*

"Jacob has officially asked him to become a partner in the business. This is such *gut* news for us. Of course, he has to say yes first."

Sadie's mouth opened and then closed. Setting her glass on the low table between the rockers, she rose, brushing past Levi.

"I'm afraid it's later than I thought. I'd best be getting home. *Danke* for the water, Rachel."

Setting his glass next to hers, Levi hurried down the porch steps after her. "Sadie, let me take you home."

She spun around so fast they bumped into each other.

She started to push him away. "I can get myself home. Don't worry about me. My house is downhill from here."

"Sadie, I know you're upset with Rachel's news."

Keeping her voice low so Rachel and Jacob couldn't overhear, she barely got out, "Rachel's news? Is that how you think of this? Jacob offered you the partnership, Levi. You." She poked a finger against his chest.

He started to take hold of her hand. Feeling as if her skin had been scorched, she took a step back, out of his reach. It seemed that no matter what he did and said to her these days, it only ended in pain and hurt. Sadie didn't know how to get him to see that together they could make anything work. Why did he continue to hold back?

"I have to go." With that, she made her way to where he'd left her bike leaning up against the side of the wagon.

"Don't go off angry."

Slowing her pace, she turned to face him.

His hands were clenched at his sides. Sadie longed to take hold of them, to feel his strength, to offer him hope. But she stood there, waiting for him to say something, anything, realizing if he were to stay here in Miller's Crossing that their lives would become intertwined.

Her heartbeat settled into a calmer rhythm as her anger dissipated. If Levi took Jacob's offer, he would be here, near her. She dared to meet his gaze, wondering if any of this had occurred to him. Wondering if he even cared. His steadfastness told her he did.

"I can't be late for dinner again."

And she rode off, arriving home to find her *vader* waiting for her. He sat on the front porch in his favorite chair, sipping from a glass of lemonade. She noticed his hands and the calluses etched in them from the years working in the fields. A straw hat covered his graying hair. His mouth was pulled into a grim line. Stepping up onto the porch, Sadie avoided his gaze.

"*Dochder.* Come, *sittsit unnah.* It's time for us to talk."

She knew better than to disobey him, even though she knew full well what he wanted to talk about. She sat on the hard bench next to the door.

"I can't wait any longer for you to make up your mind. I want a union between you and Isaiah Troyer. It will be good to bring both households together."

Her stomach twisted at his words. "Please, *Daed.* I only need a little more time."

"I've given you time. Sadie, you are the teacher at the local *schul*. You have a reputation to think about." He slapped the palm of his hand on the flat arm of the rocker. "I can't have this behavior of yours continue."

"But I don't love Isaiah."

"You will grow to love him in time."

She shook her head so hard she felt the prayer *kapp* loosen. Fighting back tears, she straightened her *kapp*. "I can't do as you ask." Not when her heart belonged to someone else.

"Sadie! I'll not have you disobeying me!"

Sucking in a breath, her mind worked to find another way to convince her *daed* that this was not the right choice for her. Isaiah Troyer could never be her Amish man.

"I'm going to speak to him tomorrow," her *vader* warned.

She covered her mouth with one hand, pushing back the sob that threatened to escape. Her stomach roiled as her heart pounded inside her chest. This couldn't be happening, not when she and Levi were so close to… *Close to what?* she wondered. She let her eyelids drop, saying a silent prayer that her *daed* would give her more time. Sadie believed with all her heart and soul that Levi had been sent here not to help out Jacob but to find her.

Behind her, she heard the creak of the screen door.

Hoping to sway her *vader* once more, Sadie said, "I need more time."

"Nee."

"Wait!"

They both jumped at the sound of her sister's

voice. Sara flew out onto the porch like a dog was nipping at her heels.

"Sadie isn't the right Fischer *dochder* for Isaiah," she blurted out. She stood in front of them, wringing her hands together. "I am."

"What is this nonsense?" their *vader* bellowed.

Sadie jumped up off the bench to stand with her sister, the life nearly scared right out of her. "Sara, what are you talking about?" Though thrilled her sister had intervened, Sadie worried that she might have gotten them both into more trouble than they were already in.

"Sadie isn't the one for Isaiah." Sara flung back her shoulders and speared their *vader* with a confident look. "I am."

Her *vader* narrowed his eyes. "You better explain yourself, Sara."

"Isaiah and I hit it off at the picnic. *Daed*, I've had feelings for him for a long time."

This admission made sense to Sadie, who'd been seeing the signs of Sara's affection toward Isaiah for months now. She recalled that Sara had been the one upset when the special dinner had to be canceled due to the storm. And Sara had been the one to put on her special dress the day of the picnic. And Sara had been the one to talk to Isaiah after church services.

Silence descended as the sisters collectively held their breath waiting for the final decision.

Their *vader* stood and walked to the far end of the porch. Placing both hands flat on the railing, he bowed his head. Sadie took hold of Sara's hand, giving it a squeeze. Even their *mamm* had come to stand in the doorway.

Sadie let out a nervous sigh. He was taking too long.

Finally, he turned to face them. "I will speak to Isaiah about you, Sara."

Sara broke away from Sadie, running to give their *vader* a hug. *"Danke!"*

Then she stepped to the side so their *vader* could deliver Sadie's fate.

"I know you think you have feelings for Levi Byler."

She didn't think it. She knew she'd fallen in love with the man.

"This should come as no surprise to you, Sadie. News like this travels fast in close-knit communities. Before you ask me, I think you know why I've wanted this for you and Isaiah. I know very little about Levi, other than he is Jacob's cousin and appears to be a good worker."

"Jacob has officially offered him a partnership." Sadie thought this bit of news might help her *vader* to see that Levi was not simply passing through Miller's Crossing. There was a good chance he might settle here.

"Again, I will remind you that you have a reputation to uphold."

"I understand." Sadie knew she'd just been given her last chance to find her true love.

Chapter Fifteen

Sadie got to work early the next morning, her mind filled with yesterday's conversations with both her *vader* and Levi. She couldn't help thinking they all wanted the same outcome. Being a woman of faith, she knew the Lord had plans. The words of her *grossmudder* Fischer popped into her head.

For faith to prosper, it must experience impossible situations.

Sadie let out a morose laugh. Her love for Levi had certainly brought her an impossible situation. But she knew as sure as the sun would rise and set each day, her faith was as solid as a rock. And just as strong as her faith in the Lord, she'd faith that she and Levi would find their way. The signs had been there yesterday when she could see his concern for her after she'd learned about his offer. At first, she'd felt betrayed that he hadn't told her, then she reminded herself that Levi assumed they were finished.

She knew different.

Glancing out a window of the schoolhouse, she

saw the *kinder* coming down the road. It was a sight that never got old. They came in groups of three and four, filtering out from their family's houses. The little girls wearing their blue *schlupp schotzli* over their dresses. Siblings and cousins helping one another to stay safe on the shared road. As soon as they hit the schoolyard, they ran across the grass and in through the basement entrance. All except for Mica. He straggled behind his group, scuffing his shoes through the tufts of grass.

Sadie hurried downstairs to the coatroom. "*Gute mariye*, everyone!"

Here and there, the children responded with their own, "*Gute mariye.*"

She kept watch over the tops of their heads, until she saw Mica join them. "Everyone, let's put your lunches in your cubbies and then settle at your desks, please."

Mica avoided making eye contact with her, which Sadie didn't like.

They filed upstairs in order of youngest to oldest. Each student took their seat and Sadie had them read aloud the morning Bible verse, then begin working on their math lessons.

The morning passed without incident. At eleven o'clock, she sent one of the older girls down to start the oven to warm the hot lunches. By noon everyone had eaten and was ready to go outside to play.

Mica had never been far from her sight. She noticed again that he didn't seem to want to read from his book. Though she did not like to stress it, obedience was one of the things they practiced here at the school. For the most part, her students behaved. Very rarely had she had to call upon a parent to come in, and heaven forbid, she'd never had to have the school board intervene on her behalf when it came to matters concerning parents and their children.

Still, her concern for Mica was growing.

"Mica, could you stop by my desk after you're done with your lunch, please?"

"Yes, Miss Sadie."

It pained her to see his mouth downturned. Sadie couldn't imagine what had gotten into him. Last year he'd been one of her best students. She didn't understand what had changed. She needed to get to the bottom of this and quickly.

She asked Mary Ellen and one of the other older girls to chaperone recess time. At twelve thirty on the dot, Mica arrived at her desk.

"Did you have a *gut* lunch?" she asked.

"Peanut butter and jelly, again." He rested his elbow on her desk, giving her a forlorn expression.

"I take it you don't like peanut butter and jelly?"

"It's okay. Not my favorite."

"I see. Now, tell me about last night's assignment. Did you get one of your parents to help with your reading?"

He shook his head.

"Why not?"

"They had chores to do."

"What about one of your older *bruders* or sisters?" Two of Mica's siblings had graduated last year, so Sadie knew they could help.

"Nee."

Bringing herself down to his eye-level, she reached across her desk and laid her hand gently on his arm. "Mica, can you tell me why you don't want to ask for help when you're at home?"

Again, he shook his head. She decided to try another tactic.

"How about you and I spend ten minutes during each recess working on your reading until you've caught up?"

"I can't do that either."

Sadie could almost feel his pain. Whatever was bothering him and keeping him from reading had to be pretty serious. "Mica? I need you to explain this to me."

"I can't do that."

His answer caused her to sit back in her chair. She watched him struggling and could tell he wanted to share his problem with her. Was he afraid of something at home? She prayed not.

An idea came upon her. "How about this. I'll read the pages from yesterday and you can follow along with me. Does that sound like a *gut* plan?" When he didn't respond, she added, "We have a test coming up on Friday, and it's going to have questions from these chapters. I know you want to do well."

His head moved up and down without looking up at her.

Satisfied that she had gotten through to him, Sadie asked him to bring his book up to her. Glancing at the clock, she saw there were fifteen minutes left of playtime. Mica would have to miss being outdoors with the other students today. Sadie felt bad about that, but it was important he kept pace with the others in his group.

While he got the book, she pulled another chair alongside hers. He sat down next to her and handed her the book. Sadie opened to the chapter he should have read and began reading to him. Every once in a while, she'd glance over to see if he were following along. At one point she paused. It seemed as if he were having problems seeing the words. Mica was leaning in close, squinting at the page.

Sadie nibbled her lower lip in thought.

The outside bell began to clang, signaling recess had come to an end. She would have to thank the girls for being so punctual with the time. Closing the book, she patted Mica on the shoulder. "Are you liking the book so far?"

He perked up a bit at her question. "I like when the boy tries to teach his sister how to fish."

Joy filled her heart. That was really *gut* to hear. It meant Mica had been paying attention even though he appeared to have trouble seeing the words. But she couldn't read to him every day. If her suspicions were correct, Mica was having trouble with his sight. She would send another note home and this time make him promise to show his parents.

The rest of the day flew by with ease. Sadie followed the routine, passing the trash can around the room for each student to toss out any papers they didn't need, and then escorted them to the coatroom, bidding them all a *gut* evening. She packed up and went home.

The next day dawned to begin the routine all over

again, with Sadie arriving at the schoolhouse an hour before the *kinder*.

Judging from the buggy parked in front of the school, Sadie assumed Mica's parents had read her note. *Gut.* The sooner they figured out his problem, the quicker they could resolve it.

She noticed a familiar wagon parked out back. Levi must be doing some final touches on the shed.

Pushing her bike to the side of the building, she gathered the lesson plans she'd brought home last night and headed inside. The Kings were sitting in two chairs facing her desk. Sadie paused, gathering her thoughts, preparing to greet them.

"It's about time you arrived!" Robert King turned to face her and stood behind his wife's chair.

From the doorway, Sadie said, "Mr. and Mrs. King. I didn't expect you."

Robert's *bruder* Amos owned the stationery store. Sadie realized they were quite different. Amos had always been kind to her, but she'd never gotten the feeling Robert was the same.

"Well, you should have after that note you sent home with Mica yesterday!" Robert's voice boomed through the room.

Calm. She needed to remain calm. Part of her job was to act on behalf of her students. She had to keep Mica's needs at the forefront. Bringing her papers with her, Sadie walked down the middle aisle. She rounded her desk and carefully set her things down. Then, raising her eyes, she faced Robert and Elenore King.

"What's this nonsense about him having problems reading?"

Sadie knew she had to tread lightly because Robert King sat on the school board. But that did not mean she wouldn't fight just as hard for Mica. As a matter of fact, Robert's stature made her want to dig in her heels to prove to him that she could handle this problem.

"Robert, Elenore. I noticed a few days ago that Mica seemed to have lost interest in doing his reading assignments."

"I'll speak to him about listening to you," Robert said.

"It's more than not listening. That's not it."

She decided it best not to mention Mica's complaint of the headache just yet. Sadie was quite certain Mica had told her that so she wouldn't push him to read in front of the class. She kept the part about the first note to herself, as well. If she needed extra leverage to convince the Kings to help him, she would tell them about the headache.

Sadie continued, "Yesterday I had him stay inside during recess to work with me. I decided to read out loud to him."

"I don't want you coddling my *sohn*," Robert admonished.

"I'm not doing that. I'm doing my job, trying to help him."

"His mother can help him."

"Robert, with all due respect, I believe that Mica's problem isn't that he can't read. It's that he's having struggles with his vision."

"What are you talking about?"

"I noticed that while he was following along, he had to lean in close to the page and then I saw him squinting. I think he needs to have his vision checked."

"You are no *doktor*! You are a teacher. Your job is to teach!"

"Robert!" Elenore put her arm on her husband's arm, stilling him. "Sadie has Mica's best interest at heart, I'm sure."

Pushing her hand away, he scolded, "Be quiet, Elenore." Continuing, he admonished Sadie, "You would do well to remember that you are still on probation here. Even if last year went fine, the school board hasn't ended their search for a new teacher."

Sadie stood there in shocked silence. She'd done nothing to deserve this kind of censure.

From outside the building, Levi heard what sounded like a male voice, raised in anger. Setting down the frame for the window box he'd been working on, he hurried to the schoolhouse.

Entering through the front door, he made his way to the threshold, just in time to hear a man say, "Perhaps it's not Mica's problem with his vision but the way you are teaching him."

Stunned, Levi walked into the classroom to see Sadie standing behind her desk visibly shaken. Her face ashen. It took every effort not to sprint over to the desk, take hold of the man at her desk and toss him outside. Coming to her defense seemed like the natural thing to do.

"Sadie Fischer is a *gut* teacher and you should consider yourself very fortunate to have her."

Sadie looked up, surprise registering on her face when she saw him standing there. She hadn't heard him come in.

The man glared at him. Levi immediately recognized Mica's *vader*. They'd met briefly after the storm. He wondered if the man remembered him. As the two of them stared at each other, Levi saw the anger simmering in Robert. The man's dark eyes narrowed, and his hands clenched at his side. Levi wondered why Robert didn't understand that Sadie only wanted the best for each and every one of her students, and Mica was no different.

Finally, Robert spoke. "I'm fairly certain you have no *kinder* in this school?"

"I do not."

"Then you have no business speaking here."

Levi stood there, weighing his options. He could apologize, or he could go back outside. Or he could strengthen Sadie's defense, not that he thought for one minute she couldn't defend herself.

"Miss Sadie does a fine job of seeing to the needs of her students."

"I imagine you know this because of all the time you've been spending here."

This was exactly why he'd told Sadie there couldn't be more between them. As long as he was around here, and they were alone working together, there would continue to be problems for her. Levi hadn't come to Miller's Crossing to find love. He'd come to rebuild his life, as a single man. Even though there had never been anything untoward between them, he knew in their community appearances were everything.

"As you know, I've been working with her since the storm blew through. As a matter of fact, your *sohn* Mica has been one of our helpers. He did a fine job with the painting and helping me build the new shed. You should be right proud of him."

Robert's ire over the reading issue seemed to soften. "*Danke*. I'm surprised he stayed focused long enough to get any work done."

"The painting he seemed to take to, but the work on the shed, not so much." Levi chuckled, hoping to break the tension in the room.

"He likes to horse around when he's outside." Robert swung his gaze back to Sadie.

"Robert, Elenore, I only want what's best for Mica," Sadie began. "As I'm sure you both do. Could you at least think about getting his eyes examined? If there is an issue, I imagine that soon it will carry over to other parts of his life. He's already complaining about headaches."

Elenore took hold of her husband's hand. "Please, Robert. We can at least think about what Sadie is saying."

"We'll discuss this at home." He stood up and then, nodding to Levi, said, "I'd like a word with you, outside."

Sadie's eyebrows rose.

Levi waited for Robert to join him and then took him down the stairs and out the basement door into the morning sunshine. Turning to face Mica's *daed*, he planted his feet about a foot apart, folded his arms across his chest and waited.

Robert's beard skimmed the top of his chest, and his gray hair reached almost to his shoulders. The man stood a good three inches taller than Levi. But even the steel gaze bearing down on him didn't intimidate him.

"Levi, I'm not one to beat around the bush, so I'll get right to the point of the matter. There's been gossip about you and Sadie Fischer. Part of my job on the school committee is to make sure the reputation of the teacher is a *gut* one, beyond reproach."

"I understand. My time with Sadie has been innocent. You can trust my word on that."

"You've been here working with her. Others saw you with her at the picnic. There may have been other times I've not been made aware of."

Levi felt his hackles raise. There had never been anything inappropriate between him and Sadie. He did not take these hints of accusation lightly. Moreover, he would never do anything to jeopardize her teaching job. Still, he found himself not liking the feeling Robert gave him. *Ja*, he knew how closely the Amish guarded their *dochders* and how many *vaders* worked hard to make the best arrangements for the good of the family. Sadie's *vader* hadn't been any different. But Levi had done nothing wrong.

This conversation left him with a sour taste in his mouth.

"I know Sadie understands this," Robert went on, "but I want to be certain that you do, too. It does not matter to me the work you've done to help out.

And even though you are a relation to Jacob, you're a stranger here."

Levi continued to hold his stance even though he felt as if he'd been sucker punched.

Robert left him standing in the shadow of the shed, and Levi watched him walk back into the schoolhouse. Only when Robert was out of sight did he let his hands fall to his side. He spun around, and his eyes fell on the window boxes. His latest surprise for Sadie. Why did he keep torturing himself when he knew he wasn't going to accept Jacob's offer of the partnership?

How could he? He'd be living near Sadie. And Levi simply couldn't trust his heart or his feelings again. The pain Anne had wrought had left him deeply wounded. And even though some of those wounds had begun to heal, Levi still didn't think he could trust himself to make the right choice. This encounter with Robert King only reinforced the reasons why Levi couldn't stay in Miller's Crossing and why he wasn't the right man for Sadie.

In all the weeks he'd been working side by side with her, he'd seen how she loved her *kinder*. Her days were devoted to making their lives better. He wouldn't be the one to destroy her happiness. He didn't want to rush headlong into another relationship.

Levi didn't know how to fix things.

He felt the ache growing inside him. He just wanted to do his work. Lord knows, he hadn't come here planning on falling in love. And yet that was exactly what had happened.

Pushing aside the pain and despair, Levi knew that the time had come for him to give Jacob an answer to his offer. But first he would finish what he started.

Picking up a two-by-eight plank, he placed it on the sawhorses, measured and cut the plank to size, two inches longer than the front of the windows. He did that one more time, and then, laying the tape measure along the wood, he measured out six inches in length and proceeded to cut four of those.

As the morning wore on, the *kinder*'s voices floated through the open window. Every once in a while, he heard the sweet sound of Sadie's voice either giving instruction or offering encouragement. When he heard the singing, he stopped his work to listen. The song, a familiar one, reminded him of home and family and of his love for the Lord. The hymn called to mind all the good that life could bring a person.

He didn't want to wallow. Shaking himself out of the doldrums, he hammered the pieces of wood into place until they resembled two long boxes. Then he hung one box beneath each window. Going to his wagon, he hefted the bag of potting soil onto his shoulder and brought it over to the work area. He filled both boxes with dirt, then gathered the pots of mums from his wagon.

He'd been first in line at Troyer's nursery this morning so he could pick out the prettiest plants. He'd chosen purple, yellow and white petunias.

Their blooms danced in the breeze. The purple reminded him of the way Sadie's eyes changed color depending on her mood. The pots of white mums brought to mind her strength, and the yellow ones made him think of how she embraced whatever came her way. And he'd not forgotten yellow was her favorite color.

Levi hoped she would like this final gift.

He placed one plant of each color in the window boxes. Patting the soil into place, Levi listened to the sounds of the *kinder* and realized he would miss them, almost as much as he would miss Sadie. Stepping back, he brushed his hands together, letting the loose dirt fall. He gave one last look to his handiwork and, satisfied that he'd done his best, began packing up the wagon.

A selfish part of him wanted to stay so he could see the look on her face when she stepped outside to see these flowers.

He'd started to untie the horse from the hitching post when he realized he'd left his tool belt on the ground by the shed. He jogged back over, picked it up and turned to see the *kinder* streaming out the coatroom door.

"Mr. Byler! How are you?" Mica ran up to him.

Patting the boy on the head, Levi said, "I'm *gut*, and how about yourself?"

"I'm doing okay, I guess." His face took on a glum expression. "I'm having trouble with my reading, so Miss Sadie has been helping me."

"I see. Well, it's important to know how to read."

"I understand, but I'd rather be outside playing."

Levi imagined he did.

"Mica!" Sadie's voice carried over on a breeze.

Levi took his hand off Mica's head and watched Sadie come out of the coatroom into the brilliant day. She raised a hand to shield her eyes from the sunlight. He saw her scan the area, looking for Mica.

Mica's *vader*'s words came back to Levi. As long as he remained here, her reputation could be at stake.

The Amish rules of courtship were strict. Levi knew them well. Sadie's *vader* had chosen for her. Watching her, he wondered what would happen if he decided to stay.

"I'm over here, Miss Sadie, talking to Mr. Levi."

Mica ran past her as she walked toward the shed, then Sadie stopped dead in her tracks.

Chapter Sixteen

"**W**ow!" she breathed out.

She stared at the beautiful petunias in the planter boxes hanging beneath each window on the front of the shed. She placed her hand on her heart. Levi's gesture was so thoughtful it brought tears of happiness. He'd been so stubborn about wanting to even give her the windows and now he'd gone and done this.

It almost made up for the earlier upset between him and Mica's *vader*. Almost. But she'd get back to that in a minute. First, she had to get a closer look at these flowers.

She couldn't keep the grin off her face as she went over to inspect the boxes. Up close the plants were even prettier. The vibrant purples along with the clean-white and sunshine-yellow flowers made her heart sing. She wondered how Levi had known to pick out her favorite colors.

She spun around to tell him how grateful she was for this gift. "Levi. *Danke. Danke* so much! You don't know how much joy this will bring the *kinder*. In the spring we can put different flowers in these boxes. And I know you didn't think any of my ideas were worth keeping in the beginning. But I can tell from the look on your..." She had to stop herself from blurting out *handsome face*.

Calming down, she said, "I can tell from the look on your face that you think these boxes and the windows look wonderful."

"I think you look wonderful."

The words had come out so softly that she thought she might have imagined them.

Her heart skipped a beat. Levi had paid her a compliment. The first one since they'd known each other. Though she tried not to get her hopes up, she wondered if this meant he wanted to move forward in their relationship. She dared not speak.

"I'm glad you like the flower boxes," he said a little louder. "And, *ja*, you were right. The windows are a *gut* fit."

Sadie didn't like his brusque new tone.

Levi took a step away from her. As sure as a dark rain cloud came over the horizon to spoil an otherwise perfect day, she watched Levi's mood shift. Sadie didn't understand what was happening.

"Well, I'm done here," he said. "I'd best be getting back over to Jacob's shop."

"Wait!" Sadie started after him. She needed to find out what Robert had spoken to him about.

Levi stopped and turned to look at her. Sadie didn't like what she saw, not one little bit. It appeared that a wall had gone up around him, worse than all those times before when she'd tried to break through to him. And when she'd so recently called him out on not telling her about the partnership offer.

Plunging ahead, she said, "I suppose I should thank you for intervening with Mica's *vader*. Honestly, I could have handled the man by myself. Dealing with distressed parents is part of my job."

His chin came up at her words. "Robert King had no business raising his voice to you."

"I agree. But he thought I wanted to tell him how to parent his *sohn*. Which I did not." Lowering her voice, so as not to have the *kinder* overhear, she confided, "I believe Mica is having trouble with his vision. He needs to see an eye *doktor*. I'm afraid Robert doesn't seem to agree with my assessment."

"That's not all he doesn't agree with."

"What are you talking about?" Sadie had a terrible feeling this had something to do with Levi.

Putting up his hand, he shook his head. "I can't talk about this."

"*Ja*, I think you need to. Tell me what Robert said to you."

"*Nee*. It will only cause trouble."

"Levi, if you are worried that I can't handle the situation, you'd be wrong. Just like when you walked in on my meeting earlier. You were wrong to interrupt. I didn't need your help. Although I appreciate your kind words on my behalf, I had the situation under control."

He leaned against the wagon. Shaking his head, he pointed a finger at her. "I don't think you did. Robert King was upset and he was standing over you and his wife, trying to intimidate you. *Es dutt mir leed*, Sadie, but I'm glad I came into the classroom when I did."

Sadie's frustration with him boiled over. The situation with this man had been tenuous for days, ever since he'd told he couldn't be the one for her. Sadie knew better. She could also tell that he was in no mind to listen to reason but that still didn't stop her from voicing her opinion.

"Levi, you can't have this both ways. You can't push me away one minute and then want to protect me the next. You can't leave me with this wonderful gift—" pausing, she looked at the window boxes "—and not think that I wouldn't see it as a sign of your affection."

They seemed to be at an impasse. Sadie fought back the heartache. This man, the only one she could ever love, stood here in his blue chambray work shirt, with his straw hat covering his light brown hair, leaning against the wagon, rubbing his hand down his face. She knew he wanted to wipe away his frustration. She clasped her hands together, not knowing what else to do. She felt her faith wavering.

Finally, Levi said, "I didn't want to tell you what Robert said. But I don't see any other way to protect you, to protect your job. He warned me to stay away from you. He said your reputation is at stake."

She started to tell him that was just Robert spewing nonsense when she heard one of the *kinder*'s cries. Her gaze quickly scanned the schoolyard to see who needed her.

Little Beth sat on the ground in front of the swing set, holding her right knee.

Without a thought, Sadie rushed over and kneeled in front of the girl. "Beth, *bischt allrecht*?"

Beth let out a sob as tears streamed down her face. "I fell off the swing," she wailed.

"There, there. Let me take a look." Sadie pushed Beth's *schlupp schotzli* off her knee and saw where her stockings had torn. Near as she could tell, this was nothing more than a scrape. But to be on the safe side, she would take Beth inside to clean it and put on a Band-Aid.

"Do you think you can walk?"

Beth's lower lip trembled. "I don't think so. I think it might be broken."

"Beth, I can assure you your knee is not broken. Now, come on and try to stand up," Sadie coaxed.

Doing as she was told, the child started to stand, and then let out a shout. Sadie knew the scrape wasn't serious. Still, she pushed herself off the ground, preparing to gather Beth in her arms to carry her inside. But before she could move, she felt a hand on her shoulder.

"Let me help." Levi's shadow covered them.

Sadie stood up the rest of the way, allowing him to move past her to scoop Beth up off the ground as if she were light as a feather. Levi cradled her in his arms as Sadie ran ahead to get the coatroom door opened.

"I've got a first-aid kit over by the sink." Sadie led them to the small kitchenette.

Levi sat Beth on the countertop.

"*Danke*, Mr. Levi." Beth batted her tear-soaked lashes at him.

Sadie thought her heart would melt at the sweet look on that little girl's face, so she could only imagine what Levi had to be thinking. He turned to her and Sadie sighed over the fact that he still appeared to be carrying that dark cloud with him.

"I'll leave this to you," he said in a brusque tone.

Sadie recognized that their situation would have to wait. Offering him her thanks, she gave her attention to Beth. For the first time since she'd met Levi and fallen in love with him, Sadie felt her resolve cracking.

Nee. She prayed for patience and strength. *I have to stay strong.*

As Levi made his way back to the shed company, he tried not to dwell on the situation with Sadie. But how could he not? At every twist and turn, no matter how hard he tried to keep them at bay, thoughts of her floated through his mind.

And it didn't help that the ride back to Jacob's seemed to take forever. The road was crowded today, with cars and eighteen-wheelers everywhere. With the fall season coming, the tourists were out and about earlier in the week. Here in Miller's Crossing, the leaves were just beginning to turn colors, the green leaves tinged with oranges and reds. A part of him wished he'd be here to see the colors at their peak.

He waited for the traffic to clear at the intersection

of Clymer Hill Road and Route Ten. When it came his turn, he turned right onto Clymer Hill.

The horse slowed as it started the ascent up the long hill. The wagon rattled along, cresting at the rise where the church stood. He remembered the day he'd first met Sadie. What a sight she'd been stuck in the mudhole. From the top of her head to the tips of her toes, she'd been a soggy mess. Even then he'd been struck by her presence and her personality.

A buggy careening around the corner at the bottom of the hill interrupted his musings.

"What on earth? Hey!" He gave a shout as the buggy came full speed up the hill. "Hey! *Was iss letz* with you! Slow down!"

The buggy pulled to a halt beside him. Levi immediately recognized one of the workers from the shop.

Mark Miller barely got the words out. "Levi! I'm so glad I found you! There's been an accident. You must come quickly!"

"Slow down. Tell me what's happened."

"Jacob took a fall outside his house. Rachel said he needed to go to the hospital."

Concern filled Levi. He prayed his friend's injuries were not serious. "All right." Seeing the young man was upset, Levi asked, "Did Rachel call for an ambulance?"

"*Nee.* Jacob insisted they call one of the neighbors. They came by and drove him away. I think he injured his arm."

"Okay, let's get back to the house."

Levi waited for the lad to turn around in the

church parking lot, and then led the way back to Rachel and Jacob's. He saw some of the workers standing around in a circle outside the shop. Their heads were bowed, and Jacob knew they were praying for their boss. He grew worried. If they had all stayed, then Jacob's condition must be serious.

Leaving the horse with some water and a bit of grain, he walked across the lot to join them.

"Levi. *Gut* you came back when you did. Jacob took a tumble down the steps coming out of his house. Rachel thinks he might have broken something."

"Did anyone else see what happened?"

"*Nee.* Most of us were inside."

"How long do you think they've been gone?" he asked.

"About half an hour."

That was too soon for any news. Levi looked at the men, who were all watching him. It took him a minute to realize they were waiting on some sort of instruction from him.

"I think it's best if we all go back to work," he said. "I'll go check to make sure Rachel didn't leave anything cooking on the stove. I'm sure she left in a hurry."

"*Ja*, she looked very upset."

The men made their way back inside the shop while Levi headed up the small incline to the house. He paused at the bottom of the porch steps. He could see multiple footprints where he guessed Jacob had fallen. He also saw the crack in the second step from the bottom. Not a *gut* thing. Skipping that step, he went on into the house.

Immediately, he could smell freshly baked bread and chicken. Hurrying through the great room, he saw two loaves of bread on a wire rack near the stove. And sure enough, simmering away on the back unit was a large black pot. Lifting the lid, he waited for the steam to clear, then peered inside. A whole chicken languished in the bubbling liquid along with celery, carrots and onions.

No doubt the beginning of the evening meal, and probably stock for later. He decided to turn it off. If he got busy outside, he didn't want to forget the pot and have the liquid cook off, scorching the chicken to the bottom. Better to be safe than sorry.

Now that he'd gotten the cooking under control, he turned his attention to fixing the step.

He went out the back door to the small outbuilding where Jacob stored his personal tools. He slid the door open, surprised to find everything neatly organized. The shovels, rakes and hoes were all hung neatly on the right side. He found a big red multi-drawer toolbox and opened a drawer marked Hammers. He picked up a medium-size one and selected a few large nails that would easily hold the repair.

Back at the porch, he tore the old step off the risers, then walked over to the scrap pile outside the shop to see if he could find something that could work as a replacement. After a bit of rummaging around, he managed to find a board that looked close enough in size. He hammered it into place, then tested the tread with his weight. This would suffice. With the job done, he returned everything back to its place in the outbuilding.

The sunlight angled through the branches of the maple trees circling the yard. Levi walked through the coolness of the shadows. He needed to check in on the workers. The end of the day was nearing, and they'd all be going home soon.

"Levi! We're wrapping up here."

He met Saul Yoder just inside the doorway. "Is there anything I need to be worried about on behalf of Jacob?"

"*Nee.* We're set with the biggest project, which is for Troyer's Nursery and Garden Center."

"*Gut.* When do you think that will be finished?"

"I'd say by the end of next week. Do you think Jacob will be out of work long?"

"I can't say until we see what his injuries are."

"For what it's worth, the others and I, well, we think you'd be a *gut* fit for Jacob's company."

Levi's eyes widened. He had no idea anyone else knew about the partnership offer.

"I can tell by the look on your face I spoke out of turn," Saul said. "I'm sorry. Nevertheless, we'd all be happy to have you join the company."

Levi decided to let the comment go. Saul had intended no harm. No one knew of his indecision when it came to accepting Jacob's offer. This was Levi's battle.

Saul and Levi made their way around the shop, checking to be sure each station had been shut down correctly and readied for the next day. He noticed a light on in the office. Like many other Amish businesses in the area, this one was powered by a combination of propane, generators and solar power. Bidding Saul good-night, Levi entered the office.

He saw the lamp on the desk and started to turn it off when his hand hit a stack of papers, sending them onto the floor. He bent down to pick them up and stopped when he saw a lawyer's letterhead on one of the papers. Knowing this was none of his business, he started to shuffle them in place. And that was when he saw his name.

Squinting, he mumbled, "What is this?"

Chapter Seventeen

He cast a quick look over his shoulder to make sure no one had seen him. This didn't make sense. Why was his name on a legal document? He stood from the floor and sat down with the paper in Jacob's chair. Going through his friend's legal papers made him feel like a criminal. But he had to see what Jacob had done.

Levi took his hat off and laid it on the desk next to some crisp white stationery. He ran his hands through his hair in frustration, and then, taking the plunge, he started to read through the document.

The top page appeared to be a cover letter. It stated the reason Jacob had contacted the attorney and detailed the scope of what Jacob would need done in order to secure a partner in the Herschberger Shed Company. One of the pages talked about the possibility of changing the name of the company to Herschberger and Byler.

As flattering as this idea was, Levi didn't understand why Jacob would go to all this trouble and not discuss this with him first. He'd seen enough. Putting the papers back in place, he turned the light off and went back up to the house to wait.

He took some leftover roast beef out of the refrigerator and made a sandwich. After pouring himself a glass of iced *kaffi*, he grabbed his plate and headed out to the front porch. While he ate, he wondered how Jacob was faring. And he mulled over this idea of the partnership. Clearly the employees didn't mind him coming on. And truth be told, the idea of finally settling down held some appeal. But could he stay here and not have contact with Sadie?

Once again, he wished he'd met her earlier in his life. Leaning back in the rocker, Levi pondered the situation. This partnership with Jacob would mean he'd leave his family permanently. He'd become a member of the Miller's Crossing church community. *Ja*, he'd see his *mamm* and *daed* on occasion, and writing letters to them helped them stay connected. He knew his parents always had his best interests at heart. They were as devastated as he had been over what had happened with Anne.

He finished the *kaffi* and sandwich, then set the plate on the table. Levi tipped his head back, closed his eyes and let the sounds of nature wash over him. Off in the distance he heard a hawk screeching and the frogs croaking in a nearby pond. Life could be *gut* here in Miller's Crossing.

He heard gravel crunching under tires and opened his eyes to see the beam of headlights sweeping across the driveway. Pushing up from the chair, he hurried off the porch.

Rachel was getting out of the back seat of a blue sedan. "Oh, Levi! I'm so glad you're here."

"How's Jacob?"

"Come and see for yourself." Rachel scurried to the passenger-side front seat.

Levi followed, anxious to see how his cousin had fared. He let out an *"ach"* when he saw Jacob's right arm in a cast and a sling.

While Rachel held the car door open, Levi helped Jacob out of the car as best he could. His friend seemed to be a bit wobbly on his feet. When Jacob swayed, Levi held on to his good arm. "Whoa. I've got you."

"Dan...ke."

Coming up behind them, Rachel advised, "He's been given a mild painkiller."

Levi nodded, taking care to guide Jacob up the porch stairs. "I fixed the step."

"*Danke! Danke*, Levi. That's the one that caused Jacob's fall," Rachel said, racing ahead of them to hold open the front door. "Take him into our bedroom. He needs to lie down and raise the arm up above his heart. The doctor said it will help keep the swelling down."

Again, she pushed her way ahead of the men, getting Jacob's side of the bed ready with extra pillows. Levi guided Jacob to sit on the bed.

"Ah." Jacob let out a relieved sigh. "I've had quite the time of it, I'm afraid. I noticed the step had cracked earlier today. I was actually coming out to fix it when I fell. Can you believe that?"

"*Ja*. These things happen," Levi answered as he helped him lie back in the bed.

"Jacob, I'm going to make you some toast," Rachel said. "The nurse said you have to take the medication with food. And how about some tea?" She tipped her head to one side, gazing down at her husband.

"*Ja*, that will be fine."

Thinking Jacob might need to rest, Levi started to follow Rachel out.

"Levi, wait. Let me have a word with you before Rachel comes back."

Levi paused at the foot of the bed, noticing the lines of fatigue around Jacob's eyes and the occasional grimace of pain on his face.

"I'm worried. The *doktor* said I fractured two bones in my wrist. One is what they called a hairline and the other is a bit more serious. They don't think I will need an operation to fix it, but the next few weeks will decide the course. I have to have this on for four to six weeks." he said, tapping on the hard cast. He started to give Levi a grin, but failed miserably.

"Look," Levi assured him, "I don't want you to worry about anything. You concentrate on resting and healing. It's getting late. I'll leave you to Rachel's care."

Softly, he closed the bedroom door behind him as he went to join Rachel in the kitchen.

"*Danke* for taking care of the pot, Levi," she said. "I completely forgot about it being on. Everything happened so fast. He was going down the steps one minute and the next he was on the ground calling out for me."

"He seems to be doing well and the *gut* news is he came back home without a stay in the hospital."

She nodded. "We were lucky that the urgent care could do everything. He needs to see a specialist in a few days. Those are all *gut* things. Did he tell you about the injury?"

"Ja."

"I'm not sure he told you everything. The nurse was very clear to me. He needs to keep that arm still. They want the fractures to heal well so they don't have to do an operation to fix them."

He saw the distress on her face and wanted to let her know that he would be here for them. "That makes sense. You know you both can count on me to help run things while Jacob heals."

"I'm glad you'll be here, is all."

The teakettle let out a shrill whistle. Rachel took it off the heat and went about fixing the tea and toast for her husband. "I know you can see to the running of the business while my Jacob recovers." Rachel put the teacup and saucer on a tray next to the plate of toast.

Remembering the papers he'd seen in the office, Levi knew he couldn't leave, not under these circumstances. He would get back to the idea of the partnership when Jacob was feeling better. But for now, temporarily, he'd stay put. A *gut* man did not walk out on his family when they were in need.

"Lizzie and I have come up with a plan to get you and Levi together."

Sadie stared dumbfounded at her sister. Sara, who had been beaming like a ray of sunshine for days now, was sitting here giving her advice on matters of the heart. Ever since their *vader* had given his blessing on her courting Isaiah, she'd been walking around with a happiness that appeared to be never ending. Meanwhile, Sadie had been existing in limbo. But today Sara had invited their friend Lizzie over for afternoon tea when all Sadie wanted was to wallow in a bit of self-pity.

She picked at the needlepoint she'd brought out to the porch to work on. There might not be enough rose-colored thread to finish. The design was a simple one: *Love is the reason behind everything God does.* She'd planned on making this for herself, hoping to hang it in her own home one day. Now she would finish it and give it to her sister as a wedding gift.

Picking up the threaded needle, she poked it through the fabric, working on the letter *o* in *Love*.

"We're going to have a potluck dinner." Sara clapped her hands together in delight.

"Rachel wants us to come to her place," Lizzie added. "She said her refrigerator is overflowing with casseroles. Everyone who stops by to visit Jacob comes with a dish in hand. I stopped by yesterday to leave a loaf of my homemade banana bread."

"And I'm to come as the extra?" Sadie hated the bitterness in her voice. Her frustration with Levi boiled over.

Both Sara and Lizzie had stricken looks on their faces.

"Sadie, you listen to me," Sara demanded. "Levi will be there."

"You seem awfully sure of yourself, Sara."

"*Ja*, I am. He's staying there, for goodness' sake. This situation between the two of you has to be resolved. The dinner will be tomorrow."

Sadie's stomach churned. "Tomorrow."

"That's right," Lizzie said, exchanging glances with Sara.

This turn of events had Sadie nibbling on her lower lip. She knew that Levi wouldn't be happy with this setup.

She wanted to confess something to Sara and Lizzie but didn't quite know how to form the words. Finally, knowing that getting this off her mind would be better than keeping it inside, she said, "I believe something is holding Levi back. I'm not exactly sure what the problem might be, but something from his past is clearly troubling him and keeping him from moving on with his life."

"Have you spoken to him about this?" Sara asked.

"Sara, I have tried every which way to get him to open up to me. This burden he is carrying is great. He doesn't trust what I know is in his heart."

"Hmm." Lizzie sipped thoughtfully at her tea. "I know one thing for sure, Sadie. God's plans should never be questioned."

"Are you thinking I should let Levi go?" Sadie got choked up just thinking it.

"That is not what I'm saying at all. Do you remember how hard I fought my love for Paul?"

Sadie laughed. "*Ja*. You were being so stubborn."

"That I was. I didn't think any man could ever love a woman who looks like I do." Lizzie rubbed her hand over the scar on her face. "But I finally gave into what my heart was telling me and what Paul knew all along. We were meant to be together."

Sadie's friend had been through a lot. The death of her *bruder* in a tragic accident, when they were young *kinder*, had left her scarred inside and out. But Lizzie had persevered and found her true love.

Setting her glass down on the low table between them, Lizzie leaned over and patted Sadie on the knee. "You will get this figured out."

A restlessness filled her. Putting the needlepoint down on the table, she stood up, stretching her arms. Nothing she did these days seemed to erase the tension that had taken root between her shoulder blades. "I'm going to go into the village to see if Decker's has the thread I need."

"Do you want company?" Sara asked.

"*Nee.* A walk might do me some good. Maybe the time will clear my head." Sadie went inside to grab her wallet. She said goodbye to Sara and Lizzie, then headed out.

She did enjoy the walk and the fresh air. By the time she arrived in Clymer, she had worked up a bit of a thirst. Going into the grocery store, she found the thread she needed in the home goods section and decided to treat herself to some root beer. She paid for the two items and stepped out onto the sidewalk.

"Yoo-hoo! Sadie!"

Chapter Eighteen

Elenore King came rushing up to her. "Oh, Sadie, I'm so glad I ran into you. I was across the street at the café."

"*Gute nammidaag*, Elenore."

"*Ja. Ja. Gute nammidaag* to you."

The woman seemed to be in a bit of distress. She was wringing her hands and could barely keep still. Sadie worried that something might have happened to Mica. "Elenore, *was iss letz*?"

Shaking her head, Elenore replied, "Nothing is wrong. At least I hope not."

This didn't sound *gut*. Sadie didn't think she could handle any more stress in her life. Clearly, this woman had something she wanted to tell her. Sadie thought asking about Mica might get her to talking. "How is Mica doing with his reading?"

"That's one of the things I wanted to tell you about. First, let me apologize again for Robert's treatment of you the other day."

"There's no need for that."

"I think there is. You are a *gut* teacher. I think one of the best Miller's Crossing has had in a long time. Robert was having a bad day. And that's no excuse for his behavior."

"I understand."

"He's been busy with work and of course providing for our family. This problem with Mica came at a bad time is all," she explained. "But I want you to know I convinced him to let us take Mica to the eye *doktor*."

"Elenore! This is wonderful news!" Sadie knew that Mica's reading would be back on track soon.

"Mica's eyes are weak. He's going to be wearing glasses while he's in school and for doing his reading and homework."

Sadie realized it had taken great courage and strength for Elenore to convince her husband to let this happen. Though she never doubted that the man cared for his family, he was known to be strict with them.

"I'm so happy for Mica."

Elenore fidgeted with the drawstring on the bag she was carrying. Her gaze didn't quite meet Sadie's eyes as she said, "There's one more thing I need to tell you."

"What is it?"

"The school board is meeting tonight. They are going to be deciding on your position."

Elenore's words hit her hard. Sadie had known this day would come. She'd understood from the beginning that this job might be temporary. Still, the idea of her fate being in the hands of three members of her community worried her.

"*Danke* for letting me know."

"*Willkomm,*" Elenore replied, and then went off, leaving Sadie standing near the intersection of Main Street and Route Ten.

She didn't know what to make of this news other than realizing she didn't want to leave the *kinder*.

The stoplight was on its third cycle of green, yellow, then red when she heard a very familiar voice say, "Are you going to stand here all day or are you crossing the street?"

She looked at Levi, blinking back tears.

"Sadie? Is something the matter?" He stepped toward her.

She backed away, blurting out, "The school board is meeting tonight."

"I see."

"They are going to be talking about me. Deciding *my* future." She poked herself in the chest. "What if I'm not the person they want to teach their *kinder*?"

"Sadie, I don't believe for one minute that they will let you go. Nor should you."

"Levi, Robert told me just last week that he'd be watching me closely. And I think he told you the same." She swallowed. "I took the job because I was looking for something to do to fill the time until I found..." She stopped talking.

Levi took a half step toward her and reached out a hand to her. But then, realizing they were in public where anyone could see them, he let the hand drop.

"Until you found what?"

"You know what I've been searching for."

He did.

"The *kinder* adore you." *I adore you.* "I've seen how they look up to you. And you bring such life into their lives. How can you think the school board won't see that?"

"I only know that my heart was in the wrong place when I began teaching last year. My reasons for accepting the temporary position were selfish. I simply thought I could walk into that classroom, do my teaching and leave. I wanted to fill this void in my life. And you know what? The *kinder* do fill my life. I love to see the expressions on their faces when they solve a problem. And one of my older students, Mary Ellen, why, she's growing up so fast and is a *gut* helper to me. Every night I go home thinking about the next day and all the new things we'll learn together."

She paused, as if remembering they were having this conversation in a very public place. She put her shoulders back and tilted her chin up to give him one of the fiercest looks he'd ever seen. "I can't lose them."

He almost cracked a smile, thinking there was the woman he loved. Levi longed to take her in his arms, to give her the comfort she so desperately needed. But he couldn't. He had decisions of his own to make. And only when he settled things in his own life would he be able to open his heart to her. A woman who richly deserved so much more than he could ever give her.

Tipping his hat back, he asked, "Will I see you tomorrow at Rachel and Jacob's?"

She seemed surprised by his question. "You know about the potluck?"

He nodded. Why wouldn't he know about the plans Rachel had made with Lizzie? "Rachel is very excited about having company. She's been so busy worrying over her husband that she's making herself crazy."

"But you've been there to help."

It wasn't a question but he answered anyway. *"Ja."*

"Gut."

Levi could almost see her mind wandering back to her problem. He hoped the board wouldn't use his friendship with her against her when making their decision. That wouldn't be fair. As far as he was concerned, they'd done nothing inappropriate.

"Listen, whatever happens at this meeting tonight, you've got your friends and family who will support you no matter what," he said.

"I know. I wish I could be there at the meeting. I'm not the most patient person."

He winked at her. She didn't need to remind him of that.

She gave him a half smile. "I guess I need to be getting back home. I'll see you tomorrow."

He wanted to offer her a ride but knew she'd turn him down. He watched her walk off, praying tomorrow would bring the answers she'd been hoping for. As for himself, he knew the time had come to settle things concerning the partnership.

He got back to the shop and was surprised to find Jacob sitting behind the desk in the office.

"So, you've finally grown tired of being cooped up?" Levi asked.

"As much as I love her, my wife has been driving me crazy with all of her coddling," Jacob admitted. "I know she's worried, but the trip to the specialist went better than we could have hoped."

"Is the cast coming off anytime soon?"

"*Nee.* Three more weeks, I'm afraid. But the bone is healing."

"I'm glad. You don't seem to be in as much pain either."

"I'm not. And that's a *gut* thing and another reason I want to get back out here—" Jacob nodded toward the shop area "—to work."

"You've got a lot of really dependable employees. They were all praying for you to have a speedy recovery."

"*Ja*, they are *gut* men. If we expand, I'll have to go outside of Miller's Crossing to find helpers. Would you be okay with that?"

The *we* part of his statement wasn't lost on Levi. His friend had been patient with him long enough. Jacob slid the contract Levi had found a week ago across the desk to him.

"I've had an attorney work on some papers. Do you want to take a look at them?"

Sitting down, Levi crossed one leg, resting the heel of his boot across the other knee. He took his time, tempering his words. "I already saw these papers."

Jacob raised an eyebrow.

"I came out here the day you fell to close up the shop, and noticed a light on in the office. When I came in, I found the documents."

"I'm assuming you looked through them."

Levi would never hold back the truth from his cousin. "I saw my name and looked at a few of the top pages."

Resting his good arm on top of the desk, Jacob studied him. Levi toyed with the cuff on the bottom of his pant leg.

"Levi, what do you think of what you've seen so far?" Jacob asked at last.

"I think it seems like a fair deal. But I'm wondering why you would want to add someone else's name to the business. The change would incur another expense. You'd have to change your branding."

"I think it's the right thing to do. My attorney advised waiting to see how a new partnership would work out before putting through that particular paperwork." Jacob leaned in, pushing the contract almost to the edge of the desk.

Levi chuckled. The man was determined. He grabbed the contract before it landed on the floor and sat back in his chair, reading through each page.

Jacob wanted a very nominal buy-in. Levi suspected it was because Jacob wanted Levi to bring something to the table other than financial strength. He got to the part about the company name change. His name looked *gut* on paper.

Still, he worried Jacob was being too generous. If this arrangement did not work out, then he'd be left with a company that bore someone else's name. The impact of the decision struck him. If he stayed here in Miller's Crossing, this would become his home. If he gave in to his feelings for Sadie, there would be no turning back.

And would either of these choices be so bad?

"I hear we're having company for dinner tomorrow night. I think the women have something planned." Jacob's voice broke the silence.

Levi shot a glance at him, thinking back on the conversation he'd had with Sadie earlier. She'd had a funny look on her face when they talked about the dinner. He began to grow suspicious.

"I don't know about your theory," he said. "I think they wanted to have a gathering is all."

Jacob shrugged. "If you say so. I still think they're up to something. You about done with your reading?"

"Give me another minute." Levi wanted to look over the last page one more time. The page with the signature line.

Jacob slid his pen across the desk.

"Sadie, did you start the bratwurst?" Sara asked.

"I'm not sure why you want to bring this. Didn't Rachel already say she has a lot of food?"

"Yes. But I think Isaiah might like it."

"Then why aren't you the one making the dish? I'm busy baking my cookies," Sadie snapped.

The day had been wearing on and still there was no word of the school board's decision. But she hadn't meant to take her frustrations out on her sister.

"Sadie! You apologize to your sister right this instant," their *mamm* ordered. Turning around from the sink, she speared Sadie with a look she hadn't seen since she was a *kinder*.

"*Es dutt mir leed*, Sara. Forgive me, please." Wiping her hands on a towel, she added, "I don't know what's gotten into me."

"This is so unlike you, Sadie," her *mamm* added.

"*Es dutt mir leed, Mamm.*" Dropping the towel on the counter, Sadie ran out of the kitchen and onto the front porch.

The pressure of waiting for the news was too much for her. So much of her life hung on the edge. Her job. Her relationship with Levi. Whether or not Levi would choose to become a partner and stay in Miller's Crossing. She leaned against a post at the top of the steps, trying to calm her nerves. But the thoughts kept coming. She feared her life would never hold the happiness she sought. She thought about her encounter with Levi yesterday.

Something about him had changed. She couldn't put her finger on exactly what, but he hadn't pushed her away. *Nee.* If anything, she'd felt closer to him.

She saw her *vader* coming up the pathway from the barn.

"*Dochder*, I have a note for you."

Sadie ran down the steps to meet him. This could be the news she was waiting for. With a shaky hand, she took the envelope he held out to her and saw her name in neat block lettering.

"Is this something important?" her *vader* asked.

"*Ja.*" Sadie's nerves were rattling so much she barely got the word out.

A million thoughts ran through her mind. If the school board was keeping her, surely they would have sent someone by to tell her in person. On the other hand, if they were going to let her go, she imagined Robert King might have taken great pleasure in delivering that news himself. She didn't know what to do.

And then a thought hit her. As sure as the sun rose and set, there was only one person she wanted with her when she opened this envelope.

She left her *vader* and ran back inside the house. "Sara, do you have everything ready to go?"

"Sadie, what's gotten into you now?" her *mamm* asked.

"Nothing. And everything." Sadie gave her *mamm* a hug, then picked up the red cookie tin with her snickerdoodles.

Sara was just putting the foil on the bratwurst. "Are we leaving? Isaiah isn't here yet. Did you forget he's driving us?"

Sadie had forgotten. "Okay, let's wait for him at the top of the driveway."

"Sadie!"

"Come on, hurry up!" She tugged her sister by the arm toward the door.

She needed to get to Levi.

Chapter Nineteen

Levi was helping Rachel put the dishes out on the picnic table in the side yard. She'd told him evenings like this were not to be wasted eating indoors. He set a dish of baked chicken in the middle of the table, along with the green bean casserole, baked macaroni and cheese, another pasta dish and a large tossed salad. The neighbors had been generous with their offerings during Jacob's recovery. And he couldn't even begin to think about the number of pies and cakes that filled the second shelf of the refrigerator.

Speaking of desserts, he hoped Sadie might bring her blue-ribbon snickerdoodles. Levi hoped she'd have good news, too.

He'd been thinking about her all day long. He prayed the school board had made the right decision, because he had a bit of his own news to share with her.

Moving to the other side of the table, he fixed the thin cushion over the bench. Rachel had insisted they use them. While the menfolk didn't mind sitting on hard benches, she assured him the ladies preferred a bit more comfort.

A buggy pulled up in front of the house, and Levi stood taller, waiting for Sadie to get out. Surprise ricocheted through him when he saw Isaiah Troyer climbing down from the front seat.

How could Sadie do this to him? Was this some sort of bad joke that life had decided to play on him a second time? He didn't think he had it in him to bear heartbreak once again.

His arms went rigid as he fisted his hands at his sides. Why on earth had Sadie brought Isaiah here?

"Levi."

The stern tone of Rachel's voice halted his dark thoughts.

"Whatever you are thinking, don't."

Sadie got out of the back seat. He watched as she tipped her head back, laughing at something her sister said. *Her sister.* Sara and Isaiah were walking side by side with Sara's arm linked through his.

Not believing what he was seeing, he glanced at Rachel, who was looking very smug. "I don't understand."

Rachel gave him a pat on the arm. "I think it best if Sadie explains the situation to you."

He left the table and crossed the lawn, meeting Sadie halfway between the buggy and the picnic area. "I think we need to talk."

She nodded.

"Let's go around to the back of the house. On the way you can tell me about your sister and Isaiah."

"The short version is Sara has always been the

Fischer *dochder* for Isaiah," Sadie said with a shrug. "I suspected her feelings for some time."

"And you didn't say anything sooner?"

"Because I needed to be sure. Look, Levi, you've known my *vader* had his mind set on a match between Isaiah and myself. I knew better."

"I see," he said, even though he didn't.

Sadie went on to explain. "Once we convinced our *vader* that Sara was meant for Isaiah, and Isaiah decided that Sara was indeed the better fit, he gave his blessing to them."

Levi still didn't understand how he hadn't seen any of this coming. "Interesting. And what about you? Has he given his blessing to you?"

Sadie stopped along the path. The look on her face told him everything. "I'm afraid not yet." She lifted her eyes to meet his.

Levi wanted to wipe away her doubt.

"He's not sure about you, Levi. But I am. I know there are things in your past—things you've kept from me. Perhaps it's time to let me in."

"Can you tell me what the school board said first?"

"All right. I have some news to share. Except I'm not sure if it's bad or *gut*. I've got the envelope here in my pocket. Someone gave it to my *vader* to give to me."

Stopping along the path, he looked down at her. He could almost read the doubt about her future in her eyes. Reaching down, he caught her hand. Her skin felt warm and soft beneath his calloused fingertips.

Giving her hand a reassuring squeeze, he said, "Remember what I said to you yesterday? How no matter what happens, you'll still have all of us to get you through?"

"I do remember." Sadie dropped his hand and took the envelope out of her pocket. She nibbled on her lower lip.

Levi felt his heart lurch. If the news was not what she'd hoped for, she'd be upset. One thing he knew for certain was her strength would get her through.

She took a deep breath, then ran her finger under the flap of the envelope. Exhaling, she pulled out a note. "I'm almost too afraid to look."

"Do you want me to read it to you?"

"Nee."

Her gaze skimmed the page. And then her face broke out into the widest smile he'd ever seen.

"Gut news, I take it?"

"Yes! Yes! I'm staying. They want me to stay!"

Levi brought his arms around her, hugging her close, feeling her trembling with excitement. He let her go, saying, "Oh, Sadie, this is the best news for you."

"The only thing that would make it better is if you were going to tell me that you've decided to stay."

He'd decided more than that. "I have something I need to tell you."

Sadie wanted more than anything to hear Levi tell her that he loved her and that he would never leave her. She let him take her hand once more, relishing the warmth and security his touch brought her.

She loved this man more than life itself. She wished this trepidation she felt every time they drew closer would leave. Only Levi could make the sensation go away.

"Does this something have to do with Jacob's offer?"

"*Ja.* And there's more." He led them to a bench under a big maple tree. "Come sit. I want to tell you about what brought me here."

She tilted her head to see him better. "I thought you came to help your cousin."

"That was part of the reason, but not all of it."

Sadie put a hand on either side of his face. Rubbing her thumbs along the hard plane of his cheekbones, she felt his strength. "Levi, in order for us to work, you need to tell me what is in your heart. I know you've been holding a pain deep inside. I saw it the first day I met you."

Sadie remembered how businesslike he'd been with her then, practically ordering her out of the wagon, and how mad he'd gotten when she didn't tell him right away where she lived. And the other times when he'd pushed her away...

But the day Robert King had come into her classroom, intent on making her at fault for Mica's learning problems, that day had been the turning point. Levi had been there for her, and now she wanted to be there for him.

"Tell me what happened to you."

Putting his hands around hers, he said, "This isn't easy for me. None of this has been easy for me." Touching his forehead to hers, his voice broke. "Falling in love with you should have come easily. And yet, I've tried to fight those feelings from the moment I set eyes on you."

"Why?"

"Because my heart had been broken." He shifted away from her, resting his hands on his knees. "This situation is difficult for me to talk about."

Sadie's heart began to race. What if she were forcing him to relive something too painful? "I'm so sorry."

"I've been in love before." He stopped and then started speaking again. "That's not right. I thought I'd been in love. I wasn't."

Sadie let the words sink in. There had been someone else before her.

"A young woman. A lot like you." He turned to look at her then. "Pretty and impetuous."

"I'm not—" She was about to say *pretty*, but Levi held up a hand, stopping her.

"Sadie, you asked me to tell you. Please, let me continue."

Folding her hands in her lap, she nodded.

"We fell in love quickly. Again, I thought at the time the feeling was love. I'd known Anne for a long time. We grew up in neighboring communities. I met her at a picnic. The time seemed right, and my family might have been pressuring me to find a wife. I know you understand."

"I do."

"To this day I'm not sure what thoughts were in Anne's head. I only know she left me a note, telling me she'd decided to leave the community."

"You mean she wanted to move?"

"*Nee.* She wanted to leave the Amish life."

Sadie gasped. She couldn't imagine walking away from the only life she'd ever known. The thought of being shunned brought tears to her eyes. The idea that she'd have to leave her family, friends and the *kinder* she taught to be all alone in the *Englisch* world? *Nee.* She couldn't fathom how someone would want to do that.

Swallowing a sob, Sadie, barely got out, "Why? Why would she want to leave?" Worse yet, why would she push a man as wonderful as Levi away?

He looked out over the yard, unable to meet Sadie's gaze. "She was in love with someone else. An *Englischer.*"

"Oh, Levi. I'm so very sorry."

"You must understand how hard this has been for me. I wanted to start a new life with her, and she had met another man and fallen in love. I can forgive her, because she never would have found happiness with me. But when it first happened, I was angry and hurt. I know now that Anne and I weren't meant to be together. But I can't forget how her actions made me feel."

"But, Levi, I'm not that woman." Sadie shook her head. "I would never treat you like that."

"I know."

"And the situation with Isaiah, well, that was my *vader*'s doing from the very beginning."

"I know that. Though I have to tell you I wasn't sure what to think when I saw him getting out of the buggy just now."

Sadie realized her mistake not telling him about Isaiah and Sara when she saw him yesterday. "I guess I should have told you about the change in plans."

"That would have been helpful."

He stood up, shoving his hands in his pockets. "I wasn't sure I'd ever be able to trust my heart to love anyone again. And then I met you, Sadie Fischer. You turned my world upside down and right side up."

Sadie's heart soared. But she had to be sure he understood, no matter what, that she wasn't like this other woman.

"Levi, I would never be like Anne who broke your heart."

"You can't deny you've had an idea of the kind of man you wanted to spend the rest of your life with. Not too old, not too young..." His voice drifted off.

She knew those words might come back to haunt her for the rest of their days together. Defending herself might not be an easy thing, but she had to at least try. "I've *never* thought of you as such. You are a kind and decent man. One who is *gut* with the *kinder*. One who delivers on his promises."

"As little as a week ago, I would have told you that none of those words matter," Levi said. "Then I heard Robert King raising his voice to you, and the only thing I could think was I needed to keep you safe."

"I told you the other day, I had the situation under control."

"I remember. But I knew then that if I left here, I might very well be leaving something *gut* behind. I've been fighting this feeling for too long." Splaying his hands wide, he said, his voice broken, "I didn't want to risk my heart again. Do you understand what I'm saying?"

This time the wrenching sob came from her. Standing, she almost couldn't bear to ask him, "Levi, then you don't deny there is something between us?"

"Oh *ja*, there is more than something between us. I've fallen in love with you, Sadie."

Sadie clung to his side. Looking up at him, she needed to know if they had a future.

"Does this mean you're staying? Before you tell me what you're about to do, let me tell you how much I love you. Levi, my world righted the day I met you. You weren't too old or too young or heaven forbid already spoken for."

Levi let out a laugh. "You're not going to let that go, are you?"

"Nope."

"I don't know why I thought I could ever leave you."

"Wait!" she said suddenly. "You need to tell me your other news."

"My other news?"

"*Ja*... Jacob's offer. Are you going to accept it?"

"I signed the papers this morning."

"*Ach!* That's wonderful!" Sadie fell into his arms. "I love you, Levi Byler."

"I love you, too, Sadie Fischer. More than life itself."

Tipping her chin up, he looked down into her eyes. Sadie's heart melted at the love she saw reflecting back at her.

Levi bent his head low. His mouth brushed against hers, his touch sending her heartbeat soaring.

"If you don't mind," he said quietly, "I want to give you a proper kiss."

She didn't mind at all. Standing on her tiptoes, Sadie met him halfway, their lips touching.

Lifting his lips from hers, he asked, "Can I tell you again how much I love you?"

"You can. Over and over and over." Sadie didn't think she'd ever been happier.

"I've finally found my home," he said with a smile.

"And I've finally found my perfect Amish man."

* * * * *

If you loved this story,
pick up Tracey Lyons's other book
A Love for Lizzie.

And be sure to check out
these other books set in Amish country:

The Baby Next Door *by Vannetta Chapman*
A Secret Amish Crush *by Marta Perry*
Amish Baby Lessons *by Patrice Lewis*

Available now from Love Inspired!

Find more great reads at www.LoveInspired.com

Sadie's Blue-Ribbon Snickerdoodle Cookies

1½ cups sugar
½ cup butter, softened
½ cup shortening
2 large eggs
2¾ cups all-purpose flour
2 teaspoons cream of tartar
1 teaspoon baking soda
¼ teaspoon salt
¼ cup sugar
2 teaspoons ground cinnamon

Heat oven to 400 degrees.

Mix the first 1½ cups sugar, the butter, shortening and eggs in a large bowl with hand mixer until light and fluffy. Stir in flour, cream of tartar, baking soda and salt until soft dough is formed.

Shape dough into 1¼-inch balls. Mix ¼ cup sugar and the cinnamon in a small bowl. Roll balls in the mixture. Place two inches apart on an ungreased cookie sheet.

Bake 8 to 10 minutes or until set. Remove from cookie sheet and cool on a wire rack.

Dear Reader,

I wrote this book during a difficult time in my life. My dad had just passed away. I remember writing the proposal for Sadie and Levi's story at the same time I was working on my dad's obituary.

My point is, we never know what life is going to bring us. But hopefully we find the happiness that lies just around the next corner.

The hero of this book had no intention of falling in love. He wanted to mend his broken heart and start fresh in a new town, while the heroine wanted nothing more than to find her perfect match. Sadie and Levi seemed to go head-to-head while repairing a damaged schoolhouse, but then found a way to work together. Circumstances brought them together and they both learned that they could set their differences aside to find true love and happiness.

I hope you enjoyed their story as much as I enjoyed writing it.

Special thanks to my editor, Melissa Endlich, and my agent, Michelle Grajkowski, who always steer me in the right direction. As always, special thanks to my husband, TJ.

Happy reading!
Tracey

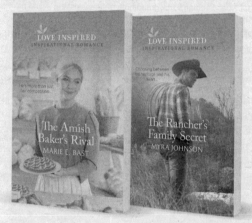

Get 4 FREE REWARDS!

We'll send you 2 FREE Books plus 2 FREE Mystery Gifts.

Love Inspired books feature uplifting stories where faith helps guide you through life's challenges and discover the promise of a new beginning.

FREE
Value Over
$20

YES! Please send me 2 FREE Love Inspired Romance novels and my 2 FREE mystery gifts (gifts are worth about $10 retail). After receiving them, if I don't wish to receive any more books, I can return the shipping statement marked "cancel." If I don't cancel, I will receive 6 brand-new novels every month and be billed just $5.24 each for the regular-print edition or $5.99 each for the larger-print edition in the U.S., or $5.74 each for the regular-print edition or $6.24 each for the larger-print edition in Canada. That's a savings of at least 13% off the cover price. It's quite a bargain! Shipping and handling is just 50¢ per book in the U.S. and $1.25 per book in Canada.* I understand that accepting the 2 free books and gifts places me under no obligation to buy anything. I can always return a shipment and cancel at any time. The free books and gifts are mine to keep no matter what I decide.

Choose one: ☐ **Love Inspired Romance Regular-Print** (105/305 IDN GNWC)   ☐ **Love Inspired Romance Larger-Print** (122/322 IDN GNWC)

Name (please print)

Address   Apt. #

City   State/Province   Zip/Postal Code

Email: Please check this box ☐ if you would like to receive newsletters and promotional emails from Harlequin Enterprises ULC and its affiliates. You can unsubscribe anytime.

Mail to the **Harlequin Reader Service:**
IN U.S.A.: P.O. Box 1341, Buffalo, NY 14240-8531
IN CANADA: P.O. Box 603, Fort Erie, Ontario L2A 5X3

Want to try 2 free books from another series! Call 1-800-873-8635 or visit www.ReaderService.com.

Arleta had tossed and turned all night ruminating over Sovilla's
and Noah's remarks. And in the wee hours of the morning, she'd
come to the decision that—as disappointing as it would be—if
they wanted her to leave, she'd make her departure as easy and
amicable for them as she could.

"Your *groossmammi* is tiring of me—that's why she wanted
me to go to the frolic," she said to Noah. "She said she wanted to
be alone. And if I'm not at the *haus*, I can't be of any help to her,
which means you're wasting your money paying me. Besides, her
health is improving now and you probably don't need someone
here full-time."

"Whoa!" Noah commanded the horse to stop on the shoulder
of the road. He pushed his hat back and peered intently at Arleta.
"I'm sorry that what I said last night didn't reflect the depth of my
appreciation for all that you've done. But I consider your presence
in our home to be a gift from *Gott*. It's invaluable. Please don't
leave because of something *dumm* I said that I didn't mean. I was
overly tired and irritated at—at one of my coworkers and... Well,
there's no excuse. Please just forgive me—and don't leave."

Hearing Noah's compliment made Arleta feel as if she'd just
swallowed a cupful of sunshine; it filled her with warmth from

her cheeks to her toes. But as much as she treasured his words, she doubted Sovilla felt the same way. "I've enjoyed being at your *haus*, too. But your *groossmammi*—"

"She said something she didn't mean, too. Or she didn't mean it the way you took it. If I know my *groossmammi* as well as I think I do, she felt like you should go out and socialize once in a while instead of staying with her all the time. But she knew you'd resist it if she said that, so she turned the tables and claimed she wanted the *haus* to herself for a while."

That thought had occurred to Arleta, too. "*Jah*, perhaps."

"I'm sure of it. I can talk to her about it when—"

"*Neh*, please don't. I don't want to turn a molehill into a mountain." Arleta realized she should have spoken with Noah before jumping to the conclusion that neither he nor Sovilla wanted her to stay. But she'd been so homesick yesterday, and she'd felt even more alone after she'd listened to the other women implying how disgraceful it was for a young woman to work out. Hannah's lukewarm invitation to the frolic contributed to her loneliness, too. So by the time Sovilla and Noah made their remarks, Arleta already felt as if no one truly wanted her around and she jumped to the conclusion they would have preferred to employ someone else. She felt too silly to explain all of that to Noah now, so she simply said, "I shouldn't have been so sensitive."

"*Neh*. My *groossmammi* and I shouldn't have been so insensitive." Noah's chocolate-colored eyes conveyed the sincerity of his words. "It can't be easy trying to please both of us at the same time."

Arleta laughed. Since she couldn't deny it, she said, "It might not always be easy, but it's always interesting."

"Interesting enough to stay for the rest of the summer?"

Don't miss
Hiding Her Amish Secret *by Carrie Lighte,*
available May 2021 wherever
Love Inspired books and ebooks are sold.

LoveInspired.com

Closing her eyes, she pressed a hand to her belly and breathed deeply, in and out.

Having inherited her mother's petite figure and danced for exercise most days of her life, her stomach had always been flat. Early though the pregnancy was, there was a noticeable swelling, just as her breasts had swollen. As dream-like as everything had felt these last few days, one thing had made itself felt with concrete certainty: she was pregnant. Her body was doing what it needed to do to bring her baby safely into this world. And Alessia would do what was needed too, and that meant marrying Gabriel.

She'd expected coming face-to-face with him to be hard, but she hadn't expected it to be that hard. She hadn't expected to feel so *much*.

Being a good, dutiful princess... That was Alessia's role in this world, her purpose, her reason for being.

Her night with Gabriel was a different matter entirely. That night, she had broken free from the bonds of duty and freed the real woman inside, and it was terrifying how strongly seeing Gabriel again relit that passionate fire inside her.

Scandalous Royal Weddings

Marriages to make front-page news!

Raised on the Mediterranean island kingdom of Ceres, Princes Amadeo and Marcelo and Princess Alessia want for nothing. But with their life of luxury comes an impeccable reputation to uphold. Any hint of a scandal could turn the eyes of the world on them...and force them down the royal aisle! Their lives may be lived in the spotlight, but only one person will have the power to truly see them...

When Prince Marcelo rescues Clara from a forced wedding, he simultaneously risks a diplomatic crisis and his heart.

Read on in
Crowning His Kidnapped Princess

Billionaire Gabriel may fix scandals for a living, but his night with Princess Alessia creates a scandal of their own when she discovers she's pregnant!

Read on in
Pregnant Innocent Behind the Veil

Both available now!

Prince Amadeo must face a stranger at the altar, when convenient royal wedding bells chime. Look out for his story, coming soon!

Don't miss this scandalous trilogy by Michelle Smart!

Michelle Smart

PREGNANT INNOCENT
BEHIND THE VEIL

HARLEQUIN
PRESENTS

Recycling programs
for this product may
not exist in your area.

ISBN-13: 978-1-335-58381-9

Pregnant Innocent Behind the Veil

Copyright © 2022 by Michelle Smart

For questions and comments about the quality of this book,
please contact us at CustomerService@Harlequin.com.

Harlequin Enterprises ULC
22 Adelaide St. West, 41st Floor
Toronto, Ontario M5H 4E3, Canada
www.Harlequin.com

Printed in U.S.A.

Michelle Smart's love affair with books started when she was a baby and would cuddle them in her cot. A voracious reader of all genres, she found her love of romance established when she stumbled across her first Harlequin book at the age of twelve. She's been reading them— and writing them—ever since. Michelle lives in Northamptonshire, England, with her husband and two young Smarties.

Books by Michelle Smart

Harlequin Presents

Stranded with Her Greek Husband
Claiming His Baby at the Altar

Billion-Dollar Mediterranean Brides

The Forbidden Innocent's Bodyguard
The Secret Behind the Greek's Return

The Delgado Inheritance

The Billionaire's Cinderella Contract
The Cost of Claiming His Heir

Christmas with a Billionaire

Unwrapped by Her Italian Boss

Scandalous Royal Weddings

Crowning His Kidnapped Princess

Visit the Author Profile page
at Harlequin.com for more titles.

This is for Mitchell. I hope life brings you an abundance of joy xxx

CHAPTER ONE

ALESSIA BERRUTI'S HAND shook as she pressed
'play' on her phone. The scene, one which had
already been viewed by over two million people
since its upload four hours earlier, was a wedding reception. Hundreds of finely dressed people were celebrating in a stateroom in the castle
where the royal family of Ceres lived. The camera zoomed in on two women. The loud music
and waves of surrounding conversation faded.

'Your brother looks smitten,' the blonde lady
in the video footage said. Her voice, although
pitched low, was clearly audible.

'He is.' The tiny, chestnut-haired woman who
answered looked over her shoulder. The camera
perfectly captured the face of Princess Alessia
Berruti.

The blonde's voice dropped even lower. 'I
wonder how Dominic's feeling right now, seeing his intended bride marry another man.'

'Who gives a...' A loud beep was dubbed

over the princess's scathing retort. 'That man's an obese, sweaty, disgusting monster.'

'Don't hold back,' the blonde said with a laugh. 'Say what you really think.'

The princess laughed too and drank some more champagne before saying, 'Okay, what I *really* think is that King Dominic of Monte Cleure should be locked behind bars and never allowed within three kilometres of any woman ever again.'

The footage ended the moment Alessia's phone buzzed in her hand. It was her eldest brother, Amadeo.

'My quarters,' he said icily. 'Now.'

Four days later, Alessia covered her flaming face and wished for the chair she was sitting on to plunge her into a deep pit.

What had she done?

Trying her hardest not to cry again, she lifted her stare to Amadeo. His features were as taut and uncompromising as she had ever seen them. To his right, their mother, her expression as unyielding as her eldest son's. To their mother's right, their father, the only person in this whole room with a smidgeon of sympathy. She couldn't bring herself to look at the man sat on the other side of Amadeo, the final link in the human chain of disappointment and anger being aimed at her.

'I'm so sorry,' Alessia whispered for the third time. 'I had no idea I was being filmed.'

It was an excuse that cut no ice, not even with her.

One unguarded moment. That's all it had been. Unguarded or not, she should have known better. She *did* know better. Her whole life had been spent having her basic human desires and reactions restrained so that she was always in total control of herself.

'I'll marry Dominic,' she blurted into the silence. 'I'm the one who's got us into this mess, I'm the one who should be punished. Not you.'

That had been the king's first demand in the Berrutis' valiant efforts to make amends. Marriage to Princess Alessia. It would show the world, so he said, that she had been jesting and that the Berruti royal family respected him. That the world had already got wind that he'd once made overtures about marriage to the princess and been politely rebuffed mattered not a jot to him. King Dominic had thicker skin than a rhinoceros. He also had the vanity of a peacock and the cruelty of a medieval despot. So atrocious was his reputation that not a single eligible female member of any European royal family had agreed to a date, let alone marriage.

Dominic's desperation for a blue-blooded bride had seen him trick a very distant relation of the current British monarch to his principality and then hold her hostage until she agreed to marry him. His victim escaped barely an hour before her forced nuptials when Alessia's other brother, Marcelo, rescued her to worldwide amazement and Dominic's fury, and married her for himself. It was at Marcelo and Clara's wedding reception that Alessia had opened her mouth and made the simmering relations between the two nations boil over.

'Don't think I've not been tempted,' Amadeo said grimly at the same moment their father stated, 'Out of the question.'

'But why should Amadeo have to give up his whole life for something that's my fault?' she implored.

'Because, sister,' Amadeo answered, 'tempting though it may be to insist you marry that man, I wouldn't marry someone I hate to him never mind my own sister.'

A tear leaked out and rolled down her cheek. She wiped it away. 'But this is *my* fault. Surely there's a way to make amends and bring peace to our countries without you having to do this?'

The man Alessia had been cursorily introduced to three days ago addressed her directly for the first time. 'This is the one resolution satisfactory to both parties.'

Gabriel Serres. The 'fixer' brought in by her parents and brother to fix the mess and bring peace to Ceres and Monte Cleure, and the most handsome man she'd ever laid eyes on. She'd taken one look at him and, for a few short moments, all her troubles had blown out of her mind.

For three days Gabriel had flown back and forth between their Mediterranean island and the European principality, negotiating between the two parties. Alessia, in disgrace for pouring fuel over the simmering tensions between the two nations, had, to her immense frustration, been cut off from the negotiations. Until now. When the deal was done.

Done deal or not, that didn't stop her arguing against it. 'How can Amadeo marrying a complete stranger be satisfactory?'

'The bride is the king's cousin. Their marriage will unify the two nations, reopen diplomatic ties and prevent a costly trade war,' Gabriel reminded the princess with deliberate indifference.

His indifference was usually effortless. A man did not reach the top of the diplomatic field by getting emotionally involved in the disputes he was paid to resolve, but he'd found himself having to work at maintaining his usual detachment since Alessia had entered the meeting room. Dressed in a pair of tight-fitted, cropped black trousers topped with a loose, white scooped top, her straight dark chestnut hair hung loose around her shoulders. A puffiness to her dark brown eyes suggested she'd been crying, and he could see she was battling to maintain her composure. Like her mother, Queen Isabella, the princess was tiny, more so in the flesh than in the constant ream of photographs the press so loved to publish of her. In the flesh, there was something about her that brought to mind the spinning ballerina in his sister's old musical jewellery box.

Since their introduction three days ago, he'd found his mind wandering to her in ways that could not be classed as professional. The few times he'd spotted her in the distance had made him give double takes, and he'd had to consciously stop himself from staring at her. Yesterday, on a brief visit back to the castle, he'd been getting out of his car when she'd appeared, flanked by her bodyguards, clearly about to head off somewhere. Their eyes had caught and held. Just for a moment. But it had been moment enough for a frisson to race through his veins. It had been moment enough for him to see the mirroring flash of awareness in her eyes.

He supposed any red-blooded man would find the princess attractive but it was a rare occasion Gabriel found himself noticing someone's desirability when working. Single-minded focus and a refusal to accept failure were traits that had helped make him one of the world's leading negotiators. There was not a top agency in the world that hadn't, at some point, called in his services. His services were simple—he acted as a bridge between warring peoples, be they businesses, government agencies or a division of the UN. His skills meant that disputes were resolved without either side losing face.

He charged a hefty fee for those services. A diplomatic Svengali who worked under the radar of the press, he also had a canny eye for start-ups with potential and, as such, his investments had made him rich beyond his wildest dreams. Gabriel Serres was the billionaire no one had heard of. Intensely private and disdaining of the celebrity-fixated world, this anonymity was exactly how he liked it. His affairs—though he disliked calling them affairs when they involved two consenting adults enjoying each other until the time came to move on—were conducted under the same intense bounds of privacy, and never with a client. To find himself attracted to his client's daughter, a woman who lived her life in the glare of a media circus, was disconcerting to say the least. Gabriel's childhood had been one huge media circus, and it was a state of being he'd actively avoided ever since.

'And what of his bride?' the object of his attraction bit out in the husky voice that evoked thoughts of dark, sultry rooms and sensual pleasure. 'Does she get a say in it? Or is she being married against her will and without her consent?'

Her anger and concern was genuine, he recognised. Princess Alessia Berruti, the darling of the European press, a woman who'd mastered the art of social media to display herself and her royal family in the best possible attention-grabbing light, was not as self-centred as he'd presumed.

'She has agreed to the marriage,' he assured her.

Gabriel's expression was indifferent, his smooth, accented voice—an accent Alessia couldn't place—dispassionate, but there was something about the laser of his brown stare and the timbre in his tone that sent a shiver racing up her spine. It was a shiver that managed to be warm and was far from unpleasant. For the beat of an instant, a connection passed between them, sending another warm shiver coiling through her. But then he snapped his eyes shut and when they next locked on hers, the dispassion in his voice was matched in his returning stare.

A man clearly used to being listened to and heeded, Gabriel Serres had a presence that commanded attention even when he wasn't speaking. Alessia had noticed him a number of times since their introduction and, though most of those times he'd been at a distance from her—apart from in the castle's private car park when she'd come close to losing her footing when their eyes had suddenly met—he'd certainly commanded *her* attention. There was something about him she found difficult to tear her gaze from, something that made her belly warm and soften even though she'd come to the conclusion that there was nothing warm or soft about him. Under the impeccably tailored grey suit lay an obviously hard, lean body that perfectly matched a hard, angular face with hooded dark brown eyes that were as warm as a frozen waterfall. Even his thick black hair had been tamed into a quiff she doubted dared escape its confines.

Anger rising that he could be so detached about a situation where a woman was required to give her entire future just to save her family's skin, Alessia eyeballed him and snapped. 'What, like Clara consented?'

'It has been agreed,' her mother said in a voice that brooked no further argument. 'Gabriel has gone to great lengths to bring a rapprochement between our nations. Your brother is in agreement, the king is in agreement and the bride is in agreement. The wedding preparations start now. The pre-wedding party will be held in two weeks, the wedding in six. You will be a bridesmaid and you will smile and show the world how happy you are for the union. We all will.' And with that, her mother rose with the innate grace only a born queen had, and swept out of the room without another look at her youngest child.

Devastated to have caused her mother such disappointment and realising she was in danger of going into a full-blown meltdown in front of her father, brother, Ice Man and the staff, Alessia got to her feet. Casting each of them a withering stare, she left the meeting room with her head as high as she could manage.

Gabriel had a tension headache, caused no doubt by three days of intense negotiations between a despotic king and a rival royal family desperately trying to salvage their own image. Having had little sleep in that period didn't help, and neither did the engine problem with his plane he'd been notified about earlier. His plan to leave the Berrutis' castle and fly home to Spain delayed, he'd accepted King Julius's offer of a bed for the night. After dining with the king and queen and the heir to the throne, he was escorted through the warren of wide corridors to his appointed quarters. Once inside, he rolled his neck and shoulders and took a shower.

As far as royal families went, the Berrutis were relatively decent. Relatively. They inhabited a privileged world where, by virtue of their births, they were exalted and deferred to from their very first breaths, and, as such, took being exalted and deferred to as their due. Compared to King Dominic Fernandes, however, they were modest paragons of virtue. Gabriel cared little either way. His job was to be impartial and broker an agreement both parties could live with and he'd done that. Negotiating a marriage was, however, a first, and had left a bad taste in his mouth, which he unsuccessfully tried to scrub out with his toothbrush. He was quite sure Princess Alessia's outrage about the marriage had contributed to the acrid taste on his tongue.

Despite his exhaustion, Gabriel was too wired to sleep. After twenty minutes of his eyes refusing to close and fighting his mind's desire to conjure the pint-sized princess, he gave up and threw the bedsheets off. Pulling on a pair of trousers, he prowled the quarters he'd been appointed, found a fully stocked bar and helped himself to a bourbon. If he wished, he could lift the receiver on the bar and call the castle kitchen, where an on-duty chef would prepare anything he desired. He would give the Berrutis their due, they were excellent hosts.

Taking the bottle of bourbon with him, he opened the French doors in his bedroom and stepped onto the balcony. The warm air of the night had lost much of the day's humidity, the distant full moon lighting the castle's extensive grounds. With a strong gothic feel, it was an intriguing castle dating back to the medieval period, and full of mysteries and secrets. In the distance he could see the ancient amphitheatre, which divided the castle's two main sections…

His thoughts cut away from him as the strong feeling of being watched made the hairs on the back of his neck rise.

Alessia had been laid in her hammock for hours. Unable to face another meal with her family, unable to bear seeing more of her mother's disappointment, unable to look at the brother whose life she'd ruined, she felt desperately alone, wracked with guilt and so very ashamed. Now, though, her heart was thumping, because a man had emerged through the shadows on the adjoining balcony, and as he turned his head in her direction her heart thumped even harder as recognition kicked in.

It was *him*. The gorgeous Ice Man who made her belly flip.

Under the moonlight, he somehow seemed even more devastatingly attractive, and she sucked in a breath as her gaze drifted over a rampantly masculine bare chest.

For a long, long moment, all the demons in her head flew away in the face of such a divine specimen of manhood.

Suddenly certain her misery had conjured him, she blinked hard to clear his image, but it didn't clear anything. That really was the gorgeous Ice Man.

Impulse took over and before she could stop herself, she called out. 'Having trouble sleeping too?'

Gabriel's heart smashed in instant recognition of the husky voice. Holding his breath, he rested an arm on the ancient waist-high stone balustrade that adjoined the neighbouring balcony, and peered into the adjoining space. There he found, laid out on a hammock in the moonlight's shadow, the woman whose unguarded words had almost caused a war between two nations and whose image had prevented him from sleeping.

He cursed silently even as his heart clattered harder into his ribs. He'd been unaware his appointed quarters adjoined hers.

'Good evening, Your Highness,' he said politely. 'My apologies for disturbing you.'

Though her spot in the shadows prevented him from seeing her features clearly, he could feel her gaze on him.

'You're not disturbing me... Is that a bottle of scotch you're carrying?'

'Bourbon.'

'Can I have some?'

The silence that fell during his hesitation was absolute. The last thing he should encourage was a late-night conversation with the beautiful princess who'd occupied so much of his thoughts these last few days.

'Please? I could do with a drink.'

What harm could a quick drink with each remaining on their respective sides of the balcony do? He would make sure it was a quick drink. Allow her one nip and then make his excuses and return to his room. 'Of course.'

She climbed off the hammock and padded barefoot to him. As she drew closer and out of the shadows, he barely had time to register that she was wearing pretty, short pyjamas before she put her hands on the balustrade—she was so short her shoulders barely reached the top of it—and, with an effortless grace, swung herself over. In seconds she stood before him, the moonlight pouring on her casting her in an ethereal light that highlighted her delicate beauty and gave the illusion of her dark velvet eyes being limitless pools.

Spellbound, for perhaps the first time in his life, Gabriel found himself at a loss for words.

CHAPTER TWO

THERE WAS AN intensity in the princess's stare before her chest rose and she indicated the bottle engulfed in Gabriel's hand. 'May I?'

A cloud of soft, fruity scent seeped into his airwaves and darted through his senses.

Dragging himself back to the here and now, he forced a tight smile and passed it to her.

'Thanks.' She unscrewed the cap and placed it to her lips. Her small but perfectly formed mouth was one of the first things he'd noticed about her. It was like a rosebud on the cusp of blooming. She took a long drink and swallowed without so much as a flinch then delicately brushed the residue with a sweep of an elegant finger. Everything about her was elegant. Graceful.

She bestowed him with a small, sad smile that did something funny to his chest. 'May I sit?'

His next forced smile almost made his face crack. 'Of course.'

Carrying the bottle to the balcony's deep L-shaped sofa, the princess sank elegantly onto the L part and stretched her legs out, hooking her ankles together. The shorts of her pale blue pyjamas had risen to the tops of her thighs and he hastily cast his gaze down. The toes at the end of feet that were the smallest he'd ever seen on a grown woman were painted deep blue. It was a colour that complemented her golden skin and set off the delicate shapeliness of legs that appeared almost impossibly smooth.

His veins heating with dangerous awareness, Gabriel dragged his gaze from the princess's feet and looked back in her eyes…only to find himself trapped again in those beguiling orbs.

Her stare fixed on him, she took another drink of bourbon. 'Don't worry, I won't stay long,' she said softly in that husky voice. She pulled another sad smile and shrugged. 'Looks like it's true that misery loves company.'

'You are unhappy?' he asked before he could stop himself.

He shouldn't encourage conversation. The moonlight, the all-pervading silence in the air around them…it lent an intimacy to the balcony setting that made his skin tingle and heightened his senses.

'I…' She cut herself off and closed her eyes. After a mediative breath, she looked back at him, her features showing she'd composed herself. She indicated the space next to her. 'Don't stand on ceremony on my account.'

He inclined his head, thinking hard as to how to extract himself from this situation but coming up with nothing. 'You're a princess. As a commoner, I thought it was my duty to stand on ceremony.'

Her cheeks pulled into a smile fractionally wider than he'd seen from her before, and in a faintly teasing voice, she said, 'Then as a princess of this castle, I invite you to sit on the sofa of your own balcony in your own quarters.'

Alessia looked into the eyes of the man standing so rigidly he could have a pole for a spine. When he finally sat, placing himself far at the other end of the sofa, it was with the same rigidity that he'd stood.

It was nothing but a mad impulse that had made her call out to him. Nothing but a second mad impulse that had made her swing over the balustrade to his balcony. And now she was sat on his balcony sofa. Sat alone with a bare-chested man in the middle of the night where the only living beings observing them were crickets and frogs and the other nocturnal creatures who played and sang and mated when the sun went down.

'I didn't realise you'd stayed,' she said when he made no effort at conversation.

'There is a problem with my plane's engine. It should be fixed by the morning. Your parents kindly invited me to stay the night.'

'That's my parents,' she said with a muted laugh, and drank some more bourbon. 'Kindness personified.'

She saw the raising of a thick, black brow at this but his firm lips stayed closed.

Feeling a stab of disloyalty for her slight on her parents, she changed the subject. Not that he'd allowed himself to be drawn into it. Was that discretion on his part or a lack of interest? She'd seen the way he looked at her, sensed he was attracted to her, but that didn't mean he liked her. After all, he had spent the last three days clearing up the mess she'd made. He probably thought her a vacuous troublemaker who'd brought shame on her family. The latter part was true but the former...? No. Alessia had put duty first her entire life. Maybe that's where the guilt at her disloyalty had come from—the Berrutis did not bad-mouth each other to outsiders. Their loyalty was to the monarchy as an institution first, and then to their people, and then to each other as family. 'Where are you from? I can't place your accent.'

Gabriel breathed in deeply. He wanted to

ask her to return to her own quarters but was conscious that this magnificent castle was the princess's home. And conscious that she was a princess used to being deferred to. She would not take kindly to being ordered about by a commoner, and his brain ticked quickly as he tried to work out how he could extract himself from this situation without offending her. A man did not reach the heights Gabriel had in the diplomatic world by offending clients or members of their families.

Those were the reasons he tried to convince himself as to why he'd not already asked her to leave. The pulses throbbing throughout his body proved the lie. Those pulses had been throbbing since the moonlight had bathed her in its silver glow, a shimmering mirage made of flesh and blood.

Alessia Berruti was a princess, yes, but she was also a woman. A highly desirable woman.

He fisted his hands and clenched his jaw.

Alessia Berruti was a highly desirable woman he couldn't touch. Shouldn't touch. Mustn't touch.

'My mother is French, my father is Spanish,' he said in his practised even tone. 'I spent my formative years in Paris but I was raised to be bilingual.'

'You're fluent in both languages?'

'Yes.'

'And you speak Italian like a native too… Impressive.'

He didn't respond. He would not encourage this conversation. Without any encouragement, she would bore of his company and leave.

'Do you speak other languages?'

He wouldn't encourage her but it would be the height of rudeness to ignore a direct question. 'Yes.'

This was like getting blood from a stone, Alessia thought, but instead of deterring her, it only intrigued her. Most people when finding themselves in a private conversation with her fawned and flattered and set out to impress. Others became tongue-tied—it was the cloud of 'celebrity' around her that caused it—but long experience at putting those people at ease usually found them loosening up quickly. Gabriel, though, was neither of those people. He was a man who dealt with powerful people and institutions on a daily basis, and carried an air of power and authority in his own right, and everything about his body language was telling her he wanted her to leave. Which only intrigued her more. Because she'd seen that expression in his eyes which had pulsed with something quite different. 'Which ones?'

'English, German and Portuguese.'

'You're fluent in six languages? That really is impressive.'

Yet more non-response.

'Do languages come naturally to you?'

There was an almost imperceptible sigh before he answered. 'Yes.'

'I speak English fluently, but that's because I went to boarding school there,' she told him. 'I can converse in Spanish as long as it's taken at a slow pace, but my French is pretty basic, my German diabolical and I've never learned any Portuguese.'

She thought she caught a glimmer of humour on Gabriel's poker face.

'I suppose good linguistic skills are essential for your line of work,' she mused into the latest bout of silence, inordinately pleased to have made his face crack into a smile, as tepid as that smile might have been. Gabriel was so serious that she wondered if he ever truly smiled. She wondered if he ever allowed himself to. He was the most intriguing person she'd met in a long, long time. Maybe ever.

'Yes.'

'And what made you choose diplomacy as a career? I don't imagine it came up on a list of career choices when you were at school.'

Another quickly vanishing glimmer of humour. 'I learned at a young age that I had an aptitude for diplomacy.'

'Who discovers something like that?'

'I did.'

'How?'

Those dreamy light brown eyes suddenly fixed on her. A charge laced her spine, even stronger than the shiver she'd experienced when gazing at him earlier. 'Forgive me, Your Highness, but that is personal.'

The sudden flash of steel she caught told her his wish for forgiveness was pure lip service. He was giving her a diplomatic answer that translated into *mind your own business*.

Another charge thrummed through her. This man was no sycophant. This man had a core of steel. That self-containment, coupled with his drop-dead gorgeous looks and tripled with the innate self-confidence that oozed from his bronzed skin, made him the sexiest man she'd ever laid eyes on.

'That's perfectly reasonable,' she assured him although she was perfectly certain he didn't want or care for her assurance. 'And please, call me Alessia.'

His jaw tightened but he inclined his head in acknowledgement.

She took another drink of the bourbon, allowing herself a glance over the sculpturally perfect chest she found so fascinating. The moonlight had turned the bronze silver, and if not for the dark hair covering so much of the chest and forearms, she could believe he'd been cast in it.

'Where do you live?' she asked, passing the bottle to him. 'If that's not considered too personal a question.'

She noticed he made sure not to allow their fingers to touch as he took it from her.

'I travel a lot with my work.' He poured a small measure into a glass she hadn't even noticed him holding.

'I'd already gathered that, but you must have a place you call home.'

She noticed his jaw clenching. 'I consider Spain to be my home.'

'Which part?'

'Madrid.'

'I've visited Madrid many times. It's a beautiful city.'

He took a large sip of the bourbon and swirled it in his mouth a long time before swallowing. His throat was as sculpturally perfect as the rest of him.

'You don't like me, do you?' she said after another bout of lengthy silence.

That strong, perfect throat moved before he answered. 'What makes you think that?'

'Just a feeling. And you didn't deny it.'

'I cannot help how you feel.' He drank the rest of his bourbon.

'Do you blame me for the mess between my family and Dominic?'

'It is not my place to cast blame.' He poured himself another measure. 'My role is only to find solutions all parties can live with.'

'Your role doesn't prevent you forming opinions.'

'It prevents me voicing them.' He extended the bottle to her.

Her fingers brushed against his as she took it from him. The electric shock that flew through her skin was so strong that her eyes widened at the same moment Gabriel yanked his hand back as if he too had felt the burn. It took her a beat to find her voice again. 'So you do have opinions?'

'Everyone has opinions. Not everyone has the sense to know when those opinions should not be voiced.'

'Like when I voiced my opinion on Dominic?'

An extremely thick black eyebrow rose but his answer was a diplomatic, 'If people only voiced their opinions at appropriate times, I would be out of a job.'

She considered this with a small laugh. 'Then you should be grateful to me...' She winced and shook her head. 'Forget I said that. It was crass of me.' She sighed. 'And I owe you an apology too, for the way I spoke to you earlier. My tone was rude. I apologise.'

There was a detectable softening in his stare and in his voice too when he said, 'You were upset.'

'There is never an excuse for rudeness.'

'But there is often a reason for it,' he countered with the ghost of a smile and a glint in his eye that said far more than would come from his mouth, and she realised that he understood.

To Alessia's horror, hot tears welled up. She didn't want to cry. She had no idea why but the last thing she wanted was to appear weak and fragile in Gabriel's eyes. She suspected he had no time for weak and fragile women. She *wasn't* a weak and fragile woman. She wasn't. Not normally. Tiny but Mighty, her brother Marcelo used to call her. But Marcelo wasn't there: the one member of her family she could usually rely on for support was abroad on his honeymoon, and she'd had to suffer days of everyone else's anger and disapproval without any respite, so to have this man of all people offer her a crumb of comfort... It only made all the guilt and anguish she'd been suffering, which had diminished in the excitement of Gabriel's appearance, rise back to the surface.

A tear rolled down her cheek. She wiped it

away and tried desperately to compose herself. In that moment it felt like one more blow could shatter her to pieces. 'I just feel so responsible about everything. Not just Amadeo's marriage but everything.'

He gazed at her for the longest time, piercingly intense eyes slightly narrowed, his mouth a straight line, as if he were weighing whether to speak what was on his mind. And then he closed his eyes briefly and inhaled. When his eyes snapped back on hers, he leaned a little closer and said in a low timbre, 'What you said at your brother's wedding was just one piece of a large jigsaw of enmity between your nation and Dominic's. You were not responsible for anything that occurred beforehand. The structural damage between the two nations had already been done.'

Alessia had no idea why this attempt at reassurance made her feel worse, but the tears she'd been fighting burst free and tumbled down her face like a waterfall before she could do anything to stop them.

With a sharp tightening in his chest and guts, Gabriel closed his eyes to the sobbing princess.

His sister had been a master at turning on the tears, using them as a weapon to manipulate their warring parents in her favour. He'd rather admired her for it. Since he'd left home, though, the women he'd chosen to acquaint himself with were women like himself: reserved, stoical and never prone to histrionics. As a result, he had no idea how he was supposed to handle this situation. He couldn't throw money or the promise of clothes or the promise of a specially wanted treat at Alessia as his parents had done when Mariella turned on the waterworks. So, when he opened his eyes and found her knees brought to her chest and her face buried in them, one hand still clinging tightly to the bottle of bourbon, he did the one thing he really didn't want to do, and moved closer to her.

First removing the bottle and placing it on the floor, he then patted her heaving shoulders in what he hoped was a reassuring manner. To his consternation, she twisted into him. A slender arm snaked around his waist, and then she sagged against him and wept into his chest.

'I'm sorry,' she sobbed. 'I don't want to cry but I just feel so bad. One unthinking comment and now Amadeo has to marry a stranger and an unwilling woman is being forced into marriage with him, and it's all my fault.'

Gabriel closed his eyes again and gritted his teeth, trying to block out the sensory overload of having this most beautiful of women crying in his arms. It had been a battle he'd fought since Alessia had joined him, uninvited, on his balcony.

He'd never been in a situation like this before. For sure, there had been women who'd invited themselves into his space through the years—the foreign minister of a Scandinavian country who'd turned up at the door of his hotel room with a bottle of Dom Pérignon came to mind—and he'd been able to disentangle himself from those potentially dangerous situations with no harm done and no hurt feelings. The difference, he knew, was that he'd not been attracted to any of those women. Gabriel was select in his choice of lovers. A celebrity princess who also happened to be a close family member of an existing client—the very reason for his being employed by that client—was as far removed as a choice of lover as he would ever make, and yet there wasn't a cell in his body that hadn't attuned itself to her since she'd called out to him from the shadows in that sexy, husky voice.

The rack of her distress, though, wove through his veins to penetrate his heart, and the instinct to comfort overrode the last of his self-preservation. Gabriel wrapped an arm around her and held her tightly to him.

Dios, his heart was thumping.

Nothing was said for the longest time as, slowly, Alessia's sobs subsided.

He could feel the heat of her breath against the dampness of her tears on his naked chest.

Swallowing hard, knowing that with every second that passed with his arms around her he was dancing with danger, Gabriel rested his chin on her head and quietly said, 'I know you're concerned for Amadeo's bride, but I assure you, she is willing.'

'How can you know that?' She squeezed her arm even tighter around him, her husky voice muffled. 'Dominic doesn't believe in giving women choices. He held Clara against her will and would have forced her down the aisle if Marcelo hadn't rescued her.'

'I know because I spoke to Elsbeth privately to satisfy myself that she was a willing participant. I do have principles and there is no sum of money on earth that would see me be party to a forced marriage.'

Slowly, the princess lifted her face and gazed into his eyes. 'How can you be so sure? Dominic might have forced her to lie. He might have guessed that you would want to speak with her privately.'

It was staring into those dark, velvet orbs that made it a sudden effort to speak and filled his veins with lava. Just unimaginable depths…

He had to clear his throat to speak. 'The eyes don't lie, Princess. You have to take my word that her eyes showed only excitement. She's glad to be leaving Monte Cleure.'

And his loins were trying to show *their* excitement. They were responding to the princess being pressed so tightly against him, the feel of her small breasts jutting into his naked chest… The telltale tug of arousal battled for supremacy against his willpower and, for the first time in decades, it was winning.

Her brow furrowed. 'Excitement?' she asked doubtfully.

He needed to extract himself from this situation right now. To stay like this would be madness. *Was* madness.

'Think about it,' he murmured roughly, clenching the silk of her pyjama vest top to stop himself from slipping a hand beneath it. 'Why did your family refuse to entertain the notion of you marrying Dominic, even before he kidnapped Clara?'

Understanding glimmered in the warm depths of her brown eyes. 'Because he's a monster,' she whispered.

Unwilling to incriminate himself verbally, Gabriel inclined his head and, for no good reason, inched his face closer to hers. Now he could smell the underlying scent of the princess's skin beneath the soft fruitiness. It was intoxicating. As intoxicating as the sight of those pretty rosebud lips barely inches from his own. 'Now put yourself in her shoes,' he said, his voice so low even he struggled to hear it. 'If you were a member of the Fernandes royal family living under Dominic's rule and the opportunity came for you to marry into another royal family with a more...' So many heady feelings were shooting and weaving through him that he had to grope for the word. '*Benign* reputation, what would you do?'

Dominic's rule over his people was absolute. His rule over his family, especially the female members, was a clenched iron glove.

And this woman, this sexy, beautiful, fragile woman, had wanted to marry him to right the wrong of the mess she'd created.

He could never have been party to negotiations in which Alessia had been the pawn, he realised hazily, soaking in every delicate feature of her face. Not even if she'd been a willing pawn as Amadeo's bride was.

Alessia had become so spellbound by Gabriel's eyes that his words had dissolved into nothing but a caress to her senses. She'd thought he had brown eyes like her own but the irises were so transparent that, this close, it was like looking into golden supernovas ringing around pulsating black holes.

To think she'd thought his eyes cold when

they contained such life and colour and fired such warmth that their radiation was heating her insides in a way she'd never felt before. Or was it the warmth of his hard body heating her veins and melting her deep in the secret place no man had touched before?

She supposed she should move her arm from around his waist but right then his solid comfort and the warmth of his flesh seeping through the thin fabric of her pyjamas made her reluctant to do what propriety said she should do.

She'd never been held by a man like this before.

Still staring into his eyes, she whispered, 'I'm sorry for making a scene.'

A finger dragged gently along her cheekbone. 'You haven't.'

She shivered and pressed herself closer.

He was divine, she thought dimly, from the thick black eyebrows to the long straight nose to the angular jaw that had been clean shaven only hours before but was now covered in thick black stubble. That stubble carried on down to his strong neck until it tapered away leaving bronzed skin so smooth that her hand tugged itself from its hold around his back to skim lightly up the hard planes of his chest to gently palm his throat and feel the smoothness for herself.

If someone had told Gabriel that morning that

he would end the day in the battle of his life, he would have laughed disdainfully, but now, trapped in the seductive gaze of this incredibly sexy and enthrallingly beautiful woman, the darts of arousal he'd been fighting had turned into flames and his efforts to remember all the reasons he needed to resist these feelings for her were fading. Thoughts themselves had become ephemeral clouds, and when the elegant fingers stroked his neck at the same moment the rose-bud lips parted, a jolt of electricity struck that vanquished the clouds leaving only the man in his rawest form.

CHAPTER THREE

ALESSIA HAD BEEN kissed only once. It had been at the leaving ball at her English boarding school at which sixth formers from the twinned boy's school nearby had been invited. Drinks had been spiked and inhibitions, which a born princess like Alessia had in spades, were dismantled. What she remembered most about that kiss was its slobberiness. In the five years that had passed, she'd looked back on that night with a certain wistfulness. If she'd known it would be her only kiss she would have made the most of it, slobberiness or not. It wasn't that Alessia prized her virginity, more that she was acutely aware of her position and that the eyes of the world followed her whenever she left the castle grounds. Many of the eligible men she came across were either sycophants or leeches or brimming with pomposity. Often all three. If she was to be linked to a man, the press would make a huge deal about it, and if she was to put herself under what would be an even greater microscope than the one dealt with on a daily basis then that man needed to be worth it. She wanted to respect the man she gave her heart to, and be confident that he wouldn't sell stories about her or her family. No such man had come into her life.

When Gabriel's firm mouth found hers, the feelings that engulfed her were so incredible that it made her five-year kissing abstinence worthwhile.

Now *this* was a kiss…

Alessia closed her eyes and sank into the headiness of a mouth that sent sensation thrumming through her lips and over her skin and then seeped beneath the flesh to awaken every cell in her body.

Wrapping her arms tightly around his neck, her hunger unleashed and she returned the kiss with all the passion that had hidden dormant for so long inside her. At the first stroke of his tongue against hers, the heat that filled her insides was strong enough to melt bone, and when his hands roamed the planes of her back there was only a dim shock that she had, at some point since their mouths found each other, shifted her body so that she was straddling his lap.

She didn't want to think, she thought dreamily as his mouth broke from hers and dipped down to the sensitive skin of her neck and his hands lifted her silk pyjama vest top up and over her head. If a touch and a kiss could evoke such wonderful pleasure then she wanted to fall into it.

For the first time in her life, she wanted to forget who she was and all the expectations she put on herself for being Princess Alessia, and let all the demons be thrown aside and just *feel*, because she'd had no idea that feeling could be so incredible.

A voice in her head whispered that she should tell Gabriel she was a virgin…

She pushed the voice away.

The moment the pyjama top was discarded, Gabriel cupped her cheeks tightly and kissed her with an ardency that sent more incredible tingles racing through her. Alessia dove her fingers through the thick black hair and moaned when his mouth assaulted her neck again, gladly letting his hands manipulate her into arching her back so he could take one of her breasts into his mouth. At the first flicker of his tongue against her erect nipple, she gasped at the thrill of pleasure, and dug her fingers even harder against his skull, and when she shifted slightly and felt the hard wedge pressing against the apex of her thighs, instinct had her press down and gasp even louder at the pulsing sensations that enflamed her.

Gabriel's arousal was such that when Alessia ground down on him, the barrier of thin clothing separating them was barrier enough to make a grown man weep for release. No woman's skin had ever tasted this good or felt this soft, Gabriel thought as he devoured Alessia's other breast. And what beautiful breasts they were, tiny and high and with dark tips as moreish as her rosebud lips.

He didn't know who was more desperate for him to take possession of her. Alessia ground down on him, cradling his head tightly against her breasts, and when she gave another of the throaty moans that added fuel to his arousal, all he could focus on was his need to be inside her. In an instant, he flipped her round so she was on her back. In an instant, her legs wrapped around his waist and she was grabbing at his buttocks, rosebud mouth finding his and kissing him with the hot sweetness that was as intoxicating as everything else about her. Mouths fused, hands grabbed down low, brushing against each other as they scrambled to undo his trousers and rid Alessia of her pyjama shorts. Without breaking the connection of their mouths, they managed to rid themselves of her shorts and then Gabriel was free from his own confines and Alessia was using her toes to yank them down to his knees. Any idea of kicking his trousers off were forgotten when she arched up with her pelvis and he felt her slickness.

Damn but she was as hot and ready for him as he was for her.

Her hands grabbed his buttocks again, and that was it for him. Spreading her thighs and pushing them up, he thrust deep into the tight, tight heat.

The discomfort was so momentary that Alessia ignored it. How could she do anything else when she was being filled so gloriously and completely?

She'd watched enough sex scenes to know what to expect but this was so much more than she could ever have known and she cried out with every hard drive inside her, Gabriel's each and every thrust filling her so greatly that her mind detached itself from her body and she became nothing but a vessel of sensual ecstasy.

Breathless groans and cries of pleasure mingled between their enjoined mouths, fingers bit into flesh and scraped through hair, the moans between them intensifying as something deep inside her wound tightly, coiling and coiling, *burning.*

Gabriel, lost in a hedonistic cloud, resisted the demand for release building inside him. Never, in all his thirty-five years on this earth, had he experienced anything like this, such complete sensory capitulation. It wasn't just the feel of being inside Alessia's tightness—and Lord, such unbelievable tightness—it was the feel of her flesh compressed so tightly to his, the seductively sweet taste of her mouth, the scent of their coupling... It was mind-blowing, and he didn't want it to end. He spread her thighs even further to reach even deeper penetration—Lord, this was something else—and lifted his face from hers so he could stare at the face of the woman as beautiful as the body he was pounding into, and when he plunged his tongue into her mouth again and heard the throaty groan as she thickened around him, he could hold on no more and, with a roar of ecstasy, Gabriel let go.

Gabriel quietly donned his clothes using the small stream of dusky light through the gap in his curtains to see by. The sun was rising. Soon it would be day. Soon the castle would come to life. He wanted to be gone before that happened.

Before he left, he gazed at the dark hair poking out above the bedsheets, the figure the hair belonged to huddled beneath. His heart clenched into a fist.

He'd never experienced a night like that before. He'd never lost himself like that before. He'd been cast under a spell, that was the only explanation for it. He usually came right back to himself after sex but with Alessia the spell had remained intact. He'd carried her delectable body to his bedroom and made love to her again. The second time, they'd taken it much slower, the combustible lust that had exploded between them reduced to a simmer that had seen them exploring each other's bodies until every inch had been discovered and worshipped. His climax had been every bit as powerful as the first time. They'd finally fallen into slumber hours after the rest of Ceres had gone to sleep. And then he'd woken up and the spell had been lifted.

All he wanted now was to leave before Alessia stirred. Self-recriminations about bedding a client's family member—a princess, no less—could wait until he was in the privacy of his own home.

She stirred beneath the sheets. He held his breath as a throb of desire stirred in his loins and closed his eyes tightly. He would not return to that bed, however deep his craving.

Only when satisfied that she was still safely asleep did he slip out of the room.

Not wishing to see any member of the Berruti family, uncertain he'd be able to look any of them in the eye, he called the driver he'd been appointed, left a note for Queen Isabella, King Julius and Prince Amadeo thanking them for their hospitality and, ten minutes later, left the castle grounds.

For the first time in Alessia's life, she didn't fight waking up. Even before her eyes opened, she thrilled to be awake, the magic of the previous night flashing through her.

For the first time in her life, Alessia had thrown propriety, duty and decorum to the wind and allowed the woman beneath the princess skin to take control. It had been sublime. If she closed her eyes she could still feel the echo of the fulfilment throbbing deep between her legs.

Joy filled her and she laughed softly as she opened her eyes, fully expecting to find Gabriel's gorgeous face on the pillow beside hers.

His side of the bed was empty.

Holding the bedsheets to her naked form, she sat up. 'Gabriel?'

No response.

Climbing out of bed, she quickly yanked her pyjama bottoms off the floor—when had *they* been brought in from the balcony?—and pulled them on and padded to the bathroom. She knocked on the door. No answer. A quick look behind the door found it empty.

Slipping the pyjama vest top over her head

and, trying hard to fight against the coldness filling her veins, Alessia left the bedroom calling out his name again.

The guest quarters Gabriel had been appointed, usually given to family members like her parents' siblings, were nearly a mirror image of her own. Laid out like an apartment, it had a bedroom and adjoining bathroom, a guest room with its own bathroom, a dayroom, a dining room, a reception room and an unused kitchen. Gabriel was nowhere to be seen. Nor were his clothes.

The quarters being on the second floor, a set of iron steps ran off the balcony and led down to the private gardens. She hurried down the steps barefoot.

Although brimming with early-morning birdsong, the garden was empty of human life.

Her heart thumping, she checked each room of his quarters a second time and then a third, her calls of his name gradually weakening to a choked whisper. Back in the bedroom, she stared at the bed. It was the very first time she'd shared a bed with another human being. She could still smell Gabriel. Could still feel his touch on her skin.

In a daze, she stepped back onto the balcony and stared at the plump sofa she'd lost her virginity on. Limbs now feeling all watery, she somehow managed to climb over the balustrade and back onto her private abode. Inside, she called the family's head of housekeeping, not even bothering to think of an excuse to explain why she was enquiring about the whereabouts of the negotiator who'd saved the Berrutis from almost certain destruction.

The answer, although expected, still landed as a blow.

Gabriel had gone.

He hadn't even left her a note of goodbye.

Alessia closed her eyes and resisted pulling at her just-done hair. She felt sick. After a few minutes spent doing breathing exercises, she felt no better, and briefly considered calling her mother and telling her she felt too ill to attend Amadeo and Elsbeth's pre-wedding party.

She couldn't miss the party. A royal princess did not bow out of engagements from something as pathetic as illness, not unless she was at death's door, which a bout of nausea did not class as. Not that it was a royal engagement as the public would recognise it. As far as the public were concerned, the party was a private affair although the carefully selected members of the press corps who'd be in attendance to document the evening—and it was a momentous occasion and not just because the heir to the throne would be showing off his new bride-to-be—would publish the usual photos and video clips to allow the public to feel a part of the event. So, a private event with as much privacy as the animals in London Zoo had. And Alessia had to smile and dance with that horrible monster King Dominic Fernandez of Monte Cleure to prove to the world that there was no bad feeling between them. She'd bet that was the cause of her nausea.

There was a knock on her bedroom door.

Opening her eyes, she stared at her reflection and brought her practised smile to her face before calling out, 'Come in.'

Rather than a member of her domestic staff, her visitor was her new sister-in-law. Immediately, Alessia's spirits lifted. Clara was the woman Marcelo had rescued from King Dominic's evil clutches. It was that rescue, photographed and leaked to the world, which had started the diplomatic war between the two countries. The fallout from the rescue had compelled Marcelo to marry Clara himself and, as a result, Alessia had a brand-new sister-in-law. What made it even better was that Marcelo and Clara had fallen madly in love for real.

There was an acute pang in her chest as Alessia wondered if a man would ever look at her the way Marcelo looked at Clara, a pang made sharper as Gabriel Serres's handsome face floated in her eyes. She willed the image away.

She'd not heard even a whisper from him since he'd snuck out of the bed they'd made love in.

For days she'd drifted around the palace in a fugue of disbelief. Disbelief that she'd fallen head over heels in lust with a man she barely knew, falling so hard and so fast that she'd given her virginity without any thought, too wrapped up in the moment to care about anything but the wonder of what they were sharing. Disbelief that Gabriel had left without a word of goodbye when they'd shared such an incredible night together. Disbelief at Gabriel's subsequent silence.

And then she'd made the fatal mistake of making excuses for his silence. After three days of this fugue-like drifting, she'd convinced herself an emergency had taken him from their bed and that he'd left without waking her because he wanted her to have more sleep. She'd convinced herself too that the only reason he hadn't called was because he didn't have her personal number and that to ask her brother or parents or any of their staff for it would lead to too many questions. Gabriel was experienced enough in her world to know a man didn't just casually ask for a princess's personal number. And so she'd decided to put them both out of their misery—because *surely* he was in as big a flux as she was after what they'd shared—and call him, asking her private secretary to obtain his number for her.

It was a business number answered by an efficient-sounding woman. Alessia left a message. For days she'd waited on tenterhooks, her heart leaping every time her phone buzzed. There had been no call back.

Her pride wouldn't let her ask her secretary to go one further and obtain his personal number, and even if it wasn't out of the question for Alessia to obtain it from her parents or brother, she finally opened her eyes and let reality sink in. It simply wasn't possible that Gabriel's assistant hadn't passed the message on. Gabriel had simply ignored it.

He'd deliberately crept out of their bed without waking her.

He hadn't called her because he didn't want to.

Despite everything they'd shared, he didn't want to see her again and didn't think her worthy of a two-minute call to tell her this.

Alessia had given her virginity to a man who was treating her like a worthless one-night stand. Now, just over two weeks on, she was well and truly done with hoping and moping.

Gabriel Serres could go to hell.

'Hi, sis,' Clara said chirpily, bounding over

to the dressing table and bringing out the first smile on Alessia's face in two weeks. 'You look fantastic! That dress is amazing! Gosh, I am so envious.'

'You can talk,' Alessia laughed, rising from her seat to embrace her tightly. Where she had chosen an elegant deep red strapless ballgown for the party, Clara had gone for a toga-style shimmering silver dress that accentuated the bust Alessia would give her left kidney for. 'You look beautiful.'

Clara beamed. 'Thank you. Call me petty but I really want to look my best tonight for King Pig. Rub his face in it a bit more.'

'You're not worried about seeing him?'

'If anyone should be worried, it's *him*. Marcelo has promised Amadeo not to make a scene and I think it's going to kill him to keep that promise. I have to keep reminding him that he got his revenge on the monster when he rescued me from him.'

'Did Amadeo make you promise not to cause a scene too?'

'I promised that voluntarily. After all, I'm trying to be the perfect princess and the perfect princess doesn't karate chop guests at a grand social function, does she?' She actually looked a touch woebegone at not being able to do this.

Alessia giggled then changed the subject.

'How did the honeymoon go?' This was the first time the two old friends had had a chance for a private catch-up since Clara and Marcelo's return from their honeymoon. 'Were the Seychelles as pretty as you hoped?'

'It was amazing! Not that we saw all that much of it as we spent most of our time in bed—'

'Hold it right there,' she interrupted before Clara could start giving details. 'I'm feeling sick enough as it is without having to listen to details about my brother's sex life.'

Clara cackled but then her brow furrowed. 'You're feeling sick? What's wrong?'

'I've just been feeling a bit off for a couple of days. Probably something I ate.'

She looked even more closely at her. 'Any other symptoms?'

'No.'

But Clara continued to scrutinise her. 'Are you wearing a padded bra?'

'I'm not wearing a bra. Why?'

'Your boobs have grown. If I didn't know better, I'd ask if you were pregnant.'

Those words set off an instantaneous reaction in Alessia. Cold white noise filled her head, cold dread prickled her skin. Instinctively, she put her hand to her abdomen and breathed hard.

'Alessia? Are you okay? Your face has gone a funny colour.'

But Clara's voice had become distant and Alessia had to lean into her dressing table to support her weak frame as the room began to spin wildly around her.

Gabriel dispassionately watched the previous evening's footage of Prince Amadeo and Lady Elsbeth's pre-wedding party in his hotel room in Rome. Italy, a country that shared a language and much cultural history with Ceres, was enthralled by the wedding between the glamorous heir to the throne and his pretty bride-to-be. The breakfast television channel he was watching as he prepared for the day's meetings with his newest client had so far devoted over two minutes to it.

He'd been invited to the party but politely declined. He had no wish to be part of a montage such as the one being televised.

His stomach clenched when the footage came to its star turn, the attendee its viewers would have been waiting for a glimpse of above all others: Europe's premiere princess, Princess Alessia. The clenching sharpened as he watched her laughing with a member of the British royal family before the camera cut to her dancing with the King of Monte Cleure. The smile on her face belied what he knew would be crawling beneath her skin to be held in the arms of a man she so despised, and Gabriel felt a stab of anger at her family for forcing this dance on her.

'I think we can safely agree that the animosity between these two nations is now a thing of the past,' a gushing reporter was saying as the cameras panned back to the studio.

Gabriel turned the television off and pinched the bridge of his nose.

A trade and diplomatic war had been averted. Any popular uprising against their royal family from the Ceresian people, who would surely have blamed them if the situation had deteriorated further and hit them economically, had been avoided. Dominic felt valued as a 'player' again. Everyone was happy.

This should be a moment of quiet satisfaction at a job well done but the discontent at seeing Alessia again was too strong. Truth was, Gabriel was furious with himself for what had happened between them and time had not abated that fury an iota. He'd had a few one-night stands over the years—he wasn't a saint—but this was the only one he truly regretted. And the only one he couldn't erase from his head.

Couldn't erase *her* from his head. He still felt the weight of his arousal for her as a memory in his loins.

He still had her number in his wallet from when she'd called the business line. His heart had thumped so hard when his PA passed Alessia's message to him that he wouldn't have been surprised if it had smashed straight through his ribcage.

The message had been brief, inviting him to call her if he wished. He'd read it a number of times, his heart deflating as the meaning had become clear.

Alessia wanted to see him again.

It was out of the question.

He should have called her back and politely made his excuses.

What he should have done before that was say goodbye and explain that as great as their night together had been, it was a one-night-only thing.

What he should have done before any of those things was rewind even further and not sleep with her in the first place.

But he should have called her back.

He'd never treated a woman so callously before. But then, he'd never reacted so strongly to a woman before or felt such a strong reaction towards him from a woman before. Or lost his mind the way he had with her.

Despite everything, he removed the folded Post-it note from his wallet and stared at the number he'd committed to memory at the first reading. It was the strength of his desire to call her back that had stopped him doing just that. Look at him now—twenty seconds of footage of her had distracted him from his preparations as effectively as a tornado hitting his hotel room.

Alessia Berruti was a princess. She was Europe's most photographed woman. She was the antithesis of what he wanted in a partner. Gabriel's childhood had been destroyed by press intrusion and he had no wish to experience the media spotlight again under any circumstance. It would be a disaster for his career too—anonymity was essential for him to be effective. Even a casual affair with the princess who seemingly loved the spotlight would bring press intrusion of unimaginable levels.

As scalding…as *fantastic*…as their lovemaking had been, he could never see or speak to Alessia Berruti again.

He had to forget her.

Another burst of unwelcome fury raged through him and he crushed the note into a tight ball. Before he could throw it in the bin—maybe burn it to ash first for good measure—his phone rang.

He gritted his teeth and took a deep breath before reaching for it. Anger was the most futile of emotions, one he rarely succumbed to. He'd suffered more of it these last two weeks than he had the whole of his life and needed to rid himself of it.

His heart managed to jolt and sink at the same time when Prince Amadeo's name flashed on the screen.

'Good morning, Your Highness,' he said smoothly, refusing to allow a trace of his emotions show in his voice. 'This is an unexpected pleasure. What can I do for you?'

'You can explain to me how the—' an expletive was shot into Gabriel's ear '—you managed to get my sister pregnant.'

CHAPTER FOUR

'HOW DO I LOOK?' Alessia asked as she checked her reflection one last time. She'd selected a pair of deep blue fitted trousers, a simple short-sleeved, high-necked silk top a shade lighter, and a thick satin band separating the two items around her waist. After much deliberation, she'd left her hair loose. She'd originally tied it into a severe bun but Clara had said it made it look like she was trying too hard. According to Clara, the bun sent the message of 'this is me *proving* that seeing you again doesn't affect me in the slightest,' instead of the 'seeing you doesn't affect me in the slightest' look Alessia was aiming for.

Clara looked her up and down and nodded approvingly. 'Perfect.'

Alessia swallowed. Her world had been thrown into chaos but she could always rely on her sister-in-law's honesty. Clara's 'perfect' answer meant Alessia had achieved what she set out to. To get through the meeting that would bring her face to face with the man who'd slipped out of her life without a goodbye and which would determine the rest of her life, she needed to look as perfect on the outside as she could. God knew she was a shambles inside.

It was Clara's comment that she could believe Alessia to be pregnant that had started it all. Alessia must have had her head in the sand because until that point, she hadn't put together the dots of a late period, tender breasts and nausea. Until that point, she hadn't registered that she had no memory of Gabriel using contraception.

What fateful naivety. What brainless stupidity.

She still had no idea how she'd got through Amadeo's party. If Clara hadn't stayed so close throughout the evening, she probably wouldn't have. Clara had come to the rescue when it came to the pregnancy test too. Knowing how difficult it would be for Alessia to buy one without detection, she'd popped to a pharmacist the next morning with her security detail. Let them think the test was for her! she'd said. She'd then sneaked it over to Alessia and sat holding her hand while they waited for the result to show, and hugged her and stroked her hair for an hour while Alessia sobbed over the positive result. Unfortunately, Clara was incapable of telling a lie, and when she'd returned to her quarters and Marcelo asked what she and Alessia had been doing, she'd felt compelled to tell him the truth. Even more unfortunately, their father happened to be there too.

There had been no time at all for Alessia to come to terms with her situation before her whole family and the majority of the palace staff knew about the pregnancy. Within two hours of the positive result an emergency family meeting was convened. For the second time in less than a month, Alessia was the subject behind said meeting.

Barely a day had passed since that positive result and she still hadn't fully come to terms with it, not on an emotional level. Her family had gone straight to damage limitation mode and she'd been carried by the panicking swell with them.

If she'd thought her mother's disappointment at her unguarded comment about Dominic had hurt, it had nothing on the cold anger she'd been hit with over the pregnancy, wounding far more deeply than Amadeo's furious diatribe.

She checked her eyes one last time to ensure the drops she'd put in them that magically disappeared redness from all the crying she'd done were still working, then slipped her feet into a pair of silver heels, dabbed some perfume to her neck and wrists and left her quarters.

If not for a lifetime of poise, just one of the many things drilled into her from the moment she could walk, her first glimpse of Gabriel in the meeting room of her mother's private offices would have knocked her off her feet. Her heart thumped so hard she couldn't breathe but she kept her back straight and her head high and strolled with all the nonchalance in the world to the empty chair.

Whatever happened in this meeting, her eyes would stay dry. She was a princess and she would remember her breeding and remain regal if it killed her.

Above all else, she would not let Gabriel know that seeing him again made her feel more violently sick than any pregnancy sickness.

She'd been nothing but a night of fun for him, quickly discarded and even more quickly forgotten.

It would be too humiliating if he guessed how deeply their night together had affected her. She could still feel the whisper of his touch on her skin. Still caught phantom whiffs of his cologne. Still felt her insides clench to remember how wonderful his lovemaking had been.

A member of staff held the chair out for her and she sat with a nod of thanks and cast her gaze around every person sat at the large oval table. Her family—her parents and two brothers, who Alessia was sandwiched between—and the family lawyer, sat at one end. At the other end sat Gabriel and a woman she assumed was his lawyer. The only person her eyes skimmed over rather than meeting their stare head-on was Gabriel. She'd intended to but at the very last second been unable to go through with it. She didn't think she could bear to see the expression in his eyes.

Skimming her eyes didn't stop the blood pumping through her body as she still somehow managed to soak in every last detail about him, from the impossibly uncreased white shirt he wore to the perfectly positioned quiff of the black hair she'd thrilled to run her fingers through.

Jutting her chin, she rested her hands flat on the table, praying no one could see the tremor in them, and purposefully faced Amadeo. Channelling their long-dead grandmother, who'd taken regal haughtiness to heights that deserved to be acknowledged as an art, she said, 'Has he agreed to accept his responsibility?'

Gabriel had watched Alessia make her grand entrance with his heart in his mouth.

Feelings he couldn't begin to describe had clawed and fisted his guts and heart since

Amadeo's bombshell. When he'd driven through the castle gates, the usual photographers on duty hoping to get a shot of a Berruti family member or newsworthy associate bound for disappointment by his blacked-out windows, the clawing and fisting had reached a pinnacle. Damn it, unless he treaded very carefully, this would be his life again.

The woman he'd never wanted to see again was pregnant with his child, and it enraged him that the blame for it was going to be laid on his shoulders by Alessia as well as her family. He'd thought better of her.

He'd thought better of himself too. But they'd both been there. They'd both got carried away and failed to use protection. After their first failure there had been little point in bothering with it, and truth was, the first time had been so damn glorious that he'd wanted to experience every single aspect of it again. Maybe that's why it had felt so good, he thought darkly. That was the first time he'd made love without a barrier. He was clean. He'd assumed the princess was too, something else that weighed on his mind—since when did he give the benefit of the doubt to anyone about anything, especially with regards to his sexual health? Keeping himself safe, aka Contraception, was his responsibility. This had the added benefit of him never having to worry that there might be miniature Gabriel Serres roaming the earth, and, as all these thoughts flashed through his mind, he found himself wondering if this had been her plan all along, to seduce him and get impregnated by him. Because she sure as hell hadn't mentioned that she wasn't on the pill. He could forgive the first time they'd made love—the madness had trapped them both—but allowing him to make love to her a second time knowing there was nothing to stop an accidental conception? Not taking action to stop any conception when there *was* still time? Unforgiveable.

Intentional or accidental, he was there, about to negotiate for his life and the life of his unborn child. He could play hardball and insist they wait until the birth for a DNA test but knew it would do nothing but delay the inevitable. He knew in his heart the child was his, but if Alessia wanted him to go along with her family's demands then she'd damned well better start showing him some respect or he would walk out of there and make the whole damn family wait until the birth for fresh negotiations.

He exhaled the anger that had spiked through him at Alessia's contemptuous tone as well as her unjustified blame. He would not allow *any* emotion to show. He needed to treat this like every negotiation he'd taken control of since he was a teenage boy negotiating his warring parents' divorce.

'I am more than willing to accept responsibility,' he informed the side of her head icily, before her brother could speak. 'The extent of that responsibility is still to be decided, but whatever the outcome of these negotiations, I will support my child and be a father to it.'

'What is there to negotiate?' Marcelo asked, his eyes blazing. 'You've got my sister pregnant. You have to marry her.'

Gabriel folded his arms across his chest. 'Actually, I don't.'

'You took advantage of her,' Amadeo spat.

'I took advantage of a twenty-three-year-old woman?' he drawled with a hint of disdain.

Angry colour stained the heir's cheeks. He would have said something else had Queen Isabella not placed her hand lightly on his. 'You have to see things from our position,' she said.

'I do,' Gabriel countered, 'and as I understand it, you fear news of the princess's pregnancy will cause a scandal in your country which, coming so close to the recent scandals, will dent your already waning popularity and lead to more voices joining the chorus for Ceres to become a republic. Is that the measure of it?'

Barely a flicker of emotion crossed the monarch's face. 'Yes.'

'Then allow me to state my position. I will marry your daughter, and I will marry her for one reason only—to enable my child to be raised with a parent who prioritises their emotional wellbeing rather than leave them to the mercy of a family who cares more about duty and public perception than what's best for them.'

There was a sharp intake of breath from every member of the royal family. With the exception of Alessia, who didn't react at all.

He failed to understand why they should be shocked at his observation. After all, Amadeo was marrying to salvage the public's perception of the Berrutis and head off talks of republicanism. Marcelo, however happy his marriage appeared to be, had married for the same reason. And now Alessia was being asked to do the same—and so was he. Three marriages to save a monarchy.

'However, before I commit myself to a loveless marriage, I have conditions that must be agreed in writing.'

There was a long beat of silence before the queen asked, 'And those conditions are?'

'That Alessia and I do not live in the castle but in a suitable dwelling elsewhere on the estate. I will not have my life dictated by protocol within my own home. I will not have my life dictated by any means. So there are no ambiguities between us or things that can be left open to interpretation, let me be clear—I will not be a working member of your family. I will not attend palace functions that have the press corps in attendance, and that includes family functions like Prince Amadeo's wedding. I will not undertake royal engagements. I will never do anything intentionally that will cause harm to your family but I will live out of the spotlight and remain autonomous in how I conduct my life.' Ignoring the latest collective intake of breath, he continued with his demands. 'My word as my child's father will be absolute. Alessia and I will raise him how we see fit and there will be no argument or interference from any of you.'

At this, Alessia's eyes finally met his. He caught the surprise in them and…was that admiration? Whatever it was, one blink and it was gone, replaced by an indifference that bordered on contempt.

'Anything else?' Amadeo asked through gritted teeth.

'Yes. If we marry, it will be a private affair, and by private I mean immediate family only. No guests, no photographers, no press, just a simple statement after the deed has been done in which you can clarify my intention to live as a private person, and which brings me to my final condition—I will only marry Alessia if I have her personal assurance that she is in agreement and, as such, I ask you all to leave the room so we can discuss the matter in private.' He deliberately held Amadeo's stare. 'I need to be satisfied that she gives her consent freely, so if you will excuse us…'

He let his words hang in the air. He doubted any member of this family had ever been spoken to in such a manner before. He wasn't being deliberately provocative or disrespectful but he knew perfectly well that he needed to set his stall out early so there could be no misunderstandings.

The queen was the first to react. Rising to her feet—she was so short that even standing while the rest remained seated she barely reached her husband's and sons' heads—she looked him in the eye. 'Speak to my daughter privately, by all means, but as you have spoken so freely, allow me the same courtesy. Whatever you think, I love my daughter. Whether you marry her or not, I will support her. We all will. And we will weather any storm that comes our way in the same way we always do—as a family.'

With only the briefest inclination of her head, she summoned the men of her family to their feet. In silence, they followed her out, the two princes towering over their mother and throwing daggers of loathing at Gabriel, and were quickly followed by the lawyers and other assorted staff.

And then it was just him and Alessia.

Huge, painful thumps in his chest made it suddenly hard to breathe but he fought through it to try and read the beautiful face of the woman he'd shared the best night of his life with.

Gabriel was excellent at reading body language. While they'd waited in tense silence for Alessia to arrive, he'd read the body language of all the Berrutis. Both princes were mountains of barely concealed rage. He sensed Amadeo's fury was at the situation as a whole. Marcelo's, he suspected, was directed entirely at him, Gabriel. The queen was steely concerned only with damage limitation. The king's body language told him that he would, once again, be the family peacemaker. It was a role Gabriel understood all too well—it was the role within his own family that had propelled him into a making a career out of peace negotiations. The reasons for needing those peace negotiations were the same reasons he kept such tight control of his emotions and had always selected his lovers from a pool of reserved, emotionally austere women. That he was on the cusp of marrying a woman who had passion embedded in her DNA and who guaranteed the press intrusion he so despised were things he must learn to handle, and quickly.

Alessia was the only Berruti who'd kept her feelings in check during their talk. Other than that flicker of surprise when he'd informed the family in no uncertain terms that they would raise their child as *they* saw fit, she'd revealed nothing of her inner feelings. Even now, when it was just the two of them at opposing ends of the large, teak table, she simply sat in her chair, back straight, hands folded neatly on the table, eyes on him, giving nothing away other than haughty disdain.

He knew though, that her haughty façade was just that—a façade.

Born princess she might be, but it wasn't possible that the woman who'd sobbed in his arms and then come undone in them, who'd exploded with a passion so strong it had to be a fundamental part of her nature, could be as cold on the inside as she was showing on the outside. And he shouldn't be wishing her to reveal it.

Alessia willed herself to hold Gabriel's hard stare. The vast space between them had shrunk to nothing and it was a struggle to think over the blood rushing through her head to console herself that he was too far away to see the thuds of her heart beating so hard and fast through her chest.

She willed even harder for the tears to stay away.

She would not let the hurt he'd put her through leech out. He would never know how his early-morning disappearing act had devastated her.

'I have to say, this feels a rather extreme method of forcing you to see me again,' she said with airy nonchalance when the silence finally became too much, and was gratified to see his jaw clench. Allowing herself a tight smile, she got down to business. 'I am grateful that you have agreed to marry me and save my family from further scandal, and grateful for your concern about whether I consent freely to us marrying. As I'm sure you remember from the night we conceived our child, when we spoke of Amadeo's marriage, consent and free will are important to me. You have my assurance that I do consent.'

One of the thick black eyebrows that had so fascinated her that night rose. 'You consent to a loveless marriage?'

'Of course.' She smiled and added with a touch of sarcastic bite, 'After all, I'm from a family that puts duty before personal feelings. In that respect, I think it can only be a good thing to marry a man who will put our child's emotional needs first because I, like the rest of my family, am far too repressed to know how to do that. What a great example you'll be able to set to him or her.' Her smile widened. 'A *great* example. One day in the future, I must remember to tell them of the time when Daddy sneaked out of the castle after spending the night having sex with Mummy and then cold-shouldered her until he came riding in to rescue the conceived child from the horrors of a family without any mercy in them.' She mock shuddered before bestowing him with another, even brighter smile. 'Let me know when it's your birthday—I'll buy you a superhero cape with *SV* for Super Virtuous emblazoned on it.'

Fearing her charade was on the verge of cracking, Alessia rose and strode to the door, opened it and invited her anxious, waiting family back inside before Gabriel could find a response.

Alessia entered 'the zone,' a place she inhabited during certain interminably boring royal engagements. Being in the zone enabled her to put her happy face on and speak brightly and clearly while a pre-marriage contract was drawn up, read through, redrafted, read through again, more clauses removed, others added... And so it went on, and on, and on, the monotony broken by a regular supply of refreshment that she made sure to consume even though her stomach was so tightly cramped she had to force the food down her throat and into it.

Occasionally a stunned voice played in her ear: *You're planning a marriage to Gabriel Serres*, but she ignored it. Everything was too fantastical and happening too fast for it to actually feel real.

She was going to have to live with him and she couldn't even begin to dissect the swell of emotions that rose in her to think of what this would mean.

Time passed in a strange alchemy of speed and slowness. Though Alessia kept strictly to her side of the table, her awareness of Gabriel's presence within these four walls was as acute as if he were standing right beside her. He was too far from her to be able to smell him but she kept catching whiffs of cologne that made her abdomen clench and her pulses soar. She fought not to gaze at him. She also fought to not march over and slap his face, which frightened her as much as the yearning to stare.

Only when Gabriel was satisfied that it protected him from actually having to be a royal did he sign the contract, and then it was her turn. She wanted to fix him with another icy stare, prove her indifferent disdain, but by then her emotions were so heightened that it was all she could do to hold the pen. She added her signature to the document without the flourish she'd so wanted to make it with. Their respective lawyers acted as witnesses and made their marks too, and then it was done.

Her composure in severe danger of unravelling, Alessia left immediately, using the excuse that she wished to rest before dinner. Leaving before anyone else, she hurried out of the room avoiding Gabriel's attempt to catch her eye.

Her nausea had returned with a vengeance and she hurried along the wide corridors to her private quarters. She climbed the stairs, closed her bedroom door and ran into the bathroom, where she threw up straight into the toilet.

It seemed to take for ever before her stomach felt settled enough for her to crawl off the floor and brush her teeth, and then she staggered back into the bedroom and collapsed on her bed.

Closing her eyes, she pressed a hand to her belly and breathed deeply, in and out. Having inherited her mother's petite figure and danced for exercise and enjoyment most days of her life, her stomach had always been flat. Early though the pregnancy was, there was a noticeable swelling, just as her breasts had swollen. As dreamlike as everything had felt these last few days, one thing had made itself felt with concrete certainty. She was pregnant. Her body was doing what it needed to do to bring her baby safely into this world. And Alessia would do what was needed too, and that meant marrying Gabriel.

She'd expected coming face to face with him to be hard but she hadn't expected it to be that hard. She hadn't expected to feel so *much*.

Being a good, dutiful princess…that was Alessia's role in this world, her purpose, her reason for being.

Her comments about Dominic had been one unguarded moment but her night with Gabriel was a different matter entirely. That night, she had broken free from the bonds of duty and freed the real woman inside, and it was terrifying how strongly seeing Gabriel again relit that passionate fire inside her.

She was a *princess*.

There was a rap on her door.

Wishing the world would leave her alone, she sighed and closed her eyes tightly before calling out. 'I'm resting. Please come back in thirty minutes.'

The door opened.

Surprised, she lifted her head, but any mild rebuke to whoever had taken it on themselves to disturb her solitude fell from her lips when Gabriel marched into her bedroom.

CHAPTER FIVE

GABRIEL NOTED THE shock at his intrusion on Alessia's flushed face as she scrambled to sit up, gripping one of the four-poster bed's posts and pressing herself into it. He'd taken her by surprise in the one room in the whole castle she could expect privacy.

Too bad, he thought grimly. They were going to be married soon. Two strangers who'd spent one perfect night together were going to be tied together for life.

'Who let you in?' she whispered, pressing her cheek to the post. 'What do you want?'

'Your staff let me in—they know that they will soon be my staff too. As for what I want…?'

Did it matter what he wanted? No, was the concise answer. He'd envisaged his child's entire future in half a minute and known at the end of that flash into the future that his or her best chance of growing into a functional adult was with Gabriel a permanent, constant part of their life. That his own life would be uprooted and upended was irrelevant. He'd failed to use protection. His child had not chosen to be conceived. Therefore his wants were unimportant.

One want that was important, though, was a want for a cordial relationship with Alessia. He had no wish for a wife who despised him. He knew first-hand from his own parents' toxic hatred of each other the damage warring parents could do to a child.

He headed to a pale blue velvet armchair placed close to the bed. It was an elaborate piece of furniture that fitted in perfectly with the feminine vibes of the princess-perfect room. His sister, he thought, would have gladly killed for a bedroom like this. Although long used to riches, he had a feeling this castle would still blow Mariella's mind.

He could take only a small crumb of solace that Alessia's room, as with the brief impression he'd obtained of the rest of her quarters, had a warmer feel to it than her parents' quarters.

'I want to talk before I leave Ceres to sort my affairs,' he said.

'Why?'

He sat down and gazed at her steadily, trying his best to block the feminine scents of this most feminine of rooms much as he was trying to block the surging of his pulses. 'Why do you think? We've pledged to spend our lives together with only cursory words exchanged between us.'

'What else is there to say?' Bitterness seeped into her husky voice. 'We've agreed to marry and raise our child together. End of story.'

'Our story is only beginning. I had hoped to discuss things properly with you when we had that time alone together earlier but you used it to take cheap shots at me and then invited your family straight back in before I could give a rebuttal.'

The burn of her angry eyes blazed enough to penetrate his skin.

Gabriel took a deep breath. He'd made his point. Time to move on to what he'd sought her out for in the first place—to diffuse tensions. 'I never meant to imply that you and your family are incapable of loving a child.'

She released her hold on the bed post and straightened, her chin jutting. Her shock at his appearance was rapidly diminishing, the regal princess remerging from the vulnerable woman who'd scrambled with shock at his appearance in her room. With a glimmer of her earlier haughty disdain, she said, 'You didn't imply it. You were explicit about it.'

'If I offended you, I apologise.' He'd spoken the truth to make his point to Alessia and her family but, he conceded, it was a point he would have softened if he hadn't reacted so strongly to seeing her again. Those same feelings were rampaging through him now but he'd prepared for it before entering her room and that mental preparation made it possible for him to choose his words with his usual care. He could look at the rosebud lips and sultry dark velvet eyes, and temper the awareness coursing through him so that it became nothing but a distant thrum.

'Apology accepted,' she said curtly, wriggling elegantly to press her back against the velvet headboard. 'Now please leave. I'm tired and wish to rest.'

'Not yet.' He rested his elbows on his thighs. 'We marry in three days and—'

The composure Alessia had only just found shattered. 'What are you talking about? I thought the wedding would be in a few weeks?'

'If you hadn't run away from the meeting, you would know this.'

'I didn't run away—I thought everything had been agreed.'

'Only the basics. Everything else is to be decided between you and me, which is why I am here.'

'Everything like what?'

'Our marriage. How we're going to make it

work so that we can live together and raise a child together.'

Icy panic clutched her chest. Three days was nothing. How was she supposed to prepare herself in that time? It was impossible. Three days! Three days until she became the wife of the man who'd ghosted her? It was too soon! She'd thought she had weeks! 'Who decided we'd marry in three days?' she demanded to know, unable to keep the agitation from her voice.

'It was a collective decision. Your family worry that news of our marriage will take the spotlight from Amadeo's wedding. We marry on Thursday and release the news on Friday. The press then have over a month to milk it until it curdles before Amadeo's wedding takes place.'

'And you agreed to this?'

He shrugged. 'Your family agreed to all my conditions. It was only fair I give them a concession in return.'

'How magnanimous of you,' she spat, hating that his composure was as assured as ever while all her turmoil was showing itself, feelings heightened by him sitting close enough to her that it wasn't the ghost of his cologne seeping into her senses as it had been during the meeting but his actual cologne, splashed on his cheeks and neck after he'd shaved that morning. It made her remember how she'd buried her face in his neck and inhaled his scent so greedily, which only made the feelings heighten. She didn't want to feel anything for this man or to show anything but the deserved contempt she'd managed earlier, but everything she'd had drilled in her the entirety of her life had slipped out of reach. They could be talking about the weather for all the emotion Gabriel was showing and she hated him for it. 'How truly *benevolent*.'

Gabriel recognised that Alessia's cool façade from earlier had been well and truly stripped away. He'd been right—it *had* all been a façade. Beneath the haughty exterior, she'd seethed with emotion. For whose benefit had she chosen to hide it? His or her family's?

He stared deep into those blazing velvet eyes again, the thrum of awareness heightening. She wanted an argument, he realised. Gabriel did not fight, physically or verbally, and never would. His parents' marriage had been too volatile even in the supposedly happy years for him to ever allow himself to follow in their shoes and lose his calm, and it was unnerving to find himself responding to the passionate emotions Alessia was brimming with.

With a sickening jolt, he realised it was this passion that had sang to him that night.

Making love with Alessia was the only time in his adult life he'd lost control of himself, and the thrumming of awareness thickened to fully realise for the first time that marriage meant he no longer had to bury his desire for her.

Closing his eyes briefly, he inhaled to control the tightening in his loins. To regain control of his thoughts. To regain control of the biting emotions.

He shifted his chair forwards and locked back onto Alessia's fiery stare. Making sure to pitch his voice at its usual modulated tone, he said, 'Considering that marrying you means I have to give up the career I excel at and move to a new country, I would say my conditions were reasonable and justified.'

'No one asked you to give up your job.'

'Once news of our marriage hits the press it will be impossible for me to continue. My clients employ me because I guarantee results and my discretion is guaranteed. Once I become a public figure, the anonymity I rely on to do my job effectively is gone.'

She pulled her knees to her chest and rested her chin on them in the same way she'd done when he'd first found himself falling under her spell. 'I'm sure you'll find a way to adapt it to the new circumstances.'

'Adaptation is always possible, of course, but continuing the business as it is will not.'

'You don't have to marry me. No one's putting a gun to your head.'

'I've put a metaphorical gun to my own head. Secrets don't stay secret. Even if we didn't marry, as soon as the pregnancy starts to show speculation about the father will start and sooner or later my name will leak, and I'll still be thrust into the spotlight I never wanted. Either way, my life as it is is over, which leaves me only two choices—marry you and be a permanent feature in my child's life, or don't and leave everything about my child's upbringing to chance. If there is one thing you will learn about me it is that I do not leave anything to chance.'

'And you don't think I'll be a loving mother,' she stated, tremulously. The implication had wounded her. Alessia had only known she was pregnant a few days but, once the tears had dried, her heart had swollen with an emotion she struggled to define, a combination of excitement and fear and love. Love for a fledging being that probably didn't as yet have a heartbeat.

Many times over the years she'd wondered what kind of mother she would be. The only conclusion she'd reached was that she'd be a different mother to her own, but she couldn't say that to Gabriel. It wasn't just a matter of disloyalty but because he wouldn't understand. How could he? A monarch wasn't an ordinary person and, even with the best will in the world, they couldn't be an ordinary parent. Their number one priority had to be to the monarchy. Alessia, though, would never be a monarch, and she thanked the good Lord every day for that.

Gabriel's eyes had narrowed but when he answered, his words were measured. 'I think you're capable of it but you're from a world where duty comes first and often to the detriment of the individual. Look at you and your brothers—all of you marrying for one reason or other to save the monarchy. I will not have our child feel forced to make those same choices.'

'It's a choice *you're* making too.'

'For their sake,' he replied in the same measured tone. 'And it is up to you and me to make the best of it and create a stable home for them. It will take many compromises and concessions on both our parts but if we are both willing, then it is achievable.'

'Will you compromise on coming to Amadeo's wedding with me?' she retorted, already knowing how humiliating it would be to attend Ceres's biggest state event in decades without her new husband by her side. People would understand someone wanting to remain private and not wanting to be a working royal, but family events, even when they were state occasions, were different. Gabriel's refusal to attend could only be interpreted as personal.

'My conditions have already been agreed but everything else is open to negotiation. The question is, are *you* willing to make the compromises and concessions necessary for our child?'

How could this be the same man who'd made love to her with such frenzied passion? Alessia wondered, gazing at him in disbelief. From the expression on Gabriel's face and the tone of his voice, he could be conducting an ordinary business meeting, not discussing the upturning of both their worlds; and his world was being upturned far more than her own.

On paper, he was everything she'd ever wanted in a husband. He was everything she'd waited for—a man she could respect, who made her feel and who wouldn't sell her out. Gabriel commanded respect just by walking in a room, and there was no denying he made her feel. In the short hours they'd spent together, he'd made her feel more intensely than she'd ever felt in her life, more than she'd believed it was possible to feel. Even now, after he'd cold-shouldered her for two weeks, the intensity of her awareness for him hadn't diminished at all. Watching his mouth as he spoke, taking in the stubble thickening on his jaw, catching those whiffs of his cologne…it all did something to her. Meeting his eye was even worse, and now she was stuck on her bed with her veins buzzing, her heart a pulsating mess, hugging her legs as tightly as she could so he couldn't see the tremors wracking her. So yes, as much as she wished he didn't, it was undeniable that he made her feel.

She knew too that he would never sell her out. His clients' loss was her gain; Gabriel's discretion was assured. And he'd made it clear he took fatherhood seriously. She should be rejoicing that he ticked all the husband boxes.

But he felt nothing for her. He wouldn't be her prince. He'd left her sleeping and disappeared from her life as if what they'd shared had never been... But it had been. The tiny life in her belly was proof of that.

She breathed in deeply and kneaded the back of her neck. It scared her how badly she wanted the man who'd created that life with her, who'd made love to her with such intense passion, who'd brought the woman out in her, to resurface.

'Alessia?' he said, one of his thick black eyebrows raising at her silence.

She blinked her thoughts away and took a deep breath before meeting his gaze. 'Yes,' she said. 'I am willing to make compromises and concessions for the sake of our child.'

'That is good to hear. It will make life easier

for all concerned if we always strive for common ground.'

Unable to speak about her marriage—an event she'd always looked forward to with rose-coloured lenses—any further in such an emotionless way, Alessia changed the subject. 'Was anything else agreed while my back was turned?'

'Yes. The converted stable block is going to be our home here. Your father tells me it is in need of modernising. Once we have agreed what we want from the renovations, the work on it will begin immediately.'

The stable block in question sat apart from the two main turreted mishmash of buildings that constituted the castle, and had initially been converted for Alessia's widowed grandmother to live in when her daughter took the throne on her husband's death. The dowager queen had been a cantankerous old boot who'd loathed living in the castle surrounded by the thing she hated most: people. And so the stable block had been converted into a seven-bedroom dwelling which she'd taken great delight in not admitting anyone into. Alessia had been terrified of her but also secretly fascinated. It had been this grandmother whose haughty spirit she'd channelled earlier to get her through seeing Gabriel again without falling to pieces. She'd tried hard to reach for that spirit again since he'd barged his way into her room but she couldn't find it any more. Knowing her grandmother, she'd probably hidden from her out of spite from her perch in heaven.

Knowing her grandmother, she would have adored Gabriel. A man who seemingly disdained the monarchy as much as she had marrying into the family would have thrilled her. The difference was that her grandmother had been from the old Greek royal family and had played her public part as queen consort until her husband's death magnificently. For all his talk about compromise, Gabriel had been very clear that when it came to royal life, he would have nothing to do with it and that there would be no compromise on this, not even for Amadeo's wedding. Alessia would be a princess with a husband but without a prince for the rest of her life.

Fearing the swelling of emotions filling back up in her, Alessia straightened her legs and spine, and lifted her chin. 'Anything else?'

'That's everything that was discussed.'

'Good. Then I would be grateful if you would leave. I'm tired and wish to rest before dinner.'

He eyed her meditatively. 'Before I go, I would like to apologise.'

'You've already apologised.'

'This is a different matter. I wish to apologise for not returning your call.'

It felt like he'd plunged an icy hand into her heart. The impulse to draw her knees back to her chest was strong, but she fought it. 'Oh. That,' she said with an airiness she had no idea how she achieved. 'Don't worry about it—it was a mere whim. I just thought if you ever came back to Ceres and was at a loose end then we could go out for drinks. I'd forgotten I even made the call.'

'Whatever your reasons for calling, it was unforgivably rude of me to not return it. I will not insult your intelligence by making up excuses. A great part of me did want to call you back but the reason I didn't is because I knew that nothing could happen between us. You're a princess and I'm a man who values my privacy and anonymity. The two are not compatible.'

How she managed to meet his stare after those words, she would never know. But she did. She forced herself to, and she forced herself to hold it. What she couldn't do was stop the tremor that came into her voice. 'Then you will have to agree it's ironic that you're being forced to marry a woman you're not compatible with.'

There was a long moment of stillness before Gabriel got to his feet. Slowly, he stepped to the bed and leaned his face down to hers.

His eyes were ringing with that beautiful supernova of golden colour she'd seen the night they'd made love and, though she tried hard to fight it, a tingle of electricity raced up her spine and tightened her skin.

His firm lips tugged into something that nearly resembled a smile but there was nothing ambiguous about the pulsating of his eyes. 'No one is forcing me to marry you, Alessia.' His face was so close to hers his hot breath caressed her face just as his tone caressed the rest of her senses. 'Our lives are not compatible and it is unlikely we have compatibility in our interests... But there is one area where we *know* we are compatible.'

The flush that crawled through her was the deepest and hottest she had ever known. She felt it crawl through every cell in her body, burning her from the inside out, and when his face moved even closer, she could no longer draw breath.

'We can have a successful marriage,' he whispered, the tips of their noses touching. 'And we can have a fulfilling one too.'

Her lips were buzzing manically even before Gabriel's mouth brushed lightly to them, but still that first touch landed like a thrill that filled her mouth with moisture and made her pelvis contract into a tight pulse.

She hadn't even realised she'd closed her eyes until the delicious pressure against her lips vanished and she opened them to find Gabriel upright and gazing down at her with that sensual, hooded expression she remembered so well.

She couldn't open her throat to speak.

His shoulders rose as he breathed in deeply, then, wordlessly, he reached into his back pocket and pulled out his wallet. From it, he plucked a business card. Eyes still boring intently into hers, he handed it to her.

She still couldn't open her throat to speak, could barely raise an eyebrow in question.

'My personal number,' he said with the hint of wry smile. 'Call me at any time. If I don't answer, I will call you back. I give you my word.'

At the door he gave one last inclination of his head. 'Until our wedding day.'

Gabriel took a moment to compose himself before going back downstairs.

The thrills racing through his loins stretched the moment to an age.

Only when certain his arousal was contained did he take the steps down.

As he left the castle, acknowledging a dozen members of staff along the way, he acknowledged too the satisfaction of a job well done.

The sexiest woman in the world was carrying his child and he'd successfully negotiated a marriage to her in which he would not be tainted by the celebrity of monarchy or controlled by her family, and in which he could continue living his life as a private man. Undeniably, he had to wind down the business that had been the biggest part of his life for such a long time, but at the end of negotiations, it was the gains you made that counted, not the losses, and his gains were ones he could live with.

He was certain too that soon Alessia would appreciate the gains *she'd* made in the negotiations. A husband and protector for their child.

And a lover for herself.

Two a.m. and Alessia was still wide awake. There was so much going through her head, so much to process, that sleep was impossible.

What a day. What a month. Part of her wished desperately that she could wind back time to Marcelo and Clara's wedding reception and gag her own mouth. But that was only a small part of her because wishing to reverse time meant wishing the life in her belly out of existence and she could never wish for that. That fledgling life was already a part of her and a growing part of her heart had already attached itself to it.

Switching her bedside light on, she reached for the business card she'd laid by her book. Her heart in her mouth, she lightly traced a finger over the numbers printed on it.

Impulse, much like the ones that had made her call out to him and swing herself over the balustrade into his balcony, had her grab her phone and dial the number.

It was answered on the third ring.

'Alessia?' His voice was thick with sleep.

Blinking with surprise that he'd guessed it was her, all she could say was, 'Yes.'

'Are you okay?'

She closed her eyes as the deep, smooth timbre poured into her ear and sent tingles racing through her, and gave a long, soft inhale. 'Gabriel…?'

'Yes?' he said quietly into the silence.

She drew her knees to her chest and took a deeper breath. 'You do know it's a huge risk that you're taking?'

'What is?'

'Marrying me. The pregnancy is at such an early stage…the most dangerous stage.' Her voice dropped even lower. 'My mother had three miscarriages between me and Marcelo. It's why there's such a big age gap between us. I'll do everything I can to bring our child safely into the world but sometimes nature has other ideas. Are you prepared for that? That our marriage might be for nothing?'

This time the silence came from him. When

he answered, his voice was the gentlest she'd ever heard it. 'I am marrying you for our child's sake, Alessia, but it is you I am committing myself to. Whatever the future holds for us, it is a commitment I am making for the rest of my life.'

Tears filled her eyes, and she had to squeeze them tightly to stop them falling. 'I'm sorry for waking you.'

'Don't be.'

Her voice was barely a whisper as she wished him a goodnight.

CHAPTER SIX

ALESSIA'S WEDDING DAY arrived in a blaze of glorious sunshine. Wearing only skimpy silk pyjamas, she stepped onto her balcony and welcomed the rays sinking into skin that had felt so cold when she'd pulled herself out of the earlier nightmare.

'Good morning, Alessia.'

Startled, she whipped her head to the adjoining balcony. Gabriel emerged to stand at the balustrade, coffee in hand. Her stomach flipped, her heart setting off at a canter at the sight of him. All he wore was a pair of low-slung black shorts that perfectly showed off his taut abdomen and snake hips, his bronzed, muscular chest bare and gleaming under the sun, hair mussed and the stubble on his face grown so thick it should rightly be called a beard.

'What are you doing here?' she asked dumbly, unable to scramble the wits together to stop herself from staring. She swore he grew more devastatingly handsome each time she saw him.

A faint curve of a smile. 'I flew in last night.'

'No one told me.'

He raised a hefty shoulder and took a sip of his coffee. 'I dislike being late. My immediate affairs were all in order so I thought it prudent to arrive early. It meant there were less things that could go wrong today. You'd already retired for the night when the decision was made.' His eyes narrowed, deep lines forming in his brow. 'You look tired. Are you still not sleeping?'

With the memory of that awful dream, which had come after it had taken her hours to fall back to sleep after the previous one, still fresh in her mind, she shook her head. 'Bad dreams.'

She'd been chasing her mother through the castle screaming for her, but her mother had been deaf to her cries. Then she'd found herself in the old, disused banqueting hall. Gabriel and Amadeo had been in there, dining together, but they'd been deaf and blind to her too.

She'd had much worse dreams before but this was the only one she'd woken from sobbing.

There was a brief flare of concern. 'Anything you wish to share?'

'It's bad luck to share a dream before midday unless you want it to come true.'

'You don't believe that superstitious non-sense, do you?'

'No. But just in case, I'm not going to risk it by telling you.'

His firm lips curved into the first real smile he'd bestowed on her. It transformed his face into something that made her already weak legs go all watery and a deep throb pulse inside her, somehow managing to make him look a decade younger despite the crinkles around his eyes and the grooves that appeared down the sides of his mouth.

Her returning smile didn't falter when a glamorous woman of around thirty dressed in a kimono-style robe and with her dark hair piled messily but artfully on top of her head appeared on his balcony and padded like a panther to stand beside him.

'Buenos días,' the woman said, rising on her toes to plant a kiss on Gabriel's cheek.

The violence of the nausea that caught hold of Alessia at this was so strong she pressed both hands to her abdomen. So loud was the roaring in her head that she almost missed Gabriel's introduction.

'Alessia, this is my sister, Mariella.'

His sister?

There hadn't been time for her to think about who this woman could be, but the spinning sensation that had her clutching the balustrade was undoubtedly relief, and she only realised Gabriel had introduced her in Spanish when Mariella's eyes widened and she dropped into a deep curtsey.

'You don't have to do that,' Alessia croaked. 'Please, Gabriel,' she added when his sister lifted her head and looked at her non-comprehendingly, and her own proficiency in Spanish had deserted her, 'tell her not to do that.'

Not taking his eyes off Alessia's flushed face, Gabriel translated while his mind whirled with what could have caused the strange turn she'd just had. Pregnancy hormones? Whatever the cause, the same needle of concern that had fired in his blood when she'd called him in the middle of the night pierced him again.

She'd sounded so vulnerable that night. He'd laid awake a long time after that call wondering whether he should fly back to Ceres. It still disturbed him how strong the pull had been.

It disturbed him too how hard a thump his heart had made when he'd recognised the number flashing on his phone and how deep the prickles that had covered his skin when her voice first seeped into his ear.

Having no need to fight himself from thinking about her any more, Alessia had unleashed in his mind a permanent vision that must have blurred because, looking at her now, she was more impossibly beautiful than his mind's eye had remembered. As his thoughts now skipped forwards to their wedding night, anticipation let loose in his blood and he came to the realisation that there was nothing disturbing in his reactions to her. Quite the opposite. He should be celebrating that he was pledging his life to a woman who aroused him more than any woman before her.

Yes, he thought thickly. Much better that he felt the pull to be with her than the alternative.

Mariella pushed herself up off the floor, and pulled Gabriel's thoughts away from the sensual delights the evening promised.

'Please,' Alessia said in that same strange croaky voice, placing a hand on the balustrade next to his, 'tell her we don't stand on ceremony.'

Unable to resist, he covered it with his own and was gratified when, though her eyes widened and more colour saturated her cheeks, she made no effort to move it. Pressing his abdomen against the cold stone, he leaned his face closer to hers and dropped his voice. 'You wish for me to lie to her?'

'But we don't,' she protested, her indignation making her sound a fraction more like her usual self.

'Perhaps not compared to your ancestors,' he agreed lightly. The compulsion to reach over the balustrade, grip her handspan waist and lift her over it and to him sent a throb rippling through his loins. She was so tiny, well over a foot shorter than him and roughly half his weight, and yet they had fit together so well. *Perfectly* well, he recalled with another throb in his loins. Like two pieces of a two-piece jigsaw...

'We don't,' she insisted, bringing *her* face closer to *his* with a piqued glare. 'Please tell your sister that I'm delighted to meet her and that I look forward to getting to know her.'

An unexpected zip of humour tugged at him at her formal tone but, remembering they had an audience, he reluctantly moved his hand, took a step back and made the translation.

The Berrutis did not expect commoners to bow and scrape to them any more, he conceded, but there was an absolute expectation of deference. From the expression on Alessia's face, this expectation was so deeply ingrained that she likely didn't realise it was there. In fairness to her, there was nothing he'd seen of her behaviour to indicate she thought herself better than anyone else. She didn't parade on her royal dignity like so many royal people were wont to do, Amadeo, her eldest brother, being one of them. But she was oblivious to how elegant and regal her bearing was, even when dishevelled, wearing pyjama shorts that perfectly displayed her toned, golden legs and a strappy pyjama top her small breasts jutted against. Her perfect breasts, he remembered thickly as he slowly swept his gaze over her again. They'd tasted so sweet. Fitted in the palms of his hands. And as he feasted his eyes on her, another flush of colour crept over her face, and the tips of those perfect breasts became visible through the silk of her pyjama top.

She was extraordinary. As desirable a creature as he had ever seen. Her dark, velvet eyes were locked on his, an expression in them he recognised: it had lodged itself in his retinas in that breath of a moment before their lips had first fused together. Unfiltered want. Want for him.

Mariella tugged at his arm, pulling him out of the strange, heady trance-for-two he'd become frozen in. Dragging his gaze from Alessia's, he stooped down a little so his sister could whisper in his ear.

He cleared his throat and translated for Alessia. 'Mariella says it's bad luck for us to see each other before the wedding.'

She blinked before responding. Then blinked again. The heightened colour still stained her cheeks but she pulled—and he swore he saw the effort it took to achieve it—a smile to her face. Taking a step back, she said lightly, 'You don't believe in that superstitious nonsense, do you?'

'I don't believe in superstition.'

'Neither to do I, but as with my dream, I don't want to take risks so I'm going to use your sister's reminder as an excuse to go back inside. I'll see you at the chapel.' Then she turned to Mariella and, in almost perfect Spanish, said, 'It was a pleasure to meet you,' before she padded into the quarters he'd be sharing with her before the night was out.

Alessia reached for the glass of water on her dressing table and tried to quench her parched mouth, but her hand trembled so hard more water ended up spilling down her chin than down her throat. A drop splashed on her wedding dress. It felt like a portent.

She'd chosen a simple white silk dress with spaghetti straps that formed a V at the cleavage and a short train that splayed behind her. The royal beauty team had worked their magic, pulling her hair into a loose knot with white flowers carefully entwined into it and loose tendrils framing her face. Subtle makeup and a subtly elegant diamond tiara placed on top of the sheer veil completed the look. The simplicity of the dress had felt fitting for the simplicity of the wedding when she'd chosen it, but looking at it now, all she felt was an unbearable sadness. The dress, like everything, was the opposite of what she'd envisaged whenever she'd daydreamed about her perfect wedding day.

Her father entered the room. Placing his hands on her arms, he kissed her temple, then stepped back to take a proper look at her. 'You look beautiful.'

She tried to smile but couldn't make her mouth work.

He looked at her awhile longer then sighed and said heavily, 'You don't have to do this.'

She met his eyes. 'I do.'

'No.' He sighed again. 'It feels wrong. No one will blame you if you change your mind.'

She thought again of the barely suppressed fury in her mother's eyes when the family had confronted her about the pregnancy. It was a look she'd never seen from her before, worse than the reproach from her unguarded comments about Dominic, and she prayed she'd never see it again. The angry censure had been in all her blood family's eyes. But not Marcelo, she remembered wistfully. His eyes had been full of sympathy. He'd known exactly how she was feeling because he'd been there himself, trying to fix a mess of his own making.

Their family, though, had never looked at him

with the same disappointment they'd looked at Alessia. Their reproval had been laced with understanding of his nature. Their forgiveness for him had come easily.

'*I'll* blame me,' she told her father, whose troubled eyes told her he, at least, had forgiven her. 'I wouldn't be able to live with myself if my actions led to the destruction of the monarchy.' The smile she'd tried to conjure finally came, small though it was, and she took her father's hand and gave it a reassuring squeeze. 'This is for the best. We can trust Gabriel with our family. If we honour our side of the deal, he'll honour his.' Of that, she was certain.

It was the only certainty she had about him.

Shortly, she would leave her quarters and marry a man she knew so little of that when a woman had appeared on his balcony on her wedding morning, Alessia's automatic assumption was that the woman had been his lover.

She knew so little about him that she didn't know if he did have a lover tucked away somewhere. She didn't know if Mariella was his only sibling.

But there was one more thing she did know, and it frightened her badly. That brief moment earlier on the balcony when she'd automatically assumed Mariella to be his lover...it had felt like she'd been hit by a truck. The relief to learn she was his sister had been dizzying, and then she'd found herself trapped in Gabriel's stare…

She'd seen the desire in his eyes. She'd seen it and been helpless to stop herself from reacting to it, no more than she'd been unable to stop the swelling of her heart when he'd smiled and his face had lit up into something heartbreaking.

So that's the one more thing she knew—how he made her feel. Like a giddy, jealous schoolgirl. And it's what frightened her so badly too.

She didn't want to feel like that for him, full stop. She believed in the commitment he was about to make to her as his wife but she couldn't forget how he'd ignored her. If not for their baby, she would never have seen him again because he didn't think her worth the bother due to their supposed incompatibility. He'd never given her a chance to find out if they could be compatible in ways that didn't involve sex for the simple reason that he hadn't wanted to.

And she couldn't forget how devastated she'd been when she woke up to find him gone.

The Berrutis royal chapel was much bigger than Gabriel had envisaged and so ancient he could feel its history seeping through the high, stone walls and dome ceiling. He could feel his sister's awe at it all as she stood next to him while they waited for the bride to arrive. He could feel the Berruti family's bemusement at his choice of a woman for a best man and that the glamorous best man had donned a feminine tuxedo to match his own. Clara, the newest family member, had clapped her hands in glee at Mariella's outfit.

Gabriel had few friends. He could travel to almost any country in the world and find hospitality from friendly acquaintances, but true friends were rare. Partly this was because of his nomadic lifestyle, always basing himself wherever his current job was located. Partly it was because he liked his own company and would much rather spend a rare evening off sipping a large bourbon and watching a film noir or reading a good thriller. The only person he was close to was his sister. Two years younger than him, they'd been as close as siblings could be since before Mariella was out of nappies. Living in their family's war zone had cemented their closeness. Trusting her implicitly, he'd confided the entire Alessia and baby situation. There had been no judgement or efforts to tell him he was being a fool to throw his life away by marrying a stranger. She knew him well enough not to bother wasting her breath like that.

'Mum would wet herself if she could see this,' Mariella murmured. 'You, marrying a princess in a royal chapel.'

He gave a subtle mock shudder. 'I can well believe it.' Their mother was the most horrendous social climber, a born attention seeker and the root cause of his media hatred. The only thing that stopped her exposing Gabriel as her son to her countless social media followers was the hefty monthly allowance he paid her. A royal wedding, though, no matter how small, would be a temptation too far for her and so he'd made the decision not to invite her. This was his last event as a private person. The circus his life was going to turn into, one that made his guts twist to imagine, could wait a few days longer.

Movement broke the stillness of the chapel and jolted his heart. The bride had arrived. His bride.

Clutching her father's arm, she walked towards him. The closer she came, the clearer she became and the greater his heart swelled.

When she reached him, he carefully lifted the sheer veil. Her eyes locked with his. The swelling in his heart stopped and his chest tightened, crushing it. His jaw locked. Alessia was simply breathtaking. He'd never imagined such beauty existed.

For a long moment she stared at him, then her shoulders rose and she jutted her chin. 'Ready?'

He nodded.

'Good.' She smiled tightly. 'Then let's do this.'

* * *

Had there ever been a more miserable excuse for a wedding? Alessia wondered morosely. No wedding march. Only six guests and a priest. She signed her name to the certificate and thought of her large, extended family. They would have loved to be here. She would have loved for them to be here. The only moment that had matched her dreams had been the wedding kiss to seal their vows. Gabriel's eyes had pulsed with a heady sensuality and the promise of more before his warm lips had brushed hers, but even that had been tainted because she couldn't forget that she wasn't his choice for a bride. He wanted her, that was obvious, and he'd said as much in words and body language, but he'd never wanted to want her.

She wished she didn't want him. She wished the woman he'd unlocked in her would go back into hiding.

The ring he'd slid on her finger felt too weighty. She wished she could wrench it off.

Once Marcelo and Clara had signed their parts of the certificate as witnesses, they all left the chapel, cutting through the chapel garden to return to the castle, where a mockery of a banquet had been prepared for them.

'Where's the photographer?' Clara asked as they walked the winding footpath.

'There isn't one,' Gabriel informed her.

'Then can I take a picture of you both? For posterity?'

'That would be nice,' Alessia said at the exact same moment Gabriel politely said, 'The agreement was no photos, but thank you for the offer.'

It was seeing the disbelief on her sister-in-law's face that made Alessia crack and, suddenly frightened she was going to burst into tears, she sped off.

She would not cry in front of Gabriel again.

A hand caught her wrist.

'What's wrong?' Gabriel asked.

'Nothing,' she muttered, loosening her arm from him and setting off again. His legs being much longer than hers, he caught her in seconds and stood before her, blocking her path.

'Clearly something is wrong.' Not an auspicious start to married life, Gabriel thought wryly. 'If I have upset you, you must tell me, else how can I fix it?'

Velvet eyes snapped onto his. 'I don't understand why you don't want pictures taken.'

He strove for patience. 'It was one of my conditions for marrying you. If you had a problem with it you should have said when you had the chance.'

'You made it very clear they were take it or leave it conditions.' She twisted as if to barge past him but then stopped and folded her arms tightly around her chest and raised her chin to meet his stare again. 'You got your way about everything with this wedding.'

'Not the date,' he said lightly, trying to defuse the head of steam she was clearly building up.

'No, that came from my family. Not from me. In fact, not once did you or any of my family ask what *I* wanted from our wedding day.'

'And what did you want?'

'It's a bit late to ask me that now, isn't it?' she suddenly shouted, before kneading the back of her neck and making a visible effort to calm herself. 'I apologise. You were upfront about your conditions and the only thing that really bothered me about them at the time was your refusal to attend Amadeo's wedding and other family events the press will be at, but I didn't really think about our wedding in emotional terms until I put my dress on this morning. I chose this dress because it fitted the simple wedding we were having but my dream was always to wear an elaborate fairy-tale dress with a twelve-foot train and to have a dozen bridesmaids. I always envisaged my entire family and all my friends being there, and a truckload of confetti being tipped over my and the groom's heads, and a huge party afterwards that went on until the sun came up, but I didn't have any of that. So many people I love forbidden to be here, and now I'm not even allowed one photo as a reminder of my wedding day.'

Gabriel stared at the hurt on her face, the same hurt that had sounded in her husky voice, and wondered if she'd been given lessons on how to make a man feel like a heel. He had nothing to feel bad about, he knew that. He'd been upfront and open, unlike his bride, who'd clearly festered about the wedding day she believed her due and which she felt had been denied her. But she'd agreed to this. As she would say, he hadn't put a gun to her head. She'd agreed to this marriage of her own free will and agreed to his conditions, so it was a bit rich to start complaining once the deed was done.

Closing her eyes, she kneaded the back of her neck again and breathed deeply. Then her eyes fluttered open and fixed back on his. 'Ignore me. I'm just feeling a little more emotional than I expected and it's making me unreasonable.'

With an apologetic smile, she set off back down the path.

Gabriel watched her. The sun high above her seemed to cast her in a golden glow. For a moment he could believe she'd been conjured by an enchantment.

'You're not being unreasonable,' he called

out, speaking through a boulder that had lodged in his throat.

She turned her head.

He breached the distance between them and gazed down at the pretty heart-shaped face and those sultry velvet eyes. A wave of desire sliced through him. Whether they could ever find common ground to build a successful marriage or not, she was now his wife, and she was breathtaking. There was not a man alive who wouldn't ache to share a bed with her.

Her chest rose, lifting those perfect, pert breasts. The desire tightened, making his skin tauten.

Colour rose on her cheeks. The tips of her breasts strained through the silk of her dress. He leaned his face closer. Her lips parted and her breath quickened. Whatever his wife's personal feelings about him, she wanted him. He could practically smell the desire radiating from her.

'And you're right,' he finally added. 'This is our wedding day. We should have photos to remember it by.' Then he placed his lips to a pretty, delicate ear and whispered thickly, 'And then, tonight, I will give you something else to remember this day by.'

The wedding banquet was as sorry an affair as the wedding itself but Alessia dragged it out as long as she could, eating at the same pace she'd done as a child when she'd wanted to annoy her brothers, who'd been forbidden from leaving the table until everyone had finished. She'd perfected the art of nibbling then and she brought those skills back out now. However, if Gabriel was annoyed at this, he hid it well, eating and drinking and conversing as if it were any meal for any occasion while she was filled with so many emotions that she didn't know how her knotted stomach was admitting food into it. All she could think was that once this banquet was done, the 'celebrations' would be over, and then she and Gabriel would go to her quarters. *Their* quarters.

As much as she tried to block them, his seductive words before he'd called Clara over to take photos of them kept ringing in her head. Every time she recalled them, heat flushed through her, a powerful throb deep in her pelvis sucking the air from her lungs. The same things happened every time she met his eye and caught the anticipatory gleam in them. Frightened at the strength of her desire for him, she tried hard not to look at him, but it was like Gabriel were a magnet her eyes were drawn to.

There were so many knots forming inside her that she couldn't work out if it was dread or excitement causing them. Or a mixture of both.

Their night together had been so wonderful that the thought of experiencing it all again was almost too tantalising to bear, but the way Gabriel had left her the next morning and then ghosted her... Her new husband had hurt her badly, and if she didn't protect herself, she feared he would hurt her again.

She hated that her body and her head, the woman and the princess, were at such odds. Until she found a way to marry the two, she didn't know how she could dare risk letting him touch her and risk losing her head like she'd done the first time with him.

'Have you decided when you're going on honeymoon?' Clara asked from across the table.

Alessia had a drink of her water, wishing it was wine. 'We're not having one.'

Clara looked like she had something to say about this but Marcelo whispered in her ear and she clamped her lips together.

A honeymoon was something else Alessia would miss out on. And being carried across a threshold... She'd fantasised about that many times, being swept into her hunky husband's arms and carried through the door and laid lovingly on their marital bed...

She grabbed her spoon and stabbed it into her ricotta and cinnamon trifle, and gritted her teeth. She needed to stop these foolish thoughts. It was done. She'd married him.

As her old headmistress had loved to espouse, she'd made her bed and now she had to lie in it. What her old headmistress had not espoused was how this was supposed to be achieved when one had to share that bed with a man it was imperative she protect her heart against.

CHAPTER SEVEN

THE BEATS OF Gabriel's heart were heavy as he followed Alessia into what was now their shared quarters, at least until the renovations of the converted stable block were completed. When he'd visited her after their marriage had been agreed, he hadn't taken much notice of any of it other than her bedroom but now he craned his neck around the high walls to take in the sumptuous furnishings, many of which he suspected were family heirlooms centuries old and much of which were too large for the rooms that were, surprisingly, the same size as the ones in the quarters he'd stayed in. They could never be described as small but in comparison to her parents' and brother's quarters, they were as pint-sized as the princess who lived in them. But there was plenty of modernity there too, the new blending perfectly with the old to create an eclectic apartment that was feminine and chic and regal all rolled into one. Although not to his taste, it was an apartment that suited Alessia perfectly and he couldn't deny the throb in his loins to know that soon—very soon—they would share that princess bed.

His new wife, who'd walked silently with her hands clasped together from the banquet room to their quarters, kicked her shoes off and hovered in the day room doorway, not looking at him. 'I need to shower so I'll leave you to familiarise yourself with the place. It's virtually the same as the quarters you stayed in so you shouldn't get lost.'

'Where has my stuff been put?' He'd been told his suitcases would be moved to his new quarters and his possessions unpacked for him.

She swallowed. 'In my dressing room. Come, I'll show you.'

He followed her up the stairs and caught the brief hesitation before she opened the bedroom door.

She padded across the room and opened the dressing room door. 'I've made as much room for you as I can but I'm afraid it's quite small—this section of the castle is four hundred years old, so relatively modern compared to other parts, and was once lodgings for courtiers until my great-grandparents had them all fiddled about with to create family apartments. This one and the one you stayed in are by far the smallest and were intended for visiting family but it was always my favourite, I don't know why, and when I came of age, I asked to have it rather than move into the one earmarked for me. The only thing missing from it was a dressing room so they stole space from the guest bedroom to create one for me.'

She paused for breath, a sheepish expression crossing her face. 'A very long-winded way of telling you that there isn't much space for your things. I'm sorry. I had all my ball gowns moved into the guest room, so if you find it all too cramped, you can put some of your stuff in there too. I hope that's okay?'

Leaning against the arch of the door beside her, Gabriel gazed at his bride.

Anticipation for what the night would bring had tortured him since he'd seen her on the balcony that morning, and now they were finally alone and all the fantasies that had sustained him through the long wedding banquet, of peeling that sheer dress from her perfect body and then kissing every inch of her soft skin before burying himself in her tight sweetness, could be acted on.

But he would keep his desire in check awhile longer. Even through his fantasies he'd sensed Alessia's nerves growing as the banquet had gone on and guessed the anticipation of their wedding night had got the better of her. It was up to him to help her relax.

'I didn't bring much with me so I'm sure it's all fine,' he assured her with a slow smile. The dressing room, long though it was, *was* small but cleverly designed to maximise every available inch of space. The left-hand side bulged with feminine colour. The right-hand side—his side—had barely a third of the available space taken. 'See, plenty of room.'

She rubbed her arm. 'When will you bring the rest of your stuff?'

'When we move into the stables. In the meantime, I'll be spending my working weeks in Madrid so will keep the majority of my stuff in my home there.'

Her eyes met his, perfectly plucked eyebrows drawing together. 'I thought you were giving up your business? You said you'd got your affairs in order.'

'No, only my affairs concerning the client I was supposed to start with this week. I will be winding my main business down but I have many other business interests too. There isn't the space for me to work here.'

A flintiness came into the velvet eyes, an edge appearing in her voice. 'I know my quarters are cramped but it's a castle with over three hundred rooms. An office can be created for you without any problem, and it can be as big as you want.'

'It's more convenient to base myself in Madrid—it's easier to travel to the countries I do business in from there,' he explained. 'By the time we move into the stables and the baby's born, my affairs will be much more straightforward and my need to travel much reduced.' Having their child and not having to live in the castle itself should hopefully make living in this royal goldfish bowl more bearable.

The flintiness sharpened. 'That sounds like an excuse to me.'

'It's a truth. The other truth is that I have no wish to live in this castle full-time. There are too many staff to have any real privacy and I suspect that being under this roof means your family and their personal staff will be incentivised to try and change my mind about being a working member of the family. If I'm out of sight then I'm more likely to be out of mind.'

'Is being a working member such an intolerable idea to you?'

'Yes.'

'And you don't think having a husband who spends his working weeks away is an intolerable idea to me?'

'It is only until the renovations are complete.'

'Which could take months.' She raised her

chin and gave a smile as flinty as the expression in her eyes. 'I shall come to Madrid with you.'

'That isn't necessary,' he stated as smoothly as he could in an effort to diffuse what his antennae was warning him: that Alessia was spoiling for an argument.

'Why not? Do you have a woman stashed in Madrid waiting for you?'

Surprised at both the question and the tone in which she asked it, he narrowed his eyes. 'Of course not.'

'Then you can have no objection to me travelling there with you.'

Gabriel closed his eyes and inhaled deeply before staring back at the face that now brimmed with what he was coming to recognise as temper. He had no choice but to add fuel to it. 'I'm afraid it's out of the question.'

'Why?'

'Because a circus follows wherever you go, and I have no wish to be a part of it. I've already made that clear.'

'The media circus is not my fault.'

'I am simply stating my reasons.'

'The moment the announcement of our marriage is made public the circus will be on you.'

'But your presence will make it more. The media love you.'

'I don't encourage that.'

'I never said you did, only that I wish to avoid it as much as I can.'

'Then you shouldn't have agreed to marry me. I'm sorry you find the thought of media intrusion so abhorrent but it is possible to have a life as a royal that isn't always accompanied by the flash of cameras, as you will learn for yourself when I accompany you on your travels.'

For the first time, visible anger darkened Gabriel's features but Alessia was too angry at his insinuations about her character and hurt at his readiness to spend the majority of his time apart from her to care about it. 'It's bad enough that I'll be humiliated by a husband who refuses to be my prince even at my own brother's wedding, but I will not be humiliated by a husband who marries me one minute then flies off without me the next too, especially when that wasn't a pre-condition of our marriage, so get used to the idea of having me by your side. If you do have any lovers stashed anywhere, warn them now that you can no longer see them because your wife refuses to be separated from you.' And with that, Alessia snatched a pair of pyjamas off a shelf and stalked into the bathroom, locking the door firmly behind her.

Alessia had never appreciated how greatly the presence of another could change an atmosphere. Her quarters, her bedroom especially, had been her favourite place in the castle since she was a little girl and would make Marcelo go exploring with her. She truly didn't know what it was that she loved so much about it other than its warm atmosphere—lots of the castle's rooms were cold and unwelcoming to a little girl—but she'd gladly foregone the much larger apartment that could have been hers for it. Gabriel's presence had changed its atmosphere markedly.

They danced cordially around each other as they readied for bed, taking it in turns to use the bathroom, giving each other privacy to undress, and all with fixed, polite smiles that brimmed with a seething undercurrent.

How many brides and grooms argued on their wedding night? she wondered bitterly. Not that they'd argued as such. She doubted Gabriel ever raised his voice. No, Gabriel preferred to make his arguments behind a smooth cordiality she was growing to detest. But she'd seen the anger in his eyes when she'd stood her ground and refused to accept being treated like a chattel. Well, tough. He'd married her. If she had to live in the bed they'd both made then so should he.

Climbing into the bed she'd never shared before, wearing long silk pyjamas with buttons running the length of the top, Alessia leaned her back against the headboard and reached for her book. She always read in bed but tonight was painfully aware she was using her novel as a prop. She imagined that, for Gabriel, sharing a bed with a woman was no big deal. She wished it wasn't a big deal for her too, but apart from the one night they'd shared, this was her first time and her nerves had grown so big that she wasn't sure if they were causing the nausea rampaging in her stomach or if baby hormones were to blame.

When he finally left the bathroom, she took one look at him and her heart juddered, the ripples spreading through her like wildfire. Wearing only a pair of snug black briefs that bulged at the front and accentuated the rugged athleticism of his physique, she doubted Adonis himself could have made a greater impact. She'd seen him entirely naked, of course, but they'd spent that night entwined, and she'd seen him in shorts on the balcony that morning, but the balustrade had hidden much of him. She hadn't had the opportunity to take in everything about him with one sweep of her eyes. All the disparate parts had come together and as he stalked to the bed, eyes softer…and yet more alive… than they'd been when she'd last looked into them, her most intimate parts became molten liquid, and all she could think was that he was the sexiest man to roam the earth or heavens.

The mattress made only the slightest movement as he slipped between the bedsheets but it was movement enough to stop her from breathing. His whispered words from the chapel garden rang in her ear again. *'Tonight, I will give you something else to remember this day by.'*

She gripped her book harder and pressed the top of her thighs together as if that could stop the pulsing heat that was spreading from down low in her pelvis.

The thuds of her heart were suddenly deafening.

She sensed his gaze turn to her. Alessia's lungs squeezed so tightly there was no chance of getting air into them even if she could breathe.

This must be the moment that he reached for her and took her in his arms...

A hard scrub of his body had finally cleansed Gabriel of the unwelcome anger inflamed by Alessia's stubborn insistence that she accompany him to Madrid.

Every time she left the castle it was under the flash of camera lenses. He accepted that those flashes and having the press on her heels—having to smile politely and answer their questions—was something she considered a normal part of her life, but she had to accept too that it was not the kind of life he was willing to live.

He'd been upfront about it and it was not something he was prepared to compromise on.

But he did accept that he would have to get used to a degree of press intrusion, at least for a short period. As Alessia had rightly pointed out, the moment their marriage was made public, the circus would begin. That didn't mean he had to feed the vultures. A refusal to engage with them or give them anything remotely newsworthy would make the press quickly bore of him.

He doubted the press would ever bore with Alessia. On top of being breathtakingly beautiful and photogenic, she was a style icon to millions. She sold magazines and generated social media clicks by doing nothing but be herself, and, he had to admit, raised great awareness for the charities she patronised as a result.

Staring at her now, he could see from the rigid way she held herself, her clenched jaw and the whites of her knuckles where she held her book, that her anger still lingered. And there was something else in her body language too, there in the tiny tremors of her body... Alessia was as aware of him as he was of her.

Having had enough of the game of silence, Gabriel plucked the book from her hand, then leaned over her to place it on her antique bedside table. He caught the intake of her breath at the same moment the soft fruity scent of Alessia hit his senses.

Had any woman ever smelt so good? Not in his lifetime.

With his back propped against the velvet headboard, he kept his gaze on her until she finally turned her face and those amazing dark velvet eyes locked onto him.

'Let me put your mind at ease,' he said. 'I don't have a lover stashed in Madrid or anywhere. My last relationship ended months ago. I'm strictly monogamous.'

He was rewarded with continued silence.

'And you?' he prompted when she did nothing but gaze into his eyes as if searching for something. 'Are you monogamous too?'

Her teeth grazed her bottom lip. 'I suppose.'

Surprised at her equivocation, he raised a brow. 'Suppose? Surely it's a question that requires only a yes or no answer.'

'Then… Yes.'

Something dark coiled inside him, as unexpected as it was disarming, but he controlled it. 'You don't look certain.'

'I am.'

He stared hard into her brown eyes. His expertise at reading people meant Gabriel knew when someone was lying to him. Alessa was not being truthful. He was certain of it. Which begged the question of why she was lying. As far as he was aware, she'd never been linked to a man so she was discreet in her affairs, probably conducting them all within the castle or in the homes of trusted friends. When it came to cheating, though, he imagined things would get trickier. There were tabloids he knew who would pay a small fortune for a story of Princess Alessia being a love cheat.

If she wasn't a love cheat then why the hesitation about being monogamous? Whatever the answer, the darkness thickened and coiled tighter, and tightened his vocal chords too, and it was a real struggle to keep his voice moderate. 'I don't care what you got up to in your past but I will not accept you taking lovers.' He bore his gaze into hers so there could be no misunderstanding. 'You don't wish to be humiliated by me travelling without you, and I will not suffer the humiliation of being cuckolded. We're married now which means it's you and me, and only you and me. Is that clear?'

Alessia fought the very real urge to laugh. She was quite sure it would come out sounding hysterical.

What would he say if she told him the truth, that he'd been her first? Which incidentally meant he would also be her last.

But how could she tell him that now when she

should have told him weeks ago, before things had gone too far between them? How could he forgive her for it? If she hadn't been so inexperienced she would have realised he hadn't put a condom on, but as it was, she'd made the fatal assumption that he'd taken care of things while she'd been in a blissful bubble of sensual feeling. If she'd told him she was a virgin then the subject of contraception would definitely have come up—one thing she knew about her new husband was that he did not leave anything to chance.

If she'd told him she was a virgin he would never have made love to her…

'Are you not going to say anything?' he asked curtly.

Pushing the bedsheets off her lap, she crossed her legs as she twisted to face him. The Ice Man stared back at her, his handsome face expressionless, large hands folded loosely against his taut abdomen. For the beat of a moment the temptation to drag her fingers through the dark hair covering his muscular chest and press down where his heart beat made her skin tingle.

'What do you want me to say?' she asked.

His eyes flashed, but other than that, his expression remained unreadable. 'Whatever's going on in your pretty head would be a start.'

She felt a flare of pleasure at the compliment.

'Trust me, you don't want to know what's in my head.' She linked her fingers together to stop herself, again, from dragging them over his supremely masculine chest. 'But let me put *your* mind at ease—I didn't take my vows lightly. I knew that making them meant I was committing myself to you for the rest of my life, and *only* you.'

His nostrils flared. 'Good.'

'But so we are clear, I am now your wife but that doesn't make me your possession.'

His wife…

'I never said you were.'

'I just wanted to make that clear.'

He leaned forwards, closer to her, a wry expression on his face. 'You did.'

Alessia had no idea why the knots in her belly had loosened so much. If she didn't know better, she would say Gabriel had sounded jealous, but then she reminded herself that if he were, it would only be from a proprietorial sense and not from a place of emotion like her own bout of jealousy had come from that morning.

Grazing her bottom lip, she suddenly blurted out, 'Do you really think I'm pretty?'

He stared at her as if she'd asked the most stupid question in the world. 'Yes.'

'Really?'

He pulled a cynical face. 'I can't be the first man to have told you that.'

'Oh, I've been told I'm pretty by lots of people but I never know whether to believe them or not.' She shrugged. 'My family are biased, and people like to ingratiate themselves with me. Then there are all the trolls out there who like to tell me that I'm pig ugly, so who knows what I should believe.'

The cynicism vanished. 'You have trolls?'

'Everyone in the public eye has trolls.' She tried not to sound too downbeat about it. If trolls were the worst thing she had to deal with in her privileged life then she had nothing to complain about. 'Nowadays, it comes with the job.'

'Who are these people?'

'Mostly anonymous. It doesn't matter.'

'Of course it matters,' Gabriel disputed roughly. The thought of anyone sitting in front of their phone or computer and targeting Alessia for their poison... He clasped her hand and leaned closer to her, staring straight into the velvet depths. 'Anyone who tells you that you're ugly needs to seek help because you're more than pretty. You're beautiful.'

She stilled, the only movement the widening of her eyes and the parting of her lips as she took a sharp intake of breath. A crawl of colour suffused her cheeks. 'Do you really mean that?' she whispered.

He drew even closer so the tips of their noses almost touched. 'You're beautiful,' he repeated. 'So beautiful that sometimes I look at you and think you must have been created by an enchantment.' And then he did what he'd been aching to do for so long, and tilted his head, brushed his lips to hers and breathed her in.

For the longest time he did nothing but allow his senses to fill with the delicate scent of Alessia's skin. Then he kissed her, gentle sweeping movements that slowly deepened until their lips parted in unison and their tongues entwined in a private dance that sent sensation shooting through him like an electric current through his veins.

All these weeks, Alessia's scent and taste had haunted him, memories so strong he'd come to believe he'd imagined just how intoxicating they were. His memories hadn't lied. Hooking an arm around her waist and pulling her to him, he fed himself on kisses that were as headily addictive and as potent as the strongest aphrodisiac could be.

With a soft sigh, she sank fully into him, returning his hunger with a ravenousness that only fed his burning arousal even more. Tightly she wrapped her arms around his neck, hands and fingers clasping the back of his head, her perfect breasts pressed against his chest, as the passion that had caught them in its grips all those weeks ago cast its tendrils back around them.

From the first whisper of his breath against her lips, Alessia had been reduced to nothing but sensation. The dark taste of Gabriel and the burning thrills of his touch raged through her flesh and veins, feeding the craving for him that she'd carried in every cell of her body since the night they'd...

'No!'

CHAPTER EIGHT

ALESSIA'S MOUTH SHOUTED the word and wrenched away from him before her brain caught up.

Her heart thumping madly, her skin and loins practically screaming their outrage at the severing of such dazzling pleasure, she disentangled herself from his arms and scrambled backwards out of reach.

Stunned eyes followed her movements, Gabriel's breaths coming in short, ragged bursts. 'What's wrong?' he asked hoarsely.

Trying hard to control her own breathing, trying even harder to control the wails of disappointment from her body, Alessia shakily shook her head. 'I can't do this. I'm sorry, but I can't. It's too soon.'

He stared at her in disbelief. 'What are you talking about? How can you say it's too soon when we've just got married?'

'It just is!' she cried, before her lips clamped together and she crossed her arms to hold her biceps, gripping them tightly as protection, not from him but from herself because like the rest of her furious body, her hands were howling to clasp themselves to his cheeks so her equally furious lips could attach themselves back to his mouth, and the whole of her could revel again in the heady delights of Gabriel. Her pelvis felt like it was on fire. Her blood burned. *Everything* burned.

His face contorted and he cursed under his breath before his chest rose as he inhaled deeply, visibly composing himself. 'You have to talk to me,' he said. She could take little comfort that the smoothly controlled voice had a ragged tone to it. 'Tell me what's on your mind. I'm trying to make sense of what you mean about it being too soon when we already know how good we are together. The night we made our child is proof of that.'

'And you walked out the next day without a word of goodbye or even a note,' she retorted tremulously, because it was remembering that little fact that had snapped her out of the sensual haze she'd been caught in.

This time his curse was more audible, and he closed his eyes.

'Are you not going to say anything?' she asked in an attempt to mimic the curt tone he'd used on her earlier, but the upset in her voice was just too strong for it to be successful.

Nausea churned heavily in Gabriel's guts. He'd apologised for not returning her call but the fact of him leaving her sleeping while he slipped out of the room had been left unsaid. He should have known this conversation would one day come.

Arousal still coursed like fire through his loins and veins, and he closed his eyes again and concentrated on tempering it. Then he locked his stare back on her. 'I left without saying goodbye because when I woke next to you, I felt like the biggest jerk in the world.'

Her chin wobbled but she didn't look away. 'Why?'

'Because your family were generous enough to give me a bed for the night when my plane was grounded and I repaid that generosity by sleeping with their daughter.'

'I'm a twenty-three-year-old woman.'

'But you're not an ordinary woman. You're a princess.'

'I'm also a woman. A woman with feelings, not some mythical creature that can't be hurt.'

'I behaved terribly. I know that. When I woke up… Alessia, I was sickened with myself, not just because of who you are and the abuse of your parents' hospitality but because I never mix business with pleasure. Never.'

Her eyes continued to search his until her

neck straightened and something that almost resembled a smile played on her lips. 'You mean I was your first? Mixing of business with pleasure, I mean?'

'Yes.'

Her gaze searched his for a moment more before the smile widened a touch. 'Should I be flattered?'

'If you like.'

'I do like.' Then the smile faded and she stilled again. 'I can understand why you felt bad about yourself for what happened. But, Gabriel, that doesn't excuse or explain your behaviour towards me.'

'It's the truth of it all.'

'Maybe, but it doesn't excuse it. It doesn't. I had the best night of my life with you and then I woke up and you were gone. Do you know how that made me feel?'

He took a long inhale.

'Dirty. I've never...' She swallowed, and drew her knees to her chest and wrapped her arms around them. 'I've never had a one-night stand before. Don't misunderstand me, I didn't fall into your arms expecting any of this—' she waved a hand absently '—to happen, but finding you gone... It hurt. To feel unworthy of even a minute of your time after what we'd shared.'

'I'm sorry,' he said, speaking through a throat

that felt like it had razors in it. 'It was never my intention to make you feel like that.'

'Then what was your intention?'

'To get out of Ceres. It felt like I'd woken from a spell and all I could do was kick myself for losing my head the way I did.'

An astuteness came into her stare. 'You don't like losing control of yourself, do you?'

'No,' he agreed.

'Why is that?'

'It's just the way I am.'

She gave a grimacing smile and rubbed her chin against her knees. 'I think we can both agree that what we shared was...madness. A child was created through it and here we are. But I'm sorry, Gabriel, I can't forget how I felt when I realised you'd gone. I kept hoping you sneaked out because you were worried about making love with a princess and my family's re-action if they found out—I guess I was partially right there—so I decided to be a modern woman and call you. I hoped you'd see my message and realise I was just a woman like any other and that there was nothing to stop us seeing each other again, but you blanked me there too, and I can't forget that. I can't forget how cheap you made me feel. I want to put it behind me—I've married you so we're stuck together now—but I've got nothing to replace those feelings with because you're still a stranger to me, and until you start opening up about who you really are, you'll continue to be a stranger.'

Alessia's heart was beating hard. Her body was still furious with her for severing the passionate connection with Gabriel and, though she knew she'd done the right thing in not letting things go any further, the ache deep inside was a taunt that she was being a prideful fool.

She didn't think she'd ever been so honest about her feelings before. 'Never complain and never explain' was a creed many royal families lived by and it was a creed she'd taken to heart at a very young age. The only person she'd ever felt able to open up to was her brother Marcelo, and even then she'd often held back because he'd suffered for being who he was born to be far more than she ever had. Alessia had never yearned to be someone else like him.

In many ways, laying her cards on the table was liberating, and she experienced a little jolt to realise that there was something in Gabriel that put her at ease enough to say what was on her mind and in her heart without sanitising or editing. There was another jolt to realise that when she was with him, she didn't have to *be* a princess. And it wasn't just about him bringing out the woman beneath the princess mask—for Gabriel, the mask dropped itself of its own accord.

And then she remembered, again, keeping her virginity from him and another spasm of guilt cut through her.

It shouldn't matter, she knew that. Her sexual history—or lack of it—was no one's business but her own. It shouldn't matter, but she suspected that for Gabriel it would.

After the longest passage of silence had passed, hands more than twice the size of hers wrapped around her fingers.

'I can see I have much to do to make amends,' he said, his expression as serious as his tone, 'and I will do my best to do that. There is much to learn about each other, but I should warn you, I'm not one for baring my soul. I have always been a private person.'

'Would you believe it, but I'm not one for baring my soul either?' She gave a rueful shrug. 'Not usually, in any case.' And then she shook her head as if disbelieving. 'And yet I cried in your arms and told you everything I was feeling that night because on some level I must have trusted you.'

It was the first time Alessia had considered that. Though there had been no forethought behind it, she'd trusted Gabriel with her feelings as well as with her body that night. She'd unbuttoned herself to him like she'd never done with anyone else on this earth, and then he'd left her life as if he'd never been in it. Was it any wonder she was so scared of getting close to him again?

The look on Gabriel's face as another long stretch of time passed told her he was thinking the same thoughts.

'Yes,' he finally said. 'I think I do believe that, and I will do whatever it takes to rebuild your trust in me.' Then he released her hands and lifted the bedsheet for her. In a softer tone, he said, 'It is late. We should get some sleep.'

She hesitated. Should she sleep in the guest room? Insist he sleep in it?

But the expression in his gaze was steady. Reassuring. And it made her mind up for her.

Her heart in her throat, Alessia slipped back under the sheets while Gabriel leaned over to turn out the lights, then her heart almost shot out of her ribs when he reached for her.

'I'm just going to hold you,' he murmured, and pulled her rigid body to him. Then, having manoeuvred her as easily as if he were manipulating play dough so that her cheek was pressed into his chest and their arms wrapped around each other, he dropped a kiss into her hair. 'Goodnight, wife.'

'Goodnight, husband,' she whispered.

The moment Alessia awoke, her eyes pinged open. There was an arm draped over her waist, the attached hand loose against her belly. A knee rested in the back of her calf.

The duskiness of the room told her the sun had already risen.

From Gabriel's steady, rhythmic breathing, he was in deep sleep.

She had no idea how long she lay there, afraid to move so much as a muscle. Afraid of the feelings swirling inside her. The deep yearn to wriggle back into his solid body and press herself to him. To wake him…

Holding her breath, she slowly inched herself out from under his arm. Once she'd inched herself off the bed too, she carefully picked up her book and her phone, and crept out of the room. Only when the door was closed behind her was she able to breathe.

Downstairs, she padded into the kitchen and fixed herself a coffee. It was the one thing she liked to do for herself, and when she had days without any engagements, she relished the solitude and independence the early mornings gave her. The days she had engagements, staff surrounded her before she'd even climbed out of bed.

Her hand clenched around her favourite coffee mug, and she squeezed her eyes shut. Hurt and anger had made her tell Gabriel she would accompany him to Madrid. She wondered if he would even pretend not to be relieved when she told him that wouldn't be possible after all?

Rolling her neck, she pulled herself together and took her coffee into the day room, opened the curtains, snuggled into her reading chair and opened the book.

Ten minutes later and she was still on the same page. It didn't matter how many times she read the same passage, the words refused to penetrate. Or should that be, her brain refused to concentrate?

With a sigh, she closed her eyes.

Her brain refused to concentrate because it wanted to think about Gabriel, and nothing but Gabriel.

Wasn't it enough that her stupid brain had taken for ever to go to sleep because Gabriel's arms had been around her and her every inhalation had breathed in the divine scent of his skin? Wasn't it enough that her body had also taken for ever to relax itself into sleep for the exact same reason? She swore it had taken at least an hour before she'd even been able to breathe properly. And then there were all the thoughts that had crowded her already frazzled mind, every single one about Gabriel, never mind the battle between her mind and her rigid yet aching body. That had been the worst of it. That yearning ache deep inside her that had spent hours begging her to wake him with a kiss.

'You're up early.'

If Alessia hadn't already finished her coffee she would have spilt the contents of her mug, which was still in her hand, all over herself.

Snapping her eyes open, she turned her head and found Gabriel in the doorway looking at her with an expression that made her heart inflate and her belly flip.

Black hair mussed, his jaw and neck thick with stubble, all he wore was a pair of low-slung black jeans that perfectly showed off the muscular chest her face had spent half the night pressed against, and the yearning that had kept her awake for hours hit her with its full force.

The hint of a smile played on his mouth. 'What does a man do for coffee here?'

Her certainty that he could sense or see the effect he was having on her sent a flush of heat thrashing through her, and she had to clear her throat to speak. 'There's a pot made in the kitchen.' Trying not to cringe at the overt croak in her voice, she straightened her back and added, 'If you're hungry, press three on any landline and it will connect you to the palace kitchen. The chefs will make you anything you want.'

The only thing I want is you, Gabriel thought.

Although the angle of Alessia's armchair hid much of her from his sight, the little he could see was enough to make his chest tighten and his pulses surge. That his appearance had such a visible effect on her only heightened the sensations, and he ground his feet into the carpet and filled his lungs slowly before speaking again. 'Have you eaten?'

She tucked a strand of her silky dark hair behind an ear. 'Not yet. I'll order something later, but please, don't wait for me. The chefs are used to preparing dishes any time of the day or night.'

'I'll wait until you eat. Did you want another coffee?'

'No, thank you. I'm limiting myself to one a day.' She pressed her belly as explanation.

The tightness in his chest loosened and expanded, and he nodded his understanding. 'Can I get you anything else?'

'No. But thank you.'

Gabriel nodded again and turned down the corridor that led to the kitchen. The aroma of freshly ground coffee greeted him, and he poured himself a cup and added a heaped spoonful of sugar while taking a moment to gather himself together.

He'd fallen asleep surprisingly easily considering everything, but had woken with a weighty feeling in the pit of his stomach. He'd felt Alessia's absence from the bed at the same moment everything that had occurred between them on their wedding night had flashed through his mind. The weighty feeling had spread to his chest as, for the first time, he had an insight into how she must have felt that morning to find him gone.

Why had he never allowed himself to think of that before? He didn't have the answer. He'd always acknowledged to himself that his behaviour that morning had been abhorrent but all the justifications he'd heaped on himself had smothered his ability to think of how it must have been for Alessia.

He wished he could say that she was overreacting. One-night stands happened all the time. Alessia wasn't his first and, princess though she was, she was a modern woman so he doubted he was hers either—although her reaction to his question about monogamy and his reaction to that reaction told him previous relationships were a subject best avoided between them—but what they'd shared did *not* happen all the time. The chemistry between them had been off the charts.

It still was.

That Alessia refused to act on the chemistry was a situation of his own making. It was on him to make things right.

Carrying his coffee back to the main living area, he took a seat on the armchair closest to her. Her eyes flickered up from the book she was reading, colour rising on her cheeks.

'I would like us to take a visit to the stables at some point this weekend,' he said. 'We need to start thinking about how we want it to be renovated.'

'Sure.' She closed her book. 'I'll ask Ena—my private secretary—to find the keys for us. She'll be at her desk in an hour.'

'What about your domestic staff? What time do they start?' All the times he'd been at the castle, whatever the time, the stone walls had contained a hive of activity, worker bees efficiently getting on with their individual tasks, unobtrusive but always in the background.

'This is an official day off for me so they won't come until I call for them.'

'Do you have many free days?'

'My weekends are normally free, but sometimes I have engagements to attend, sometimes issues crop up that need to be dealt with—my role within the family isn't something I can turn on and off. None of us can.'

'How many engagements do you go to each week?'

'It varies.'

'What do you like to do in your free time?'

Alessia studied him warily before answering. All this talk about engagements made her think there was a real irony in Gabriel making the effort to engage with her as he was currently doing when she'd been the driving force on their night together, forcing him to engage in conversation with her. She remembered thinking that he didn't seem to like her. Clearly he'd wanted her but that was physical desire. It was the liking of *her*, her personality, she'd had doubts about. She still had them. For all his excuses about ghosting her, she couldn't help but think that if he'd liked her more, he would have returned her call.

She wished she didn't feel so resentful that he was only making this effort to engage and get to know her now as part of his efforts to build trust between them so they could have some kind of harmony in their marriage rather than because he wanted to know her for her own sake as she'd so longed to know him.

But there was no point thinking like this. She had to think of their marriage as being like her headmistress's proverbial bed and imagine it having a lumpy mattress. Alessia had no choice but to lie on it and play her part in flattening those lumps, and as she thought that, she was helpless to stop the image of them naked, entwined together on a real bed, and helpless to stop another wave of longing.

She expelled a slow breath and forced herself to answer. 'Sometimes I see friends. Sometimes I go shopping. Sometimes I'll spend a whole day reading or watching boxsets. It depends.' And then, because she knew she *had* to get over her resentment and find a way to deal with her hurt otherwise she'd be condemning them both to a lifetime of misery, added, 'What about you? What do you do on your days off?'

'I don't take many days off but when I have free time I like to unwind with a bourbon and a good film or a book.' He nodded at the book on her lap. 'What are you reading?'

Bracing herself for a cutting comment, Alessia showed him the cover. It was a historical romance, the kind of book her brothers had always laughed at her for enjoying.

Gabriel didn't seem to find anything amusing about her literary choice, pulling a musing face and asking, 'Any good?'

'So far.'

'Do you read only historical books?'

'I'll read anything.'

'Me too, although I tend to lean towards thrillers and biographies. I have a library at my home in Madrid. I'm sure you'll find something on the shelves you'll enjoy.'

Caution made her reluctant to jump to conclusions. 'Does that mean you're going to let me come with you?'

'I don't remember you giving me any choice in the matter,' he said dryly. 'But you're right, I didn't make it a precondition of our marriage and, having thought about it, it would be good for you to see the place I call home. All I ask is that your presence there is kept from the press. I am serious about my privacy, Alessia, and would like any press intrusion to be kept to an absolute minimum.'

So he didn't actually want her to come. Like this whole conversation, it was a sop to her.

She lifted her chin, determined not to show the hurt. 'Our press office only notifies the press about my movements for official engagements so that won't be a problem.'

'Good.'

'But if it does become a problem, I'm sure you'll be glad to know I'll only be able to travel with you next week. After that, I'm afraid my engagement diary's full, so you will get your wish to have me out of your hair Mondays to Fridays after all. Now, if you'll excuse me, I'm going to do my dance exercises and take a shower.' Already regretting the flash of bitterness she'd had no control over, Alessia rose from her chair and, in a softer tone, added, 'Order yourself some breakfast—please, don't go hungry on my account.'

Before she could walk away, though, he said, 'Have you heard of Monica Binoche?'

She turned her face back to him. 'The French actress?' Monica Binoche was the actress Marcelo had had a crush on in his early teenage years. Alessia distinctly remembered him asking their father if she could be invited to castle so he could meet her, and their father laughing and replying with something along the lines of 'If only.'

'Yes.' Gabriel took a deep breath, and watched her reaction closely as he said, 'She's my mother.'

CHAPTER NINE

ALESSIA'S MOUTH DROPPED OPEN, her eyes widening in shock.

'Monica Binoche is my mother and the reason I value my privacy so highly,' Gabriel explained evenly. 'My father was Pedro Gonzalez. You probably haven't heard of him but he was a well-respected acting agent. He died in his sleep five years ago. Heart failure.'

She sat back on her armchair, her face expressing nothing but compassion. 'That's awful. I'm so sorry.'

He smiled grimly. 'Thank you. It was not unexpected. He was seventy-eight and not in good health. I loved him, I miss him, but it's my mother I want to talk to you about.'

He'd never discussed either of his parents with anyone but his sister in his entire adult life other than in generic terms, but Alessia wanted to know who he was and why, and until she knew, she would never trust him. He could see too that she deserved to know his past so she could understand that his refusal to play the royal media game was not anything personal or a slight against her or her family.

'There is nothing my mother enjoys more than attention,' he said. 'It's what feeds her. As children, my sister and I were accessories to her. I don't mean to paint her as a bad mother—she tried her best—but she thought nothing of using Mariella and I as props for photo opportunities. For my mother, it's a terrible day if she leaves the house and there isn't a swarm of paparazzi waiting on the doorstep. I used to have to fight my way through them just to go to school. On quiet celebrity news days, they would sometimes wait outside the school gate for us.'

'But I thought France had strict privacy laws?'

'It does. Much stricter than what you have here in Ceres. What you're not taking into consideration is that my mother encouraged it. She wanted her privacy invaded. It's how she found validation—how she still finds it.'

'That must have been rough for you,' she said softly.

'It was infuriating. And it was the reason I didn't invite her to our wedding. She hasn't used me as an accessory in twenty years, not since I gave her the ultimatum, but I didn't want to put temptation in her way. Inviting her to a royal wedding, no matter how small it was, and expecting her not to put it on her social media feeds would be like locking a recovering alcoholic in a fully stocked English pub.'

Her eyes hadn't left his face since he'd started his explanation. 'What was the ultimatum you gave her?'

'That either she stopped using Mariella and me as props for her ego or we'd move in full-time with our father.' He gave a wry smile. 'See? She does love us in her own way because it all stopped right then.'

'Your parents divorced?'

'They separated when I was twelve.'

'Because of your mother's behaviour?'

He laughed. 'His behaviour wasn't much better. My father was her agent and credited himself with ensuring her big break. As her fame grew, his jealousy grew and he started having affairs, I think to validate himself and to humiliate her. He wasn't very discreet about it. He was thirty years older than her screwing around like a teenager. She was an aging ingenue terrified of the aging process and being thought irrelevant. It was a toxic combination that eventually turned into warfare between them. Both of them blamed the other for the destruction of their marriage and both refused to move out of the marital home or give an inch on custody of me and Mariella. Neither of them was prepared to give an inch on anything.'

Alessia's head was reeling. Whatever could be said about her own childhood and upbringing, the security of her parents' marriage had never been in doubt. She'd rarely heard them exchange a cross word. 'That must have been tough to live with.'

'It was. They both tried hard to be good parents to us but there were a few years when they were too wrapped up in their mutual loathing to notice the damage they were doing.'

'What made them see sense?'

'Me.'

'You?'

He inclined his head. 'I'd listened to so many of their screaming matches that I knew exactly what their issues with each other were and what they both wanted, so I sat them down individually and brokered peace negotiations.'

'You did? When you were *twelve*?' At twelve, the only brokering Alessia had done was when trying, unsuccessfully, to negotiate the right to read books with rather more salacious material than her Enid Blyton's.

'I was fourteen at this point. It took a couple of weeks of negotiating between them but eventually they agreed to sell the house and split the profits.' He flashed a quick grin. 'That way, neither of them "won." I also got them to agree to buy a new home each within a mile of mine and Mariella's school, and drew up a custody plan that gave them equal access to us.'

'How did that work?'

'There's fifty-two weeks in a year. We spent twenty-six with each parent, with each year carefully planned to cater for their individual work schedules. We alternated Christmases and birthdays.'

'A fair compromise to them both,' she mused dubiously.

'Exactly. Neither won. Neither lost.'

'What about you and your sister, though? Wasn't it hard carving up your time between them and never being settled in one home?'

'That brought its own challenges but it was easier than living in a war zone. I also had it written into the contracts that they were forbidden from bad-mouthing each other to us.'

She rubbed the back of her head. 'You were one mature teenager.'

'My mother used to say I was born serious.'

Her eyes were searching. 'Do you agree with her? Or was it circumstances that made you that way?'

He considered this. 'A combination of both, perhaps. The circumstances certainly made me the man I am today. Pursuing a career in diplomacy felt natural after negotiating their divorce and custody arrangements.'

'And the circumstances gave you a pathological loathing of the press?' And, Alessia suspected, a loathing for conflict and a need to always be firmly in control of himself and his surroundings.

He nodded. 'I changed my surname legally when I turned eighteen—my father's name isn't as well-known as my mother's but their marriage made him a celebrity in his own right. I value my privacy because I never had it when I was a child.'

'And now you've married a princess,' she said quietly, now understanding why he was so adamant in his refusal to be a 'proper' royal. 'A life you never wanted.'

He shifted forwards in his seat and stared deep into her eyes. 'I married *you*, Alessia, and I need you to understand that though I don't want the princess, I do want the woman. I want *you*.'

So many emotions filled her at the sincerely delivered words that she couldn't even begin to dissect them. It frightened her how desperately she longed to believe him, believe that he did want her, but even that longing was fraught because she didn't know if he meant he wanted her, body, heart and soul, or just the first part, and she couldn't bring herself to ask because she didn't know if she'd be able to take the answer.

She was saved from her tortured thoughts by the ringing of the bell and the simultaneous trilling of both their phones, but there was no relief in the interruption, only a plunge in her heart as she immediately understood what it meant. It meant the media circus Gabriel so despised and had spent his adult life avoiding had come for him.

She closed her eyes briefly and sighed. 'I think the announcement of our marriage has just gone out.'

It took three days before Gabriel and Alessia were able to inspect the place that was going to be their marital home. Gabriel had expected news of their marriage to cause a sensation but, when it broke, sensation was an understatement. The east side of the castle, the half open to tourists, was so besieged by press that it had to close to visitors. The rotors of helicopters ignoring the no-fly zone above the castle was a constant noise for hours until the Ceres military put a stop to their illegality. Gabriel's phones, business and personal, didn't stop ringing. It seemed that everyone he'd ever been acquainted with felt the need to call and congratulate him. Once the press obtained his number, he'd had enough and turned it off, but not before his mother, furious not to have been invited to the wedding, cried and wailed down the phone like the good actress she was for an hour before ringing off so she could call his sister, who'd stayed for the wedding night in the castle's guest quarters, and sob theatrically down the phone to her. Alessia's phone rang non-stop too, her private secretary and other clerical staff rushing in and out of their quarters with updates and messages, the usual buzz of activity within the castle walls having turned into a loud hum.

He'd not needed to step foot out of the castle grounds to feel the impact of the circus.

Gabriel knew the stables, which had once housed hundreds of horses, had initially been converted for the reigning queen's mother to live in, but it was still much, *much* bigger than he'd expected. U-shaped with a bell tower in its centre, it was built with the same sand-coloured stone as the rest of the castle, its roof the same terracotta hue that topped the castle's turrets, and was situated close to the side of the castle where the Berruti family lived and worked but far enough from it to feel entirely separate. Even before Alessia unlocked the grand front door, he knew this would make the perfect home for them.

And then he stepped inside and knew it would

only make the perfect home if the entire thing was stripped to bare walls and started again. The high-ceilinged reception room they'd stepped into glowered—there was no other word for it—with faded glamour. It was a glamour that would have held no appeal even if it wasn't faded. Nothing had been done to mitigate the lack of natural light coming in from the small windows. If anything, the décor had been chosen to enhance the shadows. Even the exquisite paintings that lined the reception walls seemed to have been selected for the menace they exuded, and he recognised a variation of Judith with the severed head of Holofernes.

Not wanting to insult Alessia, he kept his initial impression to himself and indicated the tall archway in front of them. 'Do you want to lead the way?'

Having been staring wordlessly at a painting of the medusa turning naked men into stone, Alessia faced him, her brow creased in confusion.

'Do you want to give me the grand tour?' he elaborated.

'But I can't—I've never been in here before.'

He gazed into her velvet eyes, convinced she was joking. 'You never visited your grandmother, who lived on the same estate as you? But I thought she only died eight years ago?'

'She did but she was a miserable witch who hated people and *really* hated children.'

'That explains the décor then,' he murmured.

A glint of humour flickered over her face and then she put a hand to her mouth and giggled. 'It's *awful*, isn't it?' She shook her head, her giggles turning into a peal of laughter. 'Marcelo told me it was bad but I never guessed it was this bad. I'm glad she never let me visit. This would have given me nightmares.'

The weight in his chest lifting at the sight of Alessia with glee etched over her beautiful face and the sound of her husky laughter ringing in his ears, Gabriel couldn't stop his own amusement escaping. In his laughter was a huge dose of relief.

Since the statement had been released, Alessia had carried herself with a careful deportment around him. She was unerringly polite but meticulous about not touching him... Not until they went to bed. The moment the light went out, she would wrap her arms around him under the bedsheets and press her face to his bare chest just as they'd done on their wedding night. But, as on their wedding night, she held herself rigidly, barely drawing a breath. He could feel the fight she was waging with herself, the rapid beats of her heart a pulse against his skin, but knew better than to do anything more than hold her. As painful as it was to accept, he'd hurt her deeply. He couldn't wipe that hurt out with confidences about his childhood. She needed to learn to trust him.

And so he would lie there with her, under the sheets, her beautiful body entwined with his, holding himself back from even stroking her hair, hardly able to breathe himself with the pain of his desire cramping his lungs, having to push out the memories of the first time they'd laid entwined, both naked, fitting together like a jigsaw. When he did manage to push aside images that only fired the desire he was having to suppress, his thoughts never strayed from her. The more time he spent with her, the greater his thirst to know everything there was to know about the woman behind the always smiling, dutiful princess who so rarely smiled for him.

So to see her now, her face alight with the joy of shared absurdity, her laughter still filling his senses...

'Do you think she put these paintings here to repel people from going any further than the front door?' he asked, ramming his hands into his pockets to stop them from reaching for her.

God knew how badly he longed to reach for her.

'I'd put money on it.'

'She hated people that much?'

'More.'

'How on earth did she cope with royal life if she hated people?'

'By drinking copious amounts of gin. As soon as my mother took the throne after my grandfather's death, my grandmother announced she never wanted to endure another royal engagement or the company of another human ever again and insisted the stables be converted into a home for her. When she moved in she demanded—in all seriousness—that her new household be staffed only by mutes.' But relating this only set Alessia's laughter off again as the ridiculousness of her grandmother's behaviour really hit home, which in turn set Gabriel's laughter off again too.

Feeling lighter than she'd done in a long time—it *was* true that laughter was good for the soul—Alessia wiped the tears from her eyes. 'Come on,' she said, 'let's go and see if we can find her potion room.'

The pair of them were still sniggering when they went under the arch and entered a rectangular room with cantilevered stairs ascending from the centre. The posts at the bottom of each gold railing were topped with a gargoyle's head.

'They can go,' Alessia said, shuddering at the ugly things.

'The whole lot can go. Shall we start from the top or the bottom?'

'Let's start at the top and then we can save the dungeon for a treat at the end of it all.'

He laughed again.

He had a great laugh, she thought dreamily, a great rumble that came from deep inside him and was expelled with the whole of his body. When he laughed... Just as when he smiled, creases appeared around his eyes, deep lines grooving along the sides his mouth... Just as when he smiled, it did something to her.

She hadn't laughed like that with anyone since her school days.

'Did you have much to do with her?' he asked.

'Not really, thank God. I was six when my grandfather died so I don't have many solid memories of her before that. She would terrorise us at Christmas, Easter and family birthdays when my mother forced her to join us for celebration meals but that was the extent of my interaction with her...apart from the time when Marcelo and I were playing tennis and the ball went into what was considered to be her garden, and she chased me off like I was trespasser.'

Stepping through the first door they came to on the landing, Alessia was relieved that the worst thing about the bedroom was the blood-red wallpaper. It was replicated in all the other rooms, including the master bedroom. As she peered into the adjoining dressing room, a walled mirror reflected the four-poster bed back at her and her heart jolted to know that this suite would be the room she would share with Gabriel for the rest of her life, and as she thought this, he appeared in the reflection and their eyes met.

He stood stock-still.

The force of the jolt her heart made this time almost punched it out of her.

For a long moment, they did nothing but stare at each other. The longer she gazed at his reflection, the more the deep reds and shadows of the room reflected in the angles of his handsome face and the black clothes he wore, giving him a vampiric quality that sent a thrill rushing through her veins and dissolved the lingering humour that had bound them together in a way she had never expected.

She wanted him so badly…

Oh, why was she still resisting? Gabriel was her husband and she was his wife and that meant something.

Because you're still frightened.

Gabriel's confiding in her about his childhood and his parents' divorce had helped Alessia understand him better but it hadn't changed the deep-rooted instinct to protect herself. If anything it had made it stronger because sympathy and empathy had softened her even more towards him.

He took a step towards her.

A pulse throbbed deep in her pelvis.

The battle between her head, her heart and her body, between the princess and the woman, had been an impossible war to manage since they'd agreed to marry.

With each hour that passed, her longing for him grew stronger. When the lights went out, her weakness for him almost gobbled her up, and she would lay enveloped in his arms, breathing in his glorious scent, desire filling her from the roots of her hair to the tips of her toes, torturing herself; torturing them both because she could feel Gabriel's suppressed desire as deeply as she felt her own, which only made things worse.

She was torturing them both.

He took another step closer.

Blood roared in her head.

One more step.

She blinked and there he was, right behind her, towering over her just like a vampire from the films.

The beats of her heart tripled in an instant.

Not an inch of his body touched hers but he stood close enough for her skin to tingle with sensation.

'I don't know about you,' he murmured, 'but I think we should knock through the adjoining room. Create another dressing room and double the size of the bathroom.'

It was only when Alessia snatched a breath to answer that she realised she'd been holding it. 'That... Sorry, what did you say?'

His lips twitched but those amazing kaleidoscopic eyes didn't leave hers. He placed his mouth to the back of her ear. 'That we should double the size of our bathroom.'

His mouth didn't make contact but his breath did. It danced through her hair and over her lobe, and then entered her skin like a pulse of electricity that almost knocked her off her feet.

His eyes glimmered. 'Let's see what delights the ground floor has for us.' And then he turned and strolled out of the dressing room as if nothing had just passed between them.

It took a few beats for Alessia to pull her weak legs together.

Where she had to hold the banister to support her wobbly frame, Gabriel sauntered down the stairs with such nonchalance that she wondered if she'd just imagined the hooded pulse in his eyes and the sensuality in his voice.

And then he reached the bottom of the stairs and turned his gaze back to her, and she saw it again. His unashamed hunger for her.

CHAPTER TEN

LATER THAT EVENING, having showered and changed for dinner, Alessia found Gabriel in the dining room. The table had been set for their meal but he was sat at the other end surrounded by sheets of paper.

He looked up as she entered the room. His gaze flickered over her and she caught again that flash of desire as another smile that creased his eyes lit his handsome face.

The longing that had caught her in her grandmother's dressing room flooded her limbs again, weakening them, and it took a beat before she could close the door and cross the room to stand beside him.

'What are you doing?' she asked, glad that her voice, at least, still sounded normal. The rest of her had felt decidedly abnormal since her grandmother's dressing room, like electricity had replaced the blood in her veins. She'd been aware of every movement and every sensation her body made, from the lace knickers she'd pulled up her legs and over her thighs, to the lipstick she'd held between her fingers and applied to lips that tingled, to the perfume she'd dabbed to the pulses on her neck and wrists. Every whisper of sound she heard outside the bedroom had made her heart leap.

It was pounding now, as hard as she'd ever known it.

Why was she standing so close to him?

He looked her up and down again, this time much more slowly. His nostrils flared. 'Getting some ideas down about what we can do with the stables while the ideas are fresh in my mind. I'd like to have my office facing the garden on the ground floor.'

Her arm brushing against his, Alessia peered at the sheets. He'd sketched the floor plan in remarkable detail. How could he remember it so clearly? she wondered, awed too at how well he'd recalled the proportions of each room.

Why this should make her heart swell and ripple even more she couldn't begin to guess.

And why she'd leaned so close into him she couldn't begin to guess either.

Trying hard to cover the emotions thrashing through her, Alessia shifted away from him then turned round so her back was to the table, raised herself onto her toes and used her hands as purchase to lift herself onto it.

They were almost eye level.

If she moved her foot an inch to the left, it would brush against the calf of his leg.

'You are keen to get out of the castle,' she managed to tease. Or tried. She couldn't seem to breathe properly.

His eyes locked onto hers. 'I don't like my business belonging to everyone else.'

Somewhere in the dim recess of her mind, she understood what he meant. The family's personal wing of the castle was busy. Alessia had her own offices but they tended to blur with her private quarters, clerical as well as domestic staff in and out, her family's clerical staff often popping in to ask her questions or get her input. Everything was fluid, communication between the family's respective teams high, everyone working and pulling together for the same aim—the monarchy's success.

Right then, she couldn't have cared less about the monarchy's success. Right then, the only thing Alessia could focus on was the hooded desire flowing from Gabriel's eyes, entwining with the buzz in her veins, and the feel of his calf beneath her toes...

Large hands gripped the bottom of her thighs just above the knees. Jaw clenched, Gabriel brought his face close to hers and bore his gaze into her. 'What are you doing, Lessie?'

'I don't know,' she whispered, staring right back at him.

Had *she* kicked her shoes off so she could rub her toes against his leg?

Her head was swimming. She knew she should push his hands away but the sensations and heat licking her from the outside in were too strong. Erotic fantasies were filling her, a yearn for Gabriel's strong fingers to dip below the hem of her white, floaty skirt and slide up her thighs to where the heat throbbed the most.

Another image filled her: Gabriel lifting the strawberry-coloured bandeau top she'd paired the skirt with over her breasts and taking her nipples into his mouth.

Was that why she'd chosen to wear a top that needed no bra? she wondered hazily.

'Alessia, talk to me.'

His voice was thick, and as she gazed helplessly into his eyes, the pupils swirled and pulsed into black holes she could feel herself being pulled into.

'I... I don't want to talk,' she whispered hoarsely, unable to stop herself falling into the limitless depths.

Gabriel tightened his grip on Alessia's thighs and tried his damnedest to tighten his control.

He could feel her desire with all of his senses, feeding the thick arousal that had become a living part of him, unleashing unbound since she'd walked into the dining room, as beautiful and as sexy a sight as he had ever seen. The heat of her quivering skin burned into his flesh, its scent sinking into his airwaves. Hunger, pure, unfiltered, flashed from her melting velvet eyes into his. It was there too in the breathless pitch of her husky voice. Smouldering.

God, he wanted her, with every fibre of his being, but he would not be the one to make the first move. It had to come from her.

He drew his face even closer to hers and forced the words out. 'Alessia, what do you want?'

Her hands suddenly clasped his cheeks. Her breaths coming in short, ragged bursts, the minty taste of her warm breath flowed into his senses, making him grip even tighter as desire throbbed and burned its way relentlessly through him.

It was the control she could see him hanging onto by a thread that unlocked the last of Alessia's mental chain. She could feel Gabriel's hunger for her as deeply as she felt her own but he chose to starve than do anything without her explicit, wholehearted consent because he knew the mental agonies she'd been going through and, more importantly, he understood them.

He would rather put himself through the agony of denial than risk hurting her again, and her heart filled with such emotion it felt like it could burst out of her.

It was impossible to secure her heart against him. *Impossible.* Her heart and her body were intricately linked when it came to Gabriel and if she couldn't give one without the other then so be it. She'd committed herself to him for life, and the feelings he evoked in her were never going to subside.

What was the point in fighting the woman inside her any longer?

She was crazy for him.

Gazing deep into his eyes, she whispered, 'I want you.'

He breathed in deeply and shuddered.

'I want you,' she repeated, and then she could hold back no more and, digging the tips of her fingers into his cheeks, she kissed him with every ounce of the passion she'd been denying them.

The groan that came with his response could have been a roar.

In seconds he was off his seat, holding her tightly to him and kissing her back with a ferocity that sent her head spinning.

As if he'd looked inside her head and read her fantasies, long fingers dipped under her skirt and dragged up her thigh, and round to clasp her bottom.

Arms entwined around his neck, she closed off the world and sank into her senses…senses which were receptacles for Gabriel, for his taste, his touch… All of him.

Lips moving together, tongues duelling, fingers scraped over flesh and ripped and pulled at the intrusive fabric separating them. Grabbing his shirt to loosen it, she fumbled with the buttons before giving up and slipping her hand beneath it, flattening her palm against his hard abdomen, thrilling at the heat of his skin, the soft hair covering the smoothness. Up her hands splayed, ruching his shirt as her fingers rose until he broke the connection of their mouths to undo the top few buttons himself and yank it over his head.

Gabriel would not have believed it possible for his arousal to deepen any further but then he saw the drugged ringing of Alessia's eyes as she wantonly grazed her stare over his chest. When she put her mouth to his nipple and scraped her nails over his back, the charge that fired through his veins…

Never had he responded with such violent fever…

Apart from with Alessia.

Time had dimmed the intensity of the pleasure they'd shared that night but now, with her rosebud lips worshipping him and her hands stroking and scraping over his burning flesh, he knew that dimming had been an essential defence mechanism in him because the force of his desire was too savage and greedy to be unleashed again.

But it was unleashed now. Unleashed and frenzied and as essential as the air he breathed. *She* was as essential to him as the air he breathed, and he wanted to taste every part of her and consume her into his being.

Clasping her hair he used every ounce of his control to gently pull her head back.

Those drugged velvet eyes met his. Colour slashed her cheeks, her lips, lipstick kissed off, the darkest he'd ever seen them. He kissed them again. Hard. Thoroughly. And then he buried his mouth into her neck and pressed her down so she was laid on the table, her legs hooked around his waist, and set about consuming her.

Alessia was lost in a world of delirious pleasure. Her flesh burned and, deep inside her, pulses were converging and thickening, an urgency building that Gabriel's slavish assault only added fuel to. Her bandeau top yanked down, she cried out when his hot mouth covered her breast: sucking, biting, licking, sending her spinning until she cried out again and arched her back when he moved to the other.

The assault of his mouth continued down to her belly, his hands clasping her skirt and pushing it up to her hips. Raising his face to look at her with hooded, passion-ridden eyes, he bared his teeth with a growl and clasped her knickers. With another growl, he tugged them down her thighs and off her legs, and in moments he was on his knees with his face buried in the most feminine part of her.

This was a pleasure like no other, an all-consuming barrage of stimulation, and, closing her eyes tightly, Alessia lost herself in the flames.

The musky scent and taste of Alessia's swollen sex was the most potent aphrodisiac to Gabriel's senses. She opened herself to him like a flower in full bloom, her thighs around his neck, and with a greed he'd never known he possessed, he devoured the sweet nectar of her desire, moving his tongue rhythmically over the core of her pleasure until she stiffened beneath him and then, with shudders that rippled through her entire body, and the heels of her feet kicking him, cried her pleasure in one long, continuous moan.

Close to losing his head with the strength of his arousal, Gabriel only just managed to hold onto his control until the shudders wracking her had subsided and her moans turned into a breathless sigh of fulfilment.

Rising back to his feet, he gazed down at her pleasure-saturated face and then he could hold on no more. Working quickly at his trousers, he tugged them down with his underwear and finally let his erection spring free. The urgency to be inside her had him gripping her hips so her bottom was at the edge of the table, and then he guided himself to the place he most desperately wanted to be. And then with one long drive, he buried himself deep inside her slick tightness.

It was Gabriel's groan as he drove himself inside her that added a spark to the kindling of Alessia's spent desire. Her climax had been so powerful it had sapped all the energy that had driven her to that most glorious of peaks. It was the way his glazed eyes fixed on her as he thrust into her a second time that added fuel to the steadily increasing heat. And it was when he raised her thighs for deeper penetration and his groin rubbed against her still-throbbing nub that the flames caught all over again.

Oh, my God…

It wasn't Gabriel making love to her. It was an animal who pinned her hands to the sides of her head and laced his fingers through hers, an animal who drove so hard and so furiously into her, feeding the flames of her desire… And yet Gabriel *was* there too. He was there, behind those glazed eyes.

This animal…this beast…this was Gabriel in all his raw beauty.

She could see him. And he could see her. See right to her core.

Alessia was so taken by the animalistic beauty of the man making love to her with such ferocious passion that she was hardly conscious of her second climax building inside her until it exploded like a pulsating firework that throbbed and sparkled through her entire being and carried her away to the stars.

It was the ringing of the bell that brought Alessia crashing back down to earth.

Eyes flying open, they locked onto Gabriel's. The dazed expression she found in them perfectly matched what she was feeling inside.

'That's our dinner,' she whispered.

His brow creased as if he'd never heard of dinner before. The surround of his mouth was smeared red with her lipstick.

She laughed for absolutely no discernible reason. Maybe she was delirious? She didn't care. She felt like she could spring onto a cloud and float into the stratosphere. 'The staff will be bringing our dinner in at any second.'

Firm lips crushed against hers, teeth capturing her bottom lip as he pulled away from her with a growl.

Hastily, they scrambled to make themselves presentable. Alessia had a much easier time of it seeing as she still had her skirt and top on, and she tried to help Gabriel button his shirt but it buttoned differently to what she was used to and she was more a hindrance than a help.

She opened the dining room door and took her seat exactly ten seconds before the servers arrived.

Three days later, the paparazzi were waiting in their usual spot outside the castle grounds. That they pursued them all the way to the airfield where Gabriel's jet awaited them reinforced the impact the release of the wedding statement had had. The royal family always travelled in official cars and were always followed, but the times Gabriel had come and gone from the castle before had evoked only cursory interest from the vultures. Now, even though they were in the back of a non-official car, the paparazzi were clearly taking no chances that their cash cow might be inside it.

When they arrived at his home a few miles north of Madrid a few hours later, his heart sank to find another pack of paparazzi staked outside his estate. Fortunately, they preferred to move out of the way than get run over by his driver.

'I'm sorry,' Alessia whispered, squeezing his hand.

He gave a rueful smile. 'You have nothing to be sorry for. They will get bored soon.'

'I'll only be encroaching your space for a few days. Once I'm back home, they'll leave you alone here.'

His next smile was grim. Bringing her hand to his mouth, he kissed it and inhaled heavily. Alessia's birth and the resultant attention it brought her was not her fault. She played the media game because it went hand in glove with her role but she didn't court publicity for personal vanity like his mother did. He should never have made her feel bad for something that was beyond her control.

'You are my wife and what's mine is yours, which means this is your home too,' he told her seriously. 'Don't ever think you're not wanted here or not wanted by me.'

Her eyes held his. Her chest rising as slowly as the smile on her face, she placed a palm to his cheek and a dreamy kiss to his mouth. 'Thank you,' she said when she pulled her mouth away. 'I needed to hear that.'

He kissed her. 'And I needed to say it.'

It astounded him how quickly things could change. Opinions. Feelings. Desires.

Before their wedding a week ago, the thought of Alessia in his home had made his chest tight. Now, it was knowing that on Sunday she would fly back to Ceres without him that made it tighten.

Before their wedding, he'd known he wanted to be a good husband and a good father but they had been driven by the circumstances of their child's conception. His own father had been a good father—those two years of warfare with his mother not withstanding—and Gabriel wanted to give the same feeling of love and security to his own child. As he knew how damaging it could be for a child to witness parents at war, he knew the best way to achieve love and security for his child was by being a good husband.

The more time he'd spent with Alessia and the more he'd got to know the woman behind the princess mask, though, the more he wanted to be a good husband for her sake too. He wanted to make her happy for her own sake. Nothing made his heart lighter than to see her smile and hear her laugh.

Was he falling in love with her? It was a question he'd asked himself more and more since they'd become lovers.

Three days, that's all it had been. Three days of hedonistic bliss that had blown his mind, but it had been a hedonism that had to be rationed to the evenings and nights. Here, in his Madrid home, there was nothing to stop them spending their entire days and nights making love, and he imagined all the places they could...

'Oh, my, your *house*!'

For the first time in three days, Alessia found her attention grabbed by something that wasn't entirely Gabriel. They'd driven past the security gates and now she was trying to stop her mouth gaping open. Surrounded by high, thick trees for privacy, white-edged cubes infilled with glass were cleverly 'stacked' to create a postmodern structure like nothing she'd seen before. Where the castle her family had called home for five hundred years was believed to have had the first wing built around a thousand years ago, this home could be set a thousand years into the future.

Driven into a subterranean car park with a fleet of gleaming supercars lined up, a glass elevator took them up to the next level. A butler was there to greet them. Other than shaking his hand at the introduction, Alessia was still too dazed about the futuristic world she'd just landed in to summon her Spanish and follow the conversation.

'Are you okay?' Gabriel asked, an amused smile on his face, once the butler had left them in a vast white living area that looked as if it would repel dust from fifty paces.

She shook her head, noticing an abstract bronze sculpture taller than Gabriel that she was sure was the one that had made the news earlier in the year by breaking records when it had been sold at auction. 'I'm just trying to take everything in. I've never seen anything like your home before...' Movement caught her eye and she turned her head and did a double take. 'Is that a *waterfall*?'

She hurried over to the wall of windows the water was pouring down outside of, but before she'd reached it, the glass began to slide open. Still shaking her head, she stepped out into a vast outdoor area with plentiful seating and plentiful sun loungers that lined a long swimming pool the waterfall was falling into. Craning her neck, she gave a squeal to find there was another glass swimming pool jutting out over her.

'It's a trio of infinity pools,' Gabriel explained, standing beside her. 'The one above us extends from the private balcony in our bedroom.'

Walking to the edge of the decking area, Alessia looked down over the glass perimeter railing and saw the third swimming pool.

'That one extends from the spa,' Gabriel told her. 'There's an indoor one too, for when the weather is cooler.'

'Amazing,' she breathed, still craning her neck up and down to take the three infinity pools in. The top one was the shortest and narrowest, the bottom the longest and widest, which she guessed meant the swimmer could swim in the sun or the shade on the lower two levels. 'I've spent twenty-three years begging my parents to have an outdoor swimming pool put in but they always say no because they fear it will ruin the picture-perfect architecture of the castle. And you've got three!'

'I like to swim.'

Now she gave him all of her attention and happily let her gaze soak him in. 'I can tell.' It felt amazing to be able to do that, to let her eyes run over him whenever she wanted and say whatever was on her mind which, admittedly, had mostly been sex these last few days. It felt even more amazing that the heady feelings that had become such an intrinsic part of her were reciprocated. Alessia had fallen headfirst into lust with her own husband and it was the best feeling in the world. 'I wish you'd told me. I'd have brought a swimming costume with me.'

A lascivious gleam appeared in his eyes. 'Who needs a swimming costume when we have all this privacy?'

The mere thought made her legs go weak. 'What about your staff?' she asked, suddenly breathless.

'All chores are done in the morning. Gregor— the butler—has a self-contained apartment at the back of the kitchen that he shares with the chefs. They don't come into the main house unless I call for them.' He dipped his head and ran his tongue over the rim of her ear. 'We have complete privacy.'

Stepping onto her tiptoes, she hooked her arms around his neck and rubbed her nose into his neck, filling her senses with the scent of his skin she was rapidly becoming addicted to. 'Complete privacy?'

He clasped her bottom and pulled her to him. 'I could take you now and no one would know.'

The outline of his excitement pressed against her abdomen almost flooded her with an urgent, sticky heat.

'Then do it,' she whispered, grazing her teeth into his skin. 'Take me now.'

Minutes later, lifted and pressed against the wall, her legs wrapped tightly around Gabriel's waist as he pounded into her and the pulses of a climax thickened inside her, Alessia dreamily wondered who this wanton woman who'd taken possession of her body was.

CHAPTER ELEVEN

LATER THAT AFTERNOON, when Gabriel had to drag himself away from making love to return some of the calls he'd neglected these last few days, Alessia took herself off exploring. There was so much to see! To her delight, by the time she'd finished exploring the villa's interior, Gabriel was sitting on the balcony having a drink.

'Your home is amazing,' she said, sinking into the seat next to his and twisting round to face him, unable to keep the smile from her face. As well as the huge living area, there was a smaller, cosier living room, a cinema room with sofas so deep and wide a party of people could sleep on them, a games room with a bar, other bars inside and out, a full-blown gym and a spa area bigger than the ground floor of her quarters. On top of all that were the eight bedrooms, eleven bathrooms, an upper floor entertainment area... It was endless! Oh, and Gabriel's office, which she'd only peeked into to blow a kiss at him as he was on a call. Oh, and there were two kitchens too, an indoor one which looked like it belonged on a spaceship, and an outdoor one. She hadn't even thought of exploring the grounds yet!

His eyes crinkled. 'I'm glad you like it,' he said as he poured her a glass of iced water and passed it to her.

She thought of the intricate sketches he'd made of the stables. 'Did you design it yourself?'

'I had the vision of what I wanted but an architect put those visions into something workable.'

'It's the polar opposite of the castle. And I can't get over how quiet it is.' She closed her eyes and listened hard. The castle was quiet at night but by day, it being a place of work as well as her family's home, it bustled with the burr of people's voices, footsteps and general movement.

Large hands wrapped around her ankles and pulled her feet onto his lap. 'How would you feel about us turning the stables into something like this?'

She met his stare with a mournful sigh that turned into a sigh of pleasure when he began rubbing his thumbs over her left calf. 'We'd never be allowed—can you imagine this there?

Much as I love this, it wouldn't fit in with the surroundings.'

'Agreed, but with some clever architecture, we can get a lot more light into it.'

Relaxing under his strong, manipulating fingers, she sighed again. 'That would be nice. I've never really considered how little natural light there is in the castle. I don't suppose anyone thought about natural light when they converted the stables either. They probably thought my grandmother's personality suited living in darkness,' she added with a cackle of laughter.

'I'm still astounded by what you told me of her.'

'That she hated being a royal?'

'No, I understand that; but that she seemed to hate people including her own family.'

'She didn't *seem* to, she *did* hate people.'

'Including your mother?'

'I suppose she must have loved her,' she said doubtfully. 'That's what mother's do, isn't it? Love their children.'

His fingers were still working their magic on her legs, now massaging the muscles of her right calf. 'You don't sound sure.'

'I'm not. It's not something we really talk about. I know my grandmother was hard on my mother but she was hard on everyone. She wasn't a woman for drying a child's tears, but she knew her duty and she was the perfect queen consort. She never let my grandfather down.'

'Not until he died.'

'But when he died my mother took the throne and my father became consort. My grandmother was relegated to dowager queen. She gave forty years of her life to our monarchy so I don't blame her for wanting to retire from the public eye and wanting some privacy away from the castle.'

'You sound like you admire her.'

'I do in a way. And I feel sorry for her too. She must have really hated being a royal to go to those extremes once her duty was over.'

'And how do you feel about being a royal?'

She shrugged. 'It's just my life, isn't it? I never had a choice about it and I don't know anything different.'

'Have you ever wished for anything different?'

'Not for a long time.'

'But you used to?'

She nodded. 'When I was small.' She gave a quick smile. '*Smaller.* I used to wish my mother wasn't queen.'

'Really?'

'Really. I was six when my grandfather died and everything changed overnight. My mother took the throne but it felt to me that the throne took her. Before, when she was just heir to the throne, she had many responsibilities but she was still able to be a mother to us…in her own way. She never bathed me or read me bedtime stories—my father read me stories, though; he was always much more present, even after she took the throne—but she did take an interest in me. I remember she wanted to see my school-work every day—this was when I had a govern-ess, before I went to boarding school—and see for herself that my handwriting was develop-ing properly and that I was learning my sums. Sometimes she made me read to her. Once she took the throne, that all stopped as she just didn't have the time. There were always more important things that needed her attention.'

'That must have been tough for you.'

'It was but it's how royal life works. In our royal family, in any case. Like your mother, she did the best she could. You have to remember who *her* mother was and the upbringing she'd had. She tried hard to create a more loving en-vironment for us in comparison to what she'd endured but there were times when it was very hard. The toughest time was when she went to Australia and New Zealand for two months with my father on a state tour. I was only seven, and it was the first time I'd been properly separated from them. I can't tell you how sick I felt from missing them. It was awful.'

'What would you do if you were asked to do the same thing?'

'Leave our child on a state tour?'

He nodded.

'I wouldn't do it.'

'Why not? They'd be at home with me so they wouldn't be separated from both their parents like you were.'

'But they'd still be without their mother. Do you remember what you said that day about putting our child's wellbeing before duty?'

His eyes narrowed slightly in remembrance.

'Gabriel... I have always put my duty to my family and the monarchy first, above everything. Everything I've ever done has always been with duty and what's expected of me at the forefront of my mind.'

'And wanting approval from your mother?' he asked astutely.

'Maybe... Probably...' She grimaced. 'When I was a child I lived for my mother's attention because I got so little of it.'

'Was being a good princess a way to get it?'

'Yes. She always noticed...complimented me on my deportment and manners.' She expelled a long breath. 'I'd never allowed myself to step out of line before, and it hurts my heart that she's still angry with me about my Dominic comments and the circumstances of the pregnancy. That night… It's the only time I have ever, *ever* put my own desires first. The consequences were so great I thought I would never be able to do anything like that again but I feel the changes happening inside me and think of the child growing in my womb and the *feelings* I have for it…' She shook her head, unable to put into words how strong the emotions were. 'Our child's emotional wellbeing is more important to me than anything. My feelings are the same as yours in that regard—when you've experienced pain, the last thing you want is to put your own child through the same, and I will not make them go through what I went through. If I was asked to go on tour, I would only accept if our child could come with me.'

His hands had stopped working their magic, his stare fixed on her. There was a long pause before his shoulders relaxed and he lightly said, 'But then I would be left at home alone.'

She swallowed. On Sunday night Alessia would fly back to the castle without him, returning to her dutiful place for a full week of royal engagements. Five whole days without him.

Until the stables renovations were complete, this would be her life, only seeing him at weekends. And those precious weekends would be interrupted too, she thought with an ache, when she attended one of her frequent weekend engagements.

Would things be better when they moved into the stables and Gabriel was in a position to work from home? She would still be a princess going about her duty without her prince by her side.

For the first time, the prince of her dreams had a face. Gabriel's.

'You wouldn't have to be alone,' she whispered. 'Any time you change your mind and decide to be my prince—'

'It isn't going to happen,' he said, cutting her off. But there was no malice in his voice, just a simple matter-of-factness with a tinge of ruefulness in it.

'I know.'

'I will not be your prince but I will be your husband.'

She nodded, almost too choked to speak, but she forced herself to say what was on her mind and in her heart. 'I'd love for you to be my prince, I really would.'

Carefully placing her feet back on the floor, Gabriel gripped the sides of her chair and pulled her to him. Once their knees were touching, he ran his fingers through her hair, then gently rubbed his thumb under her chin. 'I know our marriage is not what you grew up expecting your marriage to be. It isn't what I wanted or expected of a marriage either, but we can make it work and we can be happy.'

'I want to believe that.'

Palming her cheeks, a fervour came into his voice. 'Think about it, Lessie. When we move into the stables, we can make it a real home, a real distinction between the princess and the woman. We can make it a home without any intrusion from royal life and all its demands, and our child can have the semblance of a normal life. And so can we.'

The following weekend, Alessia walked out of the bathroom after her shower with the robe wrapped around her, and stepped into the dressing room, where Gabriel had made space for her clothes. He was taking her out, something that thrilled her, just as it thrilled her to be back in his arms after five nights apart. She'd arrived in Madrid late last night and they'd gone straight to bed, making love until the sun had come up. Only when they'd finally woken at midday did he lazily announce that he would be taking her out that night. She'd assumed his aversion to publicity meant she would spend her entire marriage without a single date with her husband.

She wished she dared hope that he would one day change his mind and be her prince as well as her husband, even if it was only for those important family occasions like Amadeo's wedding. She wished so hard he would come with her, a wish that no longer had anything to do with not wanting to be humiliated. Alessia just wanted the man she was falling in love with to be a real part of her family, not the royal side of it but the human side, and to hold her hand and create the same memories of those special occasions together.

But it wasn't going to happen and there was no point upsetting herself over it. Their time together was short and she didn't want to waste it by moping.

Choosing a white, strapless jumpsuit, she happily dressed and set to work on her hair and face. It felt strange to be doing her own beauty care for a night out. Normally the castle beauty team would set to work and turn her into the princess the world expected to see. Gabriel had offered to bring in Madrid's top beautician and hair stylist for her but she'd wanted to try it herself. Here, in Madrid, she could just be Alessia, and it was a novelty that showed no sign of abating.

The thought of returning to the castle without him again sent an even stronger pang through her than it had last weekend.

The five days without him had passed quickly and yet somehow with excruciating slowness.

She'd had a couple of engagements each day and one on Wednesday evening, so in that respect, the time had flown, and yet, every time she'd sneaked a peek at her watch, she'd found the time until seeing Gabriel again still very far away.

Never mind, she told herself brightly. She was here now. Make the most of the time with him while she had him, and as she thought that, he strolled into the bedroom.

She beamed, unable and unwilling to contain her delight even though it had been less than an hour since he'd crawled out of bed after making love to her again. 'How's your sister?' she asked.

Gabriel, who'd just spent an hour on the phone to Mariella, tugged his T-shirt up. 'She's doing great. She'll be back next week.' He whipped the T-shirt over his head. Mariella was currently doing a sightseeing tour of Japan with her on-off lover. 'It's her birthday next Saturday so I've invited her to join us for dinner to celebrate.'

About to drop his shorts, he noticed Alessia's falling face in her reflection at the dressing table.

'What's wrong?' He'd thought Alessia liked his sister. Not that she knew her properly yet, but he wanted her to. Nothing would make him happier than for his wife and his sister to get along and enjoy each other's company.

'I don't think I'll be here next weekend,' she

said, reaching for her phone. Swiping, she began to type, saying, 'I'm sure I've got an engagement next Saturday night at the royal theatre. It's an annual variety night raising money for cancer research. I'm just checking now, but I'm sure it's next weekend.'

'If you've got an engagement then you've got an engagement,' he said evenly, even though his heart had sunk at the news. It meant he would have to spend the weekend at the castle, and without Alessia for a large chunk of it. 'It can't be helped.' Striding over to her, he dropped a kiss into her neck. 'I'm going to take a shower and have a shave.'

'Where are we going?'

'Club Giroud.'

'The private members' club?'

'You've been?'

'Not to the one in Madrid, but some friends and I went to the one in Rome last year… You do know it's owned by King Dominic's brother-in-law?'

'I've known Nathaniel Giroud for years.'

She blinked her shock. 'You've never mentioned it.'

He shrugged. 'We're acquaintances. His clubs are a good place to do business.'

Her phone buzzed. She swiped again then lifted her stare back to him and shrugged apologetically. 'Sorry. The theatre engagement is next Saturday.'

'It can't be helped. I'll rearrange Mariella for another weekend.'

'But it's her birthday,' she said, clearly upset about it. Then her face brightened. 'I know! She can come and stay with us at the castle. If she wants, I can arrange a ticket to the show for her.'

'I will ask her.'

She hesitated before quietly saying, 'And you can come too, if you'd like? You wouldn't have to sit with me. I can get you tickets to sit with your sister.'

'You already know the answer to that,' he said evenly. Then, placing another kiss to her neck, Gabriel went into the bathroom and stood under the shower, turning the heat up as high as he could endure.

Away from Alessia's alert eyes he took some deep breaths and willed the bilious resentment out of him.

This was the life he'd signed up for. Alessia's job was a princess. He shouldn't resent that it took her away from him on the few nights they had together.

The seductive glamour of Madrid's Club Giroud was everything Alessia had expected and more. Situated in an ordinary street with an ordinary façade, having shaken their tail of paparazzi off they entered through an unobtrusive, ultra-discreet yet heavily guarded underground car park.

An elevator took them up to the club proper and then the night began.

First they had a meal in the swish restaurant, dining on the kind of food served up at the castle when honoured guests of state were in attendance, then they explored the rooms, each with its own vibe. In some, business-suited men and women were clearly discussing business but everyone else was there to dance or gamble or sip cocktails with other members of the ultra-rich and powerful, confident that whatever took place within the club's walls stayed there. Having been in existence for almost two decades, the press still hadn't got wind of it and it remained one of the few places a man like Gabriel could let his hair down and relax.

There were many faces Alessia recognised and, as she sipped a glass of fizzy grape juice in the poker room—no alcohol for her during the pregnancy—an elegant figure caught her eye and she elbowed Gabriel. 'Look,' she hissed. 'It's Princess Catalina and her husband.'

Gabriel, about to lay a card down, followed her stare.

As if they could feel their eyes on them, Nathaniel and Catalina Giroud turned their heads in unison. In an instant, smiles of recognition lit their faces and they weaved through the crowds to them.

Rising to his feet, Gabriel shook Nathaniel's hand and, after being introduced, exchanged kisses with Catalina, who then turned her attention to Alessia and smiled widely. 'Little Alessia Berruti! Look at you all grown up...' A flare of mischief crossed her face. 'Although not much taller than I remember.'

'You two have met?' Gabriel asked.

Alessia shrugged sheepishly. 'The royal world is a small world. But it's been a long time,' she added to Catalina. 'I think I was ten when we last met.'

Almost a decade older than Alessia, Catalina took her hand. 'Yes, I remember. It was at your parents' anniversary party. I remember being sorry for you when you were sent to bed. You tried so hard to keep a brave smile on your face and not show your disappointment.'

'I guess I didn't try hard enough if you noticed it,' she laughed.

'I only noticed because I'd once been in your shoes. You carried it off far more successfully than I ever did.'

Agreeing to join them for a drink, Gabriel finished his game and then they set off to the piano room, where a session musician was playing in the corner.

After a fresh round of drinks were served, the

conversation soon turned to the one subject he would prefer not to speak of. Amadeo's wedding. Catalina was cousin to the bride. Though it was doubtful she would know of Gabriel's involvement in the setting up of the marriage, his chest still tightened.

'I'm looking forward to it,' Catalina surprised them by saying.

'You're going?' Alessia asked.

'I wouldn't miss it for the world.'

'But Dominic will be there.'

It was no secret in their circle that Dominic used to hit and tyrannise his sister and that he was the principal reason she'd fled Monte Cleure with Nathaniel.

'Forgive me, but I was under the impression you wouldn't step foot in the same country as Dominic.'

Catalina's face clouded. 'I won't ever return to Monte Cleure, not while Dominic's on the throne.' Then she brightened and looked adoringly at her husband, who gave her a meaningful look that only Catalina could understand. 'But I want to see Elspeth married and safely away from him with my own eyes. She was always a sweet little thing, and the wedding's in Ceres and Dominic can't touch me there. If he tried, Nathaniel would kill him.'

Alessia had no doubt Catalina spoke the truth.

The love this couple had for each other was as strong as the love she felt emanating from Marcelo and Clara, and she couldn't help herself from glancing at Gabriel, whose hand was wrapped tightly around hers.

Her heart sighed.

Would Gabriel ever feel such a deep-rooted, protective, possessive devotion to her?

She knew he was as crazy for her as she was for him but that was a physical, chemistry-led craziness. She knew too that the personal dislike he'd once felt for her had gone and that he did like her, very much, and that he intended to be a faithful husband to her.

But love? The kind of love that meant you would do anything for the one you loved, cherish them, and put the other's happiness before your own...?

As she thought this, Catalina said, 'I understand you're a bridesmaid, Alessia.'

Forcing a practiced smile to her face, she nodded. 'Yes. There are five of us altogether.'

'And you, Gabriel?' Catalina asked. 'What role are you playing for the wedding?'

'I'm not,' he replied smoothly. 'I won't be there.'

Even Nathaniel raised a brow at this.

'It was agreed when Alessia and I married that I would remain a private person.'

'But this is your brother-in-law's wedding...'

Catalina's voice tailed off, and she took a quick drink of her champagne to cover the awkwardness.

'I'd like you to be there,' Alessia said softly before she could stop herself.

Gabriel's eyes zoomed straight onto hers. For the first time in a long time, the expression on his face was unreadable.

Already regretting her unguarded words, she gave a rueful shrug and squeezed his hand. 'It's okay. I understand why you can't be.'

And she did understand.

But she understood too that Gabriel already knew perfectly well how much she longed for him to be the prince on her arm, especially for that one day.

That he wouldn't even entertain the idea of accompanying her for that one special day told her more than any words that he didn't love her and that, for all his talk about finding happiness and harmony together, her needs could never trump his own.

The burgeoning love growing in her heart was unlikely to ever be reciprocated.

Gabriel prowled the empty quarters of the castle he doubted he would ever feel like a home to him. The silence was more acute than usual for this early in the evening. Normally there would be background noise until around ten p.m.

With his sister having turned down Alessia's

theatre offer to take a trip to Ibiza, and unable to get into his book, he remembered Alessia saying the variety show was being televised and figured that as he couldn't be with her in person, he could try and catch a glimpse of her in the crowd.

He got his wish almost immediately. An act had just finished, the three members bowing to the audience. The camera panned to the re-action in the royal box, and he understood why the castle was so quiet. The whole family, even Clara, were in attendance.

As he attempted to digest this, his phone vi-brated. When he read the message, his mood went from bad to worse.

'What's wrong?' Alessia asked as she slipped her shoes off. After an evening she'd started with such high hopes that her mother would finally show signs of forgiveness, her hopes had been dashed when all Alessia's attempts at conversation were met with terse replies and a turned cheek. Her lifted spirits at returning home to Gabriel had sunk back down before she made it over the threshold of the dayroom where he was holed up. She could practically smell the foulness of his mood. She could certainly smell the scent of bourbon in the air.

The ardent lover who could strip her naked with a look took a long time to respond. When he finally turned his face to her, the only thing his stare would strip was acid.

Wordlessly, he held his phone out to her.

She looked at the page he'd saved on his screen and silently cursed.

Gabriel's mother had sold her story to the press. The whole world now knew the reluctant prince was the son of Monica Binoche. There was no doubt the media circus that had left him alone during the weeks when Alessia was in Ceres without him would now renew its focus. The privacy he cherished could be kissed good-bye for the foreseeable future. And all because his mother had sold him out again. She'd put her need for validation and the spotlight above her son's emotional wellbeing.

He sighed heavily. 'I should have guessed the temptation would be too much for her.'

Feeling wretched for him, she climbed onto the sofa and wrapped her arms around him.

There was a stiffness in his frame she'd not felt since the night she'd wept on his chest, right before the passion had taken them in its grip.

'I'm sorry,' she whispered, stroking his back. 'I know how hard this must be for you.'

Do you? Gabriel wanted to bite. *Then why did you give me those puppy eyes and tell me you wanted me at Amadeo's wedding? Was it to guilt me?*

But he wouldn't bite. He would never bite. His parents had always bitten at each other, the early passion of their marriage turning into passionate hatred that rained misery on everyone.

Instead, he filled his lungs with all the air he could fit in them and rested his chin on the top of her head, and waited for Alessia's soft fruity scent to work its magic on him.

It didn't.

The fury inside him refused to diminish, his mother's betrayal a scalding wound, and then there was Alessia too, failing to tell him her whole damn family were going to the theatre engagement. She wanted him to break the conditions of their marriage and attend Amadeo's wedding but refused to renege on an engagement for his sister's birthday. As a result, Gabriel had blown his sister out on her birthday so he could snatch a few hours with his wife when it turned out the engagement she 'couldn't' miss was one she actually could have missed because the rest of the damned Berruti royal family, including the queen and her heir, had been there. Alessia's absence would have been minimised.

Duty would always come first to her, he thought bitterly, and disentangled himself from her arms so he could pour himself another bourbon.

CHAPTER TWELVE

GABRIEL'S MOOD HADN'T improved the next day, and when the invitation came to dine with the queen and king in their quarters that evening for a family meal, he bit back yet another cutting remark and reminded himself that these weren't just monarchs, they were his in-laws and the grandparents of the child growing in his wife's belly.

There was a snake alive in *his* belly, a cobra fighting to rise up his throat and strike.

He would not let it out.

He was conscious from the way Alessia was walking on eggshells around him that she was aware of the darkness. Conscious too that his tone was curter than he would like, he tried hard to moderate it and respond to the affection she continued to show him.

Tomorrow morning he was flying back to Madrid. His departure couldn't come soon enough. Some time alone, away from this damn castle, would give him his perspective back. He tried to find some perspective now too.

So his mother had sold him out? Hadn't he been expecting it? Even his sister, when she'd called to commiserate, had been indulgent in her reaction to their mother's actions. But then, Mariella had never hated the media circus that had followed their childhood and adolescence. She'd hated the fights as much as him and, like him, refused to be drawn into arguments that led to raised voices, but the media didn't bother her in the slightest.

And so Alessia had attended an engagement with her family she could easily have cancelled to spend an evening with his sister for her birthday? In Madrid, Alessia was free to be Alessia. Here, in the ancient castle, she rarely removed her princess skin. It would be easier for the woman to emerge fully when they were living together full-time, and she wouldn't need or want him to be anything more than her husband.

Despite his pep talk to himself, it was with a great deal of trepidation that Gabriel set off with Alessia to her parents' quarters.

He'd dined with the queen and king in their quarters once before, the night his plane was grounded. Then, the meal had been formal, the food and wine as exquisite as anything he'd been served in a Michelin-starred restaurant.

That night the food, although served with the usual ceremony, was a lot more homely, slow roasted lamb and ratatouille. The whole atmosphere was much more welcoming and light-hearted, the conversation, too, relaxed.

The only person not relaxing into the atmosphere was Alessia. Seated across from him, she held herself with a straight-backed deportment that would be fitting if it were a state occasion and not a family meal. She wasn't speaking much either, he noted, and every time he caught her eye, her smile seemed forced. The queen, he noted too, wasn't engaging her daughter in conversation, and he thought back to Alessia's comment about her mother still being angry with her over the circumstances of the pregnancy. It was a comment he'd mulled on a number of times as there was something about that whole conversation nagging at him, a feeling that there was something about it he was missing. Something important.

'How are the wedding preparations going?' Clara asked Amadeo.

The heir to the throne pulled a disgruntled face. 'Very well.'

'The whole of Ceres has gone wedding mad,' she said with glee. 'I can't wait! It's a shame I'm not a bridesmaid but I get why I can't be—best not to antagonise King Pig!'

To Gabriel's amusement, even the queen looked like she was trying not to laugh.

'What a shame that despot had to be invited but then it would kind of defeat the purpose of the wedding not to have him there,' Clara continued before whipping her attention to Gabriel. 'Is it true you're not coming?'

'I'm afraid it is true.'

'No *way*? Why's that?'

'Because I wish to remain a private person,' he said tightly, his muscles bunching together. He took a sip of his wine. Why must he continually explain himself?

'I know that, but this is a wedding. How can anyone not love a good wedding? And this will be the wedding of the century. And Elsbeth seems really sweet,' Clara added, looking again at Amadeo, who pulled another disgruntled face. She stuck her tongue out at him, which, to Gabriel's amazement, made everyone, including the perpetually stiff-necked Amadeo, laugh.

Laughing along with them, Gabriel drank some more wine to drown the poised cobra.

'You were quiet tonight,' Gabriel said when they were back in their quarters and finally alone. 'Want to tell me what's on your mind?'

Alessia sank onto the nearest sofa and sighed forlornly. 'Just my mother's attitude towards me.

I keep hoping she'll forgive me but there's still no sign of it.'

She kneaded her aching forehead. Alessia's insides had felt knotted from the moment she'd woken. For the first time since they'd become lovers, Gabriel had shared a bed with her and not made love to her. She sensed the demons working their darkness in him and longed for him to open up to her, but she knew what the cause was: his mother's treachery in selling him out. He'd been open with her about that.

But Gabriel was not a man to spill his guts. He'd told her everything about his childhood but had relayed it matter-of-factly. He freely admitted it had made him the man he was but he never spoke about how it had made him feel or how it still made him feel.

She couldn't force it. He would tell her if and when he was ready. But she'd gone to her parents' quarters feeling knotted in her stomach for her husband, and her mother's welcoming embrace had been delivered in such a detached manner that the knots had tightened so she could hardly breathe, and suddenly she could hold it back no longer.

A jumble of words came rushing out. 'Do you know, my mother has never been angry with Marcelo before, not like she's being with me, and he's the one who started this whole mess. He dangled out of a helicopter to rescue Clara from Dominic's palace, and he was understood and forgiven even before he put things right by marrying her. I made one mistake… okay, two…and I've paid the price for it. I've done everything I can to make amends and even Amadeo's forgiven me, but I can still feel her anger. Marcelo has got away with murder—not literally—over the years, whereas I've always been the good one. I've always been dutiful, always known my place in the family and in the pecking order, never given a hint of trouble, but there's no forgiveness from her for me. She can hardly bring herself to look at me.'

Gabriel listened to her unloading in silence. When she'd got it all out, he sat next to her and took her hand. 'Do you want to know what I think?'

A tear fell down her cheek. She wiped it away and nodded.

'Your mother—all your family—have spent years learning how to temper themselves when Marcelo falls out of line, but you've never stepped out of line before. You've never disappointed them. You've always done your best to live up to your birthright. You've followed in your mother's footsteps and put duty first, above your own wants and feelings.'

'Not as much as Amadeo has.'

'We're not talking about Amadeo, we're talking about you. I don't know if you're fully aware of the impact you have on people—you, more than anyone else in your family, have carried your monarchy into the twenty-first century. You've navigated being a princess with being a modern woman in the age of social media and all without putting a foot wrong and never with a word of complaint, even when you're abused by trolls. Your mother is the queen, Amadeo the heir to the throne, but it is you who captures the public's imagination, and you who the public sees as a princess to her core. I think your family, especially your mother, see you like that too, and so when your human side was revealed so publicly, they did what they always do when the monarchy comes under threat and went straight into damage limitation mode.'

'I don't think my mother likes my human side,' she admitted with a whisper.

'Only because you've never shown it to her before. When we're living in the stables and you have breathing space to remove the princess mask you've always forced yourself to wear, your mother will learn that Alessia the woman is worth a hundred of Alessia the princess. For now, though, your mother doesn't know how to react to you about it on a personal level because...'

A strand of thought jumped at him, cutting Gabriel's words off from his tongue.

He tried to blink the thought away but then the conversation that had been nagging at him interplayed with the stray thought, and his heart began to race.

'Because?' she prompted.

Certain he must be making two plus two into five, he stared at Alessia closely.

Her eyebrows drew together. 'What's wrong?'

'You've never put a foot wrong,' he said slowly. 'Ever. You've never been linked to another man... You told me yourself that the only time you've ever put your own desires first was the night we conceived our child.' His stomach roiling, he hardened his stare. 'Alessia... Was I your first?'

It was the deep crimson that flooded her neck and face that answered Gabriel's question and sent blood pounding to his head.

Letting go of her hand, he rose unsteadily to his feet. 'Why didn't you tell me?'

Her shoulders rose before she gave a deep sigh and shook her head ruefully. 'I'm sorry. I should have told you, I know that, but at the time I was so wrapped up in the moment and all the things you were making me feel...'

Alessia shook her head again from the sheer relief that it was finally out in the open. She hadn't realised how heavily it had weighed on her conscience until now it had lifted.

Whatever had she been afraid of? Gabriel was her husband. He might not love her but he was committed to her. The truth should never be something to be feared. 'I knew if I told you I was a virgin, you would stop.'

One eyebrow rose, his stare searching. 'You're saying you *knew* I would stop?'

'Not consciously at the time. In the moment… I wasn't thinking. I remember I didn't *want* to think.' She closed her eyes as memories of their first night together flooded her. For the first time in a long time, there was no bitterness at the aftermath. At some point, she didn't know when, she'd forgiven him for that. 'You touched me and I exploded. It was the first time in my whole life that I ever threw off the shackles of Princess Alessia and became just Alessia.'

There was a long pause of silence.

'Then it's a real shame you won't throw the princess shackles off for me now, isn't it?'

It was the underlying bite beneath the smooth veneer of his voice that made her gaze fly back to him. 'What do you mean by that?'

Jaw clenched, he stared at her for an age before giving a curt shake of his head. 'It doesn't matter.'

'You wouldn't have said it if it didn't.'

'It's nothing. Excuse me but I have an early start. I'm going to bed.'

And then, to her bewilderment, he walked straight out of the room. Moments later his footsteps treaded up the stairs.

Her heart thumping, her head reeling, Alessia palmed the back of her neck wondering what on earth had just happened and what he'd just meant.

There was only one way to find out.

She entered their room as the bathroom door locked.

Gabriel brushed his teeth furiously.

The darkness he'd been fighting had tightened its grip on him, the cobra winding its way to the base of his throat.

This was unbelievable. All this time.

There had been nothing—*nothing*—to indicate Alessia was a virgin.

But you weren't thinking clearly that night, a voice whispered. *Not with your head...*

Teeth done, he took stock of his reflection, breathed deeply and gave himself another pep talk.

The past was the past. Alessia was his wife and his future...

Acrid bile flooded his mouth. He swallowed it away but the bitterness remained.

Closing his eyes, he took one more deep breath and stepped back into the bedroom.

He took one look at his wife perched on the side of the bed facing the bathroom door and all the efforts he'd made to get a grip on his emotions were overturned.

Her stare was steady. 'I need you to tell me what you meant.'

He clenched his jaw. 'Now is not the time.'

'Now *is* the time. I must have done something to warrant that remark, and as a wise half-Spanish, half-French man once said, if you don't tell me what's wrong, how can I fix it?'

The look he gave her could freeze boiling water.

'I know things are tough for you right now,' Alessia said, somehow managing to keep the steadiness in her voice through the thrashing of her heart. 'I know your mother's actions feel like a betrayal, but if I've done something to add to it then you need to tell me so I can put things right. Is it because I didn't tell you I was a virgin? Or is there something else at play?'

His chest rose and fell sharply. A contortion of emotions splayed over his face.

Gabriel gritted his teeth so hard it felt like his molars could snap into pieces. The scalding fury...he could feel it infecting every part of him.

'Did I hurt you that night?' he asked roughly.

Eyes widening, she shook her head violently. '*No.* It was wonderful. You know it was.'

'Sorry,' he bit out, 'but this little revelation has made me rethink the whole night. I suppose it explains why you weren't on the pill. Or is that another false assumption?' Somehow Gabriel was hanging onto his temper but the thread of it he clung to was fraying and the control he'd always taken with his speech was slipping out of his reach.

She closed her eyes briefly. 'No, I wasn't on the pill. But you already know that.'

'But you didn't think to tell me that then? In the moment? Before we got carried away?'

'I thought you'd taken care of it.'

'How? By wearing an invisible condom?'

There was a flash of indignancy. 'I didn't know and I didn't think to ask. I was stupid and naïve, I know that, but I wasn't thinking that night and neither were you, and you have no right to be angry with me about it because it's on you just as much as it's on me.'

The thread snapped.

'If you'd told me you were a virgin then none of this would have happened!' he snarled. 'Don't you understand that? Do you not know what you've done? I would never have touched you if I'd known! You've trapped me into a damned marriage I never wanted!'

The colour drained from her face. For the longest time she just stared at him, her mouth opening and closing but nothing coming out.

And then something in her demeanour shifted.

She got to her feet.

Somehow she stood taller than he'd ever seen her.

Padding slowly to him, her words had the same cadence as her pace but her quiet tone was scathing. 'I haven't trapped you into anything. We created a child *together*.'

'You think I don't know that? You think I don't know the blame lies with me too? You pushed aside the fact of your virginity and I pushed aside the fact you were a princess and not a mere flesh and blood woman, and I didn't have the sense to think about contraception, and now I'm trapped in a marriage to a woman I would never have married under any other circumstance. I've given up everything for this, my career, my privacy, my whole damn life!'

'You gave all that up for our child,' she snapped back. 'Remember? If you're trapped then it's in a web of your own making. You married me because you didn't trust me to put our child's wellbeing first.'

He crossed his arms tightly around his chest and leaned down into her face. 'You married me for your damn monarchy.'

'No, I married you for my family because the monarchy means everything to *them*, and so that my child could have its father in its life.'

'You married me so you could continue being the perfect princess and redeem yourself in your mother's eyes because being a princess is all you'll allow yourself to be.'

'Being a princess is who I *am*!'

'No, Alessia, you're my wife too, but you wouldn't even take one night off from your duties for my sister's birthday when no one would have missed you at that show.'

'I'd already committed to it, and how you have the nerve to say that when I gladly offered to have Mariella stay with us...' Pacing the room, she threw her hands in the air. 'You talk about everything you've had to give up, but what about all the things I've had to give up, like a whole future spent being a princess without ever having a prince on my arm? You won't even come to my brother's wedding!'

'You knew my conditions before you agreed to our marriage,' Gabriel raged. His unleashed fury and Alessia's passionate defence of herself had his blood pumping through him in a way that seemed to be feeding his anger.

'Conditions without compromise, that's what they were, and I wasn't allowed to impose any of my own, was I? As with our wedding and the home we live in, I wasn't given a say. I had no choice because you gave me no choice. You talk a good talk about compromise but you won't compromise on Amadeo's wedding, will you, even when you know how much it would mean to me to have you there.'

'I will not feed those vultures and I will not set a precedent. I don't know how many times I have to say that.'

'A precedent?' she cried. 'You call me a flesh and blood woman and then talk about precedents as if I'm nothing but some business contract?'

'The woman I made love to that night was Alessia Berruti. *She's* the woman I committed myself to, the woman I made clear to you that I was marrying, but she's not the woman I find myself married to, not when we're here. The minute you step foot on Ceres your princess mask slips back on and everything becomes about duty, but I have committed myself and so I'm condemned to spend the rest of my life on this damned island hoping every day for a glimpse of the woman I thought I'd married. But you won't throw those princess shackles off again, will you? Not if it means disappointing your mother again. I will always come second to your damned monarchy and your need to always be Princess Perfect so that you can bask in your mother's approval.'

'It's not just for her! It's who I am!'

'It doesn't have to be! Look how good things are between us when we're away from this place. If you step away from your royal duties we can have that all the time.'

She stopped pacing and stared at him with shock. 'Step away from being a princess?'

'Why not?' The thought of his wife quitting her royal duties was not something Gabriel had ever given serious consideration to, but now that the words were out, he grasped at them, for in that moment they made perfect sense. 'You've played your part for your family. Marcelo's married. Amadeo's marrying soon. That's two new beautiful Berruti princesses for the public to fall in love with, and soon no doubt new royal babies. You and I can build a new life away from here where you can be whoever you want to be.'

Alessia's early pregnancy sickness had ebbed and flowed since the hormones of conception had kicked in. The nausea in her belly was the strongest she'd known it since the day they'd agreed the contract for their marriage. 'Are you serious?'

'Yes. You, me and our baby, away from this

castle building our own private life together. You can take that princess mask off for ever and just be the woman I adore. What do you say?'

Eyes not leaving his face, she slowly wrapped her arms across her stomach. 'If I consider it, will you consider coming to Amadeo's wedding?'

He laughed. 'If you come round to my way of thinking, neither of us will have to attend his wedding. I know you still feel guilty for your part in its being.'

She held his stare for a long time, tightening her hold around her abdomen. 'But I want to go. It's my brother's wedding. And I want you to be there too, as my husband, to hold my hand and support me, because yes, I do still feel some guilt for it. But it's not just about guilt. I want you there for *my* sake, as my prince, for the biggest celebration our island's had since my mother's coronation.' She took a long breath and quietly added, 'Come with me, please. Be my husband and my prince for just that one day.'

She held her breath.

For a long time nothing was said between them. Not verbally. The flickering in his eyes told her more than words could ever say.

Now Alessia was the one to laugh, although there was no humour in it. 'You accuse me of putting you second but I wouldn't have to if you'd meet me halfway and just be my prince for family functions. I can't help that there's always press there too, but you knew it before you imposed that condition. I have no choice but to keep a huge chunk of my life separate from you because I *am* a princess, and this is the situation you've created, not me, and now you want me to give up who I am without meeting me even a fraction of the way.' She shook her head. 'You set me up for a fall right from the beginning. You engineered things in our marriage so I have no choice but to put you second.'

A flare of anger crossed his features. 'That is ridiculous.'

'Your mother always put you second, didn't she, until you gave her that final ultimatum.' Strangely, the more she spoke, the calmer she was feeling and the clearer she was seeing. 'Is that what I can expect from you as the next step? An ultimatum that you'll divorce me or take our child from me if I don't agree to step back from the world I was born into?'

'Absolutely not!' he refuted angrily.

'Maybe not consciously,' she accepted with a shrug. No, she didn't believe this had been done at a conscious level any more than she'd not told him of her virginity at the time. 'What you engineered with your conditions, intentionally or not, has become a self-fulfilling prophecy for you and an excellent excuse to keep me at a distance.'

'Do you have any idea how insane that sounds?' he sneered. But the pulse throbbing on his jaw told a different story.

'Is it? Do you realise this is the first time I've heard you raise your voice or lose your temper? You always have to be in control, don't you? The only time you let your emotions out is in the bedroom. What are you afraid of, Gabriel? That the toxicity of your parents' marriage will somehow be ours? Well, I guess that's become a self-fulfilling prophecy for us too. I don't think you're afraid of the press or that you even hate them. I think your refusal to engage with them is your way of punishing your mother because you ended the war between your parents but never dealt with its casualties—you and Mariella. You never dealt with the neglect you were put through, and you were neglected, Gabriel. You and Mariella both. So you punish your mother by refusing to play the game you hate her for but you can't hate her, can you? Not when you love her. So you punish me instead, only committing part of yourself to me, and condemning me to a life with a husband who refuses to be my husband in public, and then you dress it up to salve your conscience by trying to convince yourself that our marriage will be happy once we separate the woman from the princess…'

Alessia took another breath for the strength to continue. 'But the woman and the princess cannot be separated. The woman and the princess are one and the same thing. We cannot be separated because we are one. Ironically, you're the one who brought that woman out in me and it's through our time together that I've learned I *can* embrace both those sides of me. Maybe one day my mother will learn to embrace them too and start accepting my human side. I don't know. I don't think it even matters any more. If she loves me then she must love all of me. I am a princess. I was born a princess. I will die a princess. A princess. Woman. Human. All I have done my entire life is put everyone else's needs and feelings above my own. But for once, today, I will put myself above duty. I will not live with a man who wants to split me in two. I deserve someone who can love all of me… And that someone isn't you.'

Feeling herself in danger of crumbling, needing to keep a tight hold of her falling strength, Alessia moved her folded arms up so they covered her chest, and held his now ashen stare. 'Do you know who you remind me of? My grandmother. She hated the royal game and that twisted her and turned into hate for everyone associated with it, so let me save you a life of misery and free you from the trappings of a marriage you detest. Get in your jet and fly back to Madrid, and never come back.'

The last bit of colour in his face drained away.

'You don't need to be here any more. You know perfectly well that I will put our baby's emotional needs first even without your influence. I'm sure we can come up with a good "compromise" about custody but that's in the future. Right now, I'm going to Marcelo's quarters so you can pack your things and go.'

Marcelo, his domestic staff dismissed for the evening, opened the door to his quarters. Alessia looked into the eyes of the only member of her blood family who'd even tried to understand her and collapsed onto the floor in tears.

CHAPTER THIRTEEN

His butler's voice telling him that his sister had turned up at his home unannounced made Gabriel close his eyes and breathe deeply. He returned the phone receiver to the cradle and refocused on the documents sent by his lawyer for him to read through.

Mariella let herself into his office without bothering to knock.

'I did tell you I was too busy to see you,' he said, pre-empting her.

'You did,' she agreed cheerfully, draping herself on his office armchair. 'But seeing as it's Friday evening and you're here in Madrid and not in Ceres, and you've been avoiding me all week, I decided to put off my dinner date and ignore your edict. Going to tell me what's going on?'

'There is nothing going on.' He dropped his gaze back to his paperwork and made a point of crossing a line out in heavy black marker pen.

'Then why aren't you in Ceres? The wedding's tomorrow.'

'Yes, and as I told you and everyone else, I will not be attending.'

She was silent for such a long time that Gabriel felt compelled to look back up at her. Hunched forwards, elbows on her thighs, chin in the palms of her hands, her stare was speculative.

'What?' he asked tersely.

Her eyes narrowed. 'I know you're a stubborn thing, but I did think on this one occasion you would change your mind.'

'Then you thought wrong.'

'And what about Alessia?'

'What about her?'

'Don't play dumb, Gabriel. It doesn't suit you.'

He struck another black line through the document. He didn't even know what clause he'd just struck out. 'Alessia and I have agreed to part ways,' he told her, and blacked out another line.

His sister's unnatural silence made him look at her again.

'It's for the best,' he told her. 'Our lives are not compatible. We will agree to custody arrangements for our child nearer the—'

His words were cut off when Mariella jumped up from her seat and snatched the documents off his desk. Seconds later, she'd thrown them out of the window.

'What in hell do you think you're doing?' she raged before he could ask that very same question of her. 'What is *wrong* with you? The woman you love is thousands of miles away preparing for one of the biggest days of her life— the coverage of the wedding is *everywhere*. I know you can't stand the media but how can you let her go through that alone?'

Completely unnerved to witness his sister lose her temper, something he could never remember seeing her do before, he said, 'I just told you, we've separated.'

'Then get yourself back to Ceres and un-separate yourselves before it's too late!'

'It's already too late. She's made her mind up and I agree with her. We are not compatible. Alessia's life is one of duty and that is not—'

'And what about your duty to her as a husband?' Mariella demanded, stamping her foot for emphasis. 'What happened to your conviction that you could make your marriage work?'

'I was wrong.'

She stamped her foot again. Gabriel had the strong feeling she wished it was his head under it. 'Since when have you told lies and since when have you quit at anything? You have succeeded at everything you've ever set out to achieve and more—if you'd wanted to make your marriage work then you would have done.'

'I *did* want it to work.'

'Then why are you sitting here pretending to work while your marriage falls apart, you idiot?' Slamming her hands on his desk, she leaned over so her face was right in his. 'I have never seen you as happy as you were with her. I could even hear it in your voice. I was so *happy* for you. It gave me hope that maybe there might be someone out there prepared to take on the screw-up that is me. You found the happiness that I would *kill* for and now you're throwing it away? You married a princess, Gabriel. You knew what the deal was. Either you accept that fully and embrace it or you can look forward to a life as miserable as the one our mother leads.'

'Our mother's life is not miserable.'

'Of course it is! She has two children who both love her and have always forgiven her, and still she can only find succour from the adulation of strangers. If that's not a miserable life then what is it?'

'A selfish one.'

'That too, yes! And the path you're heading right now is going to be just as selfish and lonely and miserable as hers is.'

Gabriel couldn't stop thinking of Mariella's loss of temper. The quarter bottle of bourbon he'd drunk since she'd stormed out of his villa had done nothing to numb his brain.

As much as he wished to plead ignorance and deny any of what she'd said, he knew it was her perception that he was throwing happiness away that had made her see red. Mariella's life revolved around finding her personal Holy Grail. Happiness.

His sister's imagination was as overactive as his wife's.

His estranged wife.

His guts clenched painfully. He had another swig of bourbon.

He'd felt no need to argue back with his sister. He'd felt a little like a spectator watching a usually passive animal in a zoo suddenly start behaving irrationally. Not like it had been with Alessia.

He closed his eyes as their ferocious argument replayed itself. His blood pumped harder to remember how that had felt.

After decades spent containing and controlling his emotions, he'd finally met his match. He couldn't hide himself from Alessia. God knew he'd tried. God knew it was impossible.

Alessia brought the full spectrum of human emotion out in him...

He straightened sharply, jerking his crystal

glass so bourbon spilled over his lap. As the liquid soaked into his trousers, his mind cleared.

His sister's perception that he was throwing away happiness had been no view. It had been a fact.

And Alessia's view that he'd sabotaged their marriage had been a fact too. Her reasoning, though, was only partly right.

He'd sabotaged it because Alessia made him feel too damn much, and she had from the moment she'd stepped out of the shadows and into the moonlight on the balcony. She'd broken down every inch of barrier he'd installed to protect himself with, and slipped under his skin.

He had no reason to put those barriers back up. He didn't need to protect himself any more. Not from Alessia. She would never use him as a prop or put her needs ahead of his. He doubted she'd ever put her needs above anyone else's in her entire life. She didn't *want* him as a prop. She only wanted him for himself.

He'd been too scared to let go and give her what she needed from him: the whole of himself. She'd offered him the whole of herself, and instead of getting down on his knees and worshipping the goddess in her entirety as she deserved, he'd selfishly demanded she throw the biggest part of herself away.

Ice licked his skin as the magnitude of what

he'd done crawled through him like an approaching tsunami coming to drown him.

He'd pushed away the best thing that had ever happened to him.

He'd pushed away the woman he loved.

He'd pushed away the princess he loved.

With a guttural roar that came from somewhere unknown deep inside him, Gabriel threw the glass as hard as he could. It smashed against the wall and rained down thousands of crystal fragments. His tear-stained image reflected in every shard.

Amadeo's wedding was the first of the three Berruti siblings not to be held in the royal chapel. As heir to the throne, it had been decided with input from the Ceresian government that his position warranted a wedding in the capital city's cathedral. The whole nation had been given a day's holiday to celebrate, and they were out in force, old and young alike lining the entire route from the castle to the cathedral, many wearing the national costume that resembled a brightly coloured poncho, most waving the national flag, and all cheering.

Alessia and the four supremely excited small cousins who made up the other bridesmaids followed the horse-drawn carriage carrying the bride and the man giving her away: the King of Monte Cleure. Alessia and Clara had privately agreed earlier that morning—and Alessia made sure their conversation was entirely private—that Elsbeth would probably run down the aisle to get away from him. Any nagging fears that Elsbeth was being forced into this marriage were dispelled by the excitement shining in her eyes and all over her pretty face.

On that, Gabriel had been right.

She pushed thoughts of him away and continued waving to the cheering crowd.

Today was a day of celebration. Having spent a little time with the bride, she'd become increasingly convinced that she was a woman her brother could fall in love with...if he allowed himself to. Amadeo had a strong streak of stubbornness in him and was quite capable of denying himself happiness if it meant he didn't have to admit he was wrong.

Whether Amadeo fell in love with her or not, Alessia was determined to welcome Elsbeth into the Berruti family and make her feel that she belonged.

Gabriel could have belonged too if he'd allowed it.

Gabriel could go to hell.

The spineless coward hadn't called her. After the way he'd ghosted her before, she shouldn't be surprised. She'd sent him a message giving him the date, place and time of their baby's first scan next week. He hadn't responded. It was on him if he wanted to be there.

Little Carolina, five years old and adorable with a thick mane of black corkscrew hair, spotted someone in the crowd she knew and would have jumped out of the carriage to greet them if Alessia's reflexes hadn't been so good.

Pulling the excitable child onto her lap, she hugged her close and blinked back a hot stab of tears.

No crying today.

It didn't matter how often she told herself that he wasn't worth her tears, they still flooded her face and soaked her pillow every night.

Oh, please don't let him ghost me again. Let him come to the scan, she prayed. *As painful as it is, I can live without him, but my baby shouldn't have to live without him in its life too. That wouldn't be fair. My baby deserves its father.*

The only light in the dark that had become Alessia's life was that her mother had been markedly warmer to her, her maternal compassion roused by the sudden implosion of Alessia's marriage. For once, there had been no talk about damage limitation. Alessia suspected that was Marcelo's doing.

Her relationship with her mother felt like a fresh start.

Her marriage hadn't lasted long enough for its ending to be stale.

She missed him as desperately as if she'd spent her whole life with him.

The carriages arrived in the piazza the cathedral opened onto.

Placing a kiss on the top of her little cousin's head, she fixed a great smile onto her face and herded the other bridesmaids off the carriage, the driver helping them down one by one.

The flash of cameras was so great that it blurred into one mass of light.

Organising the bridesmaids, Alessia directed them to wave at the screaming, excited crowd and then it was time to follow the bride and King Pig into the cathedral.

The packed congregation got to its feet.

As the bridal party began its long march, Alessia's smile turned into something real as she noticed the spring in Elsbeth's feet. The bride really was fighting the urge to run to Amadeo and demand the bishop get straight to the 'I do's.

Alessia was halfway down the aisle when a tall figure in the family section at the front made her heart thump and then pump ice in her veins.

The cathedral began to sway beneath her feet. If not for the small hands clasped in hers, she would have stumbled.

It took everything she had to keep putting one shaking foot in front of the other. The closer she got, the clearer his features became.

His eyes were fixed directly on her.

The ice in her veins melted and began to heat rapidly. By the time Elsbeth took Amadeo's hand and the bridesmaids' mothers beckoned them to their seats, her whole body was burning, her heart beating like a hummingbird in her chest.

That was her family in their pride of place, the women in the perfect royal attire for a wedding, the men in identical long-tailed charcoal morning suits. Her father. Her mother. Her brother Marcelo. Her sister-in-law, Clara. Her husband…

He held a hand out to her. His features were tight but his eyes were an explosion of gold.

Her hand slipped into his without any input from her brain.

The service began.

Alessia didn't hear a word of it.

Her body went into autopilot, standing and sitting as directed, singing the hymns, clapping politely when the groom kissed the bride. It stayed on autopilot as they filed out of the cathedral, tipped confetti and rice over the happyish couple, smiled for the numerous photos that were taken. And it remained in autopilot in the carriage she shared with Gabriel, Marcelo and Clara, all waving at the cheering crowds, back to the castle and throughout the entire wedding banquet.

Gabriel could see Alessia was in shock and was working entirely in princess mode. She ate and conversed, laughed when appropriate, but she'd shut something off in herself. Even when he spoke directly to her she answered politely but there was a dazed quality to her eyes and no real engagement. It was as if he were a not particularly interesting stranger she'd been paired with for the day.

The banquet ended. The five hundred guests moved into the adjoining stateroom where the evening party was being held. Decorated in golds and silvers that shimmered and glittered from floor to ceiling, the round tables with no official place- settings quickly filled. He followed Alessia to the one she joined Marcelo and Clara at. They exchanged a significant look and then Marcelo fixed his stare on Gabriel.

The look clearly said, 'Fix things now or I will do what I would have done if my wife hadn't taken pity on you and made me help you today: I will throw you out of a window.'

He wouldn't blame him. It was nothing less than he deserved.

The bride and groom took to the dance floor.

Alessia's knuckles whitened around her glass of water.

Gabriel's heart splintered.

The first dance finished.

Gabriel got to his feet and tapped Alessia's shoulder.

She looked at him expressionlessly.

His heart beating fast, he extended his palm to her. 'May I have this dance?'

She continued to stare at him. With no movement on her face, she looked slowly down to his hand then back to his eyes. But still not seeing. Not seeing him.

By now convinced that she wasn't even going to dignify him with an answer, electricity jolted through him when she pressed her fingers into his palm and rose gracefully to her feet.

He closed his fingers around hers before she could change her mind.

Leading her to the slowly filling dance floor, cameras flashing all around them, he slid his hands around her slender waist.

There was a too-long hesitation before she looped her hands loosely around his neck and turned her cheek so that she wasn't looking at him. Other than her hands, not an inch of her body touched his.

But she was there with him. Dancing with him.

Swaying softly to the music, he spoke in a low

voice so only she could hear him. 'I love you, Princess Alessia Berruti. I love all of you, the passionate woman and the dignified princess. I love your sense of duty. I love your loyalty. I love your laugh and your sense of the absurd. I love that you can make me laugh. I love that I can make you laugh. I love your voice. I love your eyes. I love your lips and your smile. I love how it feels when I touch you and how it feels when you touch me. I love that you're carrying my child...'

Still swaying, her face slowly lifted. Her eyes locked onto his. The dazed sheen had gone but there was still no expression.

Another splinter broke off his heart and he sucked in a breath before continuing. 'But there are things I hate too. I hate that I left you sleeping that morning. I hate that I never called you back. I hate the conditions I put on our marriage. I hate that I didn't consider your feelings when I imposed them. I hate that our wedding was tiny and sparse. I hate that I was arrogant enough to think that you could ever be anything but the woman you are, and I *hate* that I let you believe you would suit me better as anything other than the woman you are.'

A tear rolled down her cheek.

'I hate that my selfish insecurities tried to hoard you all to myself. I hate that I'm a blind, pig-headed fool who pushed away the best thing that ever happened to him.'

Still holding her waist with one hand, Gabriel reached into his back pocket and pulled out a scrap of paper. Taking one of her hands in his, he placed the paper in it.

She dipped her gaze to it before closing it tightly in her fingers then locked back on him, another tear falling.

'My PA gave me this within minutes of you calling me,' he told her, staring deep into her shining eyes. 'I've kept it in my wallet ever since. I tried to destroy it once. Scrunched it up and threw it in the bin. I went back to the hotel room for it. Alessia...' A sharp lump had formed in his throat and he had to close his eyes and swallow it away before he could continue. 'Lessie, I don't know if love at first sight exists but the first time I looked at you it felt like I'd been struck by lightning. You were everything I thought I didn't want but the truth is you're everything I need. All of you. The princess and the woman. The whole of you. I can't live without you.'

His voice caught and he had to take another moment to compose himself enough to speak. 'I can't live without you,' he repeated, choking and now completely unable to control it. 'Please, Alessia, forgive me. Take me back. Please, I beg you. I am nothing without you. I can't go on like this. You are everything to me. I beg you, give me a chance to put things right. Give me a chance to prove that I can be the husband you deserve and the prince you need...'

'Shh.' A delicate finger was placed on his lips.

It took a beat for him to register that Alessia had closed the gap between them, another beat to register that her tear-filled face was shining at him.

'Oh, Gabriel.' Alessia gazed at the man she'd fallen in love with long before she'd even known it, feeling like she could choke on the emotions that had cracked through her frozen heart and were erupting inside her.

The eyes boring into hers... What she saw in them...

Oh, but it filled her with the glowing warmth of his love.

Dropping the slip of paper, she rose onto her toes, wound her arms around his neck and pressed her nose into the base of his strong throat.

He loved her.

With her lungs filled with that wonderful Gabriel scent she loved so much, she tilted her head back so she could look again into the eyes that always glistened with such wonderful colour.

She would look into them every day for the rest of her life.

'I love you,' she whispered. 'With all my heart.'

He closed his eyes as if in prayer.

Loosening one of her hands from his neck, she slid her fingers down his arm and clasped them around his hand.

She smiled up at him. 'Kiss me,' she whispered dreamily. 'Kiss me, dance with me and love me for ever.'

Then she closed her eyes as the heat of his breath filled her senses.

His lips brushing tenderly against hers, Gabriel held her in his arms on the dance floor until the music stopped. And then he loved her for ever.

EPILOGUE

Beaming so hard she thought her face might split in two, Alessia gripped tightly to Gabriel's hand as they walked back up the aisle, their vows renewed. The young bridesmaids who'd carried the twelve-foot train of her wedding dress grinned with varying degrees of gappiness. A heavily pregnant Clara, who'd been tasked with keeping the young bridesmaids in order as part of her chief bridesmaid role, looked like she was only just controlling her urge to jump over the nearest congregants and enthusiastically throw herself into Alessia's arms.

Outside in the royal chapel gardens, the sun shone down on the happy couple and their two hundred guests. To Alessia's glee, the sun's rays were diffused by the avalanche of confetti that was tipped over them, started by Gabriel's best man, his sister, Mariella. The only guest who didn't join in was Alessia's mother, but that was only because she had Alessia and

Gabriel's three-month-old daughter, Mari, in her arms. The queen's happiness radiated so strongly Alessia felt its waves on her skin every bit as much as the sun's.

After the professional photographer, who'd been paid a small fortune and made to sign a secrecy order so as to keep this special day entirely private, had finished herding them all into varying orders for the pictures, they all headed inside for the wedding banquet and after-party. When she caught Gabriel's mother surreptitiously taking photos of the party on her phone and realised he'd clocked her too, their eyes met. He shrugged in a 'what else can we expect?' way, and then burst out laughing. Her husband still loathed the press but had become far more adept at tolerating them. Once, he'd even given them a smile that didn't look completely like a grimace.

When the early hours came and the time for dancing and celebrating was over, an exhausted Alessia walked the lit path back to the stables, holding tightly to her husband's hand. Every single person she loved had been there to celebrate the love she and Gabriel had found together.

When they reached their huge oak front door, she was about to take the first step up to it when the ground moved beneath her feet and she found herself swept up into Gabriel's arms.

'I do believe it's traditional for the groom to carry the bride over the threshold,' he murmured, nuzzling his nose into her cheek.

She smiled dreamily at him. 'Thank you, Prince Gabriel.'

'No, Princess Alessia. Thank you.'

She tightened her hold around his neck and pressed her cheek against his. 'Take me to bed.'

'With pleasure.'

* * * * *

Caught up in the drama of
Pregnant Innocent Behind the Veil?
Make sure to catch up on the first instalment in the Scandalous Royal Weddings trilogy,
Crowning His Kidnapped Princess
and look out for the final instalment, coming soon!

And don't forget to check out these other incredible Michelle Smart stories!

The Forbidden Innocent's Bodyguard
The Secret Behind the Greek's Return
Unwrapped by Her Italian Boss
Stranded with Her Greek Husband
Claiming His Baby at the Altar

Available now!